THE UNCONQUERED MAGE
BOOK THREE OF CONVERGENCE

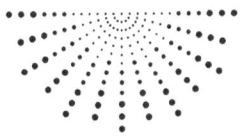

MELISSA MCSHANE

Night Harbor Publishing

Cover design by 100 Covers

www.100covers.com

AUTHOR'S NOTE

A glossary and pronunciation guide appear at the end of this book.

BOOK NINE

CHAPTER ONE

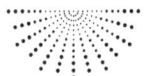

4 Hantar

This book is how I know my husband loves me. I didn't see him at all today because he was riding with Mattiak to discuss the problem of bringing an enemy army into a more or less defenseless Colosse without terrifying and panicking the populace, and he was still gone at dinnertime. I was just working out whether to be angry or worried when he appeared with this book in hand. It's fatter than the others and barely fits into my pocket, but I'm so touched I wouldn't care if it were made from tree bark and bound with braided grass.

The last time he did this, I was surprised and happy but most of all mystified that he knew to bring me one just as I needed it (no real mystery; he was secretly in love with me and had no other way to show it). This time, I'd told him my problem, trying to work out how I'd get another one, and it never occurred to me he might do it for me.

It's one of those things about love, and marriage, that I'm still learning—caring for each other's needs without having to be explicitly told what to do. Not that I expect him to always know what I'm thinking and respond appropriately. That would be ridiculous. Just—

paying attention, I guess. Having things matter because they matter to the other person.

Which is why I felt so bad about telling him I need to go back to Venetry.

It was something I was thinking about this morning, after the army started moving again and I was jostling along in my very own private wagon—private because Cederic is convinced I still need to rest after being wounded, and there's no room in the mages' wagon for a bed. Last night was overwhelming, what with Cederic becoming Emperor-elect (the main reason we're going to Colosse) and all the things that go along with that, so that's really all I was able to think about.

But this morning, my friends came by a few at a time, particularly the ~~Darssan~~ Castaviran mages, who were as stunned as I was by the development. (Sovrin teased me about losing the God-Empress's diamonds in the ruins of the palace, since now it turns out as Empress-Consort I'd have a legitimate reason to wear them.) And I remembered how Cederic had risked capture to go back and get all the mages from the Castaviran camp before the Castaviran officers could learn General Regates had defected back to the God-Empress's side.

(I know she's neither God nor Empress, but it's her aenemica now, for me, and it feels like a weapon when I write it.)

The more I thought about that, the more I thought of "my" mages back in Venetry, of Jeddan, and how they're either going to be forced to serve the God-Empress or imprisoned (or even killed?) because they refuse to do so. And I can't stop worrying about Terrael.

To Cederic's credit, when I told him this at lunchtime (he spends about half an hour with me in the middle of the day so each of us won't forget what the other looks like) he didn't get angry, or tell me I'm insane, or forbid me to even consider it. He did go totally impassive, the way he does when he's feeling a strong emotion, and sat for about a minute looking off toward the head of our procession while I waited for him to gain control.

I try not to be frustrated when he does this. I still don't know why showing anger or fear or sorrow or even great happiness is so difficult for him, or what he thinks will happen if he does, but it matters enough to him I don't push. Or maybe I *do* know, if his flying into a rage at me that one time represents what happens when he loses control. At any rate, I know he *does* feel things. He's never afraid to let me see him happy, and he seems to find it easier to make jokes and tease me these days. Though I've still never heard him laugh in public. Little steps, I guess.

Anyway. I waited—I'm learning so much patience from being married—until he was done working through his initial reaction. He said, without looking at me, "Your argument has merit. But I am afraid it is impossible. You cannot risk yourself."

"Is that because the Emperor-elect thinks his wife is too valuable, or because Cederic Aleynten can't bear to see me go into danger?" I said.

"Both," he said, "and also the fact that Renatha Torenz will certainly destroy you if she catches you. We cannot afford to lose the most powerful of the Balaenic mages."

"You know she can't hold me against my will," I said.

"She has only to keep you hemmed in until you are too exhausted to work the walk-through-walls *pouvra*," Cederic said, "and you cannot stay insubstantial forever."

"I'm not saying it isn't dangerous," I said. "And I'm still not completely healed, which I know was going to be your next objection."

"Since you never let your physical safety interfere with doing what you believe is right, I thought it irrelevant," he said with a tiny smile. "But you are correct that even if all my other objections were eliminated, I would still think this excursion too much for you in your present condition."

"It's going to be hard, true," I said. "But I still think it has to be done. And you know I'm the only one who can do it."

Cederic sighed. "Sesskia—"

"Just listen," I said. "From where we are now, it will take me nine hours to return to Venetry by flitting. That's going slowly and taking lots of breaks. I don't want to injure myself. The longer we wait to do this, the longer that trip will take and the longer it will be for all of us to return. I'm convinced we need those mages just as much as we can't leave them in the God-Empress's hands.

"And Terrael...Cederic, it's not just about friendship. He might be the only chance we have of figuring out how to bring our two magics together. You're not going to be in a position to do any of that research yourself, not anymore. *Now* is the time to go after him. If we wait until we've won this war" (I carefully didn't use the dreadful phrase "if we win this war") "he could be dead, or worse. We have to think past the short-term problems, and I know those problems are serious, but at some point it will all be over, and I don't want us regretting not taking steps to make that eventual future something we can all live with."

Cederic looked off into the distance again. "We will have no way of communicating with you," he said. "It will be days before we know if you have succeeded."

"No, see, that's the wonderful part," I said. "Once everyone is free of Venetry and headed in this direction, I'll flit back and tell you how it went. I'll be gone no more than three days. Then I can go back and forth if I have to, make sure they're on the right path to join us. It's not as if Jeddan can't lead them. And they'll travel faster than we do, so it won't take very long. I think they'll catch up to us just as we're reaching Colosse."

Cederic bowed his head and said, "You have given this much thought."

"You know I don't take unnecessary risks," I said. "I always— almost always—think things through. I wouldn't suggest this if I didn't think it was important. And you know I wouldn't volunteer myself if there were anyone else who could go."

"I know," he said. "I th

Later—That conversation ended with him saying "let me think about it" and going away. He left again after giving me this book, which is why I was writing, and he just now came back and said I should leave at first light. So I'm finishing this quickly so we can go to bed together. I'm still not well enough for anything but sleep, but I think keeping me close on this night is all he really wants.

5 Hantar

I almost changed my mind when I saw how unhappy Cederic was when I woke this morning. It felt...I don't know what that feeling was. Guilt at hurting him, probably, when we both knew this had nothing to do with the two of us.

The journey was tiring but not as exhausting as I'd feared. I haven't been totally honest with Cederic about my condition because I don't like him fretting over me—it doesn't make me recover faster and it's a burden on him. So I don't complain much even when the healing wound twinges. I took plenty of long breaks and ended up here about an hour before sunset, which is why I'm writing; I'm going to wait until near-dark to enter the city. No sense taking risks. Well, more risks than I have to.

The Castaviran camp—there's only one now—looks semi-permanent to me. Maybe what Mattiak said about them not coming after us until spring is true. The Venetrian defenders are gone, sent back to winter quarters I guess. But there's still a heavier guard presence at the gate, so things are not entirely amicable between the allies. I wonder if they let the Castavirans come into the city sometimes?

Putting this away now. Time for the first part of the plan, which is to enter the city and make my way to Fianna Manor. I hope the mages are still there, because I don't know how I'll find them if they aren't. I hope they aren't hurt. I hope they have some idea of where I can find Terrael.

6 Hantar, early

I've got about an hour before we can get the mages out. They have to pack, and even though Jeddan and I both said "pack lightly" they all have strange ideas about what "lightly" means. So he's supervising, and I'm bringing this up to date.

I got through the gate just fine. Really, I can't believe I ever bothered to wait in line to get into Venetry. Then I sneaked my way through the city center and up to where the manors begin. I don't really have a home, since Thalessa has so many painful memories attached to it, but Venetry comes close because I've spent so much time here and infiltrated so many of these manors. I remember what I took from each one, gems and coins mostly, but I also took some jewelry and a couple of curios and—oh, the silver mink statue! I haven't thought of that in years. I had to get it to trade for the Pearl of Remembrance, and I needed that for…I forget what, but it ended with me acquiring Marssik's Primer.

I put more effort into getting that book than any other and it was the last one I got semi-legitimately, tracking down all those objects to trade for other objects until I finally got the one the book's owner wanted. It was worth it, but it took me most of four months. So much easier just to steal what I need—or borrow, I suppose, since I only needed it for a couple of days. Four months in exchange for two days of reading. What was I thinking?

But that's irrelevant. The streets of Venetry were far better trafficked than they'd been the last time I was here, even though it was nearly sunset. I think martial law wasn't in effect anymore. It had been a nice day, clear and warm for early Hantar—I'd appreciated it during my journey.

It certainly didn't look like a city on the verge of war. I'd bet for most of these people, the Castaviran-Balaenic conflict was a distant… not even a worry, more like a possibility on the horizon. Which makes me wonder if the Fensadderian wars are going to spill over into our country. Venetry's not that far from the border, so it's not impossible that we could see refugees coming our way…and now I feel guilty, because my second thought there was "if the refugees cause enough trouble, the Castavirans will be too busy to come after us."

I'm so distractible right now. I think it's because I don't want to think about having to get all these mages out of the city, and then go back for Terrael, which has its own problems. But the only way out now is forward, so that's where we're all going.

When I got to Fianna Manor, I was surprised to see it guarded. Not much surprised, because one of the possibilities had always been the mages would be imprisoned because they wouldn't obey the king anymore, but I hadn't believed that would be the case. At least it meant they hadn't all been executed or transported to Solwyn Manor.

(It occurs to me now that Jeddan might have spirited them all away before I got there. I'm glad he didn't. If Terrael really is in Solwyn, Jeddan's right that I can't get him out without help.)

I went all the way around the manor at a safe distance and saw there were guards posted at every entrance point, even the large windows of the dining room. The King, or the God-Empress, wasn't taking any chances. This was a problem, because there was snow on the ground and even if I were concealed, the least alert guard would notice footprints appearing in the snow. I'd have to do this while concealed *and* insubstantial.

So I circled around, *very* carefully, looking for the best approach: the shortest distance between where I stood and the manor wall, farthest away from the guards. Naturally there was no perfect place, so I chose what I hoped was the safest of several bad options, took a deep breath, worked the walk-through-walls pouvra, and ran.

The dangerous part of this maneuver was going through the wall, because I couldn't remember what was beyond it. I could have walked right into a guard, or one of the mages, or anything. But it turned out to be a pantry near the kitchen—part of a pantry, anyway. I managed to embed myself in its wall, or would have done if I'd been stupid enough to go substantial immediately upon entering.

I took a few steps to one side, let the walk-through-walls pouvra go, and stood for a while to catch my breath. I heard people moving around next door, and the faint rattle and clank of pots being washed or put away. So the kitchen staff, and probably the rest of the servants, were still here. That combined with the presence of the guards was curious: the mages couldn't leave, but they weren't being treated as dangerous prisoners? Jeddan explained it all, but that came later.

So I sneaked out and went all the way up the servants' stair to Jeddan's room, only he wasn't there. His things were, though, so I retraced my steps and went looking for the mages on the lower floors. I'd expected them to be doing what we always used to do in the evenings—gather in the games room or the library, talk and play and generally relax after a long day of work. But both those rooms were dark. Eventually I tracked them down in the ballroom, which was a surprise, because they were practicing pouvrin even though it was, by now, full dark. I was surprised enough that I stood, concealed, in the doorway and watched them.

And they'd changed. They'd gotten better, of course, but there was a determination about them I hadn't seen before. They reminded me of our warrior mages, but where the warriors had focused on a couple of pouvrin and become exceptional at them, the defenders of Venetry had become versatile. My spies were in a corner teaching the walk-through-walls pouvra to a handful of mages I knew for a fact had shown neither inclination nor talent for it when I left. Jerussa was supervising another woman in flitting in ten-yard hops from one side of the ballroom to the other. And Jeddan stood with five or six other mages flicking ropes of fire at the walls and trying to overlay each stroke on the first mark. Every one of them was intent on his or her pouvra to the point I think I could have dropped concealment and walked into the room without being noticed.

And that turned out to be true. It was almost a minute before someone happened to glance my way. "Sesskia!" she exclaimed, which got everyone looking at me, then Jeddan grabbed me in those massive arms of his and swung me around, making me squeak in surprise (and pain).

"What are you doing here?" he said. "Where's the rest of our mages?"

"I'll tell you my story if you tell yours," I said. After a bit of wrangling over who should go first, I told what had happened (very briefly) since the Army left Venetry. I knew they had learned focus and self-control when none of them bombarded me with irrelevant questions. When I wound down, I said, "Your turn."

"Wait," Jeddan said. "You came back to get us out? Just you? That's an awful risk."

"How else could we do it, short of besieging the city and getting torn to pieces by the Castaviran Army?" I said. "I would have been sooner, but I was injured during the fight in the audience chamber. Why weren't you there?"

"I *was* there," Jeddan said. "They summoned a few of us to attend on the King and his 'bride', but I wasn't included. I don't think the King ever understood anyone but you was the leader of the mages, which was fine by me. So I sneaked in."

"I recognized your voice," Kurkis said, "and after a bit of milling around, and once Jeddan got involved, we realized who we were supposed to be attacking. Then we tried to escape with your friends, but the guards collared some of us and we couldn't get away without them being hurt. And we'd have had to leave the rest of the mages who were still here."

"So they marched us all back here and put guards on the house," Jeddan said. "I think the God-Empress wanted us killed, but the King is too afraid of us to try that. He might also hope we'll change our minds and fight on his side. He really is an idiot. It's clear the God-Empress is unstable—clear to us, anyway—but he's letting her make all sorts of decisions for him."

"We've been practicing ever since," Aelisa said. "We weren't fully prepared for the fighting on the walls, before the cease-fire. In the sense of knowing what to expect. Ten of us were killed during the week we were fighting."

I'd tried not to think about how our numbers had shrunk. "We've lost seven," I said. "Everyone else is still with the Army."

"We would have left sooner, but we needed more people who could turn the walk-through-walls pouvra on others," Jeddan said. "It will take too long otherwise."

"Well, I'm not here just for you," I said. "I have a friend who was captured before the fighting started. He brought a message to the King and then disappeared. I don't suppose you know where he is?"

"Are you sure he's still alive?" Jeddan said.

"No, but I'm not leaving until I've either rescued him or proved he's dead," I said.

"What's he look like?" Jeddan said.

I described Terrael as I'd seen him last. Jeddan said, "He hasn't been with the King or the God-Empress. If he's alive, he's in Solwyn Manor."

"That was my guess," I said. It wasn't a happy guess. I've never been inside Solwyn, but I know it's a heavily fortified prison and prisoners only rarely survive to leave when their term is up. Terrael had been inside for almost two weeks.

"So what do we do?" Jeddan said.

"We get everyone out," I said. "You'll go through the north wall, out to the old training grounds, and swing wide of the Castaviran camp until you reach the new road, the one to Colosse. Then you travel as fast as you can until you reach the Balaenic Army."

"What do you mean 'you'?" Jeddan said.

"I have to get Terrael," I said. "And I won't be able to hide that he's missing forever. Once the alarm goes up, the whole city will be alerted to the presence of an enemy, and it will be that much harder for you to get out. So you have to go first."

"You're not going into Solwyn alone, Sesskia," Jeddan said as if this were the most obvious thing in the world. "We'll get everyone out and moving, and then you and I will go back for your friend."

"Somebody needs to take charge," I said, but I was interrupted by Keonn, who said, "We're not infants, Sesskia, and some of us know how to find our way by the stars. You ought to worry more about finding *us* when you're done with your rescue mission."

That made me feel ashamed, because I *had* been thinking of them as helpless without our leadership. Sure, Keonn's not more than seventeen, but he's confident and I think Nessan's spy training has given him competence to match that confidence. "Sorry," I said, "you're right. How many of you can work the walk-through-walls pouvra on someone else?"

It turned out three of them had the ability, which impressed me. We worked out a plan that drew from Jeddan's and my freeing the Castaviran villagers from the prison camp. It means the mages' flight will be discovered sooner than if they were all capable of going insubstantial, but we hope that means the guards' attention will be drawn toward Fianna Manor and away from the prison. It's more complicated a plan than I like, but there's no help for that.

Jeddan says we're almost ready to go. Convenient, because I'm almost at the end of this entry. We're going to subdue the guards on one side of the house, run across the open space to the hedges defining the manor grounds, then split into smaller groups to cross the city. Of course Fianna Manor would be on the southern side of the city, not by much but enough that it would be easier if we could take the southern route. But that side of the city is more well-observed, and this longer route is going to be safer in the long run. We've decided on a meeting place, and Jeddan and I will stay with the group long enough to provide a few more people who can make others insubstantial, then we're going back for Terrael. I hope he's there. I hope he's alive.

CHAPTER TWO

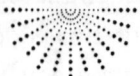

6 Hantar, not sure what time

Terrael's asleep finally. I'm not sure when he last slept, really slept ~~without being~~

It hurts to look at him. Damn the God-Empress for taking such pleasure in other people's pain! I'd have no problem killing her if she were in front of me right now. If he's permanently damaged, I might have no problem hunting her down and killing her in her sleep, never mind what Cederic says about me being no assassin. How can anyone do those things to another human being?

Jeddan volunteered to find food so I could stay with Terrael. I don't feel very hungry. My back hurts and I feel light-headed, and I think I have a fever. Nothing we can do about that except get out of Venetry as soon as it gets to be full dark. It didn't occur to either of us that Terrael might not be able to walk out with us. Now I'm so glad Jeddan insisted on coming along, because I couldn't have carried Terrael, and he needs to be carried. He's so weak, and I don't think they were feeding him hardly at all

I can't write and cry at the same time. All right. Jeddan and I knocked four guards unconscious and dragged their bodies to the hedge, then we saw everyone off—we had so much luck, all the way around, because one of our groups was actually stopped by a pair of guards in the street and Ellika had to do some fast talking to get them to leave them alone. But eventually everyone arrived, and we got them all through the wall with no problems, and Jeddan and I concealed ourselves and crossed the city to Solwyn Manor.

It looks like a prison. I don't know if it looked like a prison back when it was still just a noble's manor, but to look at it now you can't imagine it was ever anything else. It's tucked away in a fold of the hill Venetry's built on, which is no doubt why it was chosen when some long-dead King of Balaen decided he needed something to remind the citizenry of the consequences of crossing him. Nowadays people try to pretend it's not there, and most prisoners go to Gabarek instead. I don't understand why Solwyn is still even open.

The windows on the lowest two levels have been bricked over, the windows on the floor above those are narrow slits, and the walls are all slick rounded stones I wouldn't be able to climb, so getting in by way of the fourth floor windows, which are of normal size, is impossible. The grounds are broad and have been cleared of all obstructions all the way to the walls, which are also slick stone and twenty feet high. A grappling hook might get you over, but it would be a difficult climb.

Almost immediately Jeddan and I had an unpleasant surprise. The night was clear, and cold, and there was a full moon lighting up the prison yard. And we discovered our concealment wasn't proof against that bright light on the flat, smooth ground. Our shadows followed us into the yard, and while they weren't the inky black a bright sun would have cast, they weren't unnoticeable. I don't know how we managed to go all those months without discovering this quirk of the pouvra, but it makes sense—the sun and the moon can't be fooled into not seeing us.

Crossing the yard without using the walk-through-walls pouvra wasn't a problem, as the snow of the yard was trampled enough our footprints wouldn't stand out. But to keep our shadows from giving us away, we had to walk drunkenly from one side of the yard to the other, ducking to obscure our profiles. We hoped the guards observing from the balconies of the second level wouldn't figure out we were human. With luck, we'd look like small animals, of which there are a surprising number inside the walls of Venetry.

I don't know if it was because the trick worked, or if the guards were watching something else, or if they just weren't very alert, but after about five minutes we managed to reach the side of the building and pass through. Then we took a few more steps because we'd walked into a sleeping person. She didn't wake up, or die, fortunately, and we continued through the cell and into the corridor. We went down that hall, poking our heads through the cell doors, until we found an unoccupied one, which we used to make another plan.

"I don't like the idea of separating," Jeddan said. "Sure, we'd cover more ground that way, but we'd have to find each other again, and that could waste all the time we save."

"I agree," I said. "I think we need to make a search of each floor until we find him." I wasn't going to say "if."

"And hope we don't encounter any guards," Jeddan said. "I can already feel my hands going numb from the concealment pouvra. If we can keep from using it, that's better."

So we set off down the next hall, and the search took *forever*. Whatever the original floor plan was, and I'm certain this was not the original floor plan, it didn't have narrow, mazelike passages in which the cells lay at irregular angles and intervals. We got turned around several times and I'm sure we looked in the same empty cells more than once.

Finally we gave up and started marking the corners, down low where no one would immediately notice the marks. Jeddan used his pocket knife to cut scratches into the stone, and from then on we had better luck. There was a guard post near the stairs, manned by a couple of guards who were playing some card game that seemed to require lots of commentary, like "Shouldn't've played the match" and "Be past time for the royal meld, you're losing points," but the guards were preoccupied with the game and never left their post. So we had no trouble sneaking past and getting up the stairs without being seen.

That was the end of our luck. The second floor had guards

14

patrolling, alert-looking guards who walked a tight overlapping pattern. I felt confident I could move around them if I was very careful, but there was no way Jeddan could do it without making noise. So we had to find an empty cell for him (this was difficult, most of these cells were occupied) and I borrowed his pocket knife and went out on my own.

It took almost twice as long as forever for me to be certain I'd looked inside all the cells, and I accidentally brushed through a couple of guards, not their whole bodies, just their arm or shoulder. One of them just shuddered, but the other one became violently ill all over the floor and had to be helped away by another guard. I took advantage of that opening—and it gave me an idea.

I went back to Jeddan and told him what had happened. "I think we can disrupt them enough to clear a path for ourselves," I said. "They'll have no way of guessing what the real source of the problem is, and any confusion has to be for our benefit."

"Unless it makes them more alert," Jeddan pointed out.

"They're already alert enough we're having trouble moving freely," I said. "More alert isn't going to make a difference."

Jeddan hesitated. "It's not going to kill anyone," I said. "You had to pass straight through that guard for him to die. And that's never happened again."

"I hope you're right," Jeddan said, and we left our cell in search of the stairs.

This time, we weren't so careful to avoid contact. It was still slow going, because Jeddan will never be able to move quietly no matter how much he practices, and the whole strategy hinged on the guards not realizing intruders were in the prison. But we made it to the next flight of stairs, and the guard post, having made two more guards vomit and a handful of others look shaky and uncertain.

The guards at the post, like all the others on this floor, were very alert. I solved that problem by sneaking up close enough that I could work the mind-moving pouvra on one of them, blocking the flow of blood to his brain just enough that he got dizzy. While his partner was helping him, we slipped past and up the stairs.

The third floor looked more like the noble's manor this used to be and was living quarters for the guards and, I assume, the prison warden. At least there was one little suite that was nicer than the other rooms, which looked more like barracks. One of the barracks rooms was full of sleeping men. The nice little suite was also occupied. There weren't any cells on that level, and no guards, and the layout was much more straightforward: a large dining hall, a kitchen and store rooms, a couple of rooms full of things guards like to entertain themselves with (and a bookshelf, which surprised me, because I don't think of guards as literate). We checked the whole floor and found nothing of interest. A wide staircase led up to the top floor.

I'm having trouble describing what we found there. On the one hand, there were the cells—they didn't really look like cells because the furnishings were nicer, but the doors had windows with bars in them and the locks were the kind I wouldn't have wanted to have to pick to free myself. We couldn't tell for sure because they were unoccupied. They're probably for holding high-ranking prisoners before they're executed or exiled or whatever it is they do with high-ranking prisoners. As I've written before, I usually deal more with ground-level law enforcement.

That was one side of the fourth floor. The other side was taken up by the kind of rooms I'd always imagined would be underground, where what they do to people can be hidden away. I don't know why I thought that. Maybe torturers want to see their handiwork in the clear light of day. With windows like those, you'd see absolutely everything. It was sunrise when we entered, so we sure as hell did. And maybe the screams are to unnerve the other prisoners, make them want to talk, if that's why they're in prison. After all, nobody cares what lower-class prisoners have to say once they've been convicted and locked away in Solwyn. And now I've thought too much about it, and it's making me sick. Sicker.

We found Terrael in one of those rooms, chained

True God have mercy, *why* would anyone do that? Balaen is supposed to be *civilized*, why do we even *have* those rooms? I could see the God-Empress enjoying watching that, but those rooms were fitted for torture long before she seduced the King. It makes me furious and miserable and left me wanting to set the whole thing afire. The only thing that stopped me was knowing those guards would flee and leave all the prisoners locked in their cells to burn, and I don't care how evil those prisoners are, that is not a death I would wish on anyone.

So we freed Terrael, and I went and got some of the blankets from the nearest cell to wrap him in, and then we had to figure out how to get outside. The problem was, while you can work both the concealment and walk-through-walls pouvrin on yourself at the same time, you can only do one of those on another person at a time. So Jeddan could conceal them both, but if he tried to go insubstantial, Terrael would fall, and if they were both insubstantial but only Jeddan was concealed, it would look like Terrael was floating.

I was furious at this point, and I got angrier every time I looked at Terrael. This is not a good state of mind for a thief. Angry thieves get caught. But the more I thought about the situation, the more I wondered if being a thief was really the best solution. It had gotten us in here, sure, but maybe something else was needed to get us out.

"I have an idea," I told Jeddan, and explained what I wanted to do. He looked at me as if I were crazy.

"I think you're crazy," he said. "That's going to draw all sorts of attention."

"If we do it right, it will be the wrong kind of attention," I said. "And it will confuse the hell out of them."

Jeddan grinned. "It's crazy, but I like it," he said.

So he gathered Terrael up, and his weak cry of pain made me so angry I felt filled with righteous fire as I led them down the stairs all the way to the second floor, all of us concealed but substantial. Jeddan waited a few steps up and out of sight (not that he was visible) and I went to stand in front of the men at the guard post. They were having some inane discussion about a woman they both knew, and the fact that it was a little obscene made what I was about to do sweeter.

I whistled two notes—the sound a cleric makes just before

conducting a funeral dirge—and, when they'd both perked up and looked around, said, "The true God knows your evil, and *you will be punished*" and knocked one of the guards unconscious. He folded up satisfactorily, and his friend leaped up with a shout. I gave him enough time to register what I'd done before sending him unconscious too.

The shout brought another guard down the hall towards us, not quite at a run, but certainly in a hurry. "Claddik? What was that?" he called out, then came to a halt when he saw the collapsed men. I leaned in to breathe heavily in his ear, went insubstantial briefly when he whipped around to strike at me, then went around behind him and said *"You will be punished"* and repeated the trick. It's too bad it takes a few seconds to make someone unconscious that way, because he had time to scream in terror, but then he didn't make another noise until his skull hit the wooden floor.

"Let's go," I said. We went straight down the hall, not bothering to avoid the guards who were running toward us. I began keening *"Punished!"* in my eeriest voice, knocking out a few guards when it was clear they would run into us otherwise. Then someone saw us—I could see his eyes focus on me—and I started to work the (I don't know what else to call them) assassination pouvrin. But the funniest thing happened: he choked, pointing in our direction, shouted *"Harbinger!* Death has come for us!" and turned and ran.

That stirred up all manner of confusion. I can only guess he saw the barest glimpse of us before the concealment pouvra forced him to look away again, though why he thought I was Death's Harbinger I have no idea. I'm not even dressed in white. But it helped clear the path to the first floor, so I didn't think too much about it.

The first floor was crowded with guards, all of them trying to get out, and getting past them was hard. At one point we stood there waiting for an opening in the mad rush. I was glad, at that point, that I hadn't started a fire, because this was evidence that my guess about how they'd treat the prisoners in that event was right. Bastards.

Eventually we made it to the place we'd entered by. In all the commotion, we could have walked out the door, but eventually they'd figure out nothing supernatural had happened, and I didn't want to be around for that. So we risked being visible for the few seconds it took to go through the wall, and then we ran for it, not caring that our shadows, this time cast by the early morning sun, clearly marked our trail.

The guards were all making plenty of noise, some of them running out the door and not stopping when they got to the street. We probably could have dropped the concealment pouvra if it weren't for the blanket-wrapped Terrael in Jeddan's arms, they were that distracted, but that wasn't a risk I wanted to take. Instead we kept moving, invisible, until we were out of sight of Solwyn Manor and into one of the many parks in upper Venetry.

There I left Jeddan and Terrael, concealed more conventionally behind some bushes so Jeddan could get some feeling back into his toes and fingers, and went to find a place we could wait out the day. We're going to have to go directly out the front gate because Terrael needs medical care, and there's no way a surgeon in Venetry would not realize his injuries were from torture and draw the right conclusion. So we have to get him back to the Army as quickly as possible, and I don't know how we'll do that.

That's not true. I have an idea. It's probably the most insane idea I've ever had, but it might save Terrael's life. I refuse to believe it could be at the cost of my own.

Anyway, I rented us a room—I could have found us an empty shed or warehouse or something, but Terrael needed something better than bare floor padded with blankets—and Jeddan sneaked Terrael in, and now he's foraging and I

I think I'd better lie down and rest. I'm just hungry, that's why I'm light-headed. I hope Jeddan finds Terrael some clothes. And food.

CHAPTER THREE

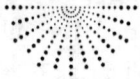

10 Hantar

Cederic hasn't let me sit up until now. He was so adamant he actually set Sovrin to watch me on the grounds that Audryn is preoccupied and Sovrin is more ruthless even than he is. I've barely been allowed to get up to relieve myself, that's how ruthless she is. I'm afraid I've pushed him too far. He was so angry, and he's barely spoken to me since I returned. Granted, I was unconscious for most of the time, it's still...I don't want him to hate me. I did the right thing and I knew what the price would be and I don't regret it. He'll understand that eventually.

I have to write this all down because my memory is fuzzy, and writing helps me put it all in order. I think—no, I know I slept before Jeddan came back, and it was a real sleep and not unconsciousness. But Jeddan let me sleep while he tended to Terrael and only woke me up when Terrael was dressed and had eaten something, though it was only watery gruel, the only thing he could manage to choke down. As starved-looking as he was, it was probably better we didn't try to feed him anything more solid. He woke long enough to recognize me and say my name, and I asked him—I don't know why I did this—if he knew his own name, which he did, so he wasn't that far gone. Then he was unconscious again.

"I don't think we'll have any trouble getting out," Jeddan said. "I liked your idea of you leaving first, then going visible so they'd be watching you while I bring him out through the gate."

"Good, because I was afraid you'd think it was too risky," I said. "But we have to get him to the camp as quickly as possible. I think he —he's not doing well. I wish they had someone who knows healing kathanas, but all the ones who did lost their magic, and it's not something Cederic can do alone."

"We can get a wagon somewhere, a light one with a couple of horses," Jeddan said. "We might be able to make twenty-five miles in a day."

"That's not much faster than the Army is going," I said. "I was thinking...maybe there's another way."

Jeddan is very smart. He was only puzzled for a couple of seconds before he said, "There's no way you can carry him while you flit, Sesskia. Even if you could carry another person, which you can't, he's got seven inches on you and is still heavier than you even in this state."

"I can carry anything I can lift," I said, "and if I can lift him, I can carry him."

"Which you can't, as I think I just pointed out," Jeddan said.

"I can if you strap him to my back," I said.

"Let me do it," Jeddan said. "He's less than a full load for me."

"*You*," I said, poking him in the sternum, "can barely flit five hundred yards at a time. It will take you forever to reach the Army. I can do it in a day and a half. Less."

"You're still injured," he said.

"Terrael's going to die if we don't get him to the surgeon," I said. "This will hurt me, yes, but it's not going to kill me, and if he dies because I didn't at least try to get him help—I can't do that, Jeddan. This is the only way."

He grimaced. "It's not the *only* way," he said, "but it's the logical way. All right. What do we need?"

It took us most of the rest of the day to find something we could use as a harness, during which time I became increasingly nervous. Suppose I couldn't do it? Suppose I exhausted myself somewhere along the road, and it took too long? I still wasn't feeling very well and I was aware there was a chance I could seriously injure myself. But I kept coming back to how bad Terrael looked, and the thought of him dying—Audryn's face if I had to tell her I'd let him die—it swept away all those worries.

It was after dark by the time we were ready to go. We stuck with the original plan to start. I went out ahead of Jeddan and Terrael, dropped the concealment pouvra and began dancing and shouting and waving to get the guards' attention. I couldn't do a lot of dancing, because my back hurt and I didn't want to exhaust myself before the real journey began, but they were definitely headed my way when I saw Jeddan and Terrael emerge through the wall and then disappear.

With my eyes watering from trying to see through the conceal-ment pouvra, I worked it myself and enjoyed the guards' consterna-tion as I "vanished" right in front of them. Then I just walked away down the road until I couldn't see Venetry's gate anymore, sat on the cold, snowy ground, and waited for the dizziness to pass and Jeddan and Terrael to arrive.

Shortly I heard a heavily-laden person approaching. Jeddan laid Terrael down carefully, but he was unconscious again and didn't make any sounds of pain. "This is not going to be easy," he told me, rolling his shoulders to get the kinks out. "Even balanced on your back, he's going to be heavy. And you'll have trouble getting him up again after your rest times."

I didn't tell him I didn't plan on there being very many rest times, nor on putting Terrael down when there were. My thought was I would get it over with quickly, push myself as hard as I could, and plan on resting when we were both safe. It was probably a bad idea, but since we're both alive, I refuse to feel guilty about it.

(This is not true. I feel horribly guilty at injuring myself and taking that risk when I promised Cederic I wouldn't. No wonder he's angry at me. I hope he'll eventually speak to me again.)

So all I said was, "I know what the risks are. I've thought it through. You just do what you can to keep up."

"I was thinking I'd try to find the other mages," he said. "Then send Jerussa on ahead to let the Army know where we are."

"All right," I said. "Help me get him up."

I was so grateful Terrael was unconscious for this part, much as his condition frightened me. I can't imagine how painful it would have been for him to be handled so roughly as we did in getting him settled on my back. My not-yet-healed wound twinged, and I had a moment's fear I would tear it open again (which ultimately turned out to be true) but I pushed that away and focused on balancing his weight. "All right," I said. "See you in a few days," and then I took a deep breath, let it out slowly, and flitted as far as I could.

It was painful when I was escaping Venetry with my back sliced open. This was ten times worse. I nearly fainted when I landed three miles down the road and had to bend over, carefully so as not to unbalance, and breathe heavily until the world stopped spinning. Then I did it again. The second time was better because I knew what to expect, and eventually I could flit almost as quickly as I usually did, though I needed to rest for a full minute between flits instead of a few seconds.

Then it was two minutes.

Then it was several.

Eventually I realized I had to stop for a longer rest or pass out, so I found a spot under a tree and settled myself. This took a lot of Terrael's weight off me, and it felt so good by comparison I felt I could sleep, so I napped. I couldn't fall fully asleep—I wasn't that comfortable—but it refreshed me somewhat.

Near sunrise, I woke out of my latest nap to hear something croaking in my ear. I turned my head, and Terrael said, "Sesskia," in a low, painfully hoarse voice.

"You're awake," I said.

He brought one nail-less hand up to grip my shoulder, lightly. "... one of us...is bleeding..." he said. It took him almost a minute to get it all out.

"It's probably me," I said. "The God-Empress's soldiers tried to carve me up. I'm not fully healed yet."

"...why...carrying me...hurts you..." he said.

I wasn't going to tell him how serious I thought his condition was. "I'm taking us both back to the Army, where the surgeon can fix us," I said. "I can carry you that far."

"...Audryn..." he said.

"She's fine. The baby's fine. She's been worried," I said.

He was silent for a moment, then he said, "Thank you."

"You're my friend," I said. "I'm sorry it took so long."

He nodded, then his head slumped, and for a few seconds I was terrified I was now carrying a corpse, but I could feel his very slow breathing on my neck. I dug into the pack strapped to my chest and got out an apple, thinking as I chewed that this wasn't going to get any easier, and if Terrael was right that I was bleeding, I didn't have a lot of time before I wouldn't be able to go on at all.

Even so, it was so hard to make myself stand, sending more pain shooting through my back as I got under Terrael's weight. I felt the wetness spreading, though it was seeping rather than flowing freely. Then I told myself to ignore the pain and made my first flit.

I don't remember much of that second journey. I stopped once long enough to eat something else, not that I remember what, and every three or four flits I checked to make sure Terrael was still alive. He never did regain consciousness, thank the true God, and I never lost consciousness even though there were times I really wanted to.

It was full night again when the camp came into view, and I was so dizzy and fuddled I thought I'd gotten turned around, and the lights of the camp were stars, and I was looking down on the sky instead of up at it. Then I made one last flit and ended up among several anonymous tents, and I was so tired I just sank to the ground and waited for someone to notice us. They did, right away, and someone took Terrael off my back, and someone else lifted me, and that person turned into Cederic, and that's when I fell asleep.

I woke up two days later, back in my not-beloved wagon warmed by several dozen th'an, and it's been nice to rest. Though it would be nicer if Cederic were here. I'm so afraid, because he hasn't come to see me except once, I've done something he can't forgive me for. Even that one time he was so distant and angry. I feel like I've broken faith with him even though there really wasn't anything else I could do, not and remain myself.

He'll come back. I know he will.

11 Hantar

Feeling much better. Sovrin's an excellent companion. She's been telling me jokes and stories about our Balaenics learning to speak Castaviran, with all the attendant misunderstandings. She's traveled quite a lot, or did before the Castaviran army set out from Colosse, and says the Balaenic villages she's visited have been mostly welcoming, though nobody, Balaenic or Castaviran, seems to believe it's possible to create a new government that will bring the two countries together instead of one conquering the other.

The Castavirans mostly like the idea of a new Emperor or Empress, whoever that might turn out to be, but most of them are afraid of God's wrath if they make the wrong choice. Hmmm. Maybe that means Cederic, as Kilios and most high priest, is a better choice than a purely secular leader.

The Balaenics are divided between wanting the King to rule both countries and wanting the government to pass to one of the other noble houses, though they don't seem to have any consensus as to which one. Convincing them Cederic

He hasn't come. I haven't seen him in two days. He must be so angry with me. I can't even cry about it because Sovrin will want to know what's wrong, and I don't want people to know my marriage is falling apart practically before it's begun. I should have known I would make a mess of it.

12 Hantar

We're nearing Colosse—should be there tomorrow afternoon. No Cederic. I wonder if I ought to leave the camp so we don't have to encounter each other, not that it matters because he's doing such a good job of avoiding me. Not that I have anywhere to go.

No idea where Jeddan and the mages are. They should have been here today. This army isn't small, and I don't know how they can miss us, so in addition to my personal misery I'm knotted up inside with worry over them. I think unhappiness is worse when you can remember what it's like to be happy. Even with Sovrin here I feel incredibly alone.

13 Hantar, noon

I'm so glad I didn't leave. It was all a huge misunderstanding. He's spent every night in this wagon by my side, but he comes to bed so late and rises so early I had no idea he was even there. They—Cederic and his aides and the Balaenic generals—have been busy planning what will happen when this foreign army comes thundering down on Colosse, so to speak, and *he* thought I was sleeping most of the day and wouldn't care if he were there or not. But something woke me before dawn today, and I rolled over and let out a shriek when I saw him because I was so surprised, which of course woke *him*. Then I burst into tears and he had to hold me until I calmed down enough to tell him, still tearfully, what I'd been thinking for the past several days.

He apologized, and kissed me, and admitted he'd been angry when I arrived back at camp because I was nearly in as bad a shape as Terrael, but he was just as angry with himself as he was with me. Once he'd reminded himself that we'd both decided this was the best course of action, he was able to let go of the anger and move on to worry.

"And I am nearly resigned to the knowledge that I will likely have cause to worry for you many, many times during our life together," he said. "Thank you for bringing Master Peressten back to us. He will recover, though I think some of his injuries will always bother him."

"I'm glad. I was afraid he wouldn't survive the journey," I said. "Was I right in taking that risk, flitting back with him?"

"You were," he said, but his arms tightened around me. "His injuries would have killed him soon. Another reason I find it difficult to be angry with your choice."

"I'm sorry," I said. "I never want to hurt you, you know."

"I know. But I think hurting each other unintentionally is part of marriage," he said, " as is apologizing afterward, and making things right," and he kissed me again. This time it was the kind of kiss that leads to other kinds of contact. It took me a while to remember I was injured, and despite the canvas cover, we were in an open wagon, and Cederic's new office meant he had to maintain his dignity, not possible if he were caught making love with his wife in the back of said wagon.

"Soon," I said, giving him a little push, "and in a real bed, please." He smiled.

"If all goes well, we will sleep in a real bed tonight, though not in the palace," he said. "It will require much repair to be habitable again."

"So what will happen when we arrive?" I said.

"The Balaenic Army will make camp outside, and we—you will attend, as Empress-Consort—" I made a face, and he laughed —"yes, your first appearance in a public role, love, because it is essential we make it clear this is to be a united country, Castaviran and Balaenic both on the Imperial throne. We, and General Tarallan and a few of his officers, and some of the Sais, will go out under flag of parley and request the presence of the rulers of the Castaviran Empire for a meeting. I will explain the situation and my reasons for accepting the Imperial crown, at which point the four former candidates for the role will begin arguing. I will allow them to argue themselves out, at which point I will convince them I am right."

"You seem awfully certain of that last thing," I said.

"I will not know what to say until I have heard their arguments, and understand what it is they want," he said, "and whether or not I can give it to them. A point in our favor is I am certain none of those candidates want the responsibility that comes with the Imperial crown. Granted, neither do I, but I understand better than they do what that responsibility is. I think, if they are guaranteed power in a new government, they will be willing to accept me as Emperor."

"Or they'll support the God-Empress and try to kill us both," I said.

"One of the things I love about you is your endless optimism," he said, and I laughed and kissed him.

"I believe in planning for the worst," I said. "What will I have to do, exactly?"

"Possibly nothing except be a visible reminder of what we are trying to accomplish," he said. "Each of those four candidates is more interested in maintaining Castaviran superiority than in bringing two countries together. They were not happy about the idea of handing our throne over to a foreign king. Now that it is again possible a Castaviran will sit on that throne, they may forget our decision and once more argue their own legitimacy. Your presence will make it difficult for them to do so. Though they may also want to know what qualifies you to be the Empress-Consort besides being married to me."

"That will be a hard question for me to answer," I said, "given that I'm not sure there *is* anything else."

"You represent a growing power in Balaen," he said, "you are, to our knowledge, the most powerful mage of your country, you have traveled extensively through Balaen without establishing ties to any one place and therefore will not privilege one area over another, and you have risked your life to defend Balaen against Renatha Torenz. Those are all reasons they will respond to."

"I should make notes," I said.

"I think your prodigious memory will make that unnecessary," he said, disentangling himself from me in preparation for rising. I made a noise of protest, and he took my hand and squeezed it gently.

"I have neglected you for far too long," he said, "and there is nothing left to do but wait until we reach Colosse in a few hours. I intend to pass the word that I will be with my wife this morning, and am not to be disturbed for anything short of Renatha Torenz's army appearing on the horizon. And then I will bring us both breakfast, and we will talk of everything except the coming conflict."

So we did. I feel so much lighter than when I was carrying around the fear that he didn't love me anymore, even if I am still nervous about the upcoming meeting. Cederic has gone to arrange everything

—the flag of parley to go first, then the rest of us to follow as soon as it's been acknowledged.

Cedric wanted me to ride my own horse—this is apparently tradition, even when going on foot makes more sense—but I flatly refused, and he decided I was right that it would look bad for the Empress-Consort to be dumped on her ass on the way in to parley. So I'll ride with him, which makes me as happy as it's possible to be when I'm on one of those animals, and we'll see what happens. I think I've mentioned that's my least favorite kind of plan.

CHAPTER FOUR

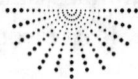

13 Hantar, evening

I didn't realize how much pain I was in until it was gone. Healing kathanas are extremely complicated and require at least three mages working together, but they're very effective. I'll still have an interesting scar, but otherwise I feel as if I'd never been wounded. Terrael's prognosis isn't as good as mine, because even the best healing kathana has its limitations, but he's conscious, and they were able to repair his tendons so he can walk again (or will when he's fully regained his strength). He looks a thousand times better than he did when we brought him out of Solwyn Manor. I don't know about his mental state, whether he'll ever truly recover from what they did to him, but Audryn doesn't seem worried, and she'd know better than anyone.

Despite what Cederic said about my prodigious memory, I really wish I'd been able to take notes. A lot happened this afternoon, and I'm sure I've already forgotten some of it, though I paid close attention to what everyone did, and didn't, say. Cederic seems to think things went better than he'd expected. I guess the next few days will show if he's right or not.

Cederic just came in from the little room where we'd put our clothes if we had any extras. He's clearly not wearing anything under that robe and he has the Look that says I won't be wearing anything in a minute either. I'm continuing to write and pretending I don't see him just to drive him mad with desire uh-oh he's

14 Hantar, early morning

I never thought about sex during the years I was traveling—I mean, not in terms of something relevant to me. I certainly never understood how it can bind two people together emotionally as well as physically. I never feel so much a part of a union as I do when Cederic and I make love, never feel so spiritually invigorated even as I'm physically so relaxed I usually fall asleep right afterward. My foundation.

I made myself wake up when Cederic did—I don't understand why he only needs about five hours of sleep a night and never exhausts himself. But it's going to be another busy day, so I wanted to write all about yesterday before I completely forget.

Our messengers came back only a few minutes after I finished writing yesterday at noonish, saying the King of Helviran would see us now. I didn't like the sound of that, as if this King were in a position to grant boons, but Cederic said, "Note that Dugan Lerongis did not style himself Emperor. He is a man easily manipulated by others and I daresay his wife encouraged him in his unsubtle and incompetent grab for power. Our messengers went to each of the candidates, all of whom are in Colosse to recognize the ascension of the new Emperor, to inform them this 'enemy' army is not here to take the city. They are to attend on me at Marloen Hall, which is as close to neutral ground as anywhere in Colosse, in one hour."

"That *does* sound like you have the power to make demands," I said.

"As Kilios, I do, though probably not to the extent I will demand their allegiance today," he said. "If there is a Kilios, he or she may choose to accept the most high priesthood, and the most high priest has the right and obligation to anoint and crown the Emperor of Castavir when that title changes hands. This also means the most high priest has the right to *choose* a new Emperor when there is no successor.

"There is nothing to say the most high priest might not decide he is the best choice for that role, but it also does not fall inevitably to him, and my decision to claim the throne for myself will be seen by some as an attempt to take power that does not belong to me. Today is for convincing these four to put their support behind me, because each has a measure of political or ecclesiastical power others will follow."

"How confident are you of success?" I said.

Cederic shrugged. "Reasonably confident. The one thing I am certain of is that each of these men and women is committed to keeping Castavir intact without it coming to war—or, at least, presenting a unified front to Renatha Torenz's army rather than being weakened by internal strife. If they can be convinced I am the superior candidate, they will probably seize on that as a satisfactory solution."

"I hope you're right," I said. At that point it was time to mount up and ride into Colosse. I kept a tight grip on Cederic's waist and tried not to wince too much at how the horse's bouncing step jarred my still-healing wound. I realize they're just animals, and not intelligent like humans, but it certainly feels as if they know ~~I'm afraid~~ I don't like them and enjoy taking advantage of that. The Kilios's robe smelled musty and sour, as if it needed washing, but I'm sure if someone tried, they'd be yelled at for damaging an important piece of history. And it would probably fall apart. So I tried not to lean too close to Cederic or think about how high off the ground I was, and paid attention to Colosse.

The streets were mostly empty when we rode into the city, probably because of the Balaenic Army massed on the horizon. It felt so strange riding into Colosse and seeing little piles of snow where the streets had been swept clear. All my memories of the city are of heat and sweat and, of course, the God-Empress. I wonder what the summer climate will be like? Surely not as hot as it was, if snow can fall here.

The farther we went, the greater the crowds, until we were surrounded on both sides by lines of people staring at us. Then someone cheered, and within minutes we were surrounded on both sides by lines of people shouting Cederic's title and waving and holding their children up so they could see. Cederic acknowledged the greeting with his usual ebullience, i.e. nodding solemnly and occasionally lifting his hand to wave. I knew they were cheering him as Kilios, since they couldn't have any idea he was their Emperor-elect, but I tried to wave at them myself and succeeded only in nearly falling off the horse.

It was a reassuring sight, because I figured if they thought Cederic was that wonderful, they might be inclined to accept him as their Emperor. I wondered what they thought of Cederic arriving surrounded by the Balaenic Army, with Balaenics in his processional. I wondered if any of them missed the God-Empress. None, I hoped.

The Marloen Hall is near the palace, south and west from where the Sais' wing used to be. Unlike most of the buildings in Colosse, where you can tell what you'll find inside by what shape it is, it's the only one of its kind. It's domed, but not like the mage buildings, which look as though bubbles are trying to emerge from them; the dome is elliptical, and bulges more at one end than the other. The building itself is a smooth oval about three stories tall, though when we went inside I discovered most of it is a single room that rises all three of those stories to the domed roof. It's full of padded chairs that all face toward the bulging end of the oval, where there's a raised circular stage bearing five of those padded chairs arranged in a circle.

There were three people, two women and a man, sitting in the chairs, none of whom turned to look at us. That was either custom, or an insult, but Cederic didn't give any clues as to what he thought of their behavior, so I'm still not sure. Probably dominance ritual of some kind.

Hah. I managed to make it sound like we rode our horses all the way inside Marloen Hall. Though the doors are big enough, and the ceilings high enough, we could have done that. No, we left them outside with the soldiers we'd brought with us to hold them. I didn't mention that even with all the cheering, you could see people edging away from the horses. The God-Empress declared, years ago, that no animals were allowed inside the city, so some of those children might never have seen a horse in their entire lives. The idea made me feel defiant, like we were making a rude gesture in the God-Empress's direction. Even if we were making that gesture with horses.

So we dismounted and went inside. There were a couple of aisles between the chairs that led to the stage, and we all followed Cederic (well, actually I was walking beside him, so they were following us) down the widest aisle. It was literally down, because it sloped a bit, probably so people sitting in those chairs could see past the people in front of them. The stage was circled by shallow steps so you could walk easily to the top, which we did, and Cederic continued on toward the circle of chairs and went around it to sit in an unoccupied seat, making a tiny gesture to me to sit next to him. Mattiak and the generals and the Sais (we'd brought a total of ten other people, evenly divided between Balaenic and Castaviran) ranged themselves behind Cederic.

The people in the circle did not look happy that I was there. "Who is—" one of the women said.

"Thank you for arriving so promptly," Cederic said, smoothly cutting her off. "Though I do not see Dugan Lerongis."

"He's always late," the man said. "Who—"

"Time enough for introductions when we do not have to repeat them," Cederic said. He was doing such an excellent job of keeping them off-balance I wanted to applaud, but that would have looked bad, so I folded my hands in my lap and tried to look serene. I'm not very good at serene, so it probably came off as something else, I'm not sure what. Hopefully not fierce, which Cederic says is my default expression when I'm intent on something.

They all subsided, though they kept glancing at me. The woman who hadn't spoken had a look of amused resignation on her face, as if this interplay was something she'd expected. She had very white hair, though her face looked too young for it, green-gray eyes, and she wore a priest's robe in honey-colored silks and satins. Two large rings adorned her hands, one a cabochon-cut star sapphire, the other the biggest ruby I'd ever seen set in jewelry in my life. (The Kerkara Ruby is twice its size, but nobody would dare set it; bad luck follows that thing like a shark follows blood.) The woman was either richer than she looked or was, like Cederic, wearing history.

The woman who *had* spoken had beautiful red hair and the beginnings of lines at the corners of her eyes; I judged her age to be mid-forties. She wore elaborate court clothing made of heavy brocade shot with gold, possibly actual gold, and a gold filigree crown set with polished red jasper perched atop her head. Her hands were constantly moving from her knees to the arm of her chair, then back to her lap where she twiddled her thumbs for a bit, but that was the only part of her that moved. I'd have thought her perfectly placid except for her hands.

The man was the youngest of the three, about Cederic's age, portly and with his dark hair cut very short in a style that suited him. He was dressed simply, but if he were Balaenic I'd have said his clothes were expensive despite their appearance. He wore a very dark stone in his left ear, either lapis lazuli or garnet, I couldn't tell in the low light. He was smiling, which unnerved me because I couldn't read his expression—amused, condescending, friendly, concealing something else? I was also unnerved at the way he kept looking from me to Cederic and back again, his gaze usually lingering on me. It was hard not to glare at him, which I would have done had I not felt it would be bad to begin this meeting in a state of antagonism, since it was so likely to end up there.

The doors at the back of the room opened again, and a man stood silhouetted against the dim light from outside. He paused for a moment so we could absorb his magnificence, or whatever, then came down the aisle at a slow pace, as if this were a ceremony and we were all here to honor him. His approach was marred by his jerking to a halt about twenty feet away from the foot of the steps, then coming toward us more rapidly.

"Why is she in my seat?" he demanded. His voice was whiny and petulant, further spoiling his magnificence, though the truth is, he wasn't all that magnificent. He was attractive enough, tall, with longish chestnut brown hair and dark eyes, dressed in ornate court costume, but he was too thin and he kept hitching at the neck of his over-robe as if to keep it from sliding off his narrow shoulders. It made him look as if he were on edge, which he probably was.

"Welcome, Dugan Lerongis," Cederic said. "We seem to have insufficient seating. Allow me to remedy that." He gestured, and the well-dressed woman and the short-haired man made little noises of surprise and consternation as their chairs scooted apart to make a space for another chair that now came floating up from the floor and settled itself there. Everyone but the older woman goggled.

I was impressed because I knew, as the rest of them did not, that despite the gesture, Cederic had used Balaenic magic, his mind-moving pouvra, to move the chairs. I hadn't seen him work *any* magic since we'd been reunited, so I didn't know he'd gotten so skilled with it. I felt smugly proud on his behalf.

"But—" Lerongis said. I knew from what they'd said before this was the King of Helviran, and the one most likely to challenge Cederic. He'd probably been hiding outside, waiting for Cederic to enter, so he could act like they'd all come at his bidding. I enjoyed seeing him flustered.

"Please be seated so our meeting can begin," Cederic said politely, but his eyes didn't look at all as if he were going to put up with Lerongis's recalcitrance. Lerongis sat.

"Thank you all for joining me," Cederic went on. "I am sure you have many questions. Allow me to answer what I have no doubt is the one uppermost in your thoughts. This lady is Sesskia of Balaen, my wife."

I was prepared for this, mostly. We'd had a long discussion about how I would be introduced, me being very reluctant to give my praenoma to a bunch of strangers who might well turn out to be my enemies, Cederic insisting we should abide by Castaviran customs in this respect because we would be urging them to make many more concessions far more important, to them, than that one. In the end, I agreed, though it didn't make me happy.

But I think he's right; we need to be prepared for the reality that each country will have customs the other finds strange or unnecessary. The idea that spending the night with someone can make you married, for example. I wonder which customs are going to be universally adopted, if any.

Anyway, that did get a reaction, even from the older woman. "The Kilios married a *foreigner*?" exclaimed Lerongis. "Impossible!"

"Congratulations," the older woman said, still with that amused look in her eye. Cederic raised his eyebrow at her and returned the smile.

"You are certainly committed to this cause," the other woman said. "I hope you didn't think this was something we expected of you."

"I doubt Cederic Aleynten has ever done anything simply because it was expected of him," the other man said. He stood and bowed to me, and said, "Moerton Taissatus, my lady, and I welcome you to Colosse." That meant more than just a greeting; Taissatus is chief consul of Colosse, which is like being head of all the Lords Governor if we had such a thing in Balaen, so his welcoming me to Colosse was a subtle political ploy whose deeper meanings were lost on me.

"She's Balaenic, Moerton, she doesn't speak Castaviran," Lerongis said.

"Yes, I do," I said, startling Lerongis. I sort of wish I'd been able to pretend I didn't, just to see what he'd say when he thought I couldn't understand. He strikes me as the kind of man who'd insult you behind your back and be sweetness and smiles to your face. But it wouldn't have been worth it.

"Thank you for your welcome," Cederic said, though most of them hadn't welcomed me at all. Taissatus sat back down, still smiling at me, which made me slightly uncomfortable because I still couldn't read his expression, except I didn't think he had a sexual interest in me. To cover my confusion, I turned in my seat and said, in Balaenic, "Cederic introduced me to them. I gather they weren't expecting him to have a wife at all, let alone a Balaenic one."

"That was a lot of conversation for just introducing you," Mattiak said. He looked extremely intimidating, which comforted me.

"Some of it was keeping them off-balance," I said. "I'll translate as best I can, but it's going to be difficult for me to keep track of two conversations."

"You can tell us the rest afterward," he said. I nodded and turned around again. The others were watching me as if they'd been waiting for me to finish. I tried not to blush with embarrassment.

"As to the rest of your urgent questions," Cederic said, "I am afraid our embassy to the King of Balaen was a failure. Renatha Torenz has convinced him of the validity of her claim, and the two of them intend to marry and rule both countries jointly."

"Hah," said Taissatus. "So she had the same idea we did."

"That doesn't explain the foreign army camped outside our capital," Lerongis said.

"Let him finish, Dugan," the white-haired woman said.

"Thank you, Sai Amaleten," Cederic said. "In our journey to the Balaenic capital city of Venetry, we encountered the main body of the Balaenic Army. Commander General Mattiak Tarallan"—he indicated Mattiak, who managed not to look startled at being suddenly included in a conversation he couldn't understand —"when presented with our purpose, agreed to support our cause. When we confronted Renatha Torenz in Venetry, he chose to break with his country and throw his lot in with ours. Since the Castaviran Army is once more controlled by the former God-Empress—"

"What happened to General Regates?" the woman whose name I didn't know said. She sounded really upset.

"She was convinced by Renatha Torenz that she would benefit greatly by rejoining her side," Cederic said. "I am sorry, Lelaena."

"I can't believe Gael would do such a thing," Osther (I didn't remember for a bit that her surname is Osther, but I knew Lelaena was the first name of the Queen of Endellavir, so I'm putting that in now) said, but in a shocked way rather than denial.

"What, because she's Endellaviran and therefore above suspicion?" Lerongis said. I liked him less with every word that came out of his mouth.

"Because most of this was her idea, Dugan," Osther shot back. "Because she has been my friend for more than twenty years. I refuse to believe she would betray us."

"I believe the General felt her life was in danger should she refuse Renatha Torenz's order," Cederic said, but the way he said, too smoothly and rapidly, told me he wasn't convinced. But they seemed to satisfy Osther, or at least help her calm down. "At any rate," he continued, "General Tarallan is committed to the cause of bringing our countries together peacefully, and has offered the services of the Balaenic Army toward that end."

"So we're supposed to put our faith in someone who betrayed his own King?" Lerongis said. "Someone like that will probably turn on us when he decides that's in his best interests."

"General Tarallan is no traitor," I said, sitting forward in my seat and startling everyone. "Garran Clendessar betrayed his country and his responsibility as King when he threw in his lot with the God—with the former Empress. *He* is the traitor."

"What did you say, Sesskia?" Mattiak asked.

"That you're a great man and Balaen's King is a traitor," I said, turning to look at him.

He grinned. "I don't know about the first, but by the sound of your voice, you're definitely someone whose good side I want to be on," he said.

"Wife of the Kilios or no, you don't have a right to speak to me that way," Lerongis sputtered.

"Sesskia has every right to correct our misapprehensions about her countrymen," Cederic said, "as she is the only one of us with any first-hand knowledge of Balaen's King. The General would find no welcome from Garran Clendessar were he to decide, as you put it, to turn on us. He has quite thoroughly and publicly burned his bridges. And he has my complete confidence."

"Well, speaking of confidence, it seems like we're back where we started two months ago," Lerongis said. "We agreed then that putting the King of Balaen on the throne of a unified country was the best solution to prevent civil war. Now he's no longer an option. What's next? More wrangling over which of us should take that role?"

"We're all reasonable people," Osther said. "We should be able to come to a decision."

"Like we did last time?" Lerongis said.

"Relax, Dugan," Taissatus said. "We all want to avoid civil war. Some of us will just have to concede personal power to reach that goal."

"'Some of us' meaning not you, Moerton?" Lerongis said.

"Enough," Cederic said, and of course they subsided. "I think you may have forgotten it is I as most high priest who will choose our new Emperor or Empress. And I have made my choice."

That got them all murmuring, even the placid Sai Amaleten. "Well, which of us is it?" Lerongis demanded.

Cederic looked at each of them in turn, waiting for silence. "I have decided I am the best choice to rule a united Castavir and Balaen," he said.

Lerongis leaped to his feet, shoving his chair back several inches. "*What?*" he shouted.

"Power grab, Kilios?" Osther said, trying and failing not to sound furious.

"That's impossible," Taissatus said. "You're ineligible. You might be the most perfect man in the world and I still wouldn't support you in this idiocy."

"I'm leaving," Lerongis said. "Helviran is withdrawing from the Castaviran Empire. I've proved I'm a better ruler than Renatha was and I don't have to endure your slight on my abilities. If you can't—"

"*Sit down,*" Cederic said. Lerongis dropped into his seat, still breathing heavily. "This is not a decision I made lightly. I have never desired political or ecclesiastical power, and my entire life is witness to that truth. But we need an Emperor who will be acceptable to *everyone*, Balaenic and Castaviran, and of the five of us, I am the only one who fits that description."

"You are also a proud man, Cederic," white-haired Sai Amaleten said, her calmness a stark contrast to everyone else's outrage. "Prone to think highly of yourself, to believe yourself superior to others because that robe declares you preeminent of the mages of Castavir. Why should we believe your assertion?"

"I did not make this choice because I believe I am a better person than the rest of you," Cederic said. "And I discovered recently how much my pride has made me weak. But it is not pride to acknowledge one's strengths. I led this city out of chaos. I am, and have always been, fair-minded when it comes to resolving conflict—one of the reasons you all agreed I should make this choice. This robe testifies to my ability as a priest-mage of the Castaviran Empire. And while I did not marry for political gain, it is true with Sesskia on the throne beside me as Empress-Consort, I will show Balaen that I—that we— are serious about bringing our countries together as equals."

"Do you honestly think anyone will believe you didn't marry this woman for political reasons?" Lerongis said.

"We were married before the convergence," I said, "before anyone knew the former Empress would be deposed and long before any of you got together and decided you were somehow perfect to rule two countries. And I don't actually give a damn what people believe. Least of all you."

"You dare speak—" he began.

"Oh, shut up, Dugan," Osther said. "Joena put you up to this, didn't she? I know she likes the idea of being Empress-Consort. You ought to listen to yourself. Demanding respect you haven't earned, claiming superiority, speaking rudely to the Kilios's wife even though she probably ranks higher than you do. You're embarrassing yourself."

Lerongis stood up again. "I don't have to take this," he said.

"No, you don't," Cederic said. Lerongis looked startled at this and froze in the act of stepping away from his chair. "You are a capable manager and Helviran has prospered these many years under your leadership. I mean no insult to your abilities when I say I believe myself to be best suited to be Emperor. You know I prize honesty— let me be honest with you. You are easily swayed by the opinions of others and quick to take offense, and those are qualities that are fatal in an Emperor. But that does not mean you cannot serve the Empire as you always have. I need your support as King of Helviran. Please."

Lerongis stared him down, breathing heavily. He swallowed. "No," he said. "Helviran is withdrawing from the Empire."

"Don't be hasty, Dugan," Taissatus said. "Helviran can't secede. It's been part of Castavir for centuries. You'd wreck both our economies, tear families apart—don't do it."

"I demand to be made Emperor," Lerongis said. "It's that, or I go."

"Don't you dare try to blackmail us," Osther said.

Cederic made a quelling motion with his hand and rose to face Lerongis. "Is that your decision?" he said quietly. "You would destroy your country to fulfil your need for glory?"

Lerongis blinked at him. "I want what's mine by right," he said, but he sounded shaky.

"Tell me what your right is," Cederic said, advancing a few steps so they were almost nose to nose. Lerongis swallowed again and glanced quickly to either side as if looking for support. "I think you have mistaken desire for rightness," Cederic said. "Renatha Torenz made the same mistake. I will be sorry to see you go, Dugan Lerongis, but *I will be damned if I turn this country over to someone just like her.*"

"I'm nothing like her," Lerongis stammered.

"Then prove it," Cederic said in a low voice. "Choose to make this Empire better rather than to exalt yourself. Or walk away." He turned and sat in his chair. I'm the only one—maybe Mattiak did too—who saw his hand tremble before he stilled it.

Lerongis continued to breathe as heavily as if he'd just run ten miles without stopping. Then he sat down again. "Helviran will stand by you, Kilios," he said.

"Thank you, your Majesty," Cederic said. "What say the rest of you?"

"After that display? I think you made the right choice, Cederic," Taissatus said with a grin. "And I can even admit I might be too easy-going for an Emperor in these times. Maybe if we were entering an era of peace, but...no. I withdraw my claim in favor of Cederic Aleynten."

"Thank you, Moerton," Cederic said, turning to look at Sai Amaleten, seated next to him. She shrugged, still smiling that enigmatic smile.

"I have known you since you first entered training, Cederic," she said, "I have seen you grow from boy to man, and I know your weaknesses as well as your strengths. You have a tendency to reach beyond your grasp, and that tendency could bring this Empire to its knees. But you," and suddenly her attention was on me, "you who want to be Empress-Consort, what do *you* say?"

"Ah," I said, "Sai Amaleten, this isn't something either of us *wanted*. Cederic was going to found a thanest, whatever that is, and I was going to learn how to bring Balaenic and Castaviran magic together. That's what we wanted. But I think it's true he's the best choice, and that means we'll face the challenge together. If that's what you're asking."

"I am asking," Sai Amaleten said, "if you believe *you* are worthy to share that throne."

"I hadn't thought in terms of *worthy*," I said, feeling irritated. "I'm Balaenic, which seems to be a criterion of worthiness *you* all thought up. I'm probably the most powerful mage of Balaen, which makes me Cederic's equal in that respect. What's most important is Cederic is going to have the most difficult task in...probably in all of history, bringing these countries together, and he can't do it alone. And I am his foundation. So I don't know if that makes me worthy, but it certainly makes me essential."

Sai Amaleten's little smile broadened just a bit. It made me wonder if Cederic learned his smile from her. "Cederic Aleynten, I will support you as Emperor," she said. "And you will make me most high priestess. This is not blackmail. It is a statement of fact."

"I accept what you offer and agree with your statement of fact," Cederic said with a nod. "Queen Lelaena?"

Osther had her elbow propped on the arm of her chair and was resting her chin on her fist. "I agree that of the five of us, you are the best candidate for Emperor," she said. "And I will withdraw my claim."

"But?" Cederic said.

Osther sighed and straightened in her chair. "The loss of the Castaviran Army is a heavy blow," she said. "I appreciate the service of the Balaenic Army, but it's a fraction of the size of the one Renatha Torenz commands, and they are still foreigners as far as Castavirans are concerned. The language barrier alone will make it hard to integrate the dispersed Castaviran forces with the Balaenic Army. We'll be fighting at a tremendous disadvantage. You'll have the support of the Castaviran people, true, but that won't give you more troops. It could even mean their deaths, if the former Empress wins this war. I think this is a mistake."

"What are you saying, Lelaena?" Cederic said.

Osther pushed herself up from her chair and bowed. "I am saying Endellavir is going to withdraw from both sides," she said. "I believe what you're doing is right, but I can't put my people at risk when I think it's unlikely you'll win. But I won't support Renatha Torenz either unless it becomes a choice between doing that or seeing Endellavir destroyed. I'm sorry, Cederic."

"I wish you would reconsider," Cederic said, standing to face her, though he didn't look at all intimidating the way he had when he faced down Lerongis. "Renatha Torenz will see anything short of immediate and total obedience as a betrayal. She will destroy you simply for having plotted her overthrow, even if you recant. Your safety, and that of your country, is at stake."

"That's true," Osther said, "but it's a lesser risk than throwing in our lot with you. My people will leave in the morning. Unless you want to force the issue."

Cederic shook his head. "We will not try to prevent your leaving," he said, "and I would wish you well if I believed at all what you are doing is the right choice."

"It's the only choice I can make," Osther said, and extended her hand to grip Cederic's. "And I pray I'm wrong."

"I understand," Cederic said. He remained standing as Osther descended the stairs and left the building. Then he said, "We will need to invent a new coronation ceremony. Obviously I cannot crown myself, so we will need a new most high priestess." He nodded at Sai Amaleten. "It must be soon. General Tarallan tells me we must find a winter home for the Army, and I would like to gather as many of the Castaviran forces as possible before spring comes. But to do that, we need an Emperor."

"I think we can come up with something that will satisfy everyone's need for pageantry," Sai Amaleten said, rising from her chair. The other men followed suit. "The palace is uninhabitable; will you stay at the Firtha thanest tonight? Or would you care to join Dugan at Moerton's home?"

"You're welcome to join us," Taissatus said. Lerongis looked petulant again. I really don't like him. I wonder what his wife's like. A real harpy, I imagine.

"Thank you for the offer, Moerton, but Sesskia was injured in our flight from Venetry and she needs healing," Cederic said. "We will meet tomorrow to plan our strategy for gaining support. Master Peressten will translate for you and Dugan, Moerton, and Sesskia, you will need to translate for General Tarallan, who will share his insights on making friends with our Balaenic neighbors. They, too, have a stake in this."

A thanest turns out to be the actual name for the domed mage buildings. The Firtha thanest is the largest one in Colosse. They're like the Darssan except with less focus on research and more on offering magical services to the citizens of Colosse. As soon as we got there I was whisked away for healing, which was uncomfortable because I had to be naked from the waist up and two of the Sais were male. But being healed made it worthwhile.

Then I went back to the camp with the healers to watch them tend to Terrael. I watched the healing with the see-inside pouvra, and then I explained about the see-inside pouvra combined with the mind-moving pouvra, and they were all very excited about that. If I had medical training, I'd be able to do what the healing kathanas do, but by myself instead of with two other people. It got me excited too

—the possibility of using those pouvrin to heal instead of to kill relieves my mind considerably.

Just before I went back to Colosse to spend the night, my mages arrived! They'd had an uneventful journey, and Jeddan found them a few days ago, so they were all together and it was a grand reunion. Now I'm impatient for Terrael to recover so he can alter his translation kathana to give the Castaviran language to the Balaenic mages. I feel guilty about sleeping in a real bed when they're all still in tents, but if the Empress-Consort can't have a few advantages, I don't see what the point of the rank is. Other than having sex with the Emperor, which from my perspective is probably the best advantage of all.

CHAPTER FIVE

14 Hantar

I got married today. Married again, I should say, because Cederic and I were married months ago, but Castavirans distinguish between the wedding promise (which is what we did in spending the night together) and the marriage vow, which is spoken before a priest-mage in a special ceremony.

It was all very abrupt. I was finishing breakfast with Audryn and Sovrin and Terrael—after the healing, he's well enough to move around on his own, though he has to rest often—and Terrael and I were preparing to join everyone for the strategy planning meeting when Cederic approached at a near-run. That was frightening. He's usually so calm that when he moves quickly, it means something is really urgent. He took me by the arm and said, "Sesskia, come with me. We have to swear our marriage vows."

I was surprised enough by his haste his words didn't make any sense to me, and I had to ask him to repeat himself. He did, all the time pulling at my arm to make me rise. I resisted, saying, "Why are you in such a hurry?"

He released me—by this time I was standing—and said, "The

Emperor must be joined to his wife by vow of marriage before they are crowned. The coronation is tomorrow. We cannot delay."

"Oh," I said. That was as far as I got before Sovrin and Audryn put themselves between me and Cederic.

"Sesskia can't make her marriage vows looking like this, Sai Aleynten," Sovrin said.

"What's wrong with the way I look?" I protested.

"It's barely past sunrise," Audryn said, ignoring me. "You can give her some time to change. This is an important day, Sai Aleynten, and you—neither of you—want to look back on it and regret being so hasty. You ought to change your own clothes, too."

Cederic glanced down at himself—he was wearing the Kilios's robe, which as I've written looks scruffy despite being a piece of Castaviran history, and his ankle boots he hasn't bothered to shine for days, and smiled one of those tiny, self-deprecating smiles. "You have a point, Master Engilles," he said. "I will ask Sai Amaleten to prepare to accept our vows at noon, if you think that will be sufficient time."

"We'll hope so," Audryn said.

"What's wrong with the way I look?" I repeated, now feeling annoyed at the idea that it might take four hours to make me presentable. But it's true I was wearing an odd mix of Venetrian and Castaviran clothing, my Venetrian shirt and coat having been ruined by the God-Empress's soldier and his so-sharp sword. I'm now very glad Audryn dragged Sovrin and me and a handful of other women mages into Colosse to a clothing store she knows.

The owner was taken aback when we all came bursting through the door, but when she understood who I was and what we were after, she became incredibly helpful. She found an unclaimed dress in my size, altered it there in the store because it was (of course) too loose in the bosom, and finally made the whole thing a present to me for my wedding day. I think she's hoping the Empress-Consort will bring business in if she's pleased with the service. That might even be true. I have no idea what kind of clothing I'll need in that position.

We went out and found shoes and jewelry while the woman was

altering the dress, dark green malachite stones and golden slippers to match the green velvet and gold lamé of the dress. It has a square-cut neckline and these odd sleeves that fit tightly through the upper arm and then bell out alarmingly (from my perspective as a thief who might have to climb walls in them) and have to be turned back and pinned to the upper sleeves by more of those malachite stones set in brooches.

We were able to do all of this in three hours, which left time for me to be fussed over by half a dozen women who (except for Audryn) had to date shown no interest in clothing or hair or jewelry, but now revealed themselves to be experts on Castaviran fashion. By the end, they were oohing and aahing over me, and when I became irritated that I was the only one who couldn't see how good I looked, they did a kathana that made a mirrored oval in front of me where I could see my whole body at once, and the sight made even me breathless.

The same women were my escort to where Cederic waited, and the sight of him made me breathless again, because I'd only once seen him in something other than a robe, and today he wore a heavily embroidered sleeveless tunic over a loose-sleeved linen shirt, and gray trousers tucked into knee boots, and he was so handsome I felt stunned. Then he turned and looked at me

I don't know why remembering that makes me emotional. Probably because no one has ever seen me the way he does. It's more than just feeling beautiful, it's that when he looks at me, I know he sees someone who makes him stronger, and being able to do that for someone—mattering that much to someone—it makes me feel stronger too.

So I took his arm, and we walked through the tents and out of the camp to where practically everyone in the combined Castaviran-Balaenic force was standing, waiting for us. It was unexpected enough that if Cederic hadn't had a tight grip on my arm, I might have tried to run out of reflex. That was when I really understood the kind of life I'd volunteered for. I'm going to live the rest of my life in the open, no more hiding, no more disappearing into the crowd. It still frightens me if I think too much about it. I hope someday it will be easier. I'm afraid it never will.

At the time, I didn't have the leisure to entertain those thoughts, because we were approaching the wagon where Sai Amaleten stood so we could be visible to everyone. I wished we were marrying in the Balaenic tradition, which is extremely private, just a votary of the true God and the two witnesses who stand as living reminders of what you promise the true God and each other. Which reminds me Cederic and I had talked about the Castaviran marriage ceremony, and we almost ended up not married right there because I was worried about swearing oath before his God when I worship a different one. It was a short but wide-ranging conversation, and the result was:

1. We don't actually know they're different Gods. Given that we both started from the same place, it's more likely we're using different concepts for the same being.

2. At no point in the ceremony do we make vows to God, so I'm not blaspheming.

3. Balaenic clerics will eventually weigh in on whether the Castaviran God is the same as the true God, or is one of the four false Gods (true God forbid this is the case), or is a different true God, and we shouldn't make that decision for them.

4. We should at some point get married the Balaenic way to satisfy the Balaenic citizens that their new Emperor respects their customs, at which point the true God can bind our union.

Even so, between the huge audience and my lingering doubts about whether the true God would strike me down for swearing these vows, I was overwhelmed enough I don't remember a lot of the ceremony. For one thing, I have no idea what I said beyond the first ritual words "To swear oath of marriage before God's representative" that you say in response to the priest-mage's inquiry as to why you're there. Everything after that is completely up to you.

I know Sai Amaleten asked some questions about what we were willing to sacrifice in order to make our marriage work, and I hope I didn't promise anything impossible, like obeying Cederic without question (hahahaha). I vaguely remember telling him I would be his foundation forever, and I don't think I was that articulate, but it was enough to satisfy both him and Sai Amaleten.

What I do remember—what I am certain I will never forget, but I'm writing it down here anyway—is Cederic taking both my hands in his, looking at me with those eyes so much like my own, and saying, "I loved you long before you knew it. Everything about you captivated me—your quick mind, your generous heart, your endless strength. Even now I will sometimes look at you and be awed at the thought that you have chosen to bind your fate to mine. I swear to be faithful to you, Sesskia, now and every day for the rest of my life."

I can't think of anything more perfect than that.

Anyway, after we'd made our vows to each other, Sai Amaleten said a few words in a language I didn't recognize Cederic said later was Kureki, a formal tongue religious ceremonies used to be celebrated in, and everyone cheered, and we kissed, and we were married. Again.

Audryn must have gotten to the camp cooks, because after all that we had a huge meal that was as nice as it could possibly be under those circumstances, and we received a lot of congratulations. Mattiak didn't even look jealous or regretful when he hugged me and said, "I wish you joy, now and in all the days to come" which is what Balaenics say to celebrate new beginnings.

Then it was over, and we changed out of our nice clothes (mine have been put away for me to wear to the coronation tomorrow) and went back to our normal routine, which for Cederic meant going over plans for the coronation and for me meant practicing with my mages. We want to work on the problem of discovering the original form of magic, but with the coronation looming up in front of me, I can't really focus.

Cederic came in about five minutes ago, asked me what I was writing, then proceeded to take off his clothes very slowly and provocatively, which is no doubt why my handwriting is so messy now. He's been waiting very patiently for me to finish, since he knows I need my record to be complete and not to skip over the important things, but I find I'm the one who's impatient now, because I feel as if this is our first night together, all over again. And this record's not nearly as important as he is.

15 Hantar

It's taken me hours to calm down enough to hold this pencil without it shaking so hard it leaves scribbles all over the page. How could I have forgotten the hold the God-Empress has on so many Castavirans? Or did I want to forget so I could cling to the belief that we're going to win in the end, despite all the disadvantages we have— small army, no support for it, no recognition by the consuls of Castavir, no allegiance from the Lords Governor of Balaen. Right now, I can't convince myself we're not going to lose.

Now I know Cederic's going to live, I can write all of this down, hoping it will calm me further. He's going to live, he's been crowned Emperor, and the raving bastard who tried to kill him is dead, thanks to the soldier in Cederic's retinue who kept his head while everyone else was screaming, me included.

I'm ashamed that my first reaction wasn't to defend my husband, especially since I was standing right beside him and could just as easily have been that man's target. My *first* reaction was confusion and shock; the man lunged out of the watching crowd with a knife in his hand and plunged it into Cederic's chest before anyone could react, even Cederic.

That's not true. Cederic had moved to put himself in front of me before the man struck, which is why the knife didn't go through his heart, and when the man raised his hand for a second blow, I worked the walk-through-walls pouvra on the blade and it fell to the floor. After that, I was busy holding Cederic up and working the ~~assassi~~ the healing pouvrin on him, trying to stop the bleeding though I had no idea what I was looking at and getting blood all over my dress and my hands

I guess I'm not as calm as I thought. Soldiers tried to take him away from me and I screamed at them and clung to his arm until they pried me off and carried me away after him. They took us to the room beneath Marloen Hall we'd waited in for the ceremony to start. I kept trying to stop the bleeding, all the while terrified I was hurting him further by my lack of knowledge.

It took forever for someone to bring healers, and then the soldiers took me away again, but only as far as the other side of the room so we weren't in the healers' way. I swear when this is all over, I'm studying medicine. I felt so *helpless*, fumbling around and not knowing what to do, and if he'd died because I didn't know how to use the pouvrin...I don't think I could have lived with myself if that had happened.

Cederic was still unconscious when they finished, but the healers assured me he was going to recover fully and thanked me for what I'd done, saying I'd probably saved his life. Which was small comfort considering I felt I should have stopped the assassin before he'd gotten that far. If I'd been paying attention, I could have made him drop the knife before he got in the first blow. I could have burned him. I could have done any number of things—but I didn't, and Cederic's alive, and I need to stop blaming myself. I can't stop blaming myself.

The soldiers took us away again, this time through a back passage where they'd brought one of those little man-powered carriages (I don't know why they didn't have a collenna) to take Cederic to the Firtha thanest for observation and possibly more healing if necessary. But it could only hold one person besides the driver.

That was when I broke down entirely. I have never felt so weak and helpless in my entire life, and I know I've never—that's wrong, the last time I gave myself over completely to grief was when Bridie died and I wasn't there for her. I couldn't bear that they were taking Cederic away from me when I felt so deeply that I'd failed him. And the soldiers just stood there like they didn't know what to do with a hysterical Empress-Consort, when their orders were to take the Emperor to safety. But Mattiak showed up—he'd come to tell me they'd confirmed the assassin was working alone—and he got angry, and in the end the soldiers found another little cart to take me to the Firtha thanest behind Cederic. I've never been so grateful to anyone in my life.

I meant to write down what happened at the coronation, but I can't remember half of it when it was driven out of my mind by what happened afterward. I'm sure people were recording the event for history, so it's not as if no one will know about it just because I didn't write it. I know, because Sai Amaleten explained it to me, that the original coronation ceremony for the God-Emperors refers to what Castavir owes them, and the rewritten one emphasizes the role of the Emperor as he *serves* Castavir. I remember after Cederic was crowned, he had to crown me as well—I'm still not sure what my role is, beyond being married to the Emperor, but it sounded as if I were some kind of Emperor-adjunct. True God forbid it means I become Empress if Cederic

He's not going to die. That's just my fear talking.

15 Hantar, later

Cederic woke up. He seems perfectly fine, if weak from blood loss. He doesn't remember anything after descending the stairs with me (he was attacked about halfway down the long aisle) and the first thing he asked when he woke up was whether *I* was all right. That made me cry again, but I stopped because it upset him. I held his hand and told him what happened, and he fell asleep in the middle of my explanation. The healers said that was perfectly normal.

15 Hantar, just after sunset

I had to change my clothes—my dress is ruined—and stand out in front of the Firtha thanest to assure the crowd that Cederic wasn't dead. It seems there was quite a lot of unrest after he was carried out unconscious and covered in blood, and somebody started a rumor he'd been killed and it was a sign he didn't have God's blessing. And *that* got people talking about whether or not it was a good idea to support someone who wasn't God as Emperor, since it had worked *so well* for them before.

When I heard about all this, I got angry. There were a lot of people gathered in front of the Firtha thanest, waiting for news, and when I came out they all started shouting questions, and so many of them sounded so...it was almost as if they were happy Cederic had been attacked, because it gave them something gruesome to talk about. That made me angrier. They probably wished I was still wearing the bloody dress.

So I summoned a great lash of fire to whip around over their heads, which made them shut up fast, and before they could start talking again, I made a speech in which I reminded them of all the evil things the God-Empress had done to them. Making them obey her whims. Punishing them when she changed her mind about what those whims were and didn't tell anyone. Executing people for disobeying her. Having people killed for no reason.

I pointed out that Cederic had sworn an oath to protect them rather than treat them as his servants and that the God-Empress (I didn't call her this to their faces because I'm not stupid) would never dream of doing anything like that. And I said if any of them wanted to challenge Cederic's claim to the throne, they could take it up with me personally.

That was more than enough to disperse the crowd. I'm sure none of them wanted to argue with a foreign mage who wielded who knew what kind of powers, let alone their anointed and sworn Empress-Consort. They won't be totally happy until Cederic can stand before them, but this should satisfy them for a few hours.

When I went back in, Cederic was awake again, more lucid this time, but still weak. He had some orange broth—I still don't recognize half the foods they have in Castavir—and was able to talk to me and hear the story of what happened. I downplayed my hysterics, partly out of embarrassment and partly because I was afraid it would worry him, and he told me it wasn't my fault he'd been nearly killed, at which point I said, "How would you know? You were unconscious and bleeding to death. It's not as if you remember any of this."

"Sesskia, you are strong and brave and selfless," he said, "but you are not invincible. You could not see the future to know that man would attack me, and your reflexes are good, but you should not expect yourself to be perfect. And I understand your pouvrin saved my life. So if you wish to blame yourself, my love, you may do so, but I refuse to engage in that behavior with you."

"Well, when you put it that way, you make me sound selfish in wanting to take all the blame," I said. I felt more cheerful than I had all day.

"Yes, you should allow me my share of blame in not realizing the possibility of such an attack," he said. "I knew already we do not have the full support of everyone in Colosse. Some will try to destroy us out of fear of what Renatha Torenz will do to them if we are defeated. Others will attack because they feel loyalty toward the madwoman as God. In either case, we are not entirely safe, and will not be until we leave Colosse. And even then we should expect these kinds of attacks to persist after we have defeated her."

"That makes me tired," I said.

Cederic set his bowl aside and lay back on his pillow. "Lie beside me," he said, "and we will sleep together and give each other comfort."

So I climbed into bed with him and held him until he fell asleep, then I got up to write all of this, and now I'm going back to bed. He's right, it gives me comfort to be next to him, listening to him breathe and being very grateful he's still able to do so.

CHAPTER SIX

17 Hantar

We've been on the road all day, which was as tiring as it ever is. We were meant to start the journey yesterday, but Cederic insisted on touring Colosse (with me, in full Imperial regalia "liberated" from the same museum the Kilios's robe came from) so everyone could see he was, in fact, not dead. It was a good idea, and drew large crowds of cheering citizens wherever we went. Reassuring to know not everyone is a potential assassin, but I for one don't remember much of the journey because I was so preoccupied with scanning the crowd, prepared to kill anyone who went after Cederic again.

My only other thought was worry for what might happen to these people if the God-Empress captured Colosse. She's capable of putting all of them to death, or trying to, because they "betrayed" her, and I wonder how ready her soldiers would be to carry out such an order, given that many of them have families here. But then I always wonder how anyone can bear to do the things she expects of her followers. It simply doesn't make sense to me.

Then Sai Amaleten in conference with the healers decided Cederic needed a day of rest before exerting himself further. But "day of rest" meant he was allowed to come back to the camp yesterday afternoon and go over some of the logistics of our journey so long as he didn't exert himself. We're going to Barrekel, where the Black and Brown divisions of the Balaenic Army are headquartered, to get the support of its Lord Governor so when winter is over and we're ready to face the God-Empress's army, we can add the Barrekellian troops to ours. Arron Domenessar, the Lord Governor of Barrekel, is supposed to be a reasonable man and one who's spoken against the King's policies in public, so Mattiak is hopeful we'll be able to get him to support us.

The real problem is Barrekel has already clashed with Castavir, specifically the Helvirite Army headquartered in Teliarne, which is about seventy miles from Barrekel in this new world. Cederic's decree (in his role as Kilios, pre-Emperor status) that the Castaviran cities not engage with the Balaenics didn't do much to stop the conflict. It was the coming of winter, and the fact that the armies were fairly evenly matched even with the Helvirite mage corps, that brought hostilities to a standstill. It took Lerongis's command added to Cederic's under the Emperor's chop to get Teliarne to agree to open diplomatic relations with Barrekel, and all we know is that they did. We don't know what kind of agreements they've come to, and there's been some discussion over whether we should go to Teliarne first, but Mattiak is convinced Domenessar needs to know we respect him, which means not appearing to give precedence to Castavir. I guess that makes sense too.

There's been a lot of discussion about how to convince the Lords Governor to follow a Castaviran ruler, and most of it is, uncomfortably, centered on me. I'm not nearly so optimistic about myself as a battle standard, or figurehead, or whatever, as Mattiak and the others are. I may be Balaenic, but I'm not noble and I'm nobody anyone would be automatically inclined to follow. Personally, I think it's likely one or more of these Lords Governor will try to raise his own standard, not that any one of them is capable of taking the throne. If anyone could, it would be Caelan Crossar, which makes me wonder what happened to him. I can't see the God-Empress being stupid enough to let him live.

After Barrekel, we're going south to Teliarne, which is the capital of Helviran, so Lerongis will be able to order the Castaviran troops headquartered there to join us. That reminds me that I met his harpy wife, Joena, and she wasn't at all what I'd expected. She's about twenty years old, a lot younger than her husband, waifish and diffident, and it isn't until you've spent some time in her presence that you realize whatever spine Lerongis has is on loan from her.

She never makes assertions, just comments on things by saying "I wonder if you've considered" and "I realize I'm not terribly informed, but it seems to me," but her comments are always on point and insightful. She's respectful of her husband, but he rarely says anything without glancing at her—I'm not sure he knows he's doing it—and I get the feeling she doesn't actually like him much. I wonder why they married.

She was polite to me, but in the way sharks are polite to each other: circling each other, recognizing a fellow predator, respectful but not remotely interested in becoming friends. It's obvious to me she thinks she ought to be the one sitting on the throne, and honestly, I can't say she wouldn't be qualified. But given that Lerongis is totally *un*qualified for the position of Emperor, the only way she could get there would be by claiming the throne herself or marrying Cederic, and even if he weren't married to me he's clearly disdainful of her method of wielding power. He prefers a straightforward, unapologetically forthright woman. Lucky for both of us I'm that.

Anyway, it seems like Lerongis will have no trouble bringing the Castaviran troops under Cederic and Mattiak's command. Even so, this makes me more worried than getting Domenessar to fall in line, because integrating the troops...I'm no military expert, but I can hear what Mattiak and the generals aren't saying, which is that it's going to be difficult even if there wasn't a language barrier. The army in Teliarne is *huge*, though, and we need all the troops we can get, especially since the western regiments of the Balaenic Army will certainly be added to the King's Castaviran forces.

(It just now struck me as so odd that we've basically swapped armies. Castavirans fighting for Balaen, Balaenics fighting for

Castavir—or maybe it's more accurate to say we've already begun integrating our countries. I'd be more cheerful about that if all our lives weren't at stake.)

Moerton Taissatus came to the meeting with Perce Aselfos, which surprised me for a few seconds until I remembered Cederic had said he'd turned out to be a capable ally, if not one with leadership qualities. It seems he's been working with Taissatus on keeping order in Colosse after the army left, turning his network of spies outward to keep track of pockets of unrest and people who still support the God-Empress. They're staying in Colosse where they can maintain contact with the consuls, some of whom are either already in enemy territory, like the one at Carinne (which is the city Mattiak was besieging before they called him back to Venetry to defend it), or are going to be overrun before we can return in the spring.

Taissatus is trying to convince them to support Cederic, but a lot of them are concerned for their cities because some of them aren't very big and certainly can't hold out against the Castaviran Army. He and Aselfos seem confident, but I'm worried for both of them. What happens if spring comes and the God-Empress reaches Colosse before we do? Much as Taissatus makes me mildly uncomfortable (only because I like being able to read people) and Aselfos makes me uncertain (because I don't totally trust him to keep faith with Cederic) they're loyal supporters so far and I'd hate to see anything happen to them.

Also to my surprise, I've become the leader not only of our mages, but the Castaviran ones as well. I'm not sure why that is, whether the Castavirans are responding to my being their ruler now, or if some of Cederic's charisma has rubbed off on me (unlikely) because I still don't understand their magic any better than I did six months ago. I *am* the only person who's successfully combined Castaviran magic with Balaenic, and maybe that's it.

Either way, they look to me for guidance, even Terrael, which is strange. He's mobile again, and able to serve as Cederic's aide, but he has to rest often, and fortunately he has Audryn to tell him when he's overexerting himself. We've talked a bit and he says, not that he wanted to be tortured or anything, but it's been good to have time to put his mental energies toward the problem we (mages) care most about, which is bringing our magic together.

"I've been thinking it can't be as simple as drawing th'an with a pouvra, like you did with that binding th'an in the Codex summoning," he said a few hours ago after we'd all eaten and were sitting around relaxing by the fire.

"Right, because that was so easy," I scoffed.

"I said simple, not easy, Sesskia," he said, scooting up where he had his head in Audryn's lap.

(He really has changed. He used to be sort of formal with her in public, tentative, like he was afraid she might change her mind about him, and now he's affectionate and loving—I saw them standing together off to one side of their tent one time, where I'm sure they thought no one could see, and he had his hand on her belly and was saying something that made her laugh. I felt shy about having witnessed it, but it made me so happy too.)

Anyway. He went on to say, "That was an obvious solution, but it's only doing two types of magic at once, not a new integrated whole."

"Do you think that's what we're looking for?" I said.

He shrugged, and said, "It's what happened to the worlds, isn't it? They've come back together and you can see the places where the landscape's a combination of what used to be in each world. What worries me is that it didn't just happen automatically. The magic reuniting, I mean."

"Maybe it has, and we haven't realized it yet," Audryn said.

"I think if it had, neither of our magics would work anymore," Terrael said. "Maybe we're looking at this the wrong way. Maybe they *can't* come back together and this new world is going to have two branches of magic."

"I don't like that," Jeddan said.

(I forgot to mention that all day yesterday, while I was off being Empress-Consort, Audryn and a handful of the other Castaviran mages were using Terrael's altered translator kathana to give the Castaviran language to all the Balaenic mages. It's been interesting to see which language people choose to speak by default, since some of the Balaenics have decided they're more comfortable with Castaviran and vice versa. It doesn't seem to matter the nationality—and maybe that's a sign we'll be able to blend our magics as easily as we have our languages.)

"At least we'd all still have magic," Terrael said, not seeming to notice he'd included himself in the magic-having group.

"*We* would," Jeddan said. "What about the children born with the ability? Your child, maybe—he or she—"

"She," Audryn said.

"She's got a good chance of being born a mage," Jeddan went on, though I wanted to override him and demand to know how Audryn could be so sure. "Suppose she's born with a pouvra the way they—" he waved his hand at Jerussa and Tobiak, sitting nearby—"developed one during the convergence. Would she even want to learn all those th'an when learning pouvrin is faster? Think of all the knowledge we'd lose if Castaviran magic disappeared. Or suppose she *doesn't* start out with a pouvra, and doesn't experience anything to trigger Balaenic magic? Pouvrin are going to stay rare, even though they're more powerful. And worse, we might end up with factions where each side believes their magic is superior and is dismissive or even antagonistic toward the other—you want the new world to look like that? I think, if it's true the magics can't come back together naturally, we ought to be looking for ways to make it happen."

Terrael sat up slowly and said, "I think you're right. But it doesn't make sense. Magic is what brought the worlds together—you can't keep it apart. But the worlds are together, and the magic still isn't."

"Which suggests there's something still keeping it apart," I said.

Terrael nodded, but he had that abstracted look he gets sometimes when his mind is already off in pursuit of some solution to an intellectual puzzle. "I can—no. That's not right. If we...or..."

"You have to say *all* the words, Terrael," Audryn said with some amusement. He glanced at her and grinned.

"Sorry," he said. "I think I should give this more thought before I say anything more—what little it seems I'm capable of saying. It's just...when you said that, Sesskia, I had the image of something propping a door open. I wonder if it's not literally true something's keeping the magic from joining."

"Or a clot of dirt in a lock that keeps the, um, key from opening it," I said, refraining at the last minute from implicating myself as a thief, even though I'm sure they all know it.

"Or a misalignment that keeps the teeth of two gears from meshing," Jeddan said.

"Nice imagery, but isn't it more likely the alterations the original kathana made to the requirements for magic aren't completely gone?" Audryn said. "Given that those mages wanted to make it possible for everyone to work magic, and that meant changing its fundamental principles."

"I hadn't thought of that," Terrael said "but it's worth considering. I'm convinced this problem is more important than it seemed at first."

"You keep saying that, but I'm not sure why," Jeddan said.

"So long as magic isn't unified, the convergence isn't complete," Terrael said. "It suggests a possibility that the worlds could diverge again, if only in pieces—though 'in pieces' might be worse than a complete divergence. But it's not just that. The Codex Tiurindi referred to those mages performing magic so powerful I could barely comprehend it. If we're going to defeat the former Empress, we'll need every advantage, and if we can use the unified magic and her battle mages can't, that's a huge advantage."

"But they'd have access to it as well," I said.

"It's unlikely anyone will be able to use it immediately," Terrael said. "It will take practice. But in making the discovery, we'll have a head start on them—more so because none of those battle mages have any experience with research."

"We still have to practice battle tactics," I said. "But if you're right, bringing magic together is another kind of battle tactic."

"That's one way to look at it," Terrael said. "And now I'm for bed, if you want to join me, my lady wife?"

That broke up the party, and I came back here to write, and now I'm looking at our bed with some distaste. It was only a few nights in

Colosse, but I got used to having a thick mattress and room to sprawl, though Cederic and I usually end up cuddled together however large the bed is. I suppose what matters isn't the size of the bed so much as who you share it with, and if I think of it that way it's a very fine bed indeed.

18 Hantar

Past midnight, so maybe technically 19 Hantar, but I'm not sure. I've been waking late at night more frequently since the assassination attempt, always with the same dream that the man is lunging at us and if I don't wake before he strikes, Cederic will die. This time I didn't feel sleepy, so I decided to do some writing—I neglected it today because Cederic came to bed at a decent hour and I think he took the hint, by the way I was lounging around in just my undershorts and breast band, that I was feeling amorous. At least, the way he stripped down to nothing in about four seconds flat makes me think that.

Today wasn't very exciting. We sent out some message riders to the villages we passed, three Castaviran, one Balaenic, with handbills explaining the coup and Cederic's ascension to the throne and the two worlds coming together. We've decided not to approach these towns along the way directly, since the Balaenic Army, while not as big as the Castaviran, is still very intimidating, even to Balaenics who don't have reason to think they're under attack by foreigners. But we do want to prepare people for the future. Hence the handbills.

I saw the mages creating them and it's a fascinating kathana, though tediously slow compared to printing and not nearly as crisp. Since we can't exactly haul a press around with the Army, this is still better than having to write it all out by hand.

It started snowing again mid-morning, though after our stop in Colosse we have covered wagons like the one I rode in while I was injured, so it wasn't so bad. I don't know why the Balaenic Army never used covered wagons. Probably they're not used to transporting anything but cargo in them, and crates don't care if they get wet.

I rode with the people I'm starting to think of as my command team, as if I were really a leader and not just the one who

No. I am the leader. I'm the one who directs our discussions and clarifies points and organizes our investigations. I'm Empress-Consort now, and I'm chief of the Balaenic mages. Even if I still don't know exactly what that first responsibility entails, and I'm not quite comfortable using the second to command the Castaviran mages in Cederic's absence, nobody seems to mind when I tell them what we're going to do next. So I think I need to get used to it and stop being dismissive of my abilities, even if they're unexpected.

I should ask Cederic about the Empress-Consort thing. At some point we will have to sit down and discuss how we're going to rule a united kingdom/empire, and I have the feeling I'm going to have to speak up on behalf of Balaenic law and custom. Fortunately for both of us I've never had a problem telling Cederic when he's wrong.

Anyway.

I rode with the people who have shown the most interest in and aptitude for solving the problem of bringing our magics together: Terrael and Audryn and Jaemis of the Castaviran mages (all good friends from the Darssan, too, and it makes me sad that Sovrin isn't with us anymore, being busy overseeing the translators), and Jeddan, Relania, Jerussa, and Tobiak of the Balaenics. Two of "ours" are old mages, two of them new, and all of them including Jeddan have non-aggressive pouvrin as their "primary" ability. I don't know if that means they're naturally more inclined toward study and introspection, but as much as that would be interesting to investigate, I don't really care right now.

Today we focused on identifying things both our magics have in common that might be part of the original, unified magic. I'm glad so few Castaviran mages attached themselves to this group, because Terrael is as intimidating in his way as Cederic is, being brilliant and quick-thinking and capable of seeing connections no one else does, and I know a lot of the Castaviran mages are inclined to defer to him. And we don't need that; we need people who are willing to challenge one another and not just accept something because the person who came up with it is a genius.

Audryn, of course, doesn't think of Terrael that way (imagine what a disaster of a marriage that would be if she deferred to him all the time) and Jaemis is a tenacious thinker who takes hold of an idea and worries at it until it either falls apart or is proven sound to his satisfaction. The Balaenic mages aren't overawed by Terrael because he may be brilliant about Castaviran magic, but he knows nothing about Balaenic magic and is (because he's Terrael) utterly humble in asking for explanations of things. Relania is the most likely to challenge him when he goes off into abstractions, and I think he likes that. After today, I feel more confident we might actually be able to figure this out.

So we discussed similarities, and came up with a list of things we know about magic we think are still true after the convergence, though we don't know what to do with them yet:

1. Magical ability. It's obvious you have to have an inborn ability to work magic. We knew that not only from how some people can't do it post-convergence, but also from what little we understand from the Codex Tiurindi about what those long-dead ~~bast~~ mages wanted to accomplish.

2. Will. Jerussa and Tobiak had a verbal tussle that led to the surprising realization that Balaenic and Castaviran magic both require a measure of will, though Balaenics have to bend their will to meet the pouvrin and Castavirans have to exert their will on magic by scribing th'an. That's too stark a contrast not to matter. So magic needs to interact with will in some way.

3. Structure. Th'an and pouvrin are so similar in the sense of having structure it's hard to believe the original magic didn't have some kind of structure too.

We also have the things we learned from the Codex Tiurindi:

4. Pre-"divergence" magic was something like th'an expressed through will rather than through writing. Which suggests some combination of Castaviran and Balaenic magic, even though we're sure it's not as simple as that.

5. The divergence kathana worked by temporarily suppressing magic, and it ended up (either on purpose or by accident) spread so thin it couldn't be used, which led us to:

6. Magic, whatever structure it has, has to have a certain level of concentration to be usable.

I have no idea what to make of all of that, but we have a lot of time in which to investigate the possibilities. We all felt exhausted when it was time to make camp. I never thought of intellectual discussion as exhausting, but it is. I told all of this to Cederic after our wild love-making—it's amazing how much cleverer I feel when I'm snuggled up with him—and he said, "You might also consider the matter of residual magic, though that is not an accurate description."

"That was in the madman's book, the one that had the conceal-ment pouvra, right?" I said. "You said it was more like pre-existing magic."

"As far as anyone knows," he said. "I'm afraid I can't tell you much about it, as I never had leisure to research it. It hints at the possibility of th'an drawing on a source of magic we are not aware of because they are so efficient at shaping magic. But it might be worth your mages looking into."

"That sounds so strange, 'my' mages," I said.

He put his arms around me and pulled me close. "They look to you because you see things as no one else does," he said, "possibility and reality. And because you have no interest in using your position for self-aggrandizement—it never even occurs to you, and I think others can see that."

"I never thought of it that way," I said. "Honestly, I can't see why anyone would go out of their way to take on that responsibility. I feel the burden and I've got fewer than a hundred people looking to me for guidance. I don't know how you do it, Emperor Cederic."

"I have a beautiful, intelligent, extraordinary Empress-Consort," he said, sliding his hand under my sleep shirt, "and I depend on her utterly."

"You should warn her you also have a jealous wife," I said, and kissed him the way any self-respecting jealous wife would.

He looks so peaceful when he's asleep in our bed. Not that I spend a lot of time watching him sleep, which would be boring, but he looks different, as if he's laid down whatever weight he has to shoulder when he's awake. Although I love him all the time, I feel so tender toward him when he allows himself to be vulnerable with me. It's times like this I truly understand the Castaviran marriage promise; that kind of trust is like a gift.

19 Hantar

More riding in the wagon, more discussion, less fruitful this time. Still, it's bringing us together as a unit, which is important.

24 Hantar

There hasn't been anything to record, so I decided not to waste pages on saying "nothing to report." I wouldn't even have written now except I wanted to remind my future self why there's so big a gap in the record.

26 Hantar

Another wedding, Audryn and Terrael this time. I know I wrote I remembered very little of the ceremony from my own wedding, but I remembered enough to note certain key differences, namely that their unborn child was explicitly made part of the union. Audryn said afterward, when I asked her, a couple who are already expecting a baby when they make their marriage vows like to recognize the child as part of the family they're creating, make it feel welcome even though it wasn't conceived after the vow like Castavirans are expected to do.

For some Castavirans, it's become a superstition that has all these horror stories attached to it, which is the other reason Audryn didn't tell anyone about being pregnant until after Terrael came out of his depression—she didn't want to deal with people criticizing her or warning her about what might happen to her baby because she'd flouted tradition. I think it's horrible that anyone might tell an expectant mother her child would be born unlucky, or deformed, or mentally deficient, just because of when it was conceived, but Audryn told me nobody takes those people seriously. Even so, it was a burden she didn't need.

It was a beautiful ceremony, much quieter than mine, but with all our friends attending, and they both looked so happy it made me cry and Cederic teased me about it. He really is less formal than he used to be, even in public, though I'm sure he still feels the pressure of maintaining the dignity of the Emperor's office. He hasn't said anything to me about maintaining the dignity of the *Empress-Consort's* office, and I haven't asked, for fear he'll tell me I have to stop making jokes in public. I'm sure if there were anything inappropriate in my behavior, he'd tell me.

No study today thanks to the wedding. We all needed a break anyway. Theory is good, but we need some way to experiment, and no one's figured out how to test our theories using actual magic. A rest day is probably what we need. (Though Terrael may be incapable of not thinking about the problem, since it's not as if he can turn off his brain. Hopefully Audryn knows how to keep him distracted, and by distracted I mean lots of legally sanctioned sex.)

27 Hantar

A big storm blew in about ten o'clock this morning, and we had to make camp and huddle in. We (the mages) discussed for most of the morning and eventually decided we will focus our efforts on discovering what's keeping the magic from fully combining, though that broke down into an intellectual argument (i.e. we weren't fighting, just passionately defending our own sides) about whether we're looking for a literal thing, or trying to identify the conditions that have to change. I finally sent everyone to their own tents to think about the points we'd all made, and we'll make a decision tomorrow.

Cedric and I spent most of the afternoon together in our own tent, talking as if we were any other married couple. We told each other stories of our childhood, him more than me, which makes sense because half the stories of my childhood aren't the kind you want to remember. He grew up in the north, in a town west of where Durran is in my world, and was a perfectly ordinary boy until he entered school and turned out to have a prodigious memory and a thirst for magical knowledge. I told him, "I can just picture you as a skinny little boy with big eyes, using long words at all your teachers."

"I was actually a very quiet student," he said, "because everything I was taught came so easily, and seemed so obvious. I thought there must be something wrong with me that I did not struggle as my classmates did. I realize that sounds arrogant, but in truth I felt awkward for many years."

"*That* I can't imagine," I said. "What changed?"

"I came to realize I had a gift I could share with others," he said. "And I was fortunate to have teachers who realized why I was so quiet in group lessons and so forthright and confident in my individual tutoring sessions. They encouraged me to take extra study in magical theory and put me on the path that led me to the Darssan, and then to the Kilios rank. Eventually I felt comfortable enough I could make friends, like Denril—"

He stopped, and rubbed his forehead as if it ached. "I still cannot understand how our friendship turned so sour," he said. "I respected his understanding of magic and his passion for the priesthood. I never thought he resented me at all."

I left my chair to sit in his lap and put my arms around his neck. The chair creaked alarmingly, but didn't collapse. "You had what he wanted," I said. "Fame and recognition. And then it wasn't enough that he had the most high priesthood—he wanted you to have nothing, or his accomplishment wasn't enough. Some people are like that."

"You are very wise," he said, putting his arms around me. "And beautiful. And you fit so nicely into my arms. I think we may have been destined for one another."

"I don't know that I believe in destiny," I said, "because how sad if you're meant for just one other person in the world and you never meet her?"

He nuzzled my neck. "But I did," he said in my ear, "and every day I hope I am becoming more perfectly someone you will want to spend the rest of your life with."

"I feel the same," I said. Then we moved on to the kind of conversation that doesn't need words.

CHAPTER SEVEN

28 Hantar

Surprisingly, the mages came to the unanimous decision that the problem is conditions aren't right for magic to come fully together, and we need to work out how to make that change. This is based on the idea that the divergence kathana was meant to alter the conditions under which magic could be worked, and the convergence might not have altered them back properly. Personally, I'm not convinced, but we have to start somewhere, and even if we take this approach and find out it's dead wrong, we'll have proved *something*.

We know those long-dead mages wanted to make it so you didn't have to be a green-eyed mage to work magic, and that condition's obviously not in force anymore. But there might be other conditions still in effect, namely the fact that th'an and pouvrin still exist; they couldn't possibly still be separate if the magic were combined. So we're going to start by analyzing both to see if they're different in some fundamental way, because that might be a hint to what conditions need to change. We hope. As I wrote, it's something.

29 Hantar

Research turned into substituting th'an for pouvrin and vice versa. Maybe this isn't the combined magic we're aiming for, but it certainly seems as if they're different versions of the same thing.

30 Hantar

Nothing new to report. I had to stop the mages from playing around with interchangeable magic this morning and focus on the real task. Time for a new approach.

2 Jennitar

Another big storm. We're only three days out from Barrekel at this point. I sat in on the strategy meeting this afternoon, though I didn't have anything to contribute, I just thought I should understand what we intend to do when we reach the city. Mattiak's plan is to send an envoy ahead of us, announcing Cederic and requesting an audience with Arron Domenessar.

(I forgot. I did have something to contribute; I asked if it didn't send the wrong message that we were making a request, and Mattiak said "We've got three divisions of the Balaenic Army behind us. He'll know it's not really a request.")

Then we will have a royal processional into the city and to Dessani Manor, the seat of government in Barrekel, and we'll sit down with Domenessar and make our case.

"Can you call out the troops if Domenessar refuses?" Cederic said.

"Possibly," Mattiak said. "If I ordered them out in my own name, I'd be charged with treason, but since I'm already a traitor—" he grinned—"I don't have anything to worry about in that quarter. However, Domenessar is the ultimate commander of the Black and Brown Armies, as the King's representative, and Roebart and Soessen may not want to go against him. And I'm not going to do anything that will pit our armies against each other. We should be prepared for the possibility we will leave Barrekel with no promise of troops in the spring."

"Without the Barrekellian troops, we're in a bad position," Drussik said.

"Nothing we can do about that," Mattiak said, "except be as convincing as possible. I think, if we can show him Balaen won't be subjugated by Castavir, and if we can promise his title isn't in danger, Domenessar will back us."

"I cannot promise he will remain Lord Governor," Cederic said, "as I have no idea whether our new government will have such a position. However, from your reports I believe him to be a capable administrator, and I intend to keep all such men and women in power, if only to minimize the pain of transition. So I can guarantee him *something*."

"I thought we were going to use her Majesty's nationality to sway him," Bronnok said.

"We will," Mattiak said, nodding at me. "A Balaenic co-regnant with a Castaviran can't help but make Balaenics feel more comfortable."

"But will they be offended that I'm Empress-Consort and not Empress?" I said.

"The Empress-Consort has power in the government," Cederic said. "The Consort may ratify laws, hold hearings, pass judgment in court and declare sentencing, speak in Council, and make political appointments in the Emperor's name. In some situations, the Emperor and Empress-Consort are expected to counsel together to make a decision. The Emperor has the final say, but he cannot effectively rule without the support of a strong Consort."

"I hope he'll understand that," I said.

"We will make certain he does," Cederic said.

I'm still not sure I'm fully qualified for this role. I don't know much about passing laws or sentencing criminals. But Cederic is so completely confident in my abilities I've resolved to prove him right. I hope it will be a while before I have to act as Empress-Consort, because I think I have a lot of reading to do.

Reading. I'm going to make Terrael teach me to read Castaviran. We can't spend all day studying magic, and I'm tired of feeling illiterate (because I am, in Castaviran anyway).

3 Jennitar

Castaviran alphabet very finicky for such a simple, straightforward language. Naturally I've been spelling everyone's names wrong, and I'm going to continue to do so, since we use a different alphabet and the words have to be transliterated anyway.

Also: horse riding lessons for when we go into Barrekel. Three soldiers, plus Nessan, who I think was there for the entertainment. I guess it was a little funny, those poor men trying to help me remember which side of the horse to mount on (there's a right side?) and how to hold the reins. All of them were no doubt in terror every time the beast sidled away from them with me on it, envisioning what might happen to them if they let the Empress-Consort get trampled or kicked or mauled or whatever the beast might decide to do. They told me she was the most docile mare they had, and assured me she would not try to toss me off, but I saw how the beast looked at me and I'm pretty sure she's just waiting for her moment.

5 Jennitar

Despite the fact that I've turned a th'an into a pouvra, we still can't repeat the trick. (Well, it's the binding pouvra, and it doesn't seem to do anything, so maybe I'm wrong that I succeeded at it.) I'm almost grateful we'll be in Barrekel tomorrow morning, because we're getting cranky and upset with each other's failings and I want everyone to leave it alone for a couple of days.

More horse riding. I was allowed to ride by myself today, with none of my helpers leading the beast. I tried not to feel too cocky about my accomplishment. That's what the beast wants. I think her name is Clover, or Pansy, or something botanical. She has them all fooled.

6 Jennitar

Positive things that came of meeting with Arron Domenessar:
1. We didn't leave at a run, pursued by his guards.
2.

I can't think of anything else. I was prepared, as I always am, for the worst to happen. It just turns out I didn't know what that was.

We reached Barrekel last night, or its outskirts anyway, and made camp on the far side of the city from the military outpost "just in case" as Mattiak said. That should have been my first warning things would not go well. Mattiak is close enough to the commanders of the

Black and Brown Armies that he uses their praenomi, but he didn't want to put us in a position where we might look like aggressors.

I asked him if he was going to meet with them that night, and he said, "I don't want it to seem like I'm trying to suborn them by meeting with them before we've talked to Domenessar. As far as they're concerned, we're still loyal Balaenic soldiers, and at worst they're going to wonder why we're this far east. I've sent messengers to let them know I'll drop by tomorrow."

"Tell me the truth. Will they follow you if Domenessar forbids it?" I said.

He sighed. "I don't know," he said. "It will depend on whether I can convince them where their loyalties should lie. Asking them to betray their King, even a weak and foolish King, to follow a foreigner may be too much."

"But we need those troops, don't we," I said.

"Do you want a comforting lie, Sesskia?" he said.

"You know I never do," I said.

"Then yes, we need those troops," Mattiak said. "At our current troop strength the Castaviran forces outnumber us three to one. King Dugan seems confident he will be able to join the Helvirite forces to ours, which narrows that gap to just over two to one. Not only do we need Black and Brown, we need them not to fall into the former Empress's hands." He took a deep breath and let it out explosively. "You might want to direct a few prayers toward the true God and hope for the best tomorrow."

So I did. I don't know if the true God wasn't listening, or if I'm not good at prayers, or if this is all part of some elaborate divine scheme, but—I'm getting ahead of myself again. I'd like to leave it at this, because I hate remembering, but I swore I'd make this as accurate as I could. So here it is.

We sent off the envoy first thing in the morning, a handful of soldiers and Terrael and two other mages (side note: Audryn told me she gets so anxious when Terrael goes off on these assignments for Cederic she has to go to their tent and lie curled up in a ball until she stops shaking and reliving memories of how he looked when I brought him back to camp. I don't blame her. Even though I'm fairly confident Domenessar isn't going to order him tortured, I can imagine how it feels watching him ride away) bearing the double flag and sealed messages in addition to the proclamation Terrael will read publicly.

Everyone in my group of researchers was too keyed up to study anything, not to mention we depend on Terrael to guide our experiments and take notes on what we discover. So I grabbed Audryn and Sovrin and had them help me dress up in my Imperial robes.

I think I wrote they came from a museum in Colosse and are about a hundred years old, but they look as if they're brand new thanks to a kathana that preserves them. Fortunately no Balaenic is going to realize how out of date our clothes are, not the way they would if I came to Dessani Manor wearing one of those high-waisted, full-skirted gowns in printed cotton and my hair wrapped around a paper cone to make it stand straight up and fountain out from the tip. Some fashions were meant to go out of style.

But I like the Imperial dress, which is a narrow-skirted underdress of fine white silk with successively shorter robes in shades of rose and violet layered over it and secured with a wide sash with tiny crystal beads embroidered onto it. Audryn told me it's tradition for Empresses to wear their hair loose with this outfit, but I told her in formal settings, Balaenic women wear their hair twisted up in back and secured in a neat roll, and going in with my hair loose would make Domenessar think he could treat me like a child.

So we finally got my hair arranged, and I was walking around, trying to get used to the short steps I had to take because of the skirt, when Cederic came in to change and I had to shoo my friends away. When they were gone, he put his hands on my waist, and said, "It is a pity you do not have time to get dressed twice, because I find myself very interested in removing those robes from your body and exploring what I find there."

"You'd mess up my hair," I said, but I put my arms around his neck. "But I will have to change later, and I *suppose* I could use some help."

"I volunteer," he said, with a little smile that dared me to kiss him, so I did. Then he kissed me. And *then* we were on our way to mussing me completely until I came to my senses and pushed him away. "We have to show self-control, Cederic, we represent an Empire now," I told him.

"You make it very difficult for me to maintain my self-possessed demeanor," he said, but he stepped away from me and undressed. "But then I remember it is beneath the dignity of the Emperor for him to sweep his wife off her feet and kiss her thoroughly in public."

"I'm glad you're allowed to do that in private," I said. Cederic's Imperial clothing is similar to mine, except he has wide-legged loose trousers and a sleeveless shirt to go under all his robes, which are gold as well as violet. "I'm still worried I won't know what to say to Domenessar. And I feel slightly awkward knowing I stole his wife's ruby bracelet five years ago, even though he can't possibly know it was me."

"Speak the truth," he said, "though of course not about the bracelet." He crouched over his trunk and came out with a couple of black velvet boxes, each about ten inches square and two inches deep. "If General Tarallan is correct, and I see no reason to doubt him, Domenessar prizes plain speaking. I imagine he will respect you for giving him direct answers."

"Unless he thinks I shouldn't speak to him at all because I'm a woman," I said.

"In which case there is nothing we can do, since I prefer you remain a woman," Cederic said. He opened one of the boxes and removed a thick circle of gold. "It would be inappropriate for us to wear the Imperial crowns, as they are for full state occasions, and the semi-formal coronets were lost in the palace's collapse. These are the Torques of Rule worn by a Castaviran Empress and her Emperor-Consort over three hundred years ago, and while Domenessar will not know their significance, I think they will be a powerful reminder to us of why we are here."

I accepted the one he held out to me. It's a semi-circle—more than a semi-circle, almost a full circle, but with a palm-width arc cut out of it—of gold that looks like a braided rope, only rigid. At both of the open ends are golden maple leaves. It has just enough give to slip around my neck, where it settles so the leaves brush my collarbones. It is *heavy*. If it really is solid gold, and why wouldn't it be, I could sell it and live off the proceeds for a year. Not that I would—oh, that's right, it's actually mine and not something I stole.

It's going to take me a while to get used to the idea that I'm wealthy now, at least in the sense of having the use of the riches of the Castaviran Empire (if we win). I don't actually own this Torque of Rule so much as have it on permanent loan. But that's so close to owning it makes no difference.

I wonder about the wisdom of putting a thief on the throne of two countries. Though…who better than a thief to safeguard the treasures of a kingdom? Something for me to think about. Maybe I need to stop calling myself a thief.

Anyway.

I put mine on, then Cederic and I examined each other's costumes for flaws (and managed not to examine anything else, thank you very much), then he offered me his arm and we went to where the Imperial party was gathering.

I wasn't looking forward to riding Buttercup, or whatever the beast's name is. Even though she'd been well-behaved during my riding lessons, I knew she was just waiting for the best, most humiliating time to drop me on my ass. This processional through the streets of Barrekel would qualify. But I smiled, and let a soldier help me mount—I don't know where they found a saddle that would accommodate my narrow skirt, but it's even less comfortable than the regular kind—and gripped the reins the way I'd been told, not clutching them like they're my worst enemy's throat, and followed Cederic and Mattiak and the flags out of the camp toward Barrekel.

Barrekel is the second-largest city in Balaen, after Venetry, and it's growing fast. A lot of people on the east coast would like it to be our capital, since it's more central (and there's some concern about Venetry being so close to the Fensadderian border), which means there are people who, without coming out and saying it, would like

Arron Domenessar to be Balaen's King. It has no city wall, just three big arches where the major roads converge on the city, that mark the unofficial city limits. Much as I feel at home in Venetry, I like Barrekel's architecture, which has a southern influence with all those big windows and covered promenades. There always seems to be some kind of construction project going on when I come here, which tells me it's a prosperous city—though from all the times I've stolen from the wealthy of Barrekel, I already knew that.

People came out to watch us as we passed. They were mostly silent, whispering to each other, but I could hear the occasional louder murmur. That was reassuring, because it was clear some of them had seen the handbills we'd sent on ahead with Terrael's envoy or heard his proclamation and were enlightening the others. On the other hand, nobody cheered our names, which satisfied Sesskia the thief perfectly, but worried Sesskia the Empress-Consort quite a lot. I'd hoped at least some of them would welcome us, but that wasn't the case. At least they weren't throwing things.

We proceeded in this manner through the arch, very slowly, giving the beast no opportunity to turn on me. The crowds were growing thick now, and the murmuring was louder. Then one of the flag-bearers shouted "Make way for Cederic, Emperor of Balaen and Castavir! Make way for Sesskia, Empress-Consort!" and the murmuring got *really* loud.

Someone shouted "What happened to the King?" and someone else shouted "Who cares?" A few people cheered. A few more people scuffled over who knows what. Cederic still had his usual public face, smooth and impassive, though he was waving at the crowd and nodding at people who didn't acknowledge him. I guess we were more entertainment than Barrekel had seen in a while.

I've never been inside Dessani Manor, but I've seen it several times. It's got a wide colonnade surrounding it, roofed against the summer sun, and its walls are stucco the way about a third of the buildings in Barrekel are, white that blinds you in the full sunlight but looks drab on an overcast day like this one.

We passed through the colonnade into a courtyard surrounded

on three sides by a covered porch that led deeper into the manor. We dismounted—I had help, but I still was awkward—and a man dressed in royal livery, with the knot of rank on the shoulder that said he was seconded to Domenessar's household, indicated we should follow. Our group was arranged in a way that was supposed to convey some subtle hints about each person's status, but all I knew was I walked next to Cederic and everyone else was arranged around us, which made me feel relieved that an assassin would have to work really hard to get at my husband.

I was surprised at how plain the inside of Dessani Manor was. Some kinds of plain are really just a type of elegance, flower arrangements with a single rose and a pile of exquisitely arranged pebbles, or a simple gold chain whose links are perfection, but this was the kind of plain that says the person who owns the house can't be bothered with interior décor. I guess that makes some sense, given that this is the center of government and not someone's home, but in all the other cities where the Lord Governor lives somewhere other than where government business is handled, the government manors at least look as if someone cares about their appearance. I don't know that it means anything, but it was strange.

We ended up at a pointed archway (this was another thing about the manor, it didn't have a lot of doors, at least on the ground level, mostly open archways and a few curtained openings) through which we found a chamber about forty feet on a side, with a dais and a carved wooden chair at the far end.

I watched Cederic for cues and stopped when he did. Terrael, at the front of our group, stepped forward and said, "Lord Arron Domenessar, the Emperor of Castavir and Balaen, Cederic Aleynten, and the Empress-Consort, Sesskia of Balaen." Then the people standing in front of us stepped to the sides, parting in the middle as neatly as a ship's prow parts the waves, and I got my first look at Arron Domenessar.

He is *extremely* handsome. I mean, I love my husband, I think he looks wonderful, but objectively, Domenessar is the sort of man people fantasize about. He has wavy light brown hair, a strong jaw, bright blue eyes, and the most perfect nose I've ever seen. My first thought, on looking at him, was *He and the God-Empress would have the most beautiful children*. My second thought was *He does not look friendly*. His perfect mouth was pinched, like he'd smelled something bad, and his brow furrowed in annoyance, which made him look marginally less handsome.

Cederic took three steps forward, so I did too. He inclined his head slightly and said, "Lord Domenessar. Thank you for your welcome."

I bowed my head too, but said nothing. We both knew he hadn't welcomed us, unless you count not having us attacked and killed as a welcome. Domenessar sat in silence, glaring at us. Cederic, as usual, looked impassive. I tried to look friendly and open. Then Domenessar said, in an unexpectedly ugly, gravelly voice, "Is this a joke?"

I looked at Cederic, who raised an eyebrow and said, "I assure you, we are entirely serious. I intend to rule Balaen and Castavir, and I assert I will do it more responsibly than Balaen's current king, something I am certain you believe."

Domenessar stood rapidly. "You come into my audience hall and mock me and my people and you expect my *compliance* with your farce?" he shouted.

Cederic didn't flinch. "No mockery was intended," he began.

"And there you do it again!" Domenessar said, and I realized what the problem was. Cederic's drawling Balaenic accent sounded exactly as if he were doing it on purpose to copy Domenessar's speech.

"Lord Domenessar, the Emperor learned our language from someone from Barrekel," I said, seizing on a lie as easier than explaining about kathanas and risking a true eruption if he were one of those afraid of magic. "His accent is in no way a mockery of you. It truly is how he speaks."

Domenessar turned on me. "You," he said, slightly calmer but still with that furrow to his brow. "You call yourself Sesskia of Balaen. What is your surname?"

"I don't have one," I said, feeling my stomach begin to churn in anxious anticipation.

"No surname? What is your placename, then?" he said.

"I am from Thalessa," I began.

"That's no answer," he said, his voice growing louder.

"You will not speak to the Empress-Consort in that tone, sir," Cederic said, his voice icy.

"She's not my Empress," Domenessar said. "What is it, woman?"

I stiffened my spine, but I knew the second the words left my lips, it was all over. "Thalessi Scales," I said.

Domenessar began to laugh. "A fishmonger?" he exclaimed. "And you choose to set her on the throne next to you? Is she really the best you could do in your grab for legitimacy?"

"Sesskia's birth is irrelevant," Cederic said. I glanced at him and saw his fist was clenched so hard the tendons were standing out on his wrist. "She is a strong, intelligent woman who will defend your country against all comers. Especially the weak, easily-led man currently sitting on your throne."

"And you think you can do better, foreigner," Domenessar said.

"I am certain of it," Cederic replied coolly. "I have the backing of the Castaviran Empire and I now request the support of the Lords Governor of Balaen. Support my claim, and you will have power in the new government. Choose to follow Garran Clendessar, and I cannot promise your safety."

Domenessar glared at him. "You, Tarallan," he said without looking aside. "What are you doing attached to this farce?"

"It's no farce, Domenessar," Mattiak said. "The King has thrown in with a madwoman who will bring Balaen to destruction. I've given my allegiance to the Emperor."

"And you've given him the forces of the Balaenic Army, no doubt," Domenessar said. "The more fool you."

"Then you will not support us," Cederic said.

Domenessar turned and flung himself back into his chair. "You've got balls of solid brass, that's for sure," he said, "but you don't have anything else. You don't have the right to rule Balaen, and your fish-monger wife sure as hell doesn't have a claim to it either. But you're right about one thing: Garran Clendessar's time is done. And I intend to do something about it."

"You will raise your standard against your King," Cederic said.

"Why not? It seems everyone is doing it," Domenessar said. "Come spring I'll raise the country against him. They already look to me as their ruler; this will simply make it official."

"You won't have the Army," Mattiak said.

"Neither will you," Domenessar said. "I've already sent word to Generals Gradden and Ellert that they're not to allow you into the military encampment. You may be Commander General, but they take their orders from me. Come spring we will ride out against that city of yours again, and from there I will bring Balaen under my rule and crush you foreigners under my boot."

"You are making a mistake," Cederic said.

"Not as big as the one you have, trying to claim superiority over Balaen when you've no authority," Domenessar said. "Get out of my hall. And be grateful I think so little of your power I don't just have you killed."

Without even thinking twice I began to work the fire-rope pouvra. *Let him think little of my power when he's writhing in pain on the floor*, I thought. But Cederic turned and looked at me, exactly as if he knew what I was thinking, and shook his head, the tiniest of gestures. I glared at him, but subsided. I still think the fire rope should be an option in the future. Fishmonger.

Cederic said, "I am sorry we could not come to an agreement. Thank you for your time," and turned and walked away too rapidly, not waiting for our escort to keep formation. I had to trot along in my tiny constrained steps to keep up with him. We swiftly left the manor and as swiftly mounted our horses and rode out of Barrekel. The crowds had dispersed somewhat while we were inside, but gathered again quickly. I half-expected them to intuit what their Lord Governor had said and scream and throw rotten vegetables at us, but they just muttered as they had before, and after what felt like two forevers we were back at the camp and dismounting. I stumbled coming off the beast, and Cederic caught my elbow to keep me from falling, but he squeezed so tightly I had to suppress a gasp. He didn't notice.

"General Tarallan, you must go immediately to the Barrekellian forces and give orders to its generals," he said. "We must claim their allegiance now, before they have time to think Domenessar's instructions over thoroughly."

"Your Majesty, if Domenessar has already sent Roebart and Soessan their orders, it's probably too late," Mattiak said.

"So long as Domenessar has not yet fielded an army, it is not too late," Cederic said. "We must gain their allegiance to join us when spring comes."

"But Domenessar's going to raise his banner in spring," I said.

"He will try. He will not succeed," Cederic said. "Now, General. If you please." It didn't sound like a polite request. It sounded like the command of an Emperor. Mattiak gestured to Bronnok and Drussik, nodded at Kalanik—sometimes I think they have some kind of mind-reading pouvra—and once more mounted and rode away from the encampment.

"General Kalanik, pass the word that we will ride out in the morning," Cederic said. "I wish to meet with the quartermasters in half an hour to assess our supply situation. We will proceed to Teliarne to gather the Helvirite Army, and we cannot depend on them to have the supplies our forces will need. Sesskia, come with me." He took my hand and pulled me along after him, forcing me again to trot to keep up with his longer stride. I yanked on his hand, which didn't make him release me—he has a grip like a clocker crab—but it did slow him down enough that he looked at me, registered the annoyance on my face, and stopped and let go of me. "I apologize," he said. "Will you walk with me?"

This time, he offered me his arm, and I hooked my hand around the crook of his elbow and we proceeded, more slowly, to our tent. Once inside, he stepped away from me, sat down heavily on the flat lid of his trunk, covered his face with one hand, and said, "I do not believe I have ever been so close to killing someone as I was in that audience hall. You should not have had to endure such insults."

"I'm sorry it didn't occur to me that would happen," I said. "I thought making the point that I'm Balaenic would matter more. I should have realized these nobles won't respect anyone who doesn't have 'ssar' after their name."

"The more fools they," Cederic said. He stood and put his arms around me. "And we cannot make the point that you are the most powerful mage of your country when we do not know if those we speak to fear magic. I have been a fool myself, in every respect. I should have remembered your countrymen are not like mine."

"We'll find a way," I said, not really believing it. "Help me out of this dress, please?"

"I am afraid we have no time for that," he said with a chuckle.

I grinned at him. "I know, but I'm not going to sit around in this getup all day, and I think we both have at least enough self-control not to attack each other just because we happen to be in our underwear. Well, *I* do. You're usually a slave to your lusts."

He laughed and began untying the sash. "I am so glad to have you with me," he said, "and I cannot imagine anyone better qualified to rule beside me, common or not."

"There's always Joena Lerongis," I said.

Cederic wrinkled his nose as if he smelled something awful. "Joena has many sterling qualities, but an Empress-Consort should not be quite so...."

"Indirect?" I suggested.

"I was thinking 'amorally self-centered,' but 'indirect' is accurate," he said. He shed his own robes and folded them neatly to go back into the trunk. "I owe you a debt of gratitude for preventing me from ascending the throne without a wife. What a nightmare that would be, all those women parading themselves for me to choose."

"Then your payment will be to come to bed at a decent hour, so I can show you the other benefits of having a wife," I said. With that we kissed each other and parted, him to meet with the quartermasters, me to find the mages and tell them what had happened. Though Terrael beat me there, so when I arrived it was in time for them to be indignant on my behalf.

It took about an hour for us to exhaust the conversational possibilities of the meeting with Domenessar, and then we spent some
time (or rather I spent some time) explaining why turning th'an into
pouvrin wasn't useful; we need to focus on identifying any unique
characteristics of each. Jaemis suggested—he's an expert at transmutation kathanas, which is probably why it occurred to him—we see if
we can use magic to turn one into the other, and he thinks he can
create a kathana that will reveal the process as it's happening, so we
can clearly see what the differences are. So that's what we're doing
next.

It's getting late and Cederic still isn't here. It's hard to remember
he has all these people bringing problems to him, far more than he
ever did in the palace or even in the Darssan, and that he would
rather be with me. That makes me feel disappointed rather than
angry, but I'm going to stay up a little longer and hope he isn't so late
all we can bear to do is sleep. I think we could both use the closeness
of sex tonight.

CHAPTER EIGHT

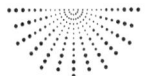

7 Jennitar

I ended up going to find Cederic last night and arrived at the command tent just as Mattiak returned from meeting the generals of the Barrekellian forces. He was in a very bad mood. "They'd follow me now, if I ordered it in my own name," he told Cederic and me and the rest of the general staff, "but they aren't ready to give their allegiance to a foreign ruler no matter how I vouch for him. Roebart's even in favor of supporting Domenessar if he tries to take the throne. Your Majesty, I think you need to speak to them."

"Will that make a difference? I will be no less foreign to them in person than I am as a distant figure in your story," Cederic said.

"I think you could convince birds to fly north for the winter," Mattiak said, "and it can't hurt."

"Very well," Cederic said. "In the morning, then."

But in the morning they tried to enter the military encampment and were turned away. I think Cederic was expecting this, because I had to stay behind, and when I argued the point, Cederic drew me to one side and said, quietly, "We cannot afford to risk both of us. If this turns ugly—"

"You don't think they'll try to kill you?" I exclaimed.

"No," he said, "but there might be fighting, and as I would prefer not to frighten our people—and they are our people, Sesskia, no matter where they think their allegiance lies—with magic, you would be helpless to defend us both. So, stay here, and we will return soon, though I hope not terribly soon."

But, as I said, they were turned away and were back in about thirty minutes. Mattiak was swearing. Cederic looked impassive. "Time enough to worry about those armies in the spring," he said.

"It's not going to be any easier then," Mattiak said.

"Much can happen in three months," Cederic said. "Now we must begin our journey to Teliarne. Dugan, what can you tell us of Brisson Rialen?"

Lerongis jumped, surprised at being addressed directly. "My cousin is lazy," he said. "He hates disruptions to his life. We're going to be the biggest disruption he's ever seen. Either he's going to bar the gates against us, or he's going to give us what we want to make us leave him alone. I think between the two of us, Cederic, we can convince him to do the latter."

"I wonder if you have considered, Dugan," Joena Lerongis said in her diffident, annoying way, "that as your heir he may see an advantage to supporting the former Empress if it means she might award him the throne of Helviran when we are defeated. Perhaps you should consider how you might reward him more satisfactorily, Cederic."

"Thank you for that insight, Joena," Cederic said. "We will discuss specific strategies in the days to come, but I anticipate greater success in Teliarne than we have found here. Now, prepare to depart."

The rest of the day was boring. There's no road that goes directly from Barrekel to Teliarne, of course, so it's going to take four or five days to get there. I plan to spend most of that time wrangling mages. We do a lot of drawing these days, the Balaenic mages trying to reproduce the shapes of the pouvrin, specifically the mind-moving pouvra because we can all do that, and the Castaviran mages trying to match th'an to those shapes. Once we feel we have two similar sets of shapes, we're going to create a kathana that reveals the underlying magic—the "residual" magic—and if we're right, they're going to look different.

I don't want to make a plan for the next step until then, because we have no idea what "different" will mean. I don't mind admitting in the privacy of these pages I'm sick of the mind-moving pouvra already. I'm still not entirely sure the pouvra is a unique shape—that is, what if it turns out each mage creates her own pouvra, that they're all roughly similar but not exactly so, and there *is* no mind-moving pouvra in the same sense that the th'an that power collennas are all identical? But I'm not saying that to them.

It's already hard enough to keep manifesting pouvrin for hours at a time. It feels like more of a struggle every time. We have to be careful to take frequent rests, though after hearing what happened to Saemon at the battle, how he collapsed and then couldn't work magic for hours, everyone's taking the need for rest seriously.

8 Jennitar

Nasty, wet, cold, miserable weather, not bad enough to make camp but enough that we're all grateful for the warming th'an scrawled all over the inside of this wagon, even if Audryn and Jaemis have to renew them every hour or so because the magic fades over time. It feels as if it's happening more quickly than before, as if the storm is leeching the power out of the th'an, though really it's just my bad mood talking.

9 Jennitar

The pouvra is its own thing and not something we're each constructing! It came together around noon, slowly, like we were dragging the knowledge out of some tar pit, but it's clear now that despite our each perceiving it differently (as a shape we're encompassing, as a shape we're on the inside of, or as a shape made of pieces that slide together) we *are* all seeing the same thing. It was such a relief we cheered and celebrated loudly enough that Cederic came to see what we were doing.

That ended with him joining us in the wagon for the afternoon while we explained our research and he made some contributions, including identifying a rare th'an even Terrael didn't know that was one of the ones that was missing. It was *so good* to have him around to talk magic with. I didn't realize how much I'd missed that. I think he misses being just Sai Aleynten (as if there was anything "just" about that role) instead of the Emperor.

10 Jennitar

Kathana almost ready. It's really very simple, or possibly that's just Jaemis's genius at work. He's stubborn, and he works by trying combinations over and over again until he finds the one that works, but he's so quick to see when something is a dead end or a failure he's as fast as someone like Terrael, who sees the thing as a whole and manipulates it in his imagination until it falls into the right shape.

But it's going to take some practicing to help our Balaenic mages, me included, to participate in the kathana. The mind-moving pouvra will be integrated with the kathana, taking the place of the th'an we identified. The result of the kathana will either be identical to the result we would expect if we'd used th'an, meaning the two are identical and interchangeable, or (more likely) there will be differences, and the kind of differences there are will tell us (we hope) what conditions still need to be altered to make th'an and pouvrin the same. I hope they're not interchangeable, because that would mean all our research to date has been wasted going down the wrong path. But everything we've learned suggests the opposite.

I hope it won't take too long. The constant working of magic combined with the bad weather (light snowfall today) and the rough living conditions are exhausting all of us, and sometimes we're tired enough it feels like the magic is fighting us. I wish I were sleeping in a real bed.

We'll reach Teliarne tomorrow afternoon—Cederic says morning, but I've been watching the skies and I'm more pessimistic. I am curious about Brisson Rialen. I didn't know he was Lerongis's heir until we left Barrekel, though it seems everyone else knew, and I want to meet this "lazy" man Dugan Lerongis, of all people, is disdainful of. Rialen is a consul of Castavir in addition to being Lerongis's heir, which to me seems like an awful lot of power to have concentrated in one place. If he really is as indolent as Lerongis suggests, he might be easily swayed to our side. On the other hand, if he's that indolent, and unsuited to rule, but we have to promise him rank of some kind to get his support, that bodes ill for our future government. On the third hand, it's early to be having those worries, so I'm going to fall back on my least favorite kind of plan and wait to see what happens tomorrow.

II Jennitar

Teliarne feels cold to me. It was clearly built for a much warmer climate even than southern Balaen, where snow in the winter is rare, and all those open courtyards and thick walls meant to keep out the summer's heat make winter seem even more dreary. It feels as if spring will never come—which is ridiculous, because we're not even halfway through Jennitar and the winter hasn't been that harsh. I've traveled rough through much nastier winters than this one. I've let the relative comfort I'm living in make me soft.

We have quarters in the royal palace, and maybe that's part of the problem. Even though Lerongis sent word ahead, Rialen didn't do anything to prepare the palace for our arrival. Lerongis was right, his cousin is lazy, and I have to insist to Cederic that we not promise him any kind of official position, because he would be a disaster. *Is* a disaster for Teliarne already. He enforces the laws only sporadically, he makes no effort to improve the lives of the citizenry, and if not for General Garatssen, Teliarne would have been overrun by Barrekel's troops.

I like Garatssen a lot. She's smart, and fair-minded, and while she isn't rude or crass she also doesn't care about making her listeners happy by telling them only what they want to hear. Rialen is afraid of her, and does a poor job of hiding it under friendly conversation and attempts to flatter her.

Lerongis looks much better by comparison—actually, it was watching him interacting with his subordinates that showed me I'd misjudged him. He's intimidated by Cederic—not by the Emperor, by Cederic himself—and I think he tries too hard to prove he's as good a man as Cederic is, and gets all weak and spineless when he fails. Once he stops puffing himself up, he's a capable administrator. I can see he has the respect of most of the people who serve him, even Garatssen, though she might only respect him as the lesser of two evils.

When we first arrived, I was so discouraged, because we met with Rialen before we did anything else, and Lerongis demanded a report on what had happened in the conflict with Barrekel. And Rialen shrugged and said, "General Garatssen knows the details. It's not really my business to interfere with the defense of the city."

"The defense of the city is one of your primary duties, Lord Rialen," Cederic said.

"You all know I'm not a military man," Rialen said. "Better for me not to step in where I'll just confuse matters."

"Surely General Garatssen reported to you," Lerongis said. He kept flicking these sidelong glances at Cederic as if worried the Emperor might hold him accountable for Rialen's failings, which was a reasonable fear.

"Of course she did," Rialen said. "But, as I said, it's not really my forte. Come, I have a meal prepared, let's all sit and eat together." And that was it. I couldn't believe this buffoon had control of one of Castavir's biggest cities. Having to work through him to get the Castaviran troops would be impossible.

That's what I thought, anyway. The food was very good—Rialen is competent when it comes to his material pleasures—but I spent most of the meal fretting over the political situation and the kathana we're planning and the impossibility of getting any Balaenic cities to follow us.

When it was over, I took Cederic's arm and we left the dining hall with our "retinue," *not* including Rialen, following Lerongis through the palace until we came to a smallish (still maybe thirty feet long) chamber containing a long table and chairs, with a nice big fireplace on one side and th'an scribed on the opposite corners to even out the heat distribution. The walls were lined with portraits of past Kings and Queens of Helviran, most of them looking very stern. Lerongis took a seat along the table without waiting for anyone else and wiped his forehead with his sleeve. "I'm sorry, Cederic, I take responsibility," he said.

"You did not appoint him consul," Cederic said, "and if you bear any responsibility for this, it is in not bringing his shortcomings to the attention of the God-Empress as was." He sat at the head of the table and added, "But I think we all know that would have been pointless, so your only other recourse would have been assassination, and we are not so desperate as to take that route."

Lerongis laughed and shook his head. "It doesn't matter anymore," he said. "With Renatha Torenz gone, I am free to act more fully in my own name—that is, with your permission, your Majesty."

"I depend on you to understand the needs of Helviran, Dugan," Cederic said. "I take it you have sent for General Garatssen?"

"She will be here shortly, and then we'll have a better idea of what went on during their little war," Lerongis said.

I could see Mattiak was getting impatient at not being able to follow this conversation. He's been learning Castaviran, but he isn't very fluent yet, and can't follow rapid speech at all. So I translated the gist of the conversation for him, and he said, "Their General is a woman?"

"I told you the Castavirans let men and women serve in the Army," I said.

He grimaced. "I still think it's a bad idea."

"You can tell it to General Garatssen right after you compliment her on her handling of her troops during the conflict," I said, "because from what I've heard, if weather hadn't been an issue she'd have walked all over your Black and Brown Armies."

"You say that as if I'm supposed to be impressed," Mattiak said, but with a twinkle in his eye that told me he was. I suppose he knows better than anyone the qualities of the Balaenic divisions, and he's honest enough that even though he wouldn't want Garatssen's troops to defeat his, and he thinks the military is no place for a woman, he can respect her for having the ability.

Right about then, Garatssen came through the door. I know I described her above, but I didn't know any of that at first, obviously, just that she's *very* young to be in command of the Helvirite Army, older than me only by a few years, and she has a strong, sharp-boned face and short brown hair that looks like it's cut to fit under a helmet. "Dugan," she said, saluting him, "welcome home."

"Raewyn," Lerongis said, "this is Cederic Aleynten, Emperor of Castavir and Balaen, and his wife Sesskia, Empress-Consort."

Her eyes went very wide for a fraction of a second, then she smiled broadly and saluted Cederic with the Imperial salute I rarely ever see, both hands clasped together at chest height, then bowing her head with a slow, respectful nod. "Your Majesty, it's a pleasure," she said, repeating the gesture to me. "The Helvirite Army is yours to command."

Lerongis made a tiny noise in the back of his throat. Garatssen said, "Oh, come on, Dugan, as if we don't all know what you're here for. I just see no reason to run through all the formalities."

"It would be nice if you'd treat me like your King for once," Lerongis muttered, and to my shock Garatssen slapped him on the shoulder and then pinched his cheek.

"Dugan is my half-brother, your Majesty," Garatssen said to my astonished face. "He's right, I have trouble treating him like the King, but he knows he has my full loyalty. Don't take this personally, your Majesty, but if Dugan hadn't thrown his support behind you, I'd have helped him take the Imperial throne myself."

"I respect your candor and your loyalty," Cederic said, "though I hope for both our sakes you have straightened out where those loyalties lie. I would hate for the Helvirite Army to come to blows with my forces again."

"I swore to serve the Empire, your Majesty," Garatssen said. Now she was deadly serious. "You are my Emperor, and my troops are, as I said, yours to command."

"Thank you," Cederic said. "Please be seated, everyone, and I will make introductions."

We went around the table, me translating for Mattiak and the rest of the Balaenics. When I got to introducing General Garatssen, Mattiak said, "*That* is their General? I suspected, from how they were all talking, but—I was expecting someone six feet tall and built like a brick sh— um, wall."

"You never say that about Bronnok, and he's so thin even I could probably break him in half," I said, grinning at Bronnok, who scowled at me (it was a friendly scowl; he's gotten used to me).

"Well, I—" Mattiak realized everyone was staring at us, and subsided. "I still have my prejudices, I guess," he said, but his eyes kept turning to Garatssen the whole rest of the meeting. She, for her part, gave him a narrow-eyed considering stare when he was intro-duced, nodded in acknowledgment, and said, in slow and well-enun-ciated Castaviran, "I hope we will deal honorably with each other, General."

"That my hope as well...General," Mattiak replied in the same language. I really hope they can get along. Mattiak got used to my being in the army, but then I wasn't ever a soldier. I don't know whether Garatssen's obvious competence is going to win him over or alienate him further. Now I can't decide whether to be relieved that it was so easy to bring the Helvirite troops to our side, or worried that we won't be able to integrate them. And what if the Balaenics don't treat the Castaviran women soldiers with respect? Wonderful. Now worry is winning out.

So we had a long discussion, the result of which is that the Helvirites aren't coming with us either.

It makes sense. First, there's the point about the Brown and Black Armies staying put rather than following us to winter quarters, where we'd have to feed them too; that applies to the Helvirite troops as well. And Garatssen was adamant that even though Domenessar says he doesn't want to fight until spring, if he sees Teliarne left defense-less, he'll attack no matter what the weather. Lerongis argued against this for a bit, but in the end he agreed with her, as did Cederic and Mattiak. I think Garatssen's eloquence and forcefulness impressed him, even if he couldn't understand most of what she said.

So the plan now is to continue on to the coast, winter over for a few months, then come back for the Helvirite Army and, Cederic said, the Barrekellian forces. I think he's overly optimistic and we're going to be *fighting* the Barrekellian forces, but he's right that a lot can change in a few months. I hope he's right that it's a good kind of change. We're leaving several of our mages to begin teaching the Castavirans to speak Balaenic. I don't envy them. Balaenic is a more complicated language than Castaviran, but the more of them speak it, the greater the chance we'll be able to integrate the troops in the spring.

Sleeping in a real bed again. I almost wanted to go back to the camp so I wouldn't get used to comfort and then have to live with the horrible disappointment of our camp bed. I think we should at least see if they make a wider one. I like sleeping close with Cederic, but there are limits, and one of them is that he sometimes wakes me when he comes late to bed, and then I can't fall asleep again for an hour. But when I suggested it (going back) Cederic said, "We should not insult our hosts by declining their hospitality. And while I enjoy sharing any kind of bed with you, I prefer one that does not creak so terrifyingly when I climb into it at night." He has a point.

CHAPTER NINE

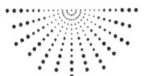

12 Jennitar, just after lunch

Off to the Castaviran city of Pfulerre. We originally planned to go further south, to Lirilla, which is a major Balaenic port city, but after our reception in Barrekel, Cederic judged it better not to risk being turned away again. We were resupplied somewhat in Teliarne, but they don't have a lot to spare because of supporting the Helvirite Army, so supplies aren't as plentiful as we'd like. We'll be pushing things to get to Pfulerre without running out of food—the journey will take most of two weeks.

It's only been a few hours (I'm writing this in the wagon) but I'm glad I have a project to occupy myself during those two weeks, because the country we're traveling through is mostly forest. That's not true, it *used* to be mostly forest, but the area around Teliarne is grassy plains and big plantations. My travels through the new combined landscape tell me that at some point we'll run into that forest, but I have no idea when that will be. So it's boring plains, and then boring forest, and then we come to the coastal region, which is beautiful even at this time of year. Or was beautiful. Who knows what it looks like now? According to the map, Pfulerre is no more than twenty miles from Lethess, which is a popular place for wealthy people to go to enjoy the warm salt breezes and bathe in the ocean. It would be a real shame if that disappeared. Not that I'm wealthy—I mean, I wasn't wealthy before, but I stayed there for about a month, recovering from a broken arm, and there's still plenty to do if you don't have money (or, like me, have money but are saving it for books).

Unfortunately, this project isn't going to require much of my time for a while, because there's only so much kathana practice you can stand in one day, so I'm looking for other things I can do to keep from going out of my mind with boredom:

1. Teach Mattiak and the other Balaenics Castaviran.

2. Practice pouvrin.

3. Ride with the other mages and bitch about how bored we all are.

4. Practice riding Acorn, or whatever the hell the horse's name is. She hasn't tried anything yet, but I think she's just waiting for me to let down my guard. My teachers insist she's a very well-behaved mare, but every one of them rides a great foaming beast with mad eyes that's about two feet taller than I am, so I think their judgments are compromised.

5. Ride with Cederic. (This is hopelessly self-indulgent. He doesn't need me clinging to him all day long.)

Back to practicing the kathana. I hope we can do it soon.

15 Jennitar

Nothing to report for the last three days. We've gotten to a point where we can't practice until we stop for the night, because the motion of the wagon is throwing us off. A few more days and we should have it.

18 Jennitar

I'm so tired, and discouraged, and the only reason I'm writing this down is that I don't want to forget any of that tired and discouraged feeling. Which sounds ridiculous, because who would want to remember such negative emotions? But it's important to me that I remember everything, not just the wonderful things but the sad and heartbreaking ones as well. Though this wasn't heartbreaking. It was just a huge setback.

It's not a very difficult or complex kathana, not like the convergence kathana, so it didn't take long for us to understand our parts and practice synchronizing them. I asked Cederic if we could camp early tonight, to give us more light to work by—we still ended up needing lanterns fueled by th'an, but the last of the daylight gave our assistants enough that they cleared a flat space of earth for us before sunset. It hasn't snowed for a while, just rained, and the ground here is clay rather than soft earth, which is perfect for a kathana circle, and after our assistants finished pulling up the sod with their trenching tools, we smoothed it down flat and marked out a double circle about two feet in diameter. Cederic, who'd asked to be present, stood nearby, watching, and I don't think I'd realized until then how much he misses doing magic. He doesn't have time, because as good as he is, there are so many other things only the Emperor can do. I wonder if I should invite him to join us occasionally. He might be busy, but he's not *that* busy. I hope.

Then Audryn, with the help of Terrael referring to a list, began marking out inert th'an in the space between the circles while the rest of us worked out the cardinal and ordinal directions and marked those off too. (You still have to be a mage to scribe even inert th'an, which infuriates me on Terrael's behalf. I'm afraid to ask him if he minds, in case I'd be rubbing salt into the wound.) Jerussa, Tobiak, and Relania moved to stand at the east, south, and west points respectively. Jeddan stood at the southeast, and I stood at the southwest, because our mind-moving pouvrin are so much weaker than the others. Jaemis went to the north and knelt in the clay with a sharpened stick in his hand. "Are you ready?" he said.

"Almost," Audryn said. In a few more seconds she stepped out of the circle and she and Terrael went to where a tambourine and a skinny piece of metal attached to a string waited. Audryn picked up the tambourine, Terrael took the metal and a steel rod about the size of his middle finger, and the two of them messed with the instruments, trying to find the best sound.

Then everything was quiet. We were far enough from the camp that the noise of so many people sounded more like waves on the beach, or that sound you get when you put a shell to your ear that's supposed to sound like waves on a beach but really only sounds like the blood rushing through your ears. I imagined I could feel Cederic's eyes on me—he was standing behind me and to the left—but all I really felt was cold. And nervousness.

Audryn struck the tambourine, lightly, then harder, then back and forth until she found a sound she liked. She gave three quick taps, then fell into a slow beat, *tap tap tap* with long pauses between the taps. After she'd done this a few times, Terrael joined in, making his chime ring out between taps and then three times after the third one: *tap ting tap ting tap ting ting ting.*

I let my breathing fall into harmony with the beat and counted. As the fifth round began, I started to work the mind-moving pouvra, slowly, letting the shape fill me as I bent my will to meet it. I couldn't tell what anyone but Jaemis was doing, but I knew I'd begun at the right time because he began scribing th'an to fill the gap at the northern point. The beat accelerated, and I embraced the pouvra and let it work more quickly, directing it at the th'an scribed in the circle rather than at the world. Any minute now, and we'd know if we were right.

On the seventh round, the ground in the center of the circle began to tremble, and I had to clench my fists to stay focused. Then, between the seventh and eighth rounds, the ground simply hunched itself and rose into a hillock about five feet tall, constrained by the kathana circle. I let the mind-moving pouvra go and sank down to sit next to the hillock. What a colossal failure.

"So they are interchangeable," Jeddan said.

"Looks like," Jaemis said.

"It could be a mistake," said Relania. "I know I was having trouble directing the magic into the kathana. We might have moved the earth with the pouvra instead."

"It's no mistake," I said. "Whatever condition isn't being met, it's not that pouvrin and th'an are different. It would have solved half our problem if they weren't interchangeable. Now we have to start over."

"It is unfortunate that we need to bring the magics together," Cederic said, "because this is a remarkable discovery. We now know we can teach each other our different magics."

"Maybe we should do that anyway, Sai Aleynten," Terrael said.

"I am happy to advise, but it is not I to whom you should look for that answer," Cederic said. He offered me his hand, and I let him pull me up.

I brushed the seat of my trousers, which were clammy, and said, "I think we shouldn't let ourselves be distracted. That was exhausting. Imagine if we tried to do both—teach each other magic *and* try to bring them together, I mean."

"It shouldn't have been this tiring," Jaemis said. "I think working together—putting th'an and pouvrin into a kathana, I mean—might be more of a burden than I anticipated. We should allow for that next time, Terrael."

"Well, at least we proved *something*," Jerussa said, then yawned. "You're right, I feel exhausted. I'm not going to think about this again until morning."

We scrubbed out the kathana circle (I don't know why, it's not as if anyone's going to care out here, and it's not as if we didn't alter the landscape, but it's part of the tradition) and went back for a late dinner and then bed. Well, it will be bed for me as soon as I finish this. I'm trying to let Jerussa's optimism carry me along and not be dragged down by my natural pessimism. We *did* prove something, even if it wasn't the something we had in mind. Tomorrow we'll look at this anew, and I'm going to keep reminding myself we're one step closer to learning the truth.

19 Jennitar

We all felt more optimistic after a good night's rest, and were able to look at our failure logically this morning. Really, we *should* be optimistic, because we're working our way down the list of conditions. Inborn ability, identical magics, the right concentration of magic—all restored. That leaves us with the problem of how will is applied to work magic, which is definitely different between Castaviran and Balaenic magic, and we're all going to think about that separately and discuss tomorrow.

We should be in Pfulerre on 21 Jennitar. We're still traveling through the forest, but the trees have gone from deciduous to evergreen, which has to be a Castaviran feature because not only was this part of Balaen not forested, there aren't (weren't?) evergreen forests until you get much further north, near Thalessa. I wonder what Thalessa looks like now. It's so bleak in the winter, and cold, with icy rain that coats the roads and makes the cobbles dangerous to walk on. I'm just as happy we're not going that far north.

I wonder if Mam's still alive. It bothers me that I don't give a damn either way. I wonder where Roda ended up. I wonder if anyone in Thalessa even remembers me.

I don't know why I'm suddenly maudlin. I'm going to think about magic now. I left my past behind a long time ago and I don't need it troubling me now.

20 Jennitar

Much discussion, much playing around with th'an and pouvrin, ultimately fruitless. This is such a big, nebulous topic—the application of will, I mean—we can't even agree on where to start discussing it. I told everyone to take a rest day, and we scattered to ride with friends in other wagons, and my wagon ended up singing Castaviran folk songs that made me laugh. I had no idea Castavirans were so dirty-minded.

21 Jennitar, afternoon

I was surprised at how relieved I felt to see the coastal landscape unchanged. I guess I think of my time in Lethess fondly. I had an excuse in my injury not to pursue my quest so doggedly as I had for the three years previous, and there's something about the coast that relaxes you. Relaxes everyone around you, too, and people are so friendly. Even the crime rate is lower in Lethess. I don't know if it's the same for Pfulerre, and I have no idea if the climate in Castavir was as lovely as it is in Balaen, but if not, the Pfulerrian citizens have to be praising their God for their good luck. The slushy snow turned into rain a few days ago, then into warm rain, and by the time we reached Pfulerre, late this afternoon, most of the clouds we've been traveling under were gone and the sun was shining—weak and watery sunshine, but by comparison to what it was like in Barrekel, very welcome. Still cold, but I'm not going to complain.

We're waiting for the envoy to return from seeing the consul of Pfulerre, Daenen Radryntor. No one in our party knows her very well, but Cederic says her relationship with the God-Empress was never very warm—never anything she could be challenged on, but she never went out of her way to court her favor. That was smart of her, because we saw, horribly, what happened to Vorantor when he tried to impress the God-Empress. So we're feeling confident she will respond favorably. (Confident but not certain, of course.)

We tried swapping will-invoking methods this morning—doing pouvrin by exerting our will on them, scribing th'an without a strong purpose in mind—and succeeded only in giving ourselves headaches. We already know if you try to force a pouvra into being, it slips away, but I was hoping we might be able to perceive *why* that happens, or see the effect. No luck.

The Castavirans were even worse off than we were, because they go through such rigorous training to learn to scribe th'an properly that trying to do it incorrectly was like trying to teach a fish to breathe air. So it didn't work. I'm marking it as one step closer to finding the truth, because I'm trying to be optimistic.

And speaking of optimism, it sounds as if Terrael's envoy is back.

21 Jennitar, evening

We've been given what I assume is the nicest room in the consul's palace. It overlooks the ocean and has actual glass windows so you can watch the waves, and the ships coming in and out of the harbor, without having to endure the salt wind that comes off the ocean constantly. It might be too warm in the summer, but right now it's very pleasant, even if the evening overcast I remember from my time here is drifting in. When the sun finally sets, it will be nearly impossible to see where the water ends and the sky begins. It's disconcerting, but in a pleasantly eerie way.

I suppose I'm in a good mood because for the first time since we began this journey, our processional came into a city and the crowds lining the road cheered us. Even Pansy, or whatever the hell the horse's name is, seemed less inclined to throw me off. Possibly she thought the cheering was for her. I was able to wave and smile at everyone, and managed not to feel awkward or nervous at all the attention focused on me. I don't know if I'm ever going to get used to being watched all the time, but if I can bluff my way into Holaen Manor, I can pretend not to feel as if I'm about to be arrested.

The consul's palace has the same southern architecture as Teliarne, except instead of big open windows, everything here has shutters or glass to protect against the spray and sand that gets blown everywhere during a storm. I wonder what it sounds like to hear the wind beating against the windows. It's too bad we can't settle here instead of Colosse. ~~Maybe we can have a summer home here.~~

True God help me, I can't believe I just thought that. I have *got* to stop taking my new affluence for granted like that. I can't be so careless about my new position. We owe a lot to the citizens of this country, and I don't want to turn into someone like Brisson Rialen, thinking only of his personal comforts, or true God forbid someone like the God-Empress, seeing everyone around her as playthings. Not that the last would ever happen; I'm not insane. But I've been poor and struggling for so long, it's like a miracle that I don't have to worry about where I'm going to find my next meal, or where I'm going to sleep—this room is so beautiful I can hardly believe it's ours.

I'm feeling tired, so I'll write about Daenen Radryntor and everything tomorrow. Cederic is still meeting with her, and I was going to join him for the discussion, but he told me I looked exhausted and I should go to bed. I don't feel exhausted, but I am tired enough I didn't argue with him.

That bed looks so soft. It makes me sleepier just looking at it.

22 Jennitar, early

This is why I shouldn't go to bed early no matter how sleepy I am; I always wake up before dawn and can't fall back asleep. On the other hand, I really was tired because Cederic didn't wake me when he came to bed, and *he* must have been tired because I didn't wake *him* when I got out of bed just now. I'm wearing this quilted satin robe I found hanging in the little room outside the *kiorka*. I hope this is what it was intended for, because it's very comfortable.

So, yesterday we came into the city to much acclaim and rode all the way to the palace, where Daenen Radryntor was waiting to greet us. She's red-headed, which told me she had at least one Endellaviran ancestor, and taller than average, and fat in a way that makes her look bold and commanding. If I were anyone else I would have found her intimidating.

She stood at the foot of the steps so she wasn't looking down on us, and waited for Cederic and me to dismount before coming forward and making the Imperial salute. "Pfulerre welcomes you, your Majesty," she said in her deep, commanding voice, and Cederic inclined his head and said, "The Empress-Consort and I are gratified by your welcome." So I hurriedly inclined my head too.

"We have prepared a reception for you, your Majesty, if you will accompany me," Radryntor said, gesturing at the door, so we went up the wide steps and through a pillared portico into the palace. It has the same mosaic walls as the palace at Colosse, though with different images, mostly of the ocean and ocean animals and ships. The wide hall had archways opening off it, curtained by blue and green gauze that made it feel even more as if we were underwater, but in a good way.

Radryntor led our group (Cederic and me, Lerongis and his wife, Mattiak and the generals, Terrael, and three Sais) through one of these arches into a vast reception hall full of well-dressed people standing around and talking quietly. They immediately turned their attention on us, and every one of them made the Imperial salute. I resisted the urge to scratch where the Torque of Rule rubbed my collarbone or fidget in some other un-Imperial way.

"Thank you for your welcome," Cederic said. "We feel honored by your presence. Pfulerre's loyalty to the Empire is well known, and we are glad to see it confirmed today."

"Allow me to make introductions," Radryntor said. I was swept along in Cederic's wake to meet a lot of people, many of whose names I don't now remember. I think they were local nobles from the surrounding area, and government officials, but I still don't know much about Castaviran government, so that didn't make a huge impression on me. I realize that's a serious failing in the Empress-Consort, but I haven't exactly had time. I'll do it once this is all over.

(I realized as I wrote that I might subconsciously be thinking "if we fail, I won't need to learn," but I don't think even I am that pessimistic.)

A lot of them were very flattering, commenting on my beauty, which made me want to laugh, because I know I'm not *that* beautiful, but it also made me nervous. It's a well-known fact that the higher you rank, the prettier you are, so it might just have been that, but now I know I have power in my own right, I'm afraid people are going to try to get me to use it in their favor. That's not going to happen—I'm too suspicious of people's motives to be easily swayed—but I dislike the idea of having to be so on my guard all the time. I'll have to talk to Cederic about this later. If we're going to spend the winter in Pfulerre, we'll have to be on show all the time, and it's time I learned what that meant.

But it was a nice reception, all things considered, and the Pfuler-rians were nice to the Balaenics in our party, and didn't say anything offensive about me being Balaenic, and then the reception turned into a dinner, which was also nice even if, as I've mentioned, half the food Castavirans serve is strange to me. In this case, it was seafood prepared in unusual ways, and I was glad because I grew up eating almost nothing but fish and kelp, and I'm usually put off by any kind of seafood. But this was all very good.

Then Cederic went to his meeting, and sent me to bed, and I was grateful for that. It's almost dawn now, and he'll be waking soon and I'll have him tell me what he learned. I'm worried that my Empress-Consort duties are going to interfere with my responsibilities to the mages, but I'll do my best to keep them balanced.

I'm hungry now. I hope it's not fish for breakfast.

CHAPTER TEN

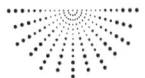

22 Jennitar, evening

Today saw a gradual erosion of the optimism I'd been feeling since we arrived in Pfulerre. This morning, when Cederic woke up, I made him sit down with me—well, no, first I finished writing and got back into bed naked, because I love the look on his face when he wakes up and finds me like that next to him. So *after* that, I made him sit down with me over breakfast (eggs, toast, bacon, pink juice, hashed potatoes, not a whiff of fish anywhere) and tell me what had happened last night.

"I am not certain our welcome was entirely genuine," he said. "Dugan and I met with Daenen Radryntor and a few of the local mayors to discuss the needs of the Army for the next few months. Lady Radryntor was very polite in acceding to our requests, but it was clear she was unhappy with our presence here."

"Well, you can't really blame her, given the kind of burden the Army will be even for those few months," I said.

"We are apportioning the supply needs among the towns near Pfulerre as well as the city itself," Cederic said. "It is the fact that it is the *Balaenic* Army she is hosting that displeases her. She will not oppose her Emperor publicly, but I am certain she will not do more than she is explicitly asked to do."

"As long as she does it, do we mind?" I asked.

Cederic sighed and forked up another piece of bacon. I have never once seen him eat with his bare hands and there's never been an opportunity for me to ask him why. This wasn't the right time either. "A reluctant consul is a consul who might be swayed to the other side if offered the right inducement," he said when he'd finished chewing. "Lady Radryntor was supportive of the God-Empress until we were crowned, at which point she decided we were the more legitimate claimants to the Imperial throne. But these talks have revealed she is also a staunch patriot, and she is not happy about the idea of Balaen being given equal treatment by someone she sees as a purely Castaviran Emperor. She might decide Renatha Torenz, despite her evil madness, will be more likely to put Castaviran interests first."

"But the former Empress is marrying the King of Balaen," I said. "Shouldn't that tell Lady Radryntor she's more interested in integrating the countries than supporting Castavir?"

"You and I know Renatha Torenz intends to control the King and ultimately subjugate Balaen to Castavir," Cederic said. "But Lady Radryntor does not, as yet, realize that. I have made your point to her and I think for now it continues to sway her to our side. That may not last."

"How does she feel about a Balaenic on the Imperial throne?" I said.

"You will have to tell me," Cederic said. "The question did not arise, and aside from greeting you on our arrival, she has not interacted with you. That might indicate disdain, or it might simply be coincidence, but in either case I have arranged for you to meet with her this afternoon to discuss Balaenic magic."

"Why would she care about that?" I said.

"She is fascinated by magic and has cultivated a large cadre of mages here in Pfulerre," Cederic said. "Apparently her interest in magic is greater than her distaste for Balaen. Whatever she may think of you as Empress-Consort, she certainly seems to respect you as a Balaenic mage."

"So should I try to be an ambassador for my country, to ease her mind about Balaen and Castavir becoming one?" I said. "That seems like it could work against us, if she thinks I'm pandering to her."

"Just be honest and forthright," Cederic said, "as you always are. Ultimately there is nothing we can do to force Lady Radryntor to believe one way or another, so we will simply go on as we have in the past. But if you can use the pouvrin to show her we have more in common than she believes, that would benefit us tremendously."

After breakfast, we went on a tour of Pfulerre—they don't have collennas yet, I mean the kind people can ride in; of course they have collennas to power things—with Radryntor and a couple of local mayors. We rode in a wheeled chariot propelled by four men seated on smaller wheeled vehicles harnessed to our chariot. Cederic said it was a type of baezrel—I know I'm spelling that wrong—which is a vehicle that was invented in Pfulerre and is very popular here, and sure enough we saw a bunch of them as we went through the streets, slimmer than the ones pulling our chariot and mostly carrying only one person. I think Balaen needs to adopt them as much as we need to have collennas, though the latter might be too big to fit comfortably in most of these streets.

Pfulerre is a very pretty, very old, very big city, maybe twice the size of Lethess and more of a port town like Thalessa than a resort. The climate here is warmer now than it was when I visited Lethess, but obviously cooler than Pfulerrians are used to, because most of the people I saw on our tour were bundled up far more warmly than I thought was necessary.

Crowds gathered wherever we passed, and everyone cheered again, calling out our names—that was a strange feeling—and not seeming to care that I wasn't Castaviran. Though they might not have realized that. It's possible they thought I was Viravonian, thanks to my hair color. I think people in Castavir don't migrate nearly as much as Balaenics do, if they assume every blond person comes from only one place in the country.

Radryntor was perfectly polite and friendly the whole time, and the mayors were even more so. I got the feeling they'd given us their unqualified support. That was reassuring, even if they aren't in positions of power that could benefit us. It was more the feeling that there *were* Castavirans who thought we were a good choice to rule, and that felt good.

We finished our tour, and had lunch, and then Radryntor said, "Your Majesty, I would love to hear more about Balaenic magic, if you wouldn't mind joining me?" and I agreed. We went to a salon decorated in blue that reminded me of a small version of the dressing room the God-Empress had brought me to the day she decided I wanted to marry Aselfos. This one didn't stink of cedar, fortunately.

Radryntor offered me a seat, sat down opposite me, and said, "I understand your magic is very unlike ours, is that true?"

"It is," I said.

"But it does the same things," she said.

"We can duplicate the effects of some th'an or kathanas," I said, "but there are things I can do that Castaviran mages can't."

"Can you show me?" she said, leaning forward in her eagerness. She was definitely acting like someone who wished she'd become a mage, though since she has hazel eyes, if she had, she would be a very frustrated mage right now.

I showed her as many pouvrin as I could, though I had to be careful with the fire pouvra because the room was filled with little wooden statues and big vases full of winter floral arrangements, all of them extremely flammable. She was most impressed with the little sphere of water I flew around the room and then dropped into one of the vases. "But you can't produce fog," she said.

"No, not yet, but we've learned Balaenic and Castaviran magic is interchangeable, so there's no reason I couldn't learn to," I said.

I don't know why that annoyed her, but she suddenly became a lot less friendly. "But Castaviran magic is capable of much more than Balaenic magic," she said.

"Castaviran magic has a tradition going back centuries," I said, "while Balaenic mages before the convergence had to stay hidden, and piece together pouvrin from ancient texts. So it's more accurate to say Castaviran *mages* are capable of more than Balaenic ones are. For the moment. But that won't last, because we're trying to find a way to combine the magics the way they're meant to be."

That definitely irritated her. "Why would that even matter?" she said.

"For the same reason it mattered that the convergence bring the worlds together as perfectly as possible," I said. "There's supposed to be only one magic, and we aren't sure why there isn't yet, but we know when it happens, magic is going to look very different than it does now, and be more powerful. It will complete the convergence."

"I see," Radryntor said. "But if Castaviran magic is more flexible, wouldn't it make sense for Balaenic mages to adapt their magic to it? That would create only one type of magic."

This was where I started to feel I should be very, very careful in what I said to her. "That's true," I said, "but history says before the worlds separated, magic wasn't like either Castaviran or Balaenic magic. Both of those developed because of the worlds being apart. We're trying to return to the pre-divergence state."

"I apologize for my bluntness, your Majesty," Radryntor said, making "your Majesty" sound close to an insult, "but that seems as if it would be a waste of both our mages' experience, if they'll have to learn a completely different type of magic. Why not let things stay as they are?"

"We hope the new magic will build on what we've already learned, Lady Radryntor," I said, managing *not* to make her name sound like an insult, "but we feel it's more important to restore the original conditions. We believe magic will be much more powerful if we do."

"I see," Radryntor said, in a chilly way, and she turned the conversation very swiftly toward asking me about Balaen, and my life, and it was obvious from her first question that she wanted to find reasons to think poorly of my country and of me. I steered the conversation away from the less savory parts of my life, downplayed my history, and did my best not to make Balaen sound superior to Castavir, even

111

though in some ways it is. The conversation made me even more convinced both countries are going to benefit by coming together. I'm not sure it changed Radryntor's mind at all.

Finally, after about an hour and a half, we ran out of things to say to each other, and I excused myself. I was tired from working all those pouvrin, which is embarrassing because I slept so well and have eaten such good food. It's not as if I haven't been practicing.

So I went and took a nap, and Cederic woke me before dinner to join him for a meeting with the mayors of the towns to the north, in the direction of Lethess. In the first weeks after the convergence, Pfulerre went through some civil turmoil Radryntor brought them out of—she may be a bigot, but she's a good leader. During that time, the northern towns clashed a few times with people from Lethess, though nothing really serious because Lethess doesn't have more than a token city guard. The Pfulerrian troops (also not much more than a token, I guess) were too busy putting down riots in the big city to be bothered to go after them.

By the time everything was settled, Lethess had withdrawn completely into itself, marshalled a city militia, and was able to drive off every attack Pfulerre sent. Now the two cities leave each other alone, but these three mayors complained that Lethess raids them occasionally, and while they're able to drive them off, it's weakened them and they're afraid they won't be able to hold out indefinitely. They want Cederic to do something about it.

Cederic said he would send a detachment of troops to each town (he told me and Mattiak afterward it would ease their supply burden too, getting some of these towns to support part of the Army) and that he would try to reason with the Lord Governor of Lethess. Not that this is likely to help, if Granea Amelessar is as unreasonable as Domenessar. She's one of only two female Lords Governor, and if the Chamber Lord Debarra Jakssar is any indication, she's going to be even more stubborn and hard-nosed than her male counterparts. But it sounds like we're going to make the attempt anyway.

23 Jennitar

I spent the day with the mages. Everyone's feeling tired these days, what with all the failed attempts at understanding why we can apply our will in such different ways and have magic still work. It took me three tries

23 Jennitar, nearly midnight

It's not us. It's the magic. It's getting weaker.

I've spent ten years—almost eleven, now—learning pouvrin, and as a result I've also learned a lot about the ideal conditions for working a pouvra. The more weary your body is, the harder it is to bend your will to the pouvra. Same thing with when you're sick, or if you're in pain—that's why I had to stay in Lethess all those years ago, because my broken arm hurt badly enough I couldn't work any pouvrin and I would have been defenseless on the road.

So I assumed, when I felt so tired working pouvrin recently, the tiredness was making them hard to manifest. It was actually the other way around: I was growing tired because it is increasingly difficult to work magic.

Because I figured this out about three hours ago, when I was already tired, I couldn't prove it myself. So I tackled Cederic. It wasn't a very good experiment, given that:

1. For all I knew, the problem was me, and every other mage had no problems;

2. Only Balaenic mages might be having problems; and

3. Cederic, as Kilios, might not struggle with magic even if there were something wrong with it in general.

But I had to try. The idea of magic getting weaker, or of pouvrin becoming less effective...it's too horrible to contemplate, and yet—anyway. I explained what I'd experienced and asked him to think of a kathana, or a th'an, that might reveal the same effects. He thought about it for a while, then did some complicated th'an on the floor with his fat writing tool that seemed to do nothing, but after a few minutes he stood up and said, "You are correct, magic has become weaker."

"But how is that possible?" I said. "Did the convergence do something?"

"I have no more idea than you what might have happened," he

said. "But I think your mages now have a more urgent problem to solve than bringing magic together."

"We need to know if the weakening is getting worse," I agreed. "Will it be all right if I don't join you for the journey to Lethess tomorrow?"

"I think we have established—my apologies—that your presence matters little to these Lords Governor who can see only that you have no surname," he said. "So I would not have asked you to come in any case. Your efforts are better spent here, at least for now."

I don't know what we're going to do. We've been complaining of tiredness, of difficulties, for weeks now without realizing it wasn't just us. If things *are* getting worse, and we missed our opportunity to keep that from happening...no, that's paranoia talking, because there's no reason to believe the worst has happened. I'm going to bed now, and in the morning I'll be able to face this better. I don't think I'll be able to sleep at all.

24 Jennitar

We did a lot of experiments today, all of which proved magic is weaker than it used to be. No way to tell if it's growing weaker over time. We all think, looking back on the past few weeks, that it has been getting harder to work magic—for example, how the warming th'an seemed to be less effective—but that could be paranoia.

Anyway, we succeeded in exhausting ourselves, physically, mentally, and spiritually, because not only do we not know what to do about it (if there's anything we *can* do about it) there wasn't any indication in all our previous research that this was a possibility. I haven't felt this discouraged since I was trying and failing to manifest the fire-rope pouvra under threat of the God-Empress's lethal displeasure. I'm doing everything I can to keep the others from picking up on it.

CHAPTER ELEVEN

25 Jennitar

No time for research, because Cederic told me this morning (I went to bed early and slept like the dead for ten hours, and he was at Lethess all day, so this was the first I'd spoken to him since yesterday around noon) all about what happened, which was a surprise on every count:

1. Granea Amelessar was cautiously welcoming of our Imperial party.

2. She had a *lot* of questions about the political situation, including the King's upcoming wedding.

2a. All the Balaenic cities have been receiving handbills announcing this blessed event, playing up the new spirit of union between our countries.

3. Amelessar thinks the King is a spineless weasel not fit to govern a herd of goats. (This was her exact phrase.)

4. She wants to meet the Balaenic woman who thinks she's capable of governing both countries.

So the result of all this is we went back to Lethess this morning specifically for me to meet the Lord Governor. I asked Cederic, "Are you sure she understands I'm a nameless nobody? This isn't at all the welcome I expected."

"I did not make the explicit point that you have no surname," Cederic said, "but I made no secret of it. Lady Amelessar did not comment on that. She is an unusual woman. When I asked about the raids Lethess had made on our Castaviran towns, she said she believed there had been misunderstandings arising from the original violence between Lethess and Pfulerre, and she put an end to those raids when she learned about them. I could not tell if she was being disingenuous, which disturbs me, as I am usually good at discerning motives. But she also seemed unconcerned about the size of the escort we brought to the meeting, which suggests she understands our security concerns and is not offended by our precautions. Over-all, she is a woman I think we would do well to ally with, even if her province is not large or tactically important."

"Having the allegiance of one Lord Governor is a step toward convincing the others to join us," I pointed out, "so it's worth doing."

"I agree," Cederic said. "We will again meet her outside the city—her suggestion. I wish I could tell you what to be prepared for."

"Then I'll just have to be prepared for anything, as usual," I said, which made him laugh.

I found out the horse's name is actually Thistle, which strikes me as a good name for her—apparently soft and pretty, but spiky if you handle her the wrong way. She's still behaving herself. For now. And I'm getting more comfortable with riding, though I don't think I'll ever love horses the way Mattiak does. He's more friendly with Thistle than I am and has chastised me for not being nicer to her. I'd tell him he can ride her if he likes her so much, but even I can tell he's far too big for her.

Anyway, she was docile enough when we rode to our meeting, which was at a pavilion set up near the city limits. Even the smallest, poorest houses of Lethess are brightly painted. It's a matter of civic pride to look good even if you're having trouble feeding yourself, which is really the only criticism I have of the place. We could see some of these houses nearby, painted yellow or turquoise or bright green like candies, and it made me sad it wasn't safe for us to ride into the city and see some of the beautiful buildings Lethess is famous for, or walk on the beach.

The pavilion was watched over by a detachment of men in the Lethess city guard uniform, something I'm glad to say doesn't strike fear into my heart, because Lethess is probably the only city I've never stolen anything from and therefore have never had to escape the local constabulary.

Huh. I never realized how much I like the place until I wrote about it.

They looked stern enough, though I know they aren't nearly as efficient as, for example, Thalessa's guardsmen, and I'm pretty sure they could have fought us off if we'd been inclined to attack Amelessar. They watched us approach without showing any nervousness, and we dismounted about twenty yards from the pavilion, a good safe distance for both of us, and Cederic and I, with Mattiak and about half a dozen soldiers, approached the tent and damn if they didn't actually salute us. Not the royal salute, but definitely one of subordinate to noble. That baffled and cheered me at the same time.

There were only four people inside the tent. Two of them were guardsmen, but bigger than the ones outside. They were also unarmed. I think they were Amelessar's personal bodyguards. I know we had them outnumbered, and our soldiers had their swords, but they stood like men who were capable of taking someone's head off with their bare hands.

The other two were women. One of them had gray hair and a deeply lined face, and wore trousers and shirt of a very fine make. The other was younger, with dark blond hair like mine but streaked with white—I think she was close to fifty—that she wore pulled tightly back from her face. She wore a silk gown with a full skirt that looked like it would be difficult to run in, and her expression was completely neutral. She was seated in one of three chairs, none of them the folding camp kind, and had her hands neatly folded in her lap.

I looked up at Cederic, who was surveying the room. He said, without turning his head, "General Tarallan, if you would ask your men to withdraw, and please give them your sword."

Now I looked at Mattiak, who clearly thought this was the worst idea Cederic had ever had, but he removed his sword belt and handed it to the nearest soldier, and that soldier and the others left the tent. Cederic inclined his head toward the younger woman and said, "Thank you for your welcome, Lady Amelessar. May I introduce the Empress-Consort, Sesskia of Balaen."

I nodded to her, trying to copy Cederic—I feel awkward not knowing how to salute people, whether there are degrees of respect I owe people of different rank—and Amelessar nodded back, equal to equal. I took this to mean she hadn't yet made up her mind how to treat us rather than a deliberate slight. She indicated the chairs and said, "Thank you for coming. Please sit."

We took our seats, and Cederic said, "I have instructed the villages who claim to have been raided by your people to cease raiding in return. I hope this will mean an end to hostilities."

"I've investigated what you told me and determined my people were to blame as well," Amelessar said. "We want to live in peace with our new neighbors." Then she smiled, and added, "We recognize we're in a weak position, given that your city—Pfulerre, is it?—is twice our size. So I admit our desire for peace isn't exactly noble."

"I do not intend to rule a subjugated Balaen," Cederic said. "But I cannot yet guarantee that every Castaviran town will be as amenable to that goal. This is why I request your fealty. Bringing our countries together requires both to desire that outcome."

"I'm not yet convinced your plan is sound, Aleynten," Amelessar said. Her face had gone back to that neutral expression. "But it's your Empress-Consort I want to talk to. Sesskia of Balaen. Are you ashamed of having no surname, that you use our country's name instead? And offer your praenoma so freely?"

"I'm not ashamed," I said, trying not to look startled at her directness. "But I think everyone should be aware I want to represent Balaen's interests in bringing our countries together rather than those of a single city. And I think—we think—an Empress-Consort ought to show her people she trusts and respects them by offering the gift of her praenoma."

"And you believe you're qualified to bring our countries together," Amelessar said.

"I've traveled Balaen for ten years," I said. "I've lived in every major city and I've visited hundreds of smaller ones. I know what our people are like and I think I know what they need, or at least what they say they need. I know what it's like to be poor and I've seen how the rich live, and I think they're not so different as we imagine. And I'm committed to seeing that Castavir doesn't dominate Balaen, and that Balaen doesn't overrun Castavir. I wouldn't say I'm the most qualified, because I don't know every person who might fill this role. But I've already risked my life to save this world, so I think that puts me at the front of the line."

"This world," Amelessar said. I kicked myself mentally for that slip. "You claim our countries were once two worlds, and our current situation is the result of them coming back together."

I had no idea what Cederic was thinking and didn't dare look at him for fear of showing weakness. "It's true," I said.

"And you were a part of this...convergence? That's what you mean when you say you risked your life?" Amelessar said.

"I was responsible for bringing them together safely, yes," I said.

The older woman said, "They had to slip into each other, correct?"

That startled me. "Yes," I said.

"Then you must know the walk-through-walls pouvra," she said. I nearly fell off my chair.

"You are a mage," Cederic said, sounding slightly shaken—probably I was the only one who noticed.

The woman raised one hand, then brought it down to slide through the back of Amelessar's chair, taking on the strange glinting shift things get when they're immaterial. I looked at her closely for the first time and realized that, yes, her eyes were green-grey behind those wrinkles.

"I have been a mage for twenty years, and Granea has protected me for five of those," she said. "It wasn't until the convergence, when all the other mages began appearing, that I dared show my abilities in public. Lethess has become a haven, these last few months, for those who need its shelter."

"We saw you had the characteristic eyes of a mage, Aleynten," Amelessar said, "but I couldn't be certain—even if you were a mage, that might not make you someone we could trust. Then you told us about the convergence, and it was clear you were downplaying your abilities as if you were afraid we'd fear you. That concerned me, because it suggested you might be concealing your powers to catch us off-guard before attacking. So I decided I had to meet your wife. I wanted to know if you'd married some Balaenic woman for a show of egalitarianism, or if you were sincere in what you claimed." She looked at me for a long moment, then said, "You should have married a noblewoman. It would boost your claim with the Lords Governor."

"We were married well before all of this, Lady Amelessar," I said, feeling irritated, "and Cederic is intelligent, but he's not a heartless pragmatist."

"I meant that as a commentary on my fellow rulers," Amelessar said, "not as a slight on you. Show me what you are capable of."

It took me a second to realize she was talking about magic, and then I despaired, remembering what we'd learned about magic weakening and how exhausting this was going to be. But I made both kinds of fire, then threw water at the back wall of the pavilion, went insubstantial, and finally concealed myself, which got a reaction out of the meaty bodyguards. "I can do others, but most of them don't have obvious effects," I said, feeling too tired for anything else—I don't think it was real tiredness, just the emotional weariness.

The older woman watched me intently, and when I was done, said, "I didn't know there were so many pouvrin in the world, let alone that a person might possess so many of them. I manifested this one at my awakening, and I learned the see-through pouvra almost by accident—by way of an old book I happened upon in the course of my work. I was a librarian in Garwin for many years."

"It took a lot of effort," I said. "Though it seems some of the new mages have learned others...by accident, I suppose you could say."

"We've seen that too," the woman said. She held out her hand, palm-first, and said, "I wish to give you the freedom of my praenoma, which is Orenna."

"And I am Sesskia," I said, saluting her and completing the ritual even though she already knew my praenoma.

Orenna and Amelessar exchanged glances, then Amelessar rose. "I will insist on keeping my position as Lord Governor of Lethess, or whatever it will be called when this transition is complete," she said, offering her hand to Cederic.

He saluted her, Balaenic-style, with no hesitation, and said, "I would be a fool to remove you from office, I think."

"You would," she agreed. "Give me a few days to spread the word, and then Lethess would like to welcome you formally...your Majesty."

"My thanks, Lord Governor," Cederic said, inclining his head to her. Amelessar turned to me and extended her hand in salute. "Your Majesty," she said, "I think you will serve both our countries well."

"I'm honored by your trust, Lord Governor," I said, "and I wish you would call me Sesskia." I was taking a chance, but I felt instinctively I wanted her as a personal ally and not just as a...I don't know what the Lords Governor and the consuls are to us; vassal sounds so archaic, subordinate sounds as if they don't wield any power. Anyway, whatever that is, I wanted something different from her.

She smiled at me, this little self-deprecating smile I've seen often on her since. "Then I offer you the freedom of my praenoma, which is Granea," she said, "and I thank you."

There wasn't much more to say, but I did talk to Orenna for a while, which resulted in me going into Lethess itself, finally, to talk to the Lethessian mages, with Mattiak as my scowling bodyguard. It was his decision, even though I fought him on the grounds the Commander General had better things to do with his time than babysit. He countered by saying if I were assassinated, Cederic would kill him and none of those things would matter.

They were a much more timid lot than ours. With no King to declare mages were not dangerous, they'd been hunted, and a lot of other mages had been killed. I think the only things that've spared our combined countries more bloodshed are the relatively great spaces between our cities and the fact that the armed forces of both countries are concentrated in only a few places. Though we've heard a few stories of places where Balaen and Castavir are getting along, which is heartening, or would be if it didn't point up so starkly how bad it was elsewhere.

Anyway. The Lethessian mages were thrilled to see me even before they knew I was their new Empress-Consort, and I'm pretty sure about half of them weren't convinced about that. But you're either a mage or you aren't, and they were all impressed at how many pouvrin I had. After demonstrating magic to them, I really was tired, which reminded me to ask if they'd noticed any changes over the last few months, and every one of them said they'd noticed it was getting harder, and more tiring, to work magic, and it had in fact been a gradually increasing problem. So I guess that's one more thing toward proving that theory.

A few of them were from Thalessa, and we talked a bit about the city, and what had happened there. There was quite a bit of destruction, they'd said, big chunks of the city just crumbling. I guess the remnants of those failed Castaviran settlements were still large enough to interfere with the convergence. It meant Thalessa was in enough turmoil those mages escaped easily by comparison to some.

None of the five had come from the poorer side of town, so we didn't have a lot of shared experiences. I think they guessed I'd been destitute, because by the end of the conversation there were a lot of pauses that said they didn't know how a pauper brat from the wrong side of town was qualified to rule anything more than a dung heap. It made me uncomfortable enough that I excused myself, saying I'd return sometime and not sure I meant it.

Then it was time for dinner, and now I'm so exhausted I can't believe I managed to write all this down. Tomorrow I have to work on this problem of magic...I hope it's not disappearing. I can't bear the thought of not having it.

26 Jennitar

Well, if magic is weakening—which is to say, we know it's weaker, yes—but if it's growing weaker over time, it's so gradual we can't see it happening. More of the mages in our camp are taking part in our research. The news that magic was fading was like a revelation—everyone had noticed the problem, but thought it was their imagination or something, and now everyone has theories about what's happening:

1. Magic is draining away and not being replenished.

2. The worlds are diverging, and taking the magic with them.

3. Magic is spreading out to a concentration too thin to be used.

4. Th'an and pouvrin are less effective because of some characteristic of the new world.

What we're working on now, though, is determining whether the effect is a result of the magic not being fully combined—and we're also working harder than ever on finding out how to make that happen.

I say "working harder" but the truth is, I'm afraid to push us to our limits because those limits seem to be closer than they used to be, and we can't afford to have anyone collapse. I'm guessing it will be as hard to recover from that as it is to work pouvrin and scribe th'an now. So I've moved our little group from the camp into the palace, which is a better environment for research, and make sure we take frequent rests and eat regularly.

I'm worried for Audryn in particular, who's already tired from her pregnancy—her stomach is visibly rounded, and she let me feel the baby kick the other day! I don't know what we'll do when spring comes and we go to war. She seems to take it for granted she'll be part of the attack, but she'll be at least seven months pregnant and the idea of risking her unborn child bothers me. It's something I've put off discussing with her, because she gets very touchy when anyone suggests she get special treatment because of her condition, like they're blaming her for her accidental pregnancy interfering with our work. But we'll have to talk about it sometime, and soon.

Things aren't going well in Pfulerre. We had dinner with Radryntor this evening, and she seemed cranky. It didn't occur to me that it might have something to do with us until she said, "You met with the leader of that Balaenic city today, yes?"

"We did," Cederic said. "I think we have resolved the issue of your towns being raided. It seems to have been a misunderstanding."

"It was a misunderstanding that left some Castavirans dead," Radryntor said. "I hope you will see justice is done."

"Balaenics were killed in those conflicts as well, Lady Radryntor," I said. "We think it's better that both sides acknowledge the mistakes they made and move forward."

"We were the ones aggressed on," Radryntor said, her tone of voice growing less friendly.

"My investigation says in two of the five instances, Castavirans attacked Balaenics," Cederic said. "I hope you are not saying you are dissatisfied with my handling of the situation."

"Of course not, your Majesty," Radryntor said, but she didn't sound any friendlier. "It's my duty to ensure the safety of Pfulerrians in these troubled times."

"That would probably be best achieved by reaching out to Lethess in friendship," I said. "I'm sure you have a lot of things you can offer each other. There are so many things Castavir has that Balaen doesn't." I caught Cederic glancing at me and hoped I wasn't laying it on too thick. Balaen has just as many things to offer Castavir, but with as prickly as Radryntor is, I figured stroking her ego wouldn't hurt.

"I'm sure you're right, your Majesty," Radryntor said, but in a way that told me she would rather chew glass than make friendly over-tures to the foreigners. "We are certainly conscious of our oaths to this new country and the duty we owe our Emperor." Which was code for *We are more valuable to you than this little Balaenic city, and you'd better not forget it.* She definitely wants us to acknowledge her importance.

I'm afraid she may get angry enough to withdraw her support

entirely, but Cederic says not to worry, she just needs to feel as if she matters. Which she does. I just wish she weren't so bigoted. She treats me with barely enough politeness not to give me any reason to object. If I could figure out a way to win her over, I would, even though I dislike her personally.

29 Jennitar

Three days of experimenting with magic, both trying to work out if it's diminishing and finding out what will has to do with bringing magic together. The current theory is that we should be exercising will the same way, either by bending our will, or exerting it, or something in between, and something in between seems most likely. It's also the hardest thing to figure out, because you'd think either you're trying to make something happen, or you're letting it happen, and there's no middle ground. But since we already know we can't work each other's magic the other way, it's all we have left.

I'm so tired all the time. Cederic keeps looking at me as if he wants to order me to stop, but he knows how important this is. Also, he runs himself to the edge of his endurance so often he'd be a hypocrite to object when I do. We're all being careful not to exhaust ourselves, to eat well and nap if and when we can. A few more mages have joined our little group, which is good except we have to take time to show them what we've done, and that feels so—not really a waste of time, but it makes everything go more slowly, and those of us who were part of the convergence kathana are starting to feel the same urgency we did back then. We need to make progress, and soon.

CHAPTER TWELVE

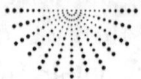

30 Jennitar

It's definitely diminishing. Slowly, barely a trickle, if magic were water or sand, but every day it's getting harder to make magic work. We're certain it's because magic isn't unified. Still no progress on figuring out how to make will work correctly. Radryntor increasingly rude to me and abrasive to Cederic. So very discouraged.

1 Teretar

Audryn collapsed yesterday and she finally, *finally* woke up an hour ago. The baby's fine, thank the true God, the healers said she didn't act as if anything were wrong with her mother, kept on moving and all that. But that's it for Audryn participating in active magic from now on. Even she had to admit I was right, though I think it was the look on Terrael's face that convinced her. I told her she could go on helping Terrael devise experiments, but that was all. It's a huge blow, losing her, but it was also a warning that we have to be even more careful about overexerting, even though she was almost certainly more at risk than the rest of us.

I asked the Pfulerrian mages if any of them wanted to join in our research, and discovered something unexpected: they tell Radryntor everything they do. I found this out at dinner (just the two of us,

Cederic busy elsewhere) when Radryntor said, "What exactly is it you're calling on my mages to do?"

Since I hadn't said word one to her about talking to the mages, let alone that magic is diminishing, it caught me off guard. "I—we're studying the nature of magic," I said.

"And how it's diminishing," she said.

"That too," I said.

She got the pinched look I see so often when she's talking to me. "Why didn't you tell me about this?" she said.

"I've been preoccupied, Lady Radryntor," I said, "and it's not as if I prepare daily reports, even for Cederic." This is not true. I write down what we learn, which isn't much, so he'll see it even if we don't get a chance to talk. I can't remember the last time we really talked about anything.

"I think I deserve to know what my mages do," she said. The pinched look was turning into an actual scowl.

"No offense intended, but isn't that up to your mages?" I said. "And since I only asked them this morning, it seems they told you what they were doing almost immediately."

She looked as if she wanted to snap at me but was afraid to so directly challenge the Empress-Consort. "I...hope they will be of use," she said.

"I think they will," I said. "They're extremely competent—that is, Terrael Peressten says they are, and I think you'd agree he's a decent judge of magical ability."

"It's a real pity he lost his magic," Radryntor said. "Such a shame that magical talent should hinge on such a ridiculous quality. It's not as if, for example, brown eyes make you an exceptional general."

"I agree completely," I said with some fervor, because it still makes me mad to think of all that talent wasted. Though I probably should be grateful for all the Balaenic mages who never would have gained their abilities if not for the convergence.

"I don't suppose you can do anything about that, in your... research?" Radryntor said.

"Unfortunately, no," I said, "because trying to do that is what caused the worlds to split in the first place. The best we can do is find ways for those mages to continue to serve our combined country."

I probably shouldn't have mentioned the combined country. Radryntor's eyes narrowed, but she didn't say anything more, just turned the conversation elsewhere. I'm definitely going to conceal the fact I asked the Lethessian mages to join our efforts too. We can't afford to lose her as an ally, even if she doesn't have the military force we need the way Teliarne does. But it bothers me that I'm almost pandering to her and her smugness about Castaviran magic being superior, which it isn't. She looks more like a liability every day.

I don't know if we can let her continue as a consul if she can't treat everyone equally. Come to think of it, Pfulerre and Lethess are too close together to justify both being the centers of whatever governing districts we come up with after the God-Empress is defeated. I don't know if it's a good idea to put Granea in charge of both cities, given that Pfulerre is about three times the size of Lethess. But we also can't cater to the bigotries of Castavirans any more than we can coddle the egos of Balaenics.

That's not to disparage Granea's abilities. She's a competent and fair-minded Lord Governor, and I have no doubt she'd be capable of ruling a larger district containing Pfulerre. Despite the difference in our ages, we've become friends, and although we haven't had our official welcome to Lethess, I've gone into the city a couple of times, mostly to talk to the mages, but once to walk on the beach. It's every bit as beautiful as I remember.

Orenna and Jaemis have developed a similar relationship, and the two of them are dogged in their quest to discover what's happening with magic. Listening to them argue (because they seem to enjoy arguing for its own sake as well as for the results it produces) is reassuring, or was right up until Audryn went pure white and collapsed like a folding chair. I haven't been that terrified in years.

3 Teretar

We made our processional into Lethess, and I realized that as friendly as Pfulerre had been, we haven't truly and wholeheartedly been made welcome until today. Granea and Cederic made speeches, and I said some things about how much I liked the city that I think everyone could tell were sincere. As nice as our room in the consul's palace is, I wish we were staying here instead. And not because I'm Balaenic.

Today was the first day I've seen Cederic in

I can't remember how long it was since we've had time to talk, other than with Radryntor's sullen presence casting a very long shadow over our dinners. We didn't have time today either, because there's been trouble north of Pfulerre again, more clashes between the cities, and Cederic had to oversee the situation because neither city is willing to let the other pass judgment. Granea wasn't happy about it either.

Today we had dinner with her, after we all returned from investigating the problem, and she said, "I can't help feeling Radryntor is opposed to a Balaenic passing judgment on cases like this because she knows she'd be partial to her own people if she were in that position."

"That has to be true," I said. "She's convinced Castavir is superior and ought to be given jurisdiction over Balaen, like a conquered country. And that's what we're trying to avoid."

"I surmise Lady Radryntor's overtures of peace aren't that," Cederic said.

Granea snorted with amusement. "They're more like demands Lethess capitulate on property ownership, or that Pfulerre be allowed to collect tolls for use of the coast road that passes within its borders," she said. "I'll bow to your decrees, your Majesty, but I expect you to keep your word that Balaen is not going to become a subject state to Castavir."

"It may come to a point where I have to make it explicit that Lady Radryntor is not the supreme ruler here, which might mean threatening her with the Balaenic Army," Cederic said.

"Because *that* will end well," I said.

"Which is why it will be our tactic of last resort," Cederic said. "And that is all I will say on the subject."

"You probably shouldn't have said that much in front of me,"

Granea said with a grin, "me being equal with Radryntor in the eyes of the government, Lord Governor and consul."

"Precisely," Cederic said, "and I trust you will not mention my slip of the tongue."

"As far as I'm concerned, we talked only of whether the King is still planning to marry your deposed Empress," Granea said, "and how long he'll survive once he has."

So we talked gossip for a while, then I went back to the mages and Cederic went to see the quartermasters about the supply situation. I'm not sure that's really his job, and I wish I'd proposed we go back to our room together instead. I can't wait until things are less busy and we can be together. I'd love to walk on the beach with him.

4 Teretar

Once again I've sat, pencil in hand, not even knowing where to begin. It seems so utterly ridiculous, the worst possible kind of coincidence, and yet—why not? My sister had to end up somewhere, and she always liked the sea. And there I was, parading happily through Lethess with thousands of people cheering me, so why shouldn't Roda have seen me? It's been sixteen years, yes, but Sesskia's not a common name, and I recognized her immediately too. I wish I didn't. I wish I'd thought to tell the messenger who came for me I didn't know anyone named Roda. That I don't have a sister. Because for all those sixteen years I felt as if I really, truly didn't.

The messenger arrived as I was finishing my breakfast (alone) and preparing for another long, tedious day with the mages. Everyone's trying different things and it's my job to look at everything they try and see if it's worth pursuing as a group. How I'm qualified to do that is one of those mysteries life comes up with sometimes. (That sounds so bitter. Well, I feel bitter right now.) The messenger was from the Army, from Mattiak actually, and he had a folded note with just a few lines on it: *There's a woman named Roda here who claims she's your sister. Her story matches what you told me. I think you should verify her claim.*

I know I read those lines several times, but I only understood them the first time. The rest was my eyes running over the characters, seeing Roda in memory—teaching me to swim, to pick the least rotten fruit from the barrow, helping me clean Bridie up after one of her seizures. And Roda telling me *It's for the best* and walking away for the last time.

I set the paper aside on the table and left the room without a word to the messenger. Mattiak knew something of my history, enough that he *would* know whether someone claiming to be related to me actually was. I guess there was a chance Roda had told her life story to a friend, or a lover, and that woman decided to get close to me by pretending to be Roda, but what would be the point other than maybe to try to assassinate me? No impostor would be able to fool me face to face. I might not have thought of Roda much in the last sixteen years—all right, the last ten, because I cursed her name every day for the first six—but I sure as hell would recognize her face.

I'm supposed to have a bodyguard wherever I go, four of Mattiak's hand-picked men, and I think they were following me when I left Pfulerre, but I wasn't paying attention to anything but the well-trodden path we'd made between the city and the camp, and I wasn't paying much attention to that. I was barely aware of startled soldiers jumping up to salute me as I passed through the camp to Mattiak's command tent and pushed the door flap aside instead of waiting for the sentries to hold it for me.

And it was her. I'd forgotten how small she is, or maybe I grew a few inches after she left, but I'm not very tall and she's truly petite. She looks like Dad and Bridie, dark-haired and blue-eyed—Dad wasn't very tall either—with that round face she and I got from Mam, only her lashes are pale and stubby and mine are thick and long. She wore her hair cut short and shaped to her head so it framed her face, and she was wearing a nice shirt and trousers and good shoes that weren't suited to walking anywhere but on a paved road.

She was facing Mattiak, but turned her head when I entered, then took a few steps so she was facing me instead. She didn't look happy, or sad, or guilty, or anything but impassive, like she was waiting for me to react so she could pick the right response. I said, "Outside. All of you. Right now."

I don't think I've ever sounded more like an Empress-Consort.

Everyone left, even Mattiak, who didn't even say anything, just clasped my shoulder and squeezed as if in support. Then it was just me and Roda. I honestly couldn't think of anything to say. Roda said, "Hello, Sesskia."

"Have you been living in Lethess?" I said. I don't know why I didn't shout at her. It wasn't as if I wasn't angry, because I was, it's just that sixteen years is a long time to hold on to a white-hot anger, and it felt as if it had dulled into something more like a toothache: painful, always there, but sometimes it stops throbbing and you forget about it until the right jab starts it up again.

"I'm here on business," Roda said. "It's good to see you."

The ache throbbed again. "Since I'm sure you never expected it, I guess you would feel that way," I said.

Her impassivity cracked. "I went back ten years ago," she said. "I looked for you."

"How generous of you," I said. "Was Mam still alive?"

"Yes," Roda said. "She didn't recognize me. Didn't recognize much of anything. Some of the neighbors were caring for her, said she didn't have much longer. I stayed long enough to bury her."

I felt a twinge of guilt I ignored. I'd already given Mam more than Roda ever had—more than she deserved, probably. "Thanks for that," I said. I meant it, too.

"Where did you go?" Roda said. "Nobody knew what had happened to you, just that you left maybe a year before I came back. I didn't think Bridie was well enough to travel."

"Bridie died two years after you abandoned us," I said. "Not that you'd give a damn about that."

"Don't you *dare*," Roda began, then swallowed, and more calmly said, "I loved her. But that wasn't enough to cure her. You know that."

"What I *know*," I said, "is you left me to take care of both of them and I was barely *twelve*, damn it, twelve years old in the slums of Thalessa with a drunken mother and a little sister who had fits, and I had to claw out a living any way I could because *you* were too wrapped up in your own needs to care about any of that!" That ache was starting to burn bright again, after all.

"I couldn't stay!" Roda shouted. "I was turning into Mam—you think that would have helped any of us? I couldn't make a living in Thalessa short of selling my body, I had to go, and I couldn't take you with me!"

"Because you didn't want to be burdened!" I shouted back.

"Because I couldn't support the three of us!" she said.

"And you think I couldn't have helped?" I said. "I was old enough to support two other people, but not to work with you to support three?"

Roda turned away. "I didn't want Mam left alone," she said, more quietly now. "I'm not saying it was the smartest decision. But I was the head of the family and I did my best. I thought I'd be back in a year or two."

"That makes me feel *so* much better now," I said. "Knowing you did your best. Like you did your best to find me. Was it a relief, knowing I was gone so you could go on with your life?"

"I *did* look for you!" she said. "I talked to everyone who'd ever known us, everyone you'd worked with—you just vanished as far as all of them were concerned. Mam didn't even remember she'd had a daughter named Sesskia. At the end all she could do was babble about—you know, how she used to go on about our family's lost glories and how we'd be living in a manor if not for Dad screwing up all our lives. I searched up and down the coast for over a year, thinking you might have stayed here, and in the end I had to give up because Balaen is huge and I'm only one person. I'm *sorry*, Sesskia."

She sounded sorry. She sounded sincere. I didn't care. "That doesn't make anything better, Roda," I said. I ignored the part of me that wanted to forgive her, the part of me that wanted her to make everything all right.

Now that I'm writing this, I feel guilty that I couldn't forgive her. It's been so long—what's the point of holding onto my anger? But I can't—I still remember how it felt the day she laid that burden on me, told me "you have to take care of them now" and then just walked away before I could do anything to stop her. And when I remember that, it's as if she did it all over again. Maybe it makes me weak. I don't know anymore.

Anyway, Roda said, "I couldn't believe it when I saw you in that procession. I thought, maybe it's some other Sesskia, because why would my sister be hailed as a ruler? But it was definitely you. It was like being given a second chance. I'm sorry, Sesskia. I'm sorry I left and I'm sorry I didn't come back in time. We're all that's left of our family. I don't want to lose that again."

My anger was slipping away no matter how hard I tried to hold onto it. I didn't want to forgive her. It felt as if doing that would be like saying everything she did to me, to us, was all right. Like I didn't have a right to be hurt by it. "What exactly do you want from me?" I said. "Money? Rank? Political power?"

She flinched. "I want my sister back," she said. "I don't care if you're a fish scaler in Thalessa or Empress of the whole damned world. I want to sit with you and find out what you've been doing all these years and how you ended up on that platform in the center of Lethess claiming to be the new ruler of Balaen and this strange new country we're cheek-by-jowl with now. I want you to forgive me, if you can."

I shook my head and realized I was crying. "I'm sorry," I said, "but I don't think I can."

Roda's shoulders slumped. She was crying too, and it was almost enough to change my mind. Almost. "I'm staying at the Salten Arms in Lethess," she said, "down by the docks. You can find me there, if you decide you want to. Goodbye, Sesskia." She left the tent, and I stood there, crying, because

I'm crying again now. I want to forgive her and I can't forgive her. I hate her and I love her. She's my sister, even though she abandoned us, and true God help me, I don't know which of those things matters more.

I couldn't talk about this at dinner in front of Radryntor, so I told Cederic I needed to talk tonight, but I don't know if he'll remember. I'm beginning to feel like he's a stranger to me.

5 Teretar

Still nothing to report. Based on the kathana Terrael created to track the decline in magic, it's not a regular decline (even though it never increases) so we can't pick a future date and say that's when it will be gone forever. It's also not happening as fast as all of us feel it is; our fears are exaggerating the truth. I barely see Cederic these days, what with me being involved in research and him dealing with an increasingly testy Radryntor. I'm wondering whether she's really that important as an ally.

6 Teretar

We got the word, finally, that the King and the God-Empress are married. Nobody in Lethess celebrated at all, but there was a funny undercurrent in Pfulerre I didn't like. Cederic and I are going to address the city tomorrow to reassure them this changes nothing. I hope it works.

I keep thinking about Roda and trying not to, because it makes me so angry and guilty and I hate both those feelings. I wish she'd never approached me.

7 Teretar

I don't know how effective that was. Cederic spoke about the God-Empress's cruelties and the oaths he swore at his coronation. I told them about the King, about his weakness and how ineffectually he'd ruled Balaen, and asked them if they wanted someone like that co-ruling them. I think that made more of a difference than what Cederic said, but mainly because a lot of Pfulerrians have picked up on their consul's bigotry. I don't know how they reconcile disliking a Balaenic King ruling them with being fine with a Balaenic Empress-Consort ruling them. I just hope they go on doing it.

We've given up on trying to reconcile the two extremes of using willpower to work magic. It's become obvious it's simply impossible for human minds to fathom, and since the point of this is to restore a unified magic humans can use, there would be no point in that magic requiring something we can't do. It feels like we've wasted so much time.

Audryn is back on her feet and looks perfectly healthy, but she got into an argument with Terrael about her coming back to active research and I had to add my voice to his. She cried a lot, then apologized, and then we hugged and I cried because I feel so overwhelmed, and I know how I'd feel if I were in her position. Unable to work magic, I mean. I have no idea what it's like to be pregnant.

I've been thinking about it a lot lately, though. I stopped taking the contraceptives after Cederic was nearly assassinated, in case the worst happens and someone—anyway, I haven't told Cederic because it feels like superstition. Nothing's happened, but sometimes I wonder what it would be like. I never pictured myself as a mother, mostly because I never dreamed I'd meet anyone I'd want to have a child with, so now I'm afraid because we have to produce at least one heir to keep all of this from sliding back into chaos when we're gone. And it's not just the giving birth; suppose I can't raise my child—children, maybe—to be a good ruler?

This is so much greater a responsibility than most parents face, where if you have a rotten kid, he or she is only going to inflict that rottenness on a few people, not on an entire country. I don't want to talk about this with Cederic right now, not with everything he's dealing with, and I probably shouldn't worry about it until we've defeated the God-Empress and brought everything, or mostly everything, under control. But it's something that worries me when I have time to spare from worrying about magic, or Radryntor, or Audryn.

I thought about going into Lethess today. Decided not to. Tried not to feel guilty.

CHAPTER THIRTEEN

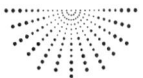

8 Teretar

Radryntor noticeably cooler toward both Cederic and me. I think the only thing keeping her from changing her mind entirely about our rule is the Balaenic Army camped outside her gates. I'm prepared for us to leave the city if that becomes necessary. Cederic—I can't believe I can't remember the last time we made love. We're just so busy...but I think we shouldn't ever be too busy for that.

Anyway, Cederic looks grim these days, or I should say, looks grim to me; I doubt anyone else will see that in his normally impassive expression. Outwardly, he's as calm and reassuring as ever, overseeing whatever Mattiak thinks needs his attention, sitting in judgment occasionally in Lethess and Pfulerre so people will see he's a just ruler, drafting handbills to send out throughout the country condemning the King's actions and reiterating his (Cederic's) claim to the throne. I cannot imagine anyone better suited to this role, and I don't think I say that just because I love him.

I'm going to wait up for him. I still haven't told him about Roda—I don't know if he even realizes she came to see me, because I bet Mattiak would think it wasn't his business to discuss *my* business with my husband, and we haven't had the right moment to talk about it yet. We need to remember we aren't just these roles we've been playing, that at heart we're two people who love and support and need each other. It's hard to remember, these days, what it was like when all we had to worry about was the God-Empress finding out we were married and using that to threaten or hurt us. As if that were anything so trivial—but it certainly feels that way now.

9 Teretar

Fell asleep before Cederic came to bed, didn't wake until after he was gone again this morning. Never had a chance to talk to him today —he was in Lethess most of the day, and I was with the mages, and then we had dinner with Radryntor and that was, of course, not a place where we could have a heartfelt conversation. Tonight for sure.

10 Teretar

See above, except this time I actively tried to speak to him and kept being called on for stupid little things I'm sure anyone could have handled, except, naturally, having the attention of the Empress-Consort makes people feel better. I wish I were just Sesskia again. I wish all of this were over. I wish Radryntor would stop being so stupid. I wish the God-Empress would drop dead and take the King with her. I wish Roda

I can't bear how cynical and vicious I've become. Something has to change. I can't quite bring myself to go into Lethess.

11 Teretar

More news out of Venetry, sickening news: the entire Chamber has been executed for "disloyalty." We're holding out hope this isn't true. It's come to us via rumor rather than official decree, but it seems so much like something the God-Empress would do it's hard to stay optimistic. Not that I really liked any of them except maybe Jakssar, and Crossar was probably an active threat to us, but I didn't wish any of them dead.

I've given up waiting for Cederic at night. Eventually, things will be less hectic, and we'll have a chance to be together again. For now, I'm so tired I can't bear it.

14 Teretar

No chance to write—well, chances to write, but not much to say.

The new kathana that will unify how we apply our will to pouvrin is coming along very slowly, as expected, and everyone's doing their best not to be impatient or worried at what that means about diminishing magic.

What I worry about all the time now is that bringing our two magics together isn't going to make a difference. That magic isn't diminishing, it's spreading out the way it did after the worlds separated, and it can't be stopped. Because, really, what does the world care if people can't use magic? It's not like it destroyed the worlds when that first stupid kathana split them apart. We just won't have magic. And I refuse to think that's inevitable. I think of how much Castaviran society depends on magic, of how many benefits Balaen might see from it, and it makes me more determined than ever to find a solution.

15 Teretar

Good progress on the kathana today. Everything else as usual. More news out of Venetry confirming the Chamber has been disbanded "in pursuit of a more unified government of our blended countries," but nothing saying the Chamber Lords were executed. Hope that's good news. Granea invited me for dinner and I made an excuse, then felt terrible. I'm not going to be magically dragged to wherever Roda is just because I step into the city. I hate this feeling.

16 Teretar

Kathana almost ready. We hope. Jaemis and Orenna seem confident; they've taken the lead on this, and by the verbal wrangling I infer they're satisfied with the results. I've never seen two people so prone to expressing their fondness for each other by shouting. They're like a couple of siblings born thirty years apart.

Radryntor is back to being cold. I think she took the expulsion of the Balaenic Chamber as a sign that the God-Empress is truly as pro-Castavir as Radryntor thinks we ought to be. I never see her except at dinner. Spoke briefly to Cederic today and he said we should definitely be prepared to force the issue.

Two more days, and we can do the kathana. I don't dare make plans beyond that.

17 Teretar

I think everyone is prepared for their role in the kathana, even our Lethessian mages, who were completely unfamiliar with Castaviran magic until recently. It's extremely complicated, so it's a good thing the Balaenic mages don't have to scribe th'an using their pouvrin or anything that would make it even more complicated. We're using the offensive pouvrin, the mind-moving and fire pouvrin, to force a shape out of the th'an that will then bind the pouvrin into something less fluid, something will can gain purchase on. Whether this will affect all pouvrin and not just the two we're using is still uncertain, as is whether this will make the magics come together, but we all feel confident about it.

Mostly confident.

I don't think I've been this nervous about magic since I learned the mind-moving pouvra and was afraid I might kill myself using it. Sleep now, kathana tomorrow.

18 Teretar, noon

I've sat here gripping my pencil, not knowing how to begin, for an hour. I feel so weary, so defeated, there almost seems no point to writing anything. So I guess I should start with the list of the dead, so their names won't be forgotten, Balaenics and Castaviran together because after this, the distinction doesn't matter anymore:

Cerran, Aelisa, Loevaron, Selwen, Elevia, Bedaeka, Harisson, Obren.

Jaemis.

So few, when I write them down, and I should be thinking of how fortunate we are it wasn't more, but every one of those names was someone I knew and cared about, even Obren and Elevia, whom I'd only just met. And I keep going over it. I know I shouldn't. I had to have Orenna sedated because I couldn't stop her trying to fix it any other way, but it's impossible not to look at that list and think we should have understood it better, or been more patient, or *something*.

We started preparing early this morning, getting a good breakfast, some of us going for a run around the camp, others meditating, whatever limbered up their bodies and minds for working serious magic. I spoke briefly to Cederic, who was headed off for yet another meeting with Radryntor, and he told me he regretted not being able to be there, and he was gone before I realized I hadn't kissed him goodbye. That felt like a bad omen, but I shook it off and went to do my own preparation ritual, which is to find a quiet spot and let my mind drift. That was hard to do today, and part of me would like to blame that for my contribution to the disaster, but I know that had nothing to do with it.

So I rested, and eventually went to where we were going to do the kathana, a big empty spot about a third of the way toward Lethess from the camp.

We needed something more permanent this time, so we we'd taken the trenching tools yesterday to dig a kathana circle out of the sod and carve out the inert th'an, which we filled with black clay we'd made by mixing white clay with charcoal. It took a lot of charcoal to get it good and black, and it left everyone's fingers filthy, but the black stood out nicely against the pale ground.

Then we all took our places at the cardinal and ordinal points, kneeling in lines of four—that is, each point had four people lined up behind it, with Balaenic mages at the cardinal points and Castavirans at the ordinal points. I was the anchor, the last person in the row, for the northern point, Jeddan was farthest from me at the southern anchor point, and Jaemis knelt in the center, with his back to me, facing south.

The most complicated part, to me, was keeping the beat: there were five "musicians" with different instruments scrounged from all over Pfulerre, and I still don't understand how they can tell the difference between two flutes that to me look and sound exactly the same, but it seems those small, nearly invisible differences matter. Maybe we used the wrong ones. I have to stop rethinking this.

Anyway, our five musicians each had a different type of instrument, drum, wooden block, fife, bell, and something that looks like a very short xylophone, and it took them about ten minutes to tune up and then get into harmony with each other. Then they began playing.

It's the first kathana rhythm I've ever heard that actually sounded like music, and one of the things we worked hardest at, in preparing for this, was learning to identify when the melody reached the end and started over. I let myself relax and fall into the rhythm, which to me felt like a dance, and I remembered how the mages had swept back and forth across the kathana that summoned the Codex Tiurindi, and how beautiful it was, and that helped me relax even further.

After three repetitions, there was a sighing noise as everyone drew breath at once, and I can appreciate that now as I didn't when I was absorbed in the rhythm, because it meant we'd passed the first obstacle, getting everyone synchronized. I was aware of movement on either side of me as the Castaviran mages to left and right brought their slates up and began scribing. I let the fire pouvra emerge from within me and began bending my will to its shape just as the mages across from our line began doing the same to manifest the mind-moving pouvra. That was how the pattern went: each pouvra in opposition to the other, with the Castaviran mages scribing th'an with the same effects, also opposite one another.

It was so difficult, as if I were trying to shape water, but eventually I felt it respond, and before it could ignite anything I let it pass from me into Davik's grip. Once it was gone I felt utterly drained, weakened, but we'd expected that, because being able to shape magic and then give it to someone else to use was so difficult we'd almost had to devise a different kathana before Relania worked out the technique. The idea was for each mage to bring the pouvra (or th'an) into shape, then give it to the next person, who would combine it with his and pass it forward until the keypoint mage, the one at the circle, was handling four times his normal ability.

It sounds dangerous. *Was* dangerous, clearly. I still don't see that we had another choice, except

Never mind that. If I write it all down, it makes their sacrifice less of a waste.

I was at the back, so I couldn't see the rest, but I knew how the kathana was meant to work. We'd never been able to get the Balaenic mages to work the pouvrin at the same speed, because some of us just take longer than others, so as each keypoint person received their burden, he or she started slapping the ground in time with the song's rhythm. As soon as everyone was doing that, Jaemis would begin his part, linking the eight magics together and essentially telling the pouvrin to act like th'an, rigid and malleable at the same time.

Like I wrote, I couldn't see any of this, but I could hear this noise begin, a range of pitches that sounded like moaning. I think it was moaning, the sound of those eight mages trying to keep the magic from escaping. I know it's not a living I don't know if magic is living or not. Maybe that's the problem. But I couldn't help picturing it trying to escape, as if we were caging it, or tormenting it.

There was the music, and the moaning, and very faintly the sound of someone dragging a knife or a stick through the hard, half-frozen earth, and then I did see something—an icy glow that sprang up around each of those keypoint mages. If winter were a color, that's what it would be, silver-white light that looked like it would burn anything it touched, except our mages weren't screaming in pain, so it was just an illusion.

And then they did start screaming.

Four of the mages at the circle went up in flames, gold mixed with that silver-white light. The other four—I couldn't see them, just that the light grew more intense and then shrank down to limn their outlines. I saw Jaemis, just barely, as he collapsed and began thrashing on the ground. That was when I tried to stand and found I needed the support of my hands to get to my feet. Everyone else was screaming, and I reached out with the extinguishing pouvra, thinking I could at least put out the fires, and it worked, but the silver light was still there, and they were all still thrashing around, and I did the only thing I could think of—flung myself forward and scrabbled at one of the inert th'an, finally prying it up and crushing it in my hands. The light vanished.

I didn't think I'd ever be able to move again. Then someone helped me stand—it was Jeddan, and he was saying something I couldn't understand. It wasn't that I couldn't hear him, but I felt addled, as if language were beyond my understanding. He had to repeat himself several times before I realized he was asking if I was all right. I nodded, though I think I was lying—it depended on what he meant by "all right." At least I wasn't injured. Then I looked around, and I thought I might never be all right again.

All the keypoint mages were dead. Four of them were blackened husks curled up on themselves from extreme heat. Four of them were crushed and mangled as if they'd been caught in a rock slide. Jaemis was unrecognizable as human. It was so silent that if Jeddan hadn't spoken to me, I'd have thought I'd gone deaf. Then someone began sobbing, and it was as if that had broken through some invisible barrier, because everyone joined in, screaming or wailing or just making these inhuman groaning sounds. Jeddan and I both sat down and held each other, crying without making a sound.

I don't know how long it took before people from our camp came to investigate the light. I had my eyes closed because it was too hard to keep them open, and because everywhere I looked I saw a dead friend, but I heard them running toward us, and then at least one person threw up. That told me I had better get control of myself, because someone would need to supervise everything, starting with taking the bodies to where they could be cared for before being buried.

It was just as hard to stand as it had been before, but Jeddan and I helped each other—well, he helped me and I tried not to weigh him down—and I was able to face the soldiers and give them instructions. Then I went to each of our mages in turn and made them calm down enough to look at me, and told them to go back to the palace and rest —in groups, if they could, because I didn't think any of us should be alone. Not that I had any choice about it, myself.

I stayed long enough to ensure the bodies were being handled with respect, then followed that horrible white-sheeted procession back to camp with Jeddan. Neither of us said anything. There wasn't anything to say, really, until we'd seen our friends cared for, and then we walked back to the palace. Once we were at the door to his chambers, Jeddan said, "I can have someone send a message to Cederic."

"He shouldn't be interrupted," I said, "and when Radryntor finds out about this, who knows what she'll think it means? I just want to sleep, Jeddan, and hope this doesn't look quite so bad later."

Jeddan didn't look convinced. "You don't look well," he said.

"Neither do you," I said. His normally tanned complexion looked chalky.

"Well," he said, "if you can sleep, sleep, but come back to the mages' quarters later. I think everyone could use some reassurance."

"I will," I said, but as I write this I'm not sure I'm capable of reassuring anyone because I can't even reassure myself.

This is the worst disaster I can imagine. Not only did we lose so many people, we failed utterly at the only thing we could think of that would make our magics whole. Magic is fading, we don't know how to stop it, it's nearly spring and we have barely any support and only a shred of an army, the God-Empress is winning, and I might as well have no husband for all we ever see each other.

I know I told Jeddan I would sleep, but I feel as if I will never sleep again, just go on putting one foot in front of the other like a puppet on strings, and writing in this book is all I can do. And it's completely pointless.

I'm going to bed now. Maybe all I can do is stare at the wall and think about my failures. Maybe that will shake something loose. Maybe not. But it's all that's left to me.

CHAPTER FOURTEEN

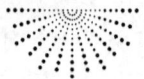

18 Teretar, evening

I don't know how long it was after I finished that last entry that I woke up—I didn't realize I'd been asleep either—to find Cederic shaking me gently and saying my name. I felt so numb, it was as if I didn't recognize him. As if he meant nothing to me. He was sitting on the edge of our bed, so I sat up to face him, and he clasped my hands and said, "Tell me what happened."

"I can't talk about it," I said.

"You have the look of someone who is being eaten from within," he said. "You need to tell someone. Please, Sesskia, let me share your burden."

Him saying that—I don't know what happened. Usually, as I've written before, I tell him everything. But it infuriated me—all those days of never seeing him, of trying to reach out and being ignored or passed over in favor of something more important, and it took nine deaths for him to decide he wanted to be with me?

I screamed at him—I won't even try to record what I said, it was horrible and vicious and I felt myself growing harder and colder with every word. He just looked at me, and before I'd fully wound down he withdrew his hands, stood and walked away, silently, his face as expressionless as always, and that shut me up. I clenched my hands and listened to his steps, listened to the door open and shut, quietly, and then I threw myself face-first onto the bed and howled.

I was making so much noise I didn't know he'd come back until he picked me up and put his arms around me, laid his cheek against mine, and held me, whispering, "I'm sorry. I'm so sorry." I cried and cried and clung to him and cried some more until my throat ached and my eyes ached and I ran out of tears. Then we sat like that, silent, until I said, "I shouldn't have said any of that. I didn't mean it."

"I think I may have deserved some of it," he said. "I have been incredibly stupid not to realize how little we were seeing of each other. Lady Radryntor has consumed so much of my time I told myself my own needs could wait—but I never thought of yours, nor that my needs are now to an extent those of the Empire and should not be neglected."

"Even so, I should never have spoken to you that way," I said. "Please forgive me."

"As you forgave me, once," Cederic said, and my heart lightened.

"I should have pushed harder," I said. "I knew we were drifting apart, but part of me was selfish and believed because I was exhausting myself, you should be the one to make the effort. So I never did anything beyond trying to stay awake until you came to bed."

He smiled. "You don't know how many times I thought of waking you," he said. "But I knew you needed your rest, and I told myself there would be time, eventually."

"I wish you'd woken me," I said.

"I wish I had too," he said, kissing me. "But we have nothing but time now."

"Even if Lady Radryntor decides to evict us from Pfulerre?" I said.

Cederic gestured, and a heavy chair flew across the room and wedged itself under the doorknob. "She will need several men with large axes to do that," he said between kisses, "and if she is able to get past that door, there are more chairs in this room I will use as projectiles."

I started unbuttoning his shirt. "Are you sure your concentration can be divided like that?" I said.

"No," he said, sliding his hands under my shirt and unfastening my breast band, "but I thought you might like the reassurance of knowing I am so committed to making you cry out in pleasure I would attack the servants of one of our vassals to ensure it."

"That is the most romantic thing you have ever said to me," I said, and then we were done talking.

I love him so much.

We made love, then we held each other, and talked, and made love again, and part of me wanted to feel guilty that I could be so happy when nine of my friends were dead, but I know it's foolish to think that way, because my being miserable isn't going to bring them back. And I needed this so much.

I told him about Roda, about what we'd said to each other, and he listened intently and held me close, and this time I didn't cry. When I finally wound down, he stayed silent, just played with my hair the way he does sometimes when we're lying close together. Eventually, I said, "Well?"

"I was not sure whether you wanted my opinion, or just a listening ear," he said.

"I—actually, I don't know," I said. "I guess I want reassurance."

"If you are looking to me to tell you whether or not to forgive your sister, you will have to ready yourself for disappointment," he said, "as I think it is not my place to tell you what to do with your pain. But I think you are wrong in believing that forgiveness means behaving as if the sin never happened."

"Then what does it mean?" I said.

"What did it mean when you forgave me the cruel things I said to you in the palace?" he said.

"That was different," I said. "That wasn't years of pain and abandonment. Besides, I was in love with you and I wanted a reason to forgive you."

He laughed. "The two may be different in, let us say, intensity," he said, "but the principle is the same. You chose to let go of the resentment you might justifiably have harbored against me. That is not the same as pretending it never happened. Much as I personally would like not to have that memory."

"And it meant being able to love you, so it's not as if nothing good came of it," I said.

"It's up to you to decide whether something good came of Roda's actions," Cederic said. "But I think, if you choose to let the past bury the past, you may feel happier. And your happiness is paramount to me."

I put my arms around his neck. "Show me," I said, and he did.

Finally, it grew dark, and we got dressed and went to eat, not with Radryntor but with the mages elsewhere in the palace. That was a lot sadder, and then I felt guilty that I'd had such a wonderful afternoon when most of them hadn't, but we remembered our dead together, and that made things easier. I think we'll be able to go back to our work soon—not before the funeral, naturally, but soon.

Cederic's right. I've been carrying around a lot of anger toward Roda for years, even though most of the time I wasn't aware of it. And it hasn't made me happier. It seems like she really does regret the choices she made, which means she's going to carry that burden whether I forgive her or not, so if I'm worried that forgiving her means pretending none of it happened, I shouldn't be. If I could forgive Cederic for his deliberate cruelty, maybe I can forgive Roda too. But I don't think anything good came of her actions.

Well, maybe. I was able to survive on my own after I left Thalessa because of what I'd had to learn to keep the three of us alive after Roda left. And it would have been harder to go out on the road the way I needed to if Roda had still been there. But I'm not ready to think like that. I'm sure as hell not going to be *grateful* to her for what she did. If she'd been with us, she would have gone for the medicine and I'd have been with Bridie when she died. I guess I'm not as over my resentment as I thought.

True God help me. I re-read that last paragraph and realized something I've failed to see all these years: it's *myself* I can't forgive.

I was supposed to take care of my baby sister and I failed her right at the end. It doesn't matter that I was only fourteen and working myself to exhaustion every day, I was doing it for her sake, because she was small even for a ten-year-old and couldn't do much more for the family than scrounge along the tide line. I had to go out for the medicine because there wasn't anyone else, and it was just stupid bad luck that's when she had her final seizure. It's just been easier, all these years, to blame Roda or Mam so I wouldn't have to face how much I blamed myself.

It doesn't change anything I wrote above, but...maybe if I can forgive Roda, I can forgive myself too.

I don't know. Letting go of this pain is hard. I'll see how I feel in the morning. And now I'm going to bed with my husband, and while we probably won't be having sex again, we will sleep close together, and bring each other comfort, and tomorrow I'll be able to face whatever the future holds. And I don't feel one bit superstitious about writing that.

19 Teretar

Today was a rest day. We each, Balaenic and Castaviran, prepared to bury our friends according to our different customs, but we also wanted to do something to honor them as mages irrespective of their nationalities. So we went into Pfulerre and bought nine blank books, and everyone wrote messages in them—nothing maudlin like "We'll never forget you," because that's either true or it isn't and writing it under these circumstances felt trivial. Instead we wrote about magic, how we felt when we used it and why we could still go on using those pouvrin and th'an that killed them because it wasn't the magic's fault what had happened.

Then we wrapped those books in red silk—red for celebration, since we already had enough white for death, and it turns out Castavirans associate white with death like we do—and laid them with the bodies. They'll be buried tomorrow, the Castavirans in one of the Pfulerrian cemeteries, the Balaenics in the burial ground outside Lethess. We'd wanted them all to be buried together where the kathana circle was, but I judged it was better they lie with the rest of the dead so their burial place wouldn't be forgotten, or disturbed by one or both of those cities expanding beyond its current boundaries.

When I wasn't participating in those things, I stayed in our room and read a book I'd borrowed from Granea, something light and mindless like I haven't read in years, and ate off a tray they brought me at lunchtime, and basically did nothing of importance. I did have dinner with Cederic and Radryntor, who wasn't quite as cold as she's been lately, probably because she's not an evil person and respected the fact that I'm in mourning. We talked about a lot of things, and I think she wanted to bring up the failed kathana but couldn't find a graceful way to do it. Probably she just wanted to be assured that Castaviran magic isn't what caused it to fail.

In two days we'll have the funeral. After that, it's time to get back to work. We still have to bring the magics together, and we still don't know how to do that, *and* there's still the problem of magic diminishing, so that's a lot of work. But we're not giving up. (I almost wrote "we're not giving up *yet*," but that implies there's a point in the future where we *will* give up, and I'm too stubborn to ever do that.)

21 Teretar

The funeral was the same as any other, which is all I'll write about that because it's bad luck to record the details of a funeral. It draws Death's attention, and I don't need any more of that. We were all able to go to both because Balaenic funerals are traditionally held at dawn, and the Castaviran funeral was mid-morning. So many of the funeral traditions are the same that for the first time, I could see how our cultures might once have been one. How terrible it's our death rituals we haven't changed in all these centuries.

It was nearly noon when the final body was laid to rest, so I went back to my room to change. Cederic had worn the Kilios' robe, and I'd been given the robe of a Castaviran priest because I'm a mage. It was uncomfortable, emotionally, like I was betraying the true God, but I didn't do anything religious so I'm sure it was all right. Then we ate in our room, without saying much, and I dawdled, and played with my food, until Cederic said, "If you wait too long, your sister may leave before you have a chance to speak with her."

"How do you know that's what I'm thinking?" I said.

"You fiddle with things when you are putting off an unpleasant task," he said, "and that shrimp is looking rather tattered now. And I know of only one unpleasant task you might have to face today, given that the mages will not be working until tomorrow."

I ate the shrimp, thinking I would need to be more careful if I wanted to conceal my emotions from Cederic. Then I realized I never wanted to do that. "You don't mind if I don't ask you to come?" I said.

"Not at all," he said. "This is a private matter. But I would like to meet her eventually."

"We'll see how this goes," I said. I kissed him and left the room.

It was tempting to slip away from my bodyguards for this. They're good soldiers, but not equipped to contain a thief with years of experience eluding men just like them. But I think they'd be disciplined severely if they lost me, even if it was my choice to elude them, and that's not fair to them. So I told them where we were going, and we set off for Lethess. I was glad Roda wasn't in Pfulerre, though why would she be? I know my bodyguards are uncomfortable in Pfulerre because they don't speak the language and because they're so conspicuously Balaenic, and the Pfulerrians aren't exactly hostile, but they're not friendly either.

We drew some attention as we made our way down to the docks, but not much. Lethess sees a lot of soldiers going in and out of town, and most of them head for the dockside entertainment despite the strong warning they're not to get into any fights with the sailors. I was inconspicuous in my regular work clothes, which are of a Balaenic design except for my trousers, but you can only make trousers so many ways and these didn't really draw the eye. So we looked like four Balaenic soldiers and a Balaenic mage headed into town for a day off. If you looked closely, you'd see they had me surrounded and looked extremely alert even for soldiers, but nobody shouted my name or told everyone to make way for the Empress-Consort.

The Salten Arms was easy enough to find because it was the largest inn near the docks. It was also fairly upscale, not the sort of place an ordinary sailor could afford, and it made me wonder what business brought Roda here. We went inside and found it had the same floor plan as most Balaenic inns built about seventy years ago: a small entry room flanked by the taproom on one side and a dining room on the other, and stairs to right and left going up to the upper floor (or, in this case, floors—it had four stories).

There wasn't anyone at the desk, but there was a bell, so I rang it. Pretty soon someone thundered down the stairs. It turned out to be a skinny man I wouldn't have imagined could make that much noise. "Yes?" he said, breathlessly.

"I—" I began, then realized I had no idea what name Roda was using. "I'm looking for a woman who's staying here," I said, and described Roda. "I'm her sister."

"What's the name?" he said, pulling a large register from under the desk and opening it.

"I, uh, don't know," I said. "We don't have a surname. We haven't seen each other in sixteen years and we...didn't have much time to talk the other day." I realized "the other day" had been most of three weeks ago, and suddenly I felt sick, remembering what Cederic had said. I didn't know if she'd even still be here. I deeply regretted all those days I'd held onto my anger.

"We register under surname or placename here," he said, shutting the book. "Can't help you if you don't know one of those. Sorry."

"Wait," I said, feeling desperate, "she would have arrived at least three weeks ago, and her praenoma is Roda."

The innkeeper regarded me curiously. "I've seen you before," he said.

"Probably," I said. "My name is Sesskia. I'm the Empress-Consort."

His mouth fell open, and he let the book fall back on the counter with a thud. "You are at that, true God defend me," he said. "Your Majesty. You said your sister? True God help me, royalty staying at my inn."

I didn't correct him. "Please say you remember her," I said.

He flushed. "I'm not sorry about this. I can't give out information to just anyone," he said, "'specially since I had no proof she's your sister. I mean, not that I don't trust your word, your Majesty, but you might have been anyone."

"That means you remember her," I said.

He blushed some more. "Wait here," he said, and rushed up the stairs again. We waited. Eventually I heard more measured footsteps, and Roda appeared. She looked awful, her hair matted, her nose and eyes red from a cold, and she moved as if she ached everywhere. "Sesskia," she said. Her voice was hoarse and as painful-sounding as the rest of her looked.

"Hi," I said. "Can we talk?"

She glanced at my bodyguards. "Alone," I said. I turned and told the soldiers, "You're going to wait here, and no one's going to tell Mattiak we were separated for a while, right?" They nodded, uncertainly, but that was good enough for me.

Roda turned and went back up the stairs, and I followed her to the third floor and into a cluttered room that smelled stuffy, like the windows had been closed for too long. I saw the innkeeper hovering at the far end of the hall just before Roda shut the door.

"I've been sick for about a week," she said, clearing some clothes off one of the room's two chairs. The bed was unmade, and there were some plates stacked on a table near the door. "Housekeeping is good here, but I told them I don't like being disturbed. Hard enough falling asleep without people banging in and out all the time. You want to sit?"

I nodded and took the newly-cleared chair. Roda sat in the other. She looked impassive again. Impassive and ill. "I'm sorry if I'm disturbing you," I said.

She waved that off. "I feel much better than I did," she said.

"You look all right," I said.

"I look like hell," she said with a short laugh. "Not that Merrikun —the innkeeper—is put off by that. Too bad for him he's not my type."

"I wondered why he looked so embarrassed when I found out he'd been stringing me along to protect you," I said.

"Well, I doubt anyone in this part of town is going to say no to the Empress-Consort," Roda said.

That dried up our conversational reserves. Finally, I said, "I thought you might have left."

"I should have left five days ago," Roda said. "The cold got in the way. I'll be leaving in three days, cold or no."

"Oh," I said. More silence. I felt really stupid about coming. I looked in the direction of the window, took a deep breath, and said, "I didn't think about how brave you were to contact me. You must have known I wouldn't be happy to see you."

"I thought it was a chance worth taking," she said.

"What did you think I'd do?" I said.

I heard her take a deep breath of her own. "Pretty much what you did," she said. "Yell at me. Blame me. Accuse me of a lot of things I was guilty of. I hoped, once you'd done that, you might be willing to forgive me."

"You think you deserve forgiveness?" I said, and memory hit me so hard I felt dizzy, me saying that to Cederic and him saying *I think we need forgiveness most when we do not deserve it.* I cut across whatever Roda was about to say with, "But it's not about deserving, is it? You can't make up for the past and I can't live the past over again. And I think maybe forgiveness is about not being angry that you can't do either of those things."

I turned my head to look at her again. Her mouth was still open from whatever she'd been about to say. "I think we both wish we'd done things differently," I said, "but right now I just want you to be my sister."

Roda wiped her nose on her sleeve and laughed, embarrassed. "When I pictured this, I wasn't quite so runny," she said. Then we were hugging and crying until I was a little runny myself. When we both calmed down, enough to sit, I said, "You don't really have to go, do you?"

Roda shrugged. "I can send word to my partners I'm taking a few weeks off. They know I'm owed it. I just—Sesskia, *why* are you the Empress-Consort? Don't they know who you are?"

"I won't say my upbringing isn't a problem for some people," I said, "but when my husband became the Emperor, I didn't have a choice."

"We have some long stories to tell each other," she said, and we did. Though there wasn't enough time today for more than me to tell her about my travels, and coming to Castavir and marrying Cederic, and for her to tell me about settling in Garwin and getting a job with a shipping company, then working her way up until she was part owner.

That was as far as we got before dinnertime, and we ordered food sent up (I arranged for my guards' dinner too, and tried not to feel too bad that they were no doubt bored out of their minds) and I tidied up the room while we were waiting for the meal. Roda didn't try to stop me. By that time she was lying down again, saying only, "That's something I remember well, you keeping that awful little shack clean right up until you had to go out to work at the fishery. And Bridie did her best to mimic you."

"She was never very good at it because she only ever wanted to read," I said. "I used to, um, *borrow* books for her and return them again when she was done. Had to be careful or Mam would sell them for gin."

"Probably just as well we didn't qualify for membership in a lending library," Roda said. "Though it sounds like you invented your own personal one. I never meant for you to become a thief, you know."

"I know," I said, feeling no resentment. It was wonderful. "But it's a skill that served me well over the years."

"Just so you made good use of it, I suppose," Roda said with a laugh. I'd forgotten how cheerful her laugh was. It's not like either of us did a lot of laughing back then. "Though putting a thief on the throne—"

"I had the same thought," I said.

"Why didn't you get someone to restore our name? Wouldn't that make your cause easier?" she said.

"I don't even know what that name was," I said. "Just what Mam always said, that we used to be wealthy and live in a manor. Dad certainly never talked about it."

"I was too young when we lost it to remember it myself, but I looked into it once," Roda said. "After Mam died, and I couldn't find you, I thought if I could regain our surname, maybe that would make up for everything. It was stupid, I know, but I was consumed by guilt. But I never got anywhere. Dad's name—it was like there were a million Aleniks of the right age." She sat up straighter against the pillows. "Though it did feel as if my not getting anywhere was on purpose. Like someone had gone out of their way to bury our family. The only thing I learned was we weren't just rich, we were noble. As in we had the "ssar" after our name."

"Not that that makes it any easier to trace us," I said, "if our name was eradicated. But I wish I could walk up to Arron Domenessar and use that name to spit in his eye."

"Somehow the idea that you have *any* relationship with Domenessar is harder to believe than the Empress-Consort thing," she said. "You know he wants to be King, right?"

"I know we're probably going to have to fight him in the spring," I said. That's when I realized it almost *was* spring. It's hard to remember because the weather's so nice here, but it's almost the end of Teretar, and that means the snows are lessening and the skies are clearing. A few weeks now, and we'll be off to Barrekel, and true God alone knows what's going to happen then.

We haven't talked about it at all, because Radryntor takes up all of Cederic's time and magic takes up all of mine, but we've made no progress toward anything that might sway Domenessar or bring the Black and Brown Armies under Mattiak's command. And I had such a nice day, too, right up until that occurred to me.

We had dinner, and talked some more, and then I had to go back to the camp because it occurred to me Cederic might have started wondering where I went, and although he knows I can take care of myself, he has a very strong protective instinct I find endearing. I told Roda I'd be back tomorrow—I think I'll ask her if she'd like to move into the consul's palace with us, so there's not so big a distance to travel. I don't know how she'll feel about that. She's not overwhelmed by my new status, probably because when you've changed someone's nappies you don't have a lot of illusions about them, but I don't know if she realizes the kind of scrutiny I'm under would necessarily be extended to her. Or maybe she does. Anyway, we'll talk about it tomorrow.

Cederic's still not here. I warned him that if he didn't come to bed by a certain time I'd track him down and drag him away by force, or at least stand in the doorway and make loud comments about how late it is and shouldn't everyone be in bed already. I think—no, I can hear him coming now. Time to put this away so when he comes in, he'll find me waiting for him wearing nothing but the quilted robe that fastens only at the waist and leaves nothing to the imagination.

CHAPTER FIFTEEN

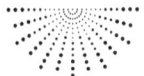

22 Teretar

It's been difficult to get back to research, and I think everyone is having trouble shaking the memory of the kathana. But we have to think about it or their deaths will have been pointless. Clearly, it did *something*, and Cederic went over the design of the kathana with me and assured me that it did, in fact, try to force a change on pouvrin. So the magic resisted that change violently, and I have to conclude that was the wrong approach.

We probably should have guessed that, since we're certain the original magic didn't look exactly like either type we have now, and we were essentially trying to alter Balaenic magic to be Castaviran, not that we thought of it that way. But we've run down our list and eliminated every possibility we came up with, which puts us back at the beginning. We still don't know why will is different, but we're afraid to try to alter it again. I don't know. I feel mentally exhausted. Maybe I'll think of something tomorrow.

Roda looked uncomfortable at the idea of moving into the consul's palace, though I think some of that was that it was in a Castaviran city full of Castavirans whose language she could only say a few words of. But she saw the sense of it, and I think neither of us wanted to be very far from each other.

It's so strange, not hating her anymore. Having her back. She and Cederic are sort of formal with each other, but *that's* probably because Cederic is formal with everyone. I've caught her watching him with this speculative look, like she's wondering what I see in him beyond him being extremely handsome, since I'm the least formal person she knows. But I think they like each other, or at least can see they have a shared affection for me.

I haven't introduced Roda to Radryntor because I think she (Radryntor) would just be snobbish toward her. And it's not as if they speak each other's language. Things are very tense in the consul's palace right now. Radryntor still eats with us, meaning Cederic and me and some of the local nobles and the Imperial Retinue (Dugan and Joena, whose praenomi I reluctantly use, Mattiak and the other generals, and Cederic's aides plus Audryn), but she barely acknowledges me and is only superficially civil to Cederic. I wish she'd challenge us already and get it over with.

23 Teretar

Big storm blew in this morning, which kept us all indoors, and that was good, because I think we've come up with something. I don't remember what got us on this track, but someone must have mentioned residual magic, because that got us all debating what we really ought to call it: foundational magic, source magic, original magic, and somewhere in there I started thinking about what it might look like. So we talked about that. The Castaviran mages were very eloquent on the subject, because it's only recently their best thinkers have determined it really is where magic comes from rather than being left over when you work magic. And the Balaenic mages came in with their thoughts about whether residual, or foundational, or original magic might be part of pouvrin as well.

That's what led me to say, "I wonder if we could do something to make it visible."

I don't know why that one sentence stopped the discussion cold.

Jeddan said, "It's where it all comes from. It has to have been around when the magics were still combined."

"That doesn't have to be true," Audryn said. "Suppose it's a symptom—" She stopped, and her eyes grew wide.

"A symptom of the divergence," Terrael finished.

"Either way, it's important," Jeddan said. "If we could see it, we might be able to figure out why the magics aren't combining."

"Can we do that?" Jerussa said. "Is that even possible? I thought residual magic was almost a myth until recently."

"So did I," said Terrael, "but we know it's there, and I'm sure we can work out a way to make it visible."

Everyone started talking at once. It felt as if a shroud had been lifted, as if we'd been wandering in the dark and suddenly seen a gleam of light—distant, but unmistakable. "What do we need?" I asked Terrael.

"The Kilios, if he's available," Terrael said. "I can come up with the beginnings of something, but I know he knows more about residual magic than I do. It's too bad we're not in Colosse, because the mages at the Kenekis thanest have been studying it for years, but with everyone's help we should be able to come up with a kathana that will do what we want."

"I'll ask Cederic," I said, "but we should start now and not wait for him, because who knows when he'll be free."

I went to find Cederic, who was preparing to sit in judgment in Lethess that morning, and told him what we'd realized. "I will not be able to give you assistance until tomorrow," he said, "but I will guarantee my presence then. No one has ever thought to do what you propose before."

"Is that code for 'it's impossible'?" I said.

He shook his head. "I mean that such a possibility has been overlooked by many thinkers for many years," he said, "and I am ashamed it never occurred to me."

"It's not as if you had time to study residual magic," I said, "and besides, you can't be expected to think of everything."

He smiled. "I am grateful to have you here to remind me of that," he said. "And I think you should come with me. The citizens of Lethess need to be reminded that their Empress-Consort is as capable of passing judgment as their Emperor. And before you object, I should point out that in the early stages of your research, most of the work is done with th'an, and you are not needed there."

"I—all right," I said. "But I don't know how useful I'll be in court. I don't know much about law."

"I am learning as I go," he said. "I have learned something of Balaenic law, thanks to Lady Amelessar's guidance, and much of what I do in these courts is observe and make plans to integrate our two legal systems, which thankfully are not so different. Most of our duties involve listening carefully, and making decisions that are as fair and just as our limited understandings can manage. You are both fair-minded and compassionate, and those are desirable qualities in a judge."

So I sat in Granea's courtroom and listened to complainants, and observed her and Cederic, and made a few comments of my own. Cederic's right that Castaviran law is similar to Balaenic. I only had to correct him once or twice in the matter of passing sentence (not punitive sentencing, we didn't hear any criminal suits, more like judgments on property ownership and things like that).

Then we had lunch with Granea, who wanted to know how things were progressing and expressed sympathy for our losses. I glossed over our latest research path, since the details are complicated even for mages, and we talked about the court and what happens when there are serious criminal charges that have to be tried. I hate the idea of being responsible for the life or death of someone.

It makes me think of what will happen when we win (see how optimistic I'm becoming?) and how we'll have to try a lot of people for treason, probably starting with Garran Clendessar. It seems strange to consider his actions treasonous, since from his perspective he's the lawful King, but if we are calling ourselves the rulers of this Empire, his resisting us really is treason. I'm still not happy with the idea.

I went back to the mages in the afternoon and wound up supervising pouvrin, everyone working them very slowly and looking for traces of residual magic. And we found it! Hard to see, because pouvrin seem to be more efficient at using it than th'an, but it's definitely there. That made everyone cheerful. We need to remember this isn't an impossible task, that we can figure this out, and when I do that I can even forget for whole minutes at a time that magic is fading and that means we have a deadline, even if we don't know what it is.

Damn. I just fell into despair again.

No, I refuse to let this discourage me. We'll figure it out eventually. I'm hanging on to that.

24 Teretar

Well, it happened. Radryntor finally defied Cederic and forced his hand. We're back in the camp now, Cederic not wanting to make things worse by taking up residence in Lethess, and there's been a lot of talk about what to do next.

That happened around noon, with an argument that started over lunch. Before that—Cederic joined me in discussion with the mages, in which we worked out pieces to a kathana that ought to show "residual" (still no good word for it) magic. Jeddan's taking the lead, with his greater experience with the see-inside pouvra, but I really can't remember much of the details because what happened later swept it all out of my mind.

It went like this: We were at lunch, which was as good as it ever is in the consul's palace, and I was thinking about pouvrin and anticipating getting back to research, when I heard Radryntor say, "Is there some reason you've allowed that Balaenic city to continue to defy me, your Majesty?"

"I am unaware of this defiance, Lady Radryntor," Cederic said, calmly even though Radryntor's voice had a shrill edge to it. "To what are you referring?"

"We've instructed the Balaenics to submit to inspection when their wagons pass our city limits along the coast road," Radryntor said. "We can't afford to have them upsetting the balance of trade."

"I see," Cederic said. "I take it they refuse."

"They've come to blows with our inspectors several times now," Radryntor said. "I thought you instructed them not to attack our people."

"I think you may be under some misapprehension," Cederic said. "I have instructed *both* cities to avoid conflict. And I believe I have told you while you are of course free to levy tariffs on trade within your boundaries, you have no authority to prevent the Balaenic merchants from passing through Pfulerre on their way to trade elsewhere."

"We can't guarantee they won't lie to us about their destination," she said. "It's my responsibility to protect this city's economy."

"As it is the Emperor's responsibility to protect the welfare of this Empire's citizens, Balaenic and Castaviran," Cederic said.

Radryntor narrowed her eyes at him. "By putting the welfare of Balaenic over Castaviran?" she said.

"I have always been even-handed in my treatment of both," Cederic said, "and I look forward to the day when we no longer draw a distinction between either."

"Balaen will never recognize you as its ruler," Radryntor said, snarling now, "and you're a fool if you think it will do you any good to crawl to them for their approval. It's a slap in the face to all good Castavirans. We expect our Emperor to respect us."

Cederic was totally impassive now. "As I demand respect from the people I govern," he said, "beginning with those to whom I have delegated some measure of rule. You set the example, Lady Radryntor. I doubt the Pfulerrians will respect their Emperor if their consul feels entitled to refer to him as a fool."

"You lack support throughout Castavir," Radryntor said, "and that will continue so long as you insist on treating these foreigners as equals."

"Do you suggest you withdraw that support?" Cederic said. I was sitting next to him, so I could see him curl his fist around the handle of his fork. An unlikely weapon, but I think he was just trying to maintain control.

"I suggest you should adhere to the oaths you swore to this

people, if you want to maintain their trust," Radryntor said.

Cedric stood up, slowly, and released his grip on the fork. "Daenen Radryntor," he said in a level voice, "do you believe you should be Empress?"

That startled her. "Of course not," she said.

"Then I wonder at your willingness to challenge me, the Emperor to whom you swore oath of fealty," he said. "You are clinging to an impossible fantasy of Castavir as was. That country is no more. *This* is the reality, Daenen Radryntor, two countries locked together, overlapping and abutting one another, and *I* have decided what our united future will be. Your support is welcome. It is not essential. Choose to follow where I lead, or I will replace you as consul, because I will not allow someone so clearly hostile to my rule to continue in *any* position of power."

He shoved his chair back and left the room, with the rest of us following as quickly as we could without looking as if we were fleeing. I got one last look at Radryntor as we left; her mouth was hanging open as if she'd just been savaged by a dog she'd thought was harmless.

Cedric led the way out of the consul's palace without stopping. "Are we leaving?" I said. "Because I left some of my favorite clothes back there. And the mages are all having lunch."

"I will send soldiers to collect our things and summon the rest of our people," he said. "I should have challenged her days ago, but I hoped she would see sense."

"At least it's over," I said. "No, wait—*is* it over? Because it's not time to head west yet."

"She has no military force to fight us," he said. "And she knows I cannot replace her, not because I have no power but because I have no other candidate for the position. We will see what she does in the coming days. It is possible she will change her mind. But if she decides to cut off support to the military…"

"That could be a real problem, since the Pfulerrian citizens don't have the power to stand up to our Army," I finished, "and the Army has to eat."

"I will make plans with General Tarallan, and we will wait and see," Cederic said. "Will you see our tent erected so we will have a place to sleep when I finally come to bed sometime after midnight?"

"Do I have to be happy about the bed?" I said.

He shook his head. "If I could think of a graceful way to bring our bed from the palace, I would arrange it," he said. Then he put his arms around me, and said, "Someday we will have a permanent home, and we will look back on the camp bed with fondness."

"That's never going to happen," I said. He kissed me and we went our separate ways.

So I never did get back to the mages, because I had to find Roda and explain what had happened, and find someone to put up our tent, which meant finding a place for the tent...basically it was a lot of work, and now I'm tired enough I'm reluctant to put this away to find Cederic and drag him out of whatever meeting he's in. But we're not going to fall into that trap again.

25 Teretar

We're teaching all the Balaenic mages the see-inside pouvra. I say "we" but it's really me, because Jeddan is working with Terrael on the kathana. It was hard work, but boring.

Someone's here to summon me to the command tent. I'm writing this because the soldier is clearly impatient to be elsewhere and I'm in just bad enough a mood I feel like annoying him. Though I'm curious about the summons.

25 Teretar, no idea when

I look back on the last thing I wrote and can't believe I was so cavalier about it all. Not that I had any idea what (who) was waiting in the command tent, but it's so—I can't find a word to end that sentence.

I followed the impatient soldier—he really wanted to be somewhere else, and I could tell he was thinking something like "the Empress-Consort knows the way, why do I have to walk with her?" He was young enough it just amused me, that and I still don't have a sense of my own importance that would let me be angry at his disrespect. When we came within sight of the command tent, he saluted and was gone as quickly as he could manage without being rude. I grinned and let the soldiers at the door hold the flap for me.

Cederic was there, and Mattiak, and a couple of soldiers flanking a man I never thought I'd see again: Caelan Crossar.

He looked awful. His hair was disheveled and his beard had grown out enough to be shaggy, and his clothes were filthy. He had a cut above his left eye that was almost healed but would certainly leave a scar. He looked like someone who'd slept rough for several weeks. Despite all that, he looked calm, even though the soldiers looked as if they thought he might be a threat and were ready to counter it.

"What is he doing here?" I said. Not my politest moment, but I was startled. It was hard reconciling this scruffy man with the powerful Chamber Lord who'd looked at me as if I were a tool.

"He has refused to speak until you were present," Cederic said.

"Well, I'm here," I said. Then I looked more closely at him, at the unnatural paleness of his skin and the almost imperceptible tic in his eye, and said, "I think we should all sit down."

Crossar accepted the seat offered him graciously and with a hint of relief. He looked worn out, not that I cared much about his comfort. I don't think my wariness was unjustified even if I didn't know at the time what news he brought. I figured he was clever enough that this might all be a trap, that he had some way of suborning the Balaenic Army and making them turn on us, or that he might try to kill Cederic, or something. I know I'm overly suspicious, but it's saved my life so many times I don't feel apologetic.

Once we were all settled, Crossar said, "Thank you for your welcome," in an ironic tone of voice that irritated me, as if we'd all come here at his sufferance.

"To my knowledge, you have done nothing in opposition to us," Cederic said. "I choose to give you the benefit of the doubt."

"Not that that's going to extend very far," I said, "because I personally don't trust you to do anything except what benefits you."

"I won't deny I'm here out of self-interest," Crossar said. "My life was in danger so long as I stayed in Venetry. I was two steps ahead of the hangman's noose when I left."

"Tell us what the usurper King and the former Empress have done," Cederic said. "We know little more than that they are married and that the Chamber has been disbanded."

Crossar clasped his hands together in his lap. "'Disbanded' is a polite word for it," he said. "At first the new Queen didn't interfere with the operation of the government, though she was made part of our Chamber meetings. Her presence made it impossible to challenge her to the King—that was definitely her intent. We had no way of getting him alone to convince him that he was acting against Balaen's interests. She has him completely enthralled, to the point that he laughs off her moments of insanity or finds ways to justify them."

"So you've seen her madness?" Mattiak said.

Crossar nodded. "Seen it, and been horrified by it. But she is just sane enough to hold onto her power. After a time, she was actively participating in our meetings. Then she was drafting laws. Jarlak Batekessar finally challenged her openly—he's never been one to mince words. The King dismissed him from the meeting immediately, had him removed by the soldiers. The next day he was discovered dead at the bottom of a flight of stairs with a broken neck. The kind of broken neck, my sources told me, that could not have resulted from such a fall.

"The day after that, the King declared that rather than replace Batekessar, he would disband the Chamber in favor of a new organizational system that would allow both our countries equal representation. Then, no doubt influenced by his lovely bride, he ordered us confined to our manors so we would not be in a position to raise up public sentiment against him. I chose not to stay and wait for whatever accident the Queen might choose for me."

"What about the others?" I said.

"I haven't heard anything. Lenssar is such a toady he might actually survive by fawning over his King and Queen. I suspect Jakssar will find a way to escape as I did," Crossar said.

"Why come here? Why not take shelter with one of the Lords Governor?" Cederic said. "You might have raised an opposition force that way."

"The Lords Governor in the west have for the most part bent the knee to the new regime," Crossar said. "Your—that is, the Castaviran Army—is powerful and none of the lords have forces that can stand up to its might. Those in the east...every one of them except Arron Domenessar is indecisive. They don't have the will to defy the King alone, they can't agree on a leader who will bring them together, and they are afraid of giving Arron power. Arron, of course, wants to be King. I knew him well when he first came to power and I'm certain he's been trying to bring those indecisive lords under his banner. You are in danger of being overwhelmed by him. He wants the Balaenic Army. In particular, he wants Mattiak Tarallan at the head of his forces. If he can't have that, he'll destroy you."

"Our forces are equal to his, Caelan," Mattiak said. "He's going to find it hard to overcome us."

"Even if he fails to destroy you, he'll inflict damages so great there's no way you will be able to face down the Castaviran Army," Crossar said. "You have no choice but to give him what he wants."

"That will not happen," Cederic said. "Our forces are sworn to protect Balaen *and* Castavir, not to allow one to dominate the other. If he persists, we will fight, we will decimate one another, and the Castaviran Army will find it easy to destroy us both. Domenessar needs to be convinced to ally with us."

"And how do you intend to do that?" Crossar said.

"He is a reasonable man," Cederic began, and Crossar laughed, a nasty sound that made me furious.

"If you just came here to mock us, you can get out now," I said. "You're so clearly capable of managing on your own. You've got no power, Crossar, no influence, nothing but a superior attitude and a really nasty personal odor. Get out. Go to Domenessar, if you're so convinced he's going to win. See if your charming personality matters to his plans."

"You may be capable of winning the Castavirans to your cause,"

Crossar said, exactly as if I hadn't insulted him, "and that might be enough. But you need those armies, and to get those armies, you need Balaenic support. Or do you deny that, Emperor of nothing and nowhere?"

I opened my mouth to shout at him again, but Cederic made a gesture that shut me up (damn it, I really need to learn not to respond to that) and said, "That is the prelude to making me an offer. What is it you want, Caelan Crossar?"

"I'd heard you were intelligent, even though that accent makes you sound like a lazy fool," Crossar said, smiling. "I can give you the Balaenic Lords Governor and the rest of the Balaenic Army."

"In exchange for what?" Cederic said.

"Find out what he knows first," I said.

"As if I'm fool enough to give away anything before I have his oath," Crossar said to me. "I want Venetry," he told Cederic. "And I don't want any weak Lord Governorship. I don't know how you're going to divide up the country if you win, but unless you're a fool you'll put viceroys over the Lords Governors and the Castaviran—consuls, is it? This country is too big and too populous to have fifty little lordlings trying to govern their fiefs. You'll make me viceroy in Venetry, and I'll give you what you need to win this war."

I grabbed Cederic's arm. "Could we discuss this in private?" I said in a low voice, though I'm not sure why because Crossar was sitting right there and could hear me clearly.

Cederic glanced at Mattiak. "General Tarallan, would you escort Caelan Crossar to a place where he can clean himself up, and send someone to find him a change of clothing?" he said. Mattiak nodded, and he stood, followed shortly by Crossar, who made it look as if he were doing us a favor. As if he were the one in control. Much as I love and respect Cederic, I was afraid for him.

So once Crossar and Mattiak were gone, taking the soldiers with them, and I judged they were far enough away to be out of earshot, I said, still in a low voice because I'm paranoid, "Cederic, we can't do that. We can't give him Venetry."

"I was unaware you were so attached to the city," he said.

"Don't make jokes," I said. "Is he right about the way we'll redistrict the country? Because he has a good point. We can't have a million different people reporting to us all the time."

"He is right," Cederic said, "and whatever else his flaws may be, stupidity is not one of them. I have already considered the question of what to do with the largest city in our new country. Making it the center of, perhaps, one of four or five 'kingdoms' is sensible given both its size and its geographic location."

"Which makes whoever rules it incredibly powerful," I said. "Crossar's dangerous, Cederic. He's smart and he's power-hungry. If we give him this, he'll find a way to use it against us. We'll end up fighting another war, probably when we're too busy bringing this country together to have any defense against it."

"You are correct that Caelan Crossar desires power," Cederic said, "but I find it interesting that he has never moved against Garran Clendessar. As Chamber Lord of Defense, he has, or had, control of the Balaenic Army; he is General Tarallan's friend, as far as a man like him has friends; and he is far more intelligent than Balaen's King. He might have made himself King twenty years ago. I think if he were interested in moving against whoever wins this war, he would not have asked us for the direct power he would receive by ruling Venetry's new district."

"Unless he's trying to trick us into lowering our guard," I said. "I don't trust him."

"Neither do I," Cederic said, "at least not in the way I trust, for example, Granea Amelessar. But I do trust him to act in his own best interests, and so long as I know what those interests are, I can predict how he will behave toward us."

"What if whatever it is he knows is worthless?" I said. "Suppose you promise him all that and he's lying?"

"Then he will receive nothing," Cederic said. "I would never make a promise like this without stipulating his information must deliver on what he claims. He is the one taking a risk, Sesskia, because he cannot know whether I am honorable enough to fulfil my promise. I might easily take his information and then have him killed, as far as he knows anything of me."

I sighed, and said, "I don't like this."

"To be honest, neither do I," Cederic said, "but—" He drew me closer and lowered his voice. "I have no plan for swaying Arron Domenessar to our side," he said. "He is stubborn and greedy and there is no benefit to him in joining us. We will return to Barrekel and take the Black and Brown Armies by force, if we cannot convince their leaders our cause is just. General Tarallan feels certain he can sway at least one of them, but no matter what happens, unless we are very lucky, we will come to blows with the Barrekellian forces. If Caelan Crossar has information that will bring Domenessar to our side..."

"I think he might be overly ambitious," I said, "because I can't imagine Domenessar bowing to anyone. He barely gave respect to the King, and then only because he had to."

"We have to take this chance, Sesskia," he said.

At that point the tent flap opened, and Crossar and Mattiak came back in, followed by Crossar's guard. Crossar looked better, though his beard was still shaggy and his clothes didn't fit quite right. He immediately went to his chair and sat without waiting for an invitation. "Have you made a decision?" he said.

Cederic and I both sat, me slowly as if daring Crossar to take offense at my rudeness. He ignored me in favor of watching Cederic, which annoyed me enough I almost wanted to tell Cederic to send him packing. Cederic, as calm as ever, said, "If your information proves as useful as you claim, you will be given what you ask. But I will not consider myself bound by that promise unless it brings Arron Domenessar to my banner."

"It will," Crossar said.

Cederic spread his hands in invitation for Crossar to speak. Crossar nodded, slowly. Then he looked at me. "I know your family name," he said.

It felt like a blow to the chest. I'd been expecting...actually, I hadn't been expecting anything, because I thought he was lying about having *anything* we could use. "But we lost our surname," I said. "Just knowing it isn't going to restore my family's status, if Dad was stripped of power."

"Your father did not legally lose his surname," Crossar said. "He was forced to leave it behind, and may have chosen not to use it, but you are still entitled to it."

"How is that supposed to matter?" I said. "Domenessar might respect me more if I'm noble, because he's a snob, but he doesn't defer to any of the other nobles and he certainly won't defer to me, knowing my past."

"It matters," Crossar said, "because your father was Alenik Daressar."

I think he was going for an awed or shocked reaction. What he got was Cederic's polite incomprehension and me saying, "Am I supposed to be impressed by that?"

"Sesskia," Mattiak said. I turned to look at him because he sounded choked. "Sesskia, Alenik Daressar nearly took the throne of Balaen twenty-six years ago."

"He did not," I said. Then I felt stupid. It was just—It's still the only reaction I can summon up. My Dad, who never did anything in his life but go out on that boat and bring home his catch to keep us from starving—I knew he had a life before that, but not

He never acted like someone who might have ruled a kingdom. I mean, he never did anything to stand out, was always humble to that fat bastard he worked for before he could afford his own boat. I guess, based on what Crossar

I'm not thinking about that, because it makes me want to set Crossar on fire, anything to make him suffer, and there's still a rational part of me that knows that's wrong. So I'm just going to go on and tell this the way it happened, and save my anger for the right place.

So—right. I said, stupidly, "He did not."

Mattiak said, "It was just as Garran Clendessar was coming to power. Everyone knew he was the weakest of the Clendessar family, and there was a lot of unrest. And Daressar saw an opportunity. He had a lot of quiet support among the families in Venetry. I guess—I was young then, but Venetry was in turmoil and we all knew there was conflict centered on the throne. And then Daressar's support collapsed, no one knew why, he and his family disappeared, and the King acted as if his rule had never been challenged. He went out of his way to make sure anyone who even talked about Daressar suffered. So people just...stopped talking about him. But no one's ever forgotten the man who nearly ruled Balaen. In the last, I'm not sure, maybe five years, his name has started coming up again as Garran Clendessar's rule became harsher and more erratic."

"That's insane," I said. "I've never heard anything like that."

"You wouldn't have," Crossar said. "Only those at the highest levels of government even whisper about it. The missing Alenik Daressar and his family. Everyone believes the King had them killed, but a lot of the Lords Governor would love to be proven wrong on that."

I was still gaping at him. "Cederic," I said, but I wasn't sure what I wanted from him. Reassurance? For him to punch Crossar for making up this story?

"I think he is telling the truth," Cederic said. "He stands to lose too much if his story is disproven."

"I think he ought to have some proof other than just his say-so," I said. "Do I have some kind of distinctive birthmark? Not that I'd be thrilled if you knew about it, if I did."

"I can name five men and one woman, all Lords Governor past or present, who were witness at your sanctification before the true God when you were five days old," Crossar said. "They know that Alenik's second daughter was born with those green-gray eyes. You were given the name Sesskia on that day. And you are the very image of Cessily Daressar, your mother. She was the premier hostess in Venetry and there is a painting of her in Iyannka Manor; it was spared Clendessar's purge because your grandmother hid it."

I was shaking, because an awful feeling had started to come over me. "You're not my grandfather," I said.

He shook his head. "No. Your grandparents passed away years

ago. You—and presumably your sister and your mother—are all that's left of the Daressars."

"And yet you know all of this," I said. "Tell me why."

"You already know," he said.

I leaped out of my chair and flung myself at him, knocking him over and landing hard on his chest, and got my hands around his throat. *"You betrayed him!"* I screamed, shaking him hard as he clawed at my hands. "You're the reason his plan failed! You're why we had to hide—why we lived in poverty—damn you, it's *your fault he died!"*

Cederic took me by the arms and pulled me off Crossar. I fought him, but his grip was too strong, and eventually I let him lead me back to my seat. Mattiak helped Crossar up, but the former Chamber Lord remained standing. "I did betray him," he said, hoarsely. "I wanted to rule Balaen behind the scenes. Alenik Daressar would never have allowed me to manipulate him, and I saw in Clendessar an opportunity to control the Chamber. So I sent word of his attempted coup to those who could stop it. Then I helped him escape Venetry, and buried his trail so no one would find him or his family. I saved your life."

"You expect me to be *grateful?*" I shouted, trying to leap out of my chair again and being once again restrained by Cederic. "Dad died in a fishing accident—he would never have been there if not for *you*. Mam drank herself to death because she couldn't stand the loss of our wealth and status. Bridie—" I choked. "She'd have lived if we could have afforded real doctors. What you did nearly destroyed my family. How *dare* you stand there and suggest you did *anything* for us?"

"That coup might have killed you anyway," Crossar said. "If Daressar had attacked and failed, Clendessar's men wouldn't have been merciful just because you were barely able to talk. And suppose he'd succeeded, and become King? By your account, yours was the magic that brought our worlds together safely. If you had been nothing but a princess, our worlds would be destroyed now. I don't expect you to love me for what I did, and I don't regret my actions. But, *your Majesty*, your life would look very different now if your father had succeeded...and you can't guarantee it would have been better."

I stopped fighting Cederic long enough for him to relax his grip. Then, once his attention was on Crossar again, I stood up and ran out of the tent. I came straight back here to write this all down, hoping it would calm me. It did, a little, but now I feel adrift, out to sea without rudder or sail and having no land to set my sights on.

Crossar's telling the truth, I'm certain of that. My being a Daressar suits his agenda or he'd have gone on never telling anyone who I was. But it doesn't change anything about my life. Though it makes sense why Dad was always so quiet and easy-going; he couldn't afford to give anyone a hint that he'd been something other than a fisherman once. And Mam...I still blame her for a lot of things, for her weaknesses and her inability to support us, but I feel sorry for her now, too, because she couldn't possibly have been ready for the kind of life Crossar's treachery threw us into.

The thing is, I may have the name, but there's nothing noble about my upbringing. Everything I've learned about being a leader, what little there is, came from working with the mages and watching Cederic. I doubt Domenessar is going to drop to his knees no matter who my father was. He'll believe I'm not qualified to sit on the throne, and he'll still go to war against us. So I've learned all of this, and Crossar will get nothing, because Domenessar won't become our ally. Good. I hope he gets nothing. I hope he has to bury himself in a tiny town where he'll have to scrounge a living like we did. That would be justice. Not that there's really anything in the world I'd accept as balancing the kind of life I had to live because of him.

I'm trying to decide if I should go back to the command tent. On the one hand, I think if I see Crossar again, I might attack him, this time with fire. On the other hand, I'm the Empress-Consort and it's my responsibility to know our plans with regard to ruling the Empire. I'm going to sit here and think about it for a while, then make a decision. I'm glad Cederic didn't come after me. He always seems to know when I need to be alone.

CHAPTER SIXTEEN

26 Teretar

I decided to go back. The part of me that's Empress-Consort realized I can't afford to indulge in self-pity. I also wanted to hear Crossar's plan. Not that I trust him, but I was certain he wouldn't have come here and made that offer unless he was certain he could deliver on it. And I was also concerned that Mattiak and Cederic aren't sufficiently cautious, and Crossar is still a wily bastard who will get away with as much as he possibly can unless someone gets in his way. I'm pretty sure that someone has to be me. (I'm so glad he's not my grandfather. For the tiniest moment I entertained the possibility before realizing it was just too tidy for real life. Besides, he doesn't resemble any of my family, not even a little bit, and though I realize families don't have to look like each other, ours really does.)

(I can't believe Crossar thinks I look like Mam. We do have the same round face, and the same thick blond hair, but she was so thin and worn down...maybe it's just that I don't want to have anything in common with her. It's why I almost never drink. I wish I could see the painting of her in that manor, whatever he called it, see her before time and liquor ground her down.)

Anyway.

I went back to the tent and they were all still there, Cederic, Mattiak and Crossar. I sat down and glared at him, but said nothing. Mostly I knew they'd been talking while I was gone and I didn't want to say anything that would make them have a discussion, or an argument, all over again. Cederic said, "We have a plan for bringing Domenessar to our side, Sesskia."

"What is it?" I said. I thought I sounded polite, but all of them, Cederic included, were looking at me warily, as if they expected me to throttle Crossar again or something. Which I admit was a reasonable fear.

"Domenessar must be convinced trying to claim the throne won't give him the power he wants," Crossar said. He didn't look at all uncomfortable or guilty, which roused my anger again, but I kept quiet because I do have self-control. "He's already facing a battle he'll likely lose, and will suffer heavy casualties even if he doesn't. You will explain to him who you are and that the other Lords Governor will see in you someone to rally behind. Domenessar knows the others are afraid of what might happen if he became King, and he is rapidly running out of time to consolidate his power. Then offer him an alternative, something that gives him a measure of power, and he'll see the logic behind following the...Emperor."

"What do you mean, *I* will explain?" I said. "You're the one who will have to vouch for my identity, and Cederic's the public speaker."

"It must be you, Sesskia, because you must show him you are a strong leader whom others will follow," Cederic said. "He knows the other Lords Governor must be convinced you can hold the throne, because if they think you are merely a token presence in the Imperium, they will refuse to follow your Castaviran husband."

"I'm not sure this is a good idea," I said.

"It's the only way, Sesskia," Mattiak said. "And you can't tell me you don't know how to address a crowd. I was there outside the Firtha thanest when the Emperor was injured. You were pretty damn eloquent."

"I also cracked a whip of fire over their heads and made them cower in terror," I said. "I can't do that to Domenessar. Much as I'd like to."

"It may still be a possibility, if Domenessar refuses to be reasonable," Cederic said. "Though it should be the last possibility we resort to."

"If you offer him the right incentive, he'll be reasonable," Crossar said.

"And I take it you know what that incentive should be," Cederic said coolly.

"Give him the governance of the region," Crossar said.

"Not a chance," I responded promptly.

"We cannot remove him from office entirely, and he will not be satisfied simply with what he holds now," Cederic said.

"I know that," I said, "but if you make him a viceroy, or a district governor, or whatever we end up calling it, that's way too much power. He'll wait until you're preoccupied and then make a play for the Imperial throne. If having *him*—" I jabbed my thumb in Crossar's direction—"as viceroy is bad, giving Domenessar that rank is ten times worse."

"We may have to take that risk," Cederic said.

"What risk are you willing to take to win this war?" Crossar said to me.

"Shut up," I said. "Cederic, this is dangerous."

"So is fighting the Castaviran Army at a three to one disadvantage," Cederic said. "We will simply have to arrange things to prevent Domenessar from exercising too much power."

"Or teach him to use that power on this country's behalf," Crossar said.

"I think that unlikely," Cederic said, "but this appears to be our only recourse."

I sighed. "When are we leaving?"

"In two days," Cederic said. "The weather is still against us, but we need to reach Barrekel before Domenessar is capable of sending out messengers, and soldiers, to threaten the other Lords Governor who might be intimidated into supporting him. I think it will be more difficult to convince them to change sides if they are already committed to him."

"And what's the plan for if Domenessar is unreasonable and tries to kill us?" I said.

"Your optimism is truly endless," Cederic said with a small smile. "As I said, we fight to defend ourselves, and if Domenessar dies in that fighting, then our problems are different."

"Starting with how the other Lords Governor will see you as a threat to them, and refuse to follow you, your Majesty," Mattiak said.

"As I said, different problems," Cederic said. "General Tarallan, would you find Lord Crossar a place to sleep? We will meet again in the morning to continue planning for the march."

Mattiak nodded, and once the tent was empty but for Cederic and me, I said, "That wasn't how I imagined this evening going."

Cederic put his arms around me and held me close. "I don't know what to say to you," he said. "That was quite a revelation."

"I don't know what to think," I said. "It doesn't change who I am, but it will change how a lot of other people see me. And Roda...what will *she* think? She's head of a noble family now!"

"I suppose some will insist I release you from your marriage oaths and marry her instead," he teased.

"You're not her type," I said. "Besides, she'd have to fight me for you, and I fight dirty."

He laughed. "I have just imagined you fighting some other woman for my affections. I find the idea incredibly arousing. I hope you are not offended."

"Of course not," I said, "so long as you remember who you're supposed to bestow those affections on."

We went to bed, but it took me a while to fall asleep, and when I did sleep, I had unsettling dreams—not about Crossar's revelation, or facing Domenessar, or anything else I might reasonably dream about, but about the palace at Colosse and its many passages that grew and divided as I walked through them. So I've been foggy all day. It feels strange, as if we invented my noble rank to give us an edge in this war. I can't tell if the Balaenics in the camp don't know yet, or if they already respect me as Empress-Consort and therefore this doesn't make a difference. Though since most of the soldiers are younger than I am, they're probably just as uninformed about Alenik Daressar as I was.

I told Roda about it first thing this morning, and she laughed because she thought I was joking. Then she went very quiet when I insisted that no, it wasn't a joke, she was Roda Daressar and head of our family. Then I said, "I suppose I should have gotten your permission to marry. Or something. I don't actually know what the rules are about noble families. But it's all true."

"No wonder I couldn't find anything about Dad," she said. "Sesskia, what am I supposed to do with this?"

"I don't know," I said. "It's not like we have money or property. Though I suppose when this is all over, we can find out if there's anything you're entitled to. All we have now is the name."

"I like my life, Sesskia," Roda said. "I don't want to get tangled up in political intrigue. But—I don't want to lose this. It's all we have left of Dad."

"I don't know if you have to give up your life," I said, "though you...well, you'd have to have children if you don't want the name to disappear, since my children will all be heirs to the Imperial throne."

Roda made a face. "I suppose I could endure that, in Dad's memory," she said. "Damn Crossar for everything. I just hope it helps in the war, the name, I mean."

"Me too. I'm not looking forward to facing Domenessar again. I'm still not confident he's going to care what my name is," I said.

"You can convince him," she said. "I can't believe how much more confident you are. I mean, it's been a long time, you were just a kid, and of course people change over time, but you always sort of faded into the background, and now people look to you."

"It's uncomfortable. I don't like being noticed," I said, "but you're right, people look to me now, and I have to accept that."

Which I mostly have. I guess Domenessar scares me, probably because, having seen Barrekel and heard about his rule, I know he'd be good at ruling all of Balaen. My not liking him doesn't change that.

But he won't be able to rule a united Castavir and Balaen, and that's why we have to get him on our side.

After I talked to Roda, I went into Lethess to meet with Granea. I'd hoped she knew something of my Dad, but she said she'd never met him. "But everyone knew Alenik Daressar was a man of honor," she said. "You can be proud to be his daughter."

"I already was proud," I said, "but it's good to know he wasn't just like that because he was forced to be humble."

"He was Lord Governor of Hasskian before he—you—disappeared," Granea said. "I came to power about five years after that. None of the Lords Governor ever talked about him when we met in council twice a year, but sometimes someone would slip and say something about an innovation he'd made, or some policy he'd proposed. So he was a legend even then."

"I've been trying not to wish things were different," I said. "If he'd lived, Roda and I wouldn't have had a reason to leave Thalessa, and none of this would have happened."

"It's not wrong to wish you'd known your father better," Granea said.

"That's true," I said. "But it sounds like there are a lot of people who did know him, and I hope we don't have to go to war against them."

I spent the afternoon with the mages, who are working on a kathana to reveal residual magic. None of them care about my newly revealed status, since magic is more important to all of us, and things are moving along really well. We should have no trouble working on this as we travel to Barrekel, though Jeddan won't say how long he thinks it will take. He's getting to where he understands Castaviran magic as if he'd been born Castaviran, though he can't scribe th'an, and overall there's a sense of optimism we haven't felt in a long time.

Naturally, this worries me. What will we do if this new kathana fails? We're running out of possibilities to try, and you can only endure so many failures before you lose hope entirely. So I'm being encouraging and positive in public, keeping my pessimism to myself and making plans for what I'll do if everything starts falling apart again. I wonder if that's the job of every leader or if it's just my own unique approach.

Leaving for Barrekel in the morning. Cederic went in to talk to Radryntor today and I haven't seen him, but he's supposed to join us for dinner in Lethess and we'll find out what happened. Personally, I think he should ignore her, go win this war and then put someone else in her place, but he said he wanted to give her a chance to rethink her attitude toward Balaen. Sometimes Cederic's optimism astonishes me.

27 Teretar

It feels as if we're moving backward in time, leaving behind the pleasant if chilly weather of the coast for the snows and sharp winds of the inland. It was a clear day, though, and we made good time.

I helped teach the see-inside pouvra to the Balaenic mages today. It's exhausting, studying pouvrin, and more exhausting trying to demonstrate the shapes when none of us can actually see them. I think that's why everyone's so eager for this kathana to work. Being able to see pouvrin will make a huge difference.

Cederic said Radryntor welcomed him, but cautiously. It was the kind of welcome that said she was worried about losing her status rather than that she'd changed her mind and was now firmly on our side. We discussed it in bed last night, and Cederic said, "She will have to go, once we are in a position to reorganize the government."

"She's not going to be happy about that. Not that I care about her happiness, but does she have any power to fight us?" I said.

"She can create discord in the towns under her rule," he said. "She is a popular and effective ruler, and her citizens will not be happy to see her go. They might rise up against whomever we put in her place."

"Well, that doesn't sound like a good reason to keep her," I said. "I mean, I'm in favor of people having a say in government, but we can't let them bully or blackmail us into doing whatever selfish thing they want."

"And they will resist the changes we make even if we do not

remove Lady Radryntor from power," Cederic said. "I am afraid we are facing many years of strife, even after we defeat Renatha Torenz."

"I notice you never say 'if we defeat her,'" I said.

"I try not to let myself think in those terms," he said. "Failure in this will be fatal not only for us, but for our country. So I act, and believe, as if we have won. It reminds me of the commitment we have both made."

"I like it," I said. "You're teaching me optimism."

"And you are teaching me perseverance," he said. "I believed myself dedicated until I met you and realized what it truly meant to pursue a goal with unflinching determination."

"That's a nice way of saying I'm stubborn and pig-headed," I said. He laughed, and we snuggled up together and went to sleep.

28 Teretar

It's not a kathana. It's a pouvra.

The theory at this point, thanks to Terrael and Jeddan, is that th'an soak up too much foundational magic (our new name for residual magic, still clunky but more accurate) for it to be visible. Making a kathana to reveal it would be like getting a closer look at water by soaking it up with a sponge—what you're looking at is concealed by the container holding it. But pouvrin, being themselves structures of magic, don't obscure the foundational magic, and we think we might be able to create a pouvra that will actually reveal it.

This is much harder than I've made it sound. I'm the only person who's ever invented a pouvra, and I needed the th'an to give me a starting place. Jeddan thinks if we start with the see-inside pouvra, we can add to it or alter it to create a pouvra that lets us "see inside" the magic. I think he's right. This leaves our Castaviran friends with nothing to do but observe, but they also go through the camp renewing the healing th'an and performing other little tasks. Only the crucial little tasks, though, because we all still become exhausted far more quickly than before. Magic is still fading, and that gives our efforts more urgency.

It's strange how I don't feel the way I used to when I worked pouvrin, that fear and excitement and the sense of being filled to bursting with power. It feels...faded. Distant. As if I'm reaching for a memory of power. It frightens me, because for so long magic was all there was to me, and even though I have friends and a husband and rank and responsibility now, magic is still at the core of my identity, and I can feel it slipping away. I refuse to believe this is inevitable. We *will* find a solution.

We all work separately now (the Balaenic mages, I mean) with me teaching the see-inside pouvra to those who don't know it yet and the ones who do experimenting with creating new shapes from it. I think most of them aren't really sure what they're doing, and only about half of us know the pouvra, but this is the best approach we could come up with, so it's what we're doing. Terrael and Audryn stay with us, Terrael sketching out th'an that might represent shapes that could be added to the pouvra and Audryn keeping me company when I have to rest. She looks so much better now she's not working magic all the time. Better, and happy, and very pregnant. I asked her yesterday how she knew the baby was a girl, and she said there's a kathana that reveals the baby's sex. Of course. I wonder if that will still be possible when I'm pregnant, since we hope to reunite the magic before the two sides clash and who knows what it will look like then. I try not to think about it, pregnancy I mean, but with Audryn right there all the time it's hard not to.

I practice the binding pouvra a lot these days, because it's the least draining and that makes it easier to see the foundational magic attached to it, or coming off it, or whatever. It would be nice if it were what we need to bring the magics together, but there's still nothing for it to hold onto. Once we can finally see the foundational magic, maybe that will change, but I think if it were that easy, the binding pouvra would have worked already.

I don't see Roda much during the day, though we usually have lunch together. I know she hasn't spoken to Crossar, and when I asked her about it, she said she wasn't sure she could meet him without trying to kill him. I think the knowledge of what he did has exacerbated her guilt over leaving us. And she's also told me she doesn't see any point to it, because it's not as if it will change anything, her confronting him. She's more well-adjusted than I am, I think, but then she always was rational in her decision-making. She's going to stay with us until Teliarne, then head south to Garwin, but she promised she'll keep in touch. I don't know how her life is going to change now—it's something I have to find out once our rule is mostly secure—but it's got to be as much a shock to her as becoming Empress-Consort was to me.

1 Shelet

There hasn't been anything worth writing about for the last several days. All but three of our Balaenic mages have learned the see-inside pouvra, which means in a day or two I'll be done teaching and can begin experimenting with the rest of them. Cederic rode with me for a while today while I rested, and he and Audryn and Terrael told stories of the Darssan, and people they knew there. I've never seen Cederic so relaxed around any of the mages. Which is probably why, when we were eating alone in our tent tonight, he said, "I wish I had your gift for making friends. I have worked closely with Master Engilles and Master Peressten for many months now, and I... consider them friends. But I fear they still feel the barrier between us that is my hieratical rank. I don't know how to break that barrier."

"You could ask them to use your first name," I said. "That's how our friendship began. Yours and mine, I mean."

"Did it?" he said, raising one eyebrow. "For me that was the beginning of falling in love with you."

"Well, for me it let me feel as if you weren't so distant," I said, "though it took me a while to get past how awkward I felt using your praenoma when we *weren't* really friends yet."

"Any awkwardness I felt around you was a result of being completely indecisive as to whether I should pursue you openly," he said. "What would you have done if I had?"

I laid my fork and knife down and leaned back in my chair. "I don't know," I said. "I didn't feel anything for you for a long time, not even friendship, but if I'd known you were interested in me...that might have started me thinking along those lines. Or it would have made me feel more awkward, and I would have told you I wasn't interested, and we wouldn't be here now. Just as well I didn't find out until I'd already fallen in love with you."

He reached across the little table and took my hand. "I count myself fortunate you did," he said, "and that you forgave me so completely when I expected nothing from you but anger and recrimination. I have never known anyone with such a generous heart as yours, Sesskia."

"You mean the generous heart that kept me from forgiving Roda for most of three weeks?" I said with a grin.

"The generous heart that eventually forgave what most others would see as unforgivable offenses," he said. "And chose to allow Caelan Crossar to live. Don't think I did not realize his death was a possible outcome of that meeting."

"I don't know if that was generosity or just pragmatism," I said. "I haven't forgiven him."

"And I do not expect you to," Cederic said, "because that is a choice you alone can make. I think in some cases, refusing to pursue vengeance is all that forgiveness can manage, and that is also admirable."

"Good, because I'm not going to forgive him," I said. "Do you have another meeting tonight?"

"I do not," he said, tightening his grip on my hand, "because I intend to spend the evening with you, and I intend us both to be naked for it. If you agree."

"Well," I said, standing up and moving to put my arms around his neck, "I *was* planning to sit around staring at the walls, but your idea has merit."

So we did that, and then I wrote for a bit while Cederic went off to ask someone about our itinerary, then he came back and is rubbing my back while I finish this entry. I wonder if he knows I sometimes watch him while he's talking to our advisors, or giving a speech, and remember moments like this one—where he's just Cederic Aleynten who loves Sesskia Daressar. That's the strangest feeling, writing my surname. Castavirans don't have a tradition of one spouse taking his partner's name, which is why Terrael and Audryn still have different surnames; girl children take their mother's name and boys take their father's. But I know anyone who married into the God-Empress's family took the name Torenz, so maybe I'm Sesskia Aleynten. Something to ask him later—I've already ignored him long enough, because his hands are straying away from my back, and as I think I've written before, this book isn't nearly as important as he is.

3 Shelet

Finally, all the Balaenic mages know the see-inside pouvra. I was going to start experimenting today, but I'm so exhausted from teaching that I'm going to write this and then sleep.

4 Shelet

We'll be at Barrekel tomorrow, and I'm so nervous I can't focus on pouvrin. We—Cederic and Mattiak and, ugh, Crossar—have gone over what I need to say to Domenessar, or rather the points I need to touch on, as all of us agree a prepared statement would sound weak and ridiculous. What I need to tell him:

1. My name and my father's name. (Obviously. Crossar (ugh) will attest to my identity too.)

2. I intend to gain the support of the other Lords Governor, starting with Granea, because they all remember Alenik Daressar and will like the idea of putting his daughter on the throne. (Not totally sure about this, but Crossar (ugh) says it's plausible.)

3. If he decides to raise his own standard to take the throne of Balaen or of a combined Balaen and Castavir, he'll be without support, and he needs that support. (Not totally sure about this either, but I don't have to believe it, I just have to sound convincing about it.)

4. If he throws in his lot with us, and turns the Black and Brown Armies over to us, we promise him the viceregency, or whatever we call it, of one-fourth of the Empire when we win. (We won't be keeping the traditional borders of the Castaviran Empire, but dividing the new Empire into four pieces, five if you include Viravon, but no one's talking about them yet, makes sense.)

I'm still not sure this is going to work. A lot depends on the power of a name, and we didn't have time to gather the support of anyone but Granea. But I've had plenty of time to think about this, and over the last eight days I've become increasingly convinced they're right, and I'm the only one who can do this. Somehow that doesn't frighten me—it makes me feel strong. Domenessar is powerful, and smart, but he's not omnipotent and he has no better right to rule this Empire than we do. And I refuse to be intimidated by him.

CHAPTER SEVENTEEN

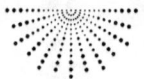

5 Shelet

Well, I wasn't intimidated by him. Unfortunately, he wasn't intimidated by me either until it was too late. The only good thing that came of this is Crossar isn't going to get what he wanted. Domenessar is never going to follow us.

We reached Barrekel a few hours before sunset, having sent our envoy ahead of us to request a meeting with Domenessar. While we were making camp (on the side of the city away from the Barrekellian forces, to show good faith) the envoy returned with the message that Arron Domenessar welcomed us to Barrekel and invited us to wait on him at Dessani Manor in one hour. That irritated me, him thinking he had a right to order us around, but Cederic, calm as always, sent back our acceptance and told everyone who would be going to be ready to go into Barrekel in an hour. When I got Cederic alone in our tent, I said, "What are we going to do if this is a trap?"

"I am certain it could become a trap if Arron Domenessar chooses to make it one," Cederic said, "which is why we are bringing so many Balaenic mages skilled in the offensive pouvrin. We do not know if he has any mages of his own, but even if we cannot take him by surprise, our mages are almost certainly more skilled fighters than his. And if he chooses to assault us, you and I, my love, are not exactly helpless."

"It's still a huge risk," I said. "We should have insisted on a halfway camp."

"It's unlikely he would have agreed to that, since he wants to display his power over us," he said. "Better to allow him his pride, since we are about to pull his support out from under him."

"I hope you're right," I said. We changed our clothes and went to meet with the others. Thistle makes a good show of being glad to see me these days, but I'm not letting my guard down. Mattiak and Bronnok were dressed in their formal uniforms (Drussik and Kalanik were staying behind in case Domenessar got ideas about cutting off the head of our army) and Crossar was wearing something that actually fit, though it wasn't as fancy or formal as I'm sure he's used to. I don't spend any more time near him than I have to, but tonight I was going to pretend I liked him so Domenessar wouldn't think we weren't completely united.

Cederic and I were in simplified versions of our Imperial garb, less ornate and easier to fight or run in. We looked elegant, and fierce, and completely competent. Not that any of that mattered, in the end.

Our progress through Barrekel drew a lot of attention of the muttering type. Mostly they all watched us as if they didn't know what to make of us, which made sense. Cederic behaved as if they were warmly welcoming. I kept my eyes open for assassins.

This time, our heralds didn't announce our identities, and the attention didn't turn ugly, and we reached Dessani Manor with no incidents. Again we followed a liveried man through the manor and into Domenessar's audience chamber, and again Domenessar faced us from his seat at the far end of the room, with soldiers standing at attention against the walls (outnumbering us, I saw). He looked as handsome, and as irritated, as ever.

"Arron Domenessar," Cederic said before Domenessar could speak, "thank you for your invitation. We hope this means you have changed your mind."

Domenessar ignored him, focusing with some surprise on

Crossar. "Caelan," he said. "They told us you'd been executed for treason."

"I escaped Venetry before that could happen," Crossar said.

"What are you doing here, with these people?" Domenessar said, in a tone of voice that clearly said what he thought of "these people."

"I have decided Cederic Aleynten is the best choice to rule our combined countries," Crossar said.

Domenessar looked even more surprised. Then he laughed. "Caelen, you're not a fool," he said. "This man has no chance of ruling Balaen."

"I disagree," Crossar said coolly. "I'm here to ask you to throw your support behind him."

Domenessar laughed harder. "Throw my support—" he said, then couldn't speak for laughing again. I started to think seriously about circling him with fire. I don't like being laughed at. "Oh, Caelan," he finally said. "He's got no support and barely any army. Why are you backing him? Join me, and be part of the winning side."

"You have no more support than he does," Crossar said. "And we have something that will convince the Lords Governor to support Aleynten over you."

That killed his laughter. "I already have the support of Lirilla and Garwin," he said, "and in a few weeks I'll have the northern cities. Nothing you can say will convince them to follow a foreigner, especially since I've already demonstrated my leadership."

"I wonder how long you'll have their allegiance once they know the future Empress-Consort is the daughter of Alenik Daressar," Crossar said.

I hate Crossar, but I had to admit it was perfect drama. Domenessar didn't register his words at first. Then he snapped his gaze to me. Fortunately, I was ready for it, and didn't flinch. "That's a lie," he said. "You expect me to believe this fishmonger is anything but a wharf rat? You're making this up to support your claim."

"Do you call me a liar, Arron Domenessar?" Crossar said. The coolness of his voice had gone icy. Domenessar went pale. "I guarantee you the Lords Governor will take my word for it. Aeleen

Vrenssar was witness at this woman's sanctification. She knew Alenik Daressar. Garwin's support for you will vanish when she learns the truth."

"Irrelevant," Domenessar said, looking at me again. "You may be his daughter, but you know nothing of ruling. Your presence on the throne would be a disaster."

"I know who I am, Domenessar," I said. "I've traveled this country for years, learning how to be something other than a wharf rat. I'm capable of leading others and I know how to judge fairly and impartially. Cedric and I together are committed to bringing our countries together peacefully. We want you to be a part of that."

"Do you," Domenessar said, leaning back in his chair. "As your servant?"

"As viceroy of the southeast," I said. We hadn't actually decided what we'd call it, but better to sound as if we had an actual plan. "You support us as Emperor and Empress-Consort. You give us command of the Barrekellian forces. You help us gain the allegiance of the other Lords Governor. And you get to rule a quarter of the Empire."

"What makes you think I'll be satisfied with that?" he said.

"Because you can't take this kingdom—these kingdoms—alone," I said. "You need the support of the Lords Governor, and we're going to take that away from you."

Domenessar regarded me with narrowed eyes, as if he were considering something. "You think you can make promises like that?" he said.

"We are sworn rulers of this new Empire," I said. "You just haven't accepted that yet."

Domenessar stood and strode toward us, stopping inches from me. I could almost feel Cedric tense. "You challenge me in my own hall?" he said.

"I doubt you'd have been willing to meet us on our own terms," I said.

He was close enough that I felt his breath on my face. It smelled nasty. "Brave words," he said.

"An Empress-Consort who's afraid of her own subjects is a poor ruler," I said. And it was true, I wasn't afraid of him. Maybe that was the confidence of the surname, maybe it was realizing I could defend myself against him, but I just wasn't afraid.

And then everything went to hell.

Domenessar shouted a command, and the soldiers came alert and moved on us so quickly there wasn't time to do more than draw weapons. They stopped about a foot away from our group, forcing us to draw closer together, and I looked to Cederic for direction, but he had his attention on Domenessar. "Arron Domenessar, you are making a mistake," he said.

"You have no right to rule this country, foreigner," Domenessar said. "I'm not going to let your fishmonger wife, whatever her surname, sway the rulers of Balaen to your side. Caelan, I'm sorry about this, but if you've chosen to follow him, you're a traitor to Balaen and I can't allow you to live. Kill them all."

The soldiers lunged. Mattiak threw himself in front of me. Cederic swept three soldiers away to go flying into the wall. The mages behind me began to work the offensive pouvrin. And I brought up a great sweep of fire to circle Domenessar and shouted, "Stand down or he dies!"

It still took a minute for them to figure out what was going on, but then soldiers were backing away, lowering their swords, some of which were stained with blood. A few men lay motionless on the floor, but no one could look away from the fire long enough to tend to them. Domenessar himself stood motionless, his handsome face distorted with fear. "Sorcerer," he said.

"Mage," I said, "and you're going to tell your soldiers to move well away from us or you'll find out just how hot I can make this burn."

Domenessar made a signal I thought was abbreviated thanks to the confines of his fiery cage, and the soldiers backed away until they were ranged against the rear wall, behind the dais. Cederic said, in a low murmur, "They will attack us when you extinguish that fire, and you are *not* to stay behind here to protect our escape."

"I have a plan," I murmured back. "Walk forward," I told Domenessar. His eyes widened with fear. "Just do it," I said. I began moving

194

the fire forward so he was forced to do as I said. "Everyone else, out the door," I added, and heard them moving behind me. Cederic took hold of my elbow and guided me so I could keep the fire in view. Domenessar was sweating from the heat and taking very short steps, and I sped the fire up so he had to walk at a normal pace. I was sweating myself, not from heat but from exertion. I've gotten better at maintaining fire without fuel as I've improved at making bigger fires, but it's still difficult and exhausting. I really, really hoped I wouldn't collapse before we all got out safely.

We made a terrifying group, soldiers bristling with weapons in case Domenessar's men decided to follow us, mages prepared to work pouvrin, Cederic guiding me, and Crossar, for some reason, walking behind Domenessar with this smirk on his face I couldn't understand. Still don't understand. I had Domenessar walking fast enough the floor couldn't actually ignite, but the whole hall smelled of burnt wood, and the air looked hazy from the smoke rising up from the scorched floor. By the time we reached the door, I was lightheaded and needed Cederic's support.

The man who'd led us to the audience chamber was at the door, too terrified to move. "Please ask someone to ready our horses. We intend to depart," Cederic said, and the man fled.

"You'll never get out of the city," Domenessar said, his voice barely more than a whisper.

"You're not coming with us, if that's what you're afraid of," I said. "You're just a temporary hostage. A good one, too."

He swore at me. I ignored him and said, "Cederic, he's helpless, and his words can't hurt me, so please don't kill him."

That shut Domenessar up—well, that and he could see Cederic's face, which I couldn't, but I could guess how he looked. He really doesn't like people insulting me. It's sort of romantic, even though he knows I can defend myself. Especially since I was proving it right then.

Eventually the horses were led to the front door, and everyone mounted. I backed toward Thistle, hoping someone would help me mount, but instead Cederic lifted me onto his horse, where I perched awkwardly and tried not to faint. "Arron Domenessar, this is your last chance," Cederic said. "We will not hold it against you that you wanted power. Join us, lend us your support, and we will give you that power."

"The bitch is almost unconscious from keeping me captive," Domenessar snarled, "and when I'm free, I'll set my soldiers on you and we'll see how far your power will protect you."

Cederic raised his hand, and Domenessar flew backward through the fire and into the stucco wall of the manor, so hard it knocked him unconscious. "Ride," he said. I let go the pouvra and sagged into his arms. I didn't fall unconscious, but I don't remember much of the ride, just being jostled along sideways in front of Cederic, and then Mattiak lifting me down from the horse, and I found I could stand well enough that no one had to carry me to my tent. About halfway there, though, I tried to pull away from Cederic, who was supporting me. "We need to discuss this," I said.

"We will, when you are more comfortable," he said.

"Not the two of us, I mean our staff," I said. "We need a plan because Domenessar is certainly going to send the troops after us in the morning."

"You would fall down if I were not supporting you," Cederic said. "You should rest for an hour or so, then join us. Sleep if you can." He steered me through the tent door and to the bed, where he gently pressed me down onto it. "I will return for you soon. Promise me you will rest."

"If you promise not to make any decisions without me," I said. He nodded. So I lay down, but discovered I was tired but not sleepy, so I got up and wrote all this down. I know I did the right thing, because Domenessar was never going to agree to our plan, but there's a part of me that wishes we—I—could have found a way to persuade him, if only because everything would have been so simple. As if any of this has been simple. Radryntor, Domenessar, even Crossar...I just wish people could see Cederic is the best man for the job and follow along. But, again, that would be too simple.

Cederic's not back yet. I'm giving him five more minutes and then I'm going to the command tent myself.

6 Shelet, morning

I can't believe it. We have the Black and Brown Armies.

No. What I can't believe is that they were willing to follow me.

Cederic came almost exactly five minutes after I wrote that last and we went to the command tent. It looked as if people had been arguing. I sat in my chair and said, "Somebody please sum up the arguments for me, because I'm still tired and angry and not interested in listening to the actual arguments."

They were quiet for a bit, looking at each other like they were all waiting for someone else to speak first. Finally, General Drussik said, "Your Majesty, we need to move the Army quickly to surround the Barrekellian forces. The Gray Army will remain here to protect you and the Emperor, and the Blue and Green Armies will flank the enemy—"

"They are *not* the enemy, Drussik!" Mattiak shouted. "Those are my men you're talking about, and we are *not* going to attack them!"

"We have no alternative!" Drussik shouted back. "You think Domenessar won't order them to turn on us the moment the sun hits the horizon? It's either that or run away with our tails tucked under our asses!"

"Leaving to gain a better tactical position isn't running away, Drussik," Kalanik said.

"We're never going to have a better tactical position," Drussik said. "General Tarallan, you know what we have to do."

"Leaving is what we have to do," Mattiak said. "We're going to strike camp and head for Teliarne. If Soessen and Roebart follow us, we need those Castaviran troops even if half of them don't speak our language."

"Are you certain there is no way to reason with them, General Tarallan?" Cederic said.

"If I could speak to them, maybe," Mattiak said. "They weren't willing to listen to me before, but maybe if they know the missing Daressar heir was with us...Roebart and Soessen both knew Alenik

Daressar. Roebart was head of the Hasskian detachment before he was promoted. It might make a difference."

"It's too bad the Daressar heir can't talk to them directly," I said. Excitement started bubbling up inside me.

"If we could get to them...but Domenessar's given orders. They'd only attack us before we could explain what we were there for," Mattiak said.

"That's true," I said with a grin. "If only the Daressar heir could turn invisible and walk through walls. Wouldn't that be nice?"

Mattiak stared down at me, then looked at Cederic. Cederic raised one eyebrow. "She has a point," he said.

"Aleynten, are you actually going to allow your wife to walk into an enemy camp to talk to a couple of men who may not even believe she is who she claims to be?" Mattiak shouted.

"I don't think 'allow' is the word you're looking for," I said.

"Sesskia," Cederic said. I sobered at the serious look on his face. "This is a tremendous risk. General Tarallan is correct that these men may not believe you. You will be in great danger and we will not be able to rescue you."

"I'll go with Jeddan," I said, "just in case, and I'll be very careful. You know I always am."

"I know you think little of your personal safety when you are in pursuit of your goal," he said, "and while you may be the only one who can do this, you are also our only Empress-Consort. And my only wife."

"Cederic, if we don't have these forces, the former Empress will likely destroy us," I said, "and then it won't matter. You know you'd risk yourself if our positions were reversed."

He sighed. "I know," he said, kissing me. "You should go immediately, so they will have no time to react."

"Then have someone find Jeddan, and I'll get changed," I said, because I'd rested while still wearing my Imperial clothes. Cederic came with me to help me dress, possibly because you need help getting out of the Imperial garb, but more likely because he wanted to keep me near him as long as possible. That made me feel guilty and sad, because I don't like hurting him and I know how devastated he is when something happens to me. But one of the things I love most about him is how he never stops me doing what we know is right, no matter how dangerous it is. I couldn't stay married to him if he tried to protect me by never letting me do anything.

When I was dressed—that took a while, because there was kissing, and hugging, and quiet endearments—we went back to the command tent, where Jeddan was waiting. I squeezed Cederic's hand once more, and then Jeddan and I set off for the far side of Barrekel, and the Black and Brown Armies.

I never have found out why they name the divisions of the army after colors. There's no White Army, of course—that's the name given to Nessan's elite forces, the color of death—and the army at Durran is just called the Northern Army, but I'd think they would run out of colors that sound strong and defiant. There's certainly no Pink Army.

Anyway, the Black Army is under the command of General Roebart Gradden, and the Brown Army is commanded by General Soessen Ellert. We approached the Black Army because, as Mattiak said, General Gradden knew my Dad well, and would probably be the most responsive to my claim to be his daughter. It was a long walk to their headquarters, and we couldn't take horses—that reminds me I never did find out what happened to Thistle when we left Dessani Manor. I'm surprised to discover I'm worried about her. I hope I'm not going soft.

We had to walk, and it was full dark when we reached the outer perimeter. I could tell the soldiers had no idea fighting was imminent, and I could also tell they were used to perimeter duty being boring, because I think we could have sneaked past them without concealing ourselves. Not that we were that bold. No point taking unnecessary risks.

Jeddan and I held hands so we wouldn't get separated, and made our way almost-invisibly through the camp. It's permanent, not a collection of tents, and the people definitely had the look that says they don't expect to have to move anytime soon. There are actual roads between the buildings, and a lot of women who clearly live there, probably wives rather than camp followers, and even children running around, ignoring their mothers' cries for them to come to bed. It made me sick to think Drussik wanted us to attack them unawares.

It took us a while to find the center of camp, but the command center was obvious by how well lit it was and how much activity was going on there. The rest of the camp might be oblivious, but it sure looked as if Domenessar had sent General Gradden some very upsetting orders. Jeddan and I found a quiet corner still within sight of the command building and had a whispered discussion.

"I think if I go in there with you, I'll look like a threat," Jeddan said. "On the other hand, the Emperor will kill me if I let you get injured because I wasn't there."

"Then you'll have to be invisible," I said. "Go in through the back wall when I come in the front, so they'll be distracted and won't be looking your way."

"If someone sees through the concealment pouvra, it's going to look like treachery," Jeddan said. "But I think it's the best plan we can manage."

"Be careful," I said. I tried to watch him walk away and only succeeded in making my eyes water. I counted to ten to give him time to get into place, then dropped concealment and walked casually toward the door of the command building.

The sentries saw me, but didn't do anything at first. They probably thought I was somebody's wife. Then, when it was clear I was headed for them, they came alert and brought their weapons up (swords but no shields). "What do you want?" one of them asked.

"I have a message for General Gradden," I said.

"Message from who?" the other one said.

"It's a private message, and it won't take me long to deliver it," I said. This was the trickiest part of the plan, convincing the sentries to let me in, and I prayed I wouldn't have to work the pouvrin on them, or run away and circle back around to enter the building through the wall.

"You think you can just walk up and see the General?" the first soldier said.

"No, but I think *you*," I said, pointing at him, "can walk in there and ask if General Gradden will take a message from his old friend Mattiak."

"Who?" he said. I suppressed a sigh. Of course I had to deal with a stupid soldier.

"Mattiak," the other soldier said, as if he were trying to remember the name. I waited. Finally, the second soldier said, "Old friend?"

"All you have to do is tell him he has a message from Mattiak," I said, "and if he doesn't want it, I'll leave."

"I don't get it," the first soldier said.

"Because you're an idiot," the second soldier said. "Wait here," he told me, and disappeared inside. I smiled politely at the first soldier, who continued to frown at me in puzzlement. The hum of noise from within, the sound of a few people talking, got louder. Then several men left the building, and the soldier returned and said, "General Gradden wants to speak to you."

I went inside and down a short hall to the only open door, through which bright lamplight shone. The only person in that room was a man wearing uniform trousers and a white shirt. He had faded red hair and looked to be about sixty years old. "Why is a woman tossing Mattiak Tarallan's name around like she owns it?" he said, glowering at me.

"General Gradden, Mattiak sends his regards and asks you to listen to what I have to say," I said. "Could we sit down?"

"How did you get into this camp?" he said, not moving.

"That's not important now," I said. "Please, General. Just give me five minutes."

Gradden stared at me for a few seconds, then waved me at a seat and pulled another chair around to face me. "I'm listening," he said, in a tone that indicated he wouldn't be listening for long.

I took a deep breath and prayed one last time he would listen. "General, my name is Sesskia Daressar, and I am the Empress-Consort of Balaen and Castavir."

His eyes went wide. "You—what kind of claim is that? Sesskia Daressar died twenty-six years ago with Alenik!"

"Caelan Crossar smuggled my family out of Venetry when my father's attempt to take the throne was betrayed," I said, wishing I could tell him what other part Crossar had had in that fiasco. "I grew up in Thalessa. My father was killed nineteen years ago. My sister Roda and I are all that's left of the Daressars."

"You're lying," he said. "And what's this nonsense about Empress? Is Mattiak out of his mind?"

"He supports my husband and me in our claim to the throne," I said.

"Then he knows we've been ordered to be prepared for an attack," Gradden said.

"Yes," I said. "I'm here to see if we can't come to a different arrangement."

"You want me to betray Lord Domenessar," he said.

"I want you to fight for the rightful rulers of this country," I said. "You know the Lords Governor don't want to follow Domenessar because they're afraid to give him that much power. You know they'll follow me because a Daressar heir on the throne is preferable to the alternative. If you continue to lead your troops in Domenessar's name, you will lead this country to chaos."

"You can't prove what you claim," Gradden said. He sounded shaky.

"Mattiak says you served my father when he was Lord Governor of Hasskian," I said. "That you were good friends. You must have known his wife. General, you may not believe I'm Alenik Daressar's daughter." I took another deep breath. "But you can't look at me and not see Cessily Daressar's face."

Gradden's gaze swept me from my head to my feet, then settled on my face. His belligerence slipped away, replaced by astonishment. "True God help me, you look just like her," he said quietly. "What—where is she?"

"She died ten years ago," I said, just as quietly.

To my shock, tears came to his eyes. "Poor Cessily," he said. "I can't believe your family survived. Everyone thought the King had had you killed."

"I grew up not knowing the truth," I said. "Just that my Dad was a good and honorable man. I want to honor his legacy. I think Cederic and I will rule this country justly. Please, General, help us do that."

Gradden stood up and began to pace the tent. I hoped Jeddan was well out of his way. "Alenik Daressar," he muttered. "Mattiak Tarallan. Your husband is a foreigner?" he said to me.

"He's Castaviran," I said. "Those people you were fighting last fall? Their country is called Castavir. Magic brought our countries, our worlds, together, and I know you probably think of magic as evil or frightening—"

"My son was a sorcerer," Gradden said. "He left home twenty years ago because he couldn't keep it hidden. It didn't matter to us. He would never have hurt anyone, but he could make fire—it's all about what you choose to do with it, I think. How could magic make another country appear like this?"

"It's...complicated," I said, "and something I can explain to you when we have plenty of time. But it sounds like we don't have much time now. Though...your camp doesn't look much like it's preparing to go to war."

"I'm reluctant to follow the orders I've been given," Gradden said. "Those are our comrades over there, and Lord Domenessar has no idea of the tactical situation. He may be our ultimate commander, but he's no soldier. I don't want to disobey orders, but I also don't want to follow orders that will result in mass destruction."

"Then come to our side," I said. "Mattiak needs you. The Castaviran Army is huge and we don't stand a chance without more troops. Right now, you're fighting for Domenessar's glory. You're the Balaenic Army. You ought to be fighting for your country. For what it can become."

Gradden sighed. "You've got your father's silver tongue to go with your mother's lovely face," he said. "I'll send for Soessen and we'll convince him together. I wish we could meet with Mattiak. It's not going to be easy, leaving Barrekel—I presume that's what you want?"

"We have to go to Teliarne—that's the city you were fighting—for the troops headquartered there," I said, "and then...actually I don't know what happens next, because I don't understand military strategy very well. But yes, you're going to have to break camp. I know that will be hard."

"This is the military. Hard is our specialty," Gradden said. "Excuse me."

He left the room, and I said, "Jeddan."

Jeddan became visible, crouched in a corner. "That's uncomfortable," he said, standing and stretching. "I'm glad I found the right room."

"Will you go tell Mattiak what's happened? And ask him to come here? I'll make sure the sentries let him through," I said.

"Just Mattiak? Not the Emperor?" he said.

"Uh...better not have both of us here at the same time, just in case," I said. "But tell him I'm safe and I'll be back soon."

Jeddan nodded and vanished again. I waited a while longer, impatiently, until Gradden finally came back. "General, I've sent for Mattiak, but you should probably tell your sentries to let him through," I said.

"How could you send for him?" Gradden said.

"Um...magic, actually," I said, which was close to the truth. "But you did say you wished you could strategize with him."

"This is a night of wonders," Gradden said, shaking his head. "Soessen will be here soon. I didn't tell him anything but that I wanted to talk. He'll be harder to convince, but that's balanced against how he's even more reluctant to go to war against our own people than I am."

"Thank you for being reasonable, General," I said.

"Lady Daressar, I don't think you understand how the men and women of my generation felt about your father," he said. "There were a lot of people who wanted him to be King and were devastated when he disappeared. They'll follow you in his name, if you're even halfway competent as a leader."

"I hope I am," I said, feeling very nervous. "General...could you tell me about him? He died when I was nine, and...I wish I'd known him better."

So the General and I talked about Dad, and I cried a few tears, but he didn't hold it against me. Then Mattiak arrived—I didn't know how he managed to get there before General Ellert, but then Ellert came in and he looked so ill I was amazed he was out of bed. Mattiak and Gradden didn't seem put off by it, as if this were something they'd expected, and I pieced together the explanation that Ellert deals with stress by developing severe intestinal trouble, and he was under a lot of stress just then.

Convincing Ellert went faster than I'd been led to believe by Gradden, mainly because Mattiak was there and Ellert really wanted to be convinced. I think he might not totally believe I'm who I say I am, but as long as he leads the Brown Army into battle behind our standard, he doesn't have to.

Once we had them both convinced, I excused myself, because I was so tired by that time—working that fire pouvra and then the concealment pouvra had drained me. I walked back through the camp and didn't bother to conceal myself even when I passed the perimeter sentries; even in my exhausted state it was easy to avoid them. Then I kept walking until I reached our camp, and I had enough sense to go to the command tent where Cederic would be rather than to our tent, so he could stop worrying. He took me to our tent and helped me get undressed and into bed, then snuggled up next to me so I fell asleep in his arms, which is my favorite way to fall asleep.

When I woke up, he was gone, and I still felt weary enough I didn't want to get up. So I wrote this for a while, until someone brought me breakfast—is it bad that I'm getting used to the benefits of being Empress-Consort?—and then I wrote the rest. And I'm still astonished it all worked. That is, I assume it worked, and there weren't any setbacks, and nobody changed his mind and went crawling back to Domenessar. But if that had happened, I doubt my morning would have been so peaceful. So I'm going to assume for once, everything worked out fine.

CHAPTER EIGHTEEN

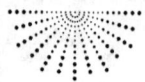

6 Shelet, evening

I'm grateful, right now, to have this book, because I need to write all this out. It's funny—before I got out my pencil I read back over the other books, just a few of the entries, and I never realized how much I was defining myself by what I worked out in these pages. Cederic thinks I have a generous heart, but right now I feel vindictive and cruel and I hate those feelings but I can't set them aside. Crossar betrayed my family and he might as well have murdered my parents and Bridie. And now that I have the power to destroy him, I want to see him suffer. I want him to know what it's like to lose everything. It would be justice, I think. But I don't know who I'd become if I went through with it.

It was after dinner. Cederic and I ate alone in our tent, which we do more frequently now. I think both of us feel the need for privacy after spending the day being public figures. Cederic was very quiet, but I didn't feel much like talking either, so I didn't think anything was wrong.

Today was long, and full of discussions and messengers going back and forth between the armies and between the Barrekellian forces and the city. I don't know what Gradden told Domenessar about why he hadn't followed orders—possibly that they needed time to break camp. True God knows what Domenessar thought of the Balaenic Army not moving either. I guess they're still working out the logistics of combining the divisions.

It was fun to imagine Domenessar getting more and more furious, and wonder when that fury was going to turn into apprehension and then fear. But it's not as if he had the forces to do anything about it. I'm happy, because having to give him a quarter of the Empire would have been disastrous, worse than giving Crossar Venetry. If that's what happens.

Anyway, Cederic was quiet, and it wasn't until the meal was nearly over that he said, "Sesskia," in a way that told me he was gearing up for an unpleasant conversation. I felt my meal begin to roil in my stomach. "Sesskia," he repeated, "there is something we should discuss."

"What is it?" I said, holding on to my calm demeanor.

He looked away from me. "It is about our promise to Caelan Crossar," he said.

Now I felt really sick, because I hated thinking about that. "He did what he said he would," I said. "We can't go back on our word."

He shook his head. "The agreement was that he would deliver us Arron Domenessar," he said. "He failed to do that."

"But," I said in surprise, "we have the troops. He brought us support."

"Sesskia," he said, "what I am telling you is we are not technically bound by that promise. I told him what the terms of our agreement were and he did not keep his side of the bargain."

I opened my mouth to protest and then it hit me. We didn't have to keep that promise. We didn't have to give Crossar power. I wouldn't have to see my family's betrayer elevated to the rank my father had tried to secure. I grinned. "I like that," I said. "Can I tell him?"

Cederic didn't smile. "I said 'technically,'" he said. "But it is dishonorable. The spirit of our agreement has not been broken. We should not take advantage of this."

I clenched my fist under the table. "He'll be a terrible ruler," I said. "He'll use his power to benefit himself and he might even challenge you someday. We can't afford to let him have it."

"It would cost us our honor to refuse," Cederic said.

"It would not," I said. "How is it dishonorable to protect the Empire?"

Cederic looked at me in silence for a moment. Finally, he said, "I am going to let you decide."

"What?" I exclaimed. "Shouldn't we decide this together?"

"Your heart is bound up in this," Cederic said. "You say you want justice when what you want is revenge. I don't want you resenting me for forcing you to reward a man you justifiably hate. You need to decide where our honor lies: keep our word, or protect the Empire. You were the one wronged, Sesskia, and if choosing not to keep that promise is what will satisfy your need, I will not speak against it and I will accept your judgment as the honorable thing. I trust you to do what's right."

"You're just saying that to make me feel guilty so I'll keep that promise," I said.

"No, I am not," he said. "I want to use that loophole as much as you do. Caelan Crossar could be disastrous for our rule. But this is not about the kingdom. This is about how you were hurt by him. If he becomes viceroy, we will have to deal with him often, and I don't want you to have to face him with hatred and bitterness in your heart, because that will make you someone you are not. I will not tell you to forgive him, but I think you need to find a way to break the power he has over you."

"He doesn't have any power over me," I said.

"He controls your emotions simply by his presence," he said, "and he is a reminder of what you have lost. You are stronger than he is, but I think you've forgotten that." He stood up from the table. "This is your choice, and I trust you to make a good one," he said, "because I love you and I have faith in you." He left the tent, left me gaping and unable to say a word. The noises of the camp seemed muted now, as if they were coming from farther away. I sat there for a few minutes, not thinking of anything, and then I found my book and wrote this.

I don't care what Cederic says, I don't think it would be dishonorable to hold Crossar to the letter of his agreement

That's not true. There's a part of me hidden deep inside that knows we'd be cheating him. The information he provided did give us the allies we needed, because the truth is Domenessar was only important because he could order the Black and Brown Armies to join us, and knowing about my Dad let us bypass him and go straight to the generals. That couldn't have happened if I were still just Sesskia the wharf rat.

But...I really think it's a bad idea to give Crossar so much power! Maybe he *is* a competent ruler, I don't know. But I know he's always going to put his own interests ahead of those of the Empire, and if he decides his interests mean betraying us to take the Imperial throne for himself, he'll do it, and he's clever enough he might even succeed.

No. I can't lie to myself. I don't give a damn about what kind of ruler he'll be. Well, I do, but what I really care about is crushing him into the ground. If I let him win, I'll be betraying my family as much as he ever did. How can he be rewarded for that? How can I stand to see him triumph after what he's done? I can't do it. I don't care if it's not honorable. I can't.

It's been fifteen minutes since I wrote the last and I'm more confused than ever. I feel as if I'm at war with myself: part of me wants to see Crossar humiliated, but then there's the part of me that cringes at what I'd become if I do that. It's the part of me that felt guilty at not being able to forgive Roda—but she was penitent, and she only made a mistake. Crossar doesn't care that he destroyed my father and he did it on purpose. Don't I have a right to avenge him?

Cederic was right; this is about what I need. I just can't tell which decision will make me whole again. Will satisfy the pain he's caused me. I wish I could talk to Roda, but even though she's entitled to a say in what kind of justice Crossar deserves, she doesn't have the authority to make this decision for the Empire. So it's down to me. And I'm a selfish, vindictive woman who can't let go of the past.

6 Shelet, midnight
I sat for about half an hour after finishing that last entry, staring

at the page and wondering if there were anything else to write. When I finally concluded there wasn't, I put the book away in my pocket and went to find Cederic, who was standing outside the picket lines talking to Gradden. "I've made a decision," I said.

Cederic immediately broke off his conversation and saluted Gradden, who mounted his horse and rode off in the direction of the Black Army. I know now we're moving out in the morning, and I wish I could see Domenessar's face when he sees the Barrekellian forces leaving the city. His loss, since he was too greedy to make the right decision.

"Should I summon Caelan Crossar?" Cederic said.

"Yes. I want us to speak to him privately," I said.

"May I ask what you've decided?" he said.

"I'm afraid if I tell you, I'll change my mind," I said, "because I'm still not totally sure I've made the right decision."

He took my arm and we walked through the camp together. "I am certain you have," he said, "because I trust you. And I will support you no matter what you tell Caelan Crossar."

At the command tent, I sent a messenger to find Crossar, and Cederic told everyone they were done for the day—it was nearly sunset, so that wasn't so strange, except Cederic usually works until midnight. But no one wanted to argue with the Emperor, especially since most of them had other, more enjoyable things to do. We went into the empty tent and sat and waited. Finally Crossar arrived. "I assume this couldn't wait until morning," he said.

"You assume correctly," I said. "Have a seat."

He sat without a trace of nervousness. He clearly didn't think we could do anything to him. "Your information proved essential," I said. "Thank you."

"I live to serve my country," he said, with a smirk that said he was lying.

"And now you want to serve in a grander capacity," I said.

"I gave you the Armies, you give me Venetry," he said.

I leaned forward. "That was not the agreement," I said. "You were to give us *Domenessar*. I notice he's not riding with us. You failed."

Crossar's eyes narrowed. "A technicality," he said. "We both know the nature of the power you wanted."

"Nevertheless, you failed to deliver on your promise," I said, "and we don't feel bound by that agreement. You get nothing."

Crossar leapt to his feet. "How *dare* you cheat me!" he shouted. "I gave you what you needed and you betray me!"

"Like you betrayed my father?" I said. "You ought to know how it works, Crossar. All that matters is getting what you want, no matter how many promises you have to break. You don't deserve to rule in Venetry because you're a lying traitor who will only keep faith with your Emperor as long as it benefits you."

"I swore an oath," Crossar said, breathing heavily. "I want this kingdom to prosper. I only turned on your father because he was in the way of that. You will give me what you promised or I'll—"

"*Sit down*," I said. To my surprise, he dropped back into his seat. "I'm not finished. You betrayed my father. You're a lying opportunist and you only keep the promises that benefit you. And I'll be damned if I turn into someone like you."

I had his full attention. I went on, "I would be completely within my rights not to keep that promise, and you were a fool to make a vow that specific. But I'm not dishonorable. And you gave me a heritage I never expected. So we're keeping that promise. You get what you asked for. But listen closely, Crossar."

I stood up and took two steps to loom over him. "You're not getting this because you earned it or because you forced us into it," I said. "You're getting it because I choose to give it to you. Everything you have, everything you are from this moment on, is thanks to me. If you have power, it's because Alenik Daressar's daughter gave it to you. Without me, you are *nothing*, and I can take all of that away just as easily. So think carefully before you decide to betray this Daressar, Crossar, because I'm not my Dad, I'm suspicious and distrustful and I love this Empire, and if I so much as suspect you're trying to use it for your own selfish purposes, I'll destroy you." I took a step backward. "You're dismissed, Lord Crossar."

Crossar looked in Cederic's direction. I could have told him he wouldn't get any sympathy from that quarter. He stood, slowly, then bowed to me, vassal to ruler. "Your Majesty," he said, and left the tent.

Cederic put his hand on mine. "That was not the decision I expected," he said, "but it was clearly the right one."

"Was it?" I said. "Or will it just motivate him to strike at us sooner?"

"That is a man who responds to power," he said, "and I think he has finally realized that in coming to us, he can no longer exercise that power through others. He has lost what power he had in Balaen, and he will never be satisfied with being an ordinary man. He thought to deal with us from a position of power without remembering he has none. You reminded him he rules at our sufferance and that there are consequences arising from that, namely that he can lose his power at any time. Not that we would be so autocratic, but the possibility is there."

"That makes me feel better," I said. "And I think my Dad would approve."

"I think your father loved you, and would be proud of the woman you've become," he said.

"I hope so," I said. "And thank you for having faith in me. I was close to making the wrong decision."

He gripped my hand tighter. "You are as human as anyone, love, but you have a generous heart and I have never known you to be cruel," he said. "You might have been a good choice for Empress without me."

I hugged him, and said, "Don't ever say that again. It fills me with horror that I might not have you with me."

"Then, as I have sent everyone away for the night," he said, "I think we should retire to our tent and remind each other of why we need one another so much."

So we did. I do love him. Sometimes I think back on how we first met and I'm astonished that we were able to go from that to love and marriage and trust and everything we have together. I'm worried it can't last, that we're going to run up against something too big for us to get past, and start fighting, and discover character flaws we can't endure, because this seems too good to be true. And yet it is.

I read some of this book to Cederic while we were snuggled up together, before I wrote this, the part about going to Venetry to rescue Terrael, and he said, "I was even angrier than you realized. It was fortunate you were unconscious, because I lost my temper and would have turned it on you instead of on the soldiers who brought you to me. And I never want you to be the recipient of my anger again."

"But am I any better than those soldiers, really?" I said. "They didn't deserve it either."

"No, but with you, added to the guilt and shame of having lost my temper would be the agony of seeing you look at me in pain and betrayal," he said. "And the fear that you might not be willing to forgive so readily a second time."

"I understand that," I said. "You have a temper, and I have a tendency to run away when things are bad."

He tightened his arms around me and said, "If you run away, I promise I will follow you and make things right."

"I know," I said. We lay still and quiet together until we both dozed off. Then I woke up and had trouble falling asleep again, so I wrote even though I'd planned to record this in the morning. Writing helps me relax, though I think it's the contrast between sitting here in the chilly tent and lying cuddled up in a warm bed that helps me fall asleep again. So I'm going to do that, because tomorrow's going to be a busy day, heading out to Teliarne.

7 Shelet

So we're not going to Teliarne after all. We were breaking camp when a scout arrived, looking as if he'd ridden for days without rest. His horse didn't look much better. I don't think I've ever felt sympathy for a horse before, but it was hard not to feel sorry for the animal. He brought terrible news which I'll sum up:

1. The God-Empress's troops (they call it the New Army, but we all know who's driving it) left Venetry a week or two ago even though the snows are still fairly heavy in the north.

2. They went to Duberin, which is a Castaviran city west of

Colosse and one of our allies, and demanded they swear allegiance to the God-Empress. (The scout only heard rumors about the details, but he was certain they did not say "allegiance to the God-Empress and the King of Balaen.)

3. Duberin, which is a heavily fortified if not heavily defended city, defied them. I think this was insane. They should have pretended to swear allegiance and then turned on the God-Empress later. Cederic said that was out of character for Castavirans. I told him Castavirans are crazy. He agreed with me. I think he was proud of his countrymen.

4. The God-Empress set the entire Castaviran Army on Duberin, which was overwhelmed in days. Then she let the troops destroy it. Raping, looting, killing—there's almost nothing left of the people of Duberin. The consul who defied her was disemboweled and left to die in the city square.

5. The God-Empress sent out messengers describing what she'd done and promising the same to any city that failed to acknowledge her rule.

This changes a lot. She's almost certainly on her way to Colosse and if we don't get there quickly, it's going to suffer the same fate. So we sent messengers to Teliarne and we set out as fast as we could for Colosse, or rather for a ford across the Myrnala that will let us cross over so we can go to Colosse. The Helvirite Army is going to meet us there, and I hope it moves quickly, because we are heavily outnumbered right now, even with the Barrekellian forces. Mattiak doesn't look happy at all. He and the generals have been in conference with Cederic and his advisors, going over maps of Colosse and trying to plan a defense of a city the Balaenics have barely seen. That's assuming we get there in time to set up a defense as opposed to having to fight street-to-street.

The whole thing makes me sick because I'm helpless right now. All I can do is work with the mages to figure out how to stop magic from fading. Our army may be outnumbered, but we definitely have more mages than they do, since all the Balaenic mages left Venetry and Cederic "retrieved" his mages from the Castaviran Army. Unfortunately, Cederic's mages aren't battle mages, and the Balaenic mages still don't have a lot of experience. And with magic becoming so weak, we'll be even less effective. So we're all focused on figuring out the pouvra that makes magic visible, and we'll see what happens next.

8 Shelet

We're in contact with the Firtha thanest now, fearing the day when the message will be *We're overrun* and then silence. Duberin's closer to Colosse than Barrekel is, and we're all pushing ourselves as hard as we can without collapsing. We make only a minimal camp each night, though we still eat well, since no one wants the army to be starving and exhausted when we meet the enemy.

It's as if this pouvra doesn't want us to master it. To me it feels like it's slipping away even if I don't try to exercise my will on it. I'm having to be cheerful and positive so no one gets discouraged, but privately I feel on the verge of despair. We'll reach Colosse in nine or ten days, which seems like forever when we're thinking about how fast the God-Empress's army can move, but it's almost nothing when we're trying to discover, or create, or shape a pouvra we can barely comprehend. My biggest worry is we'll get it to work, and it won't matter because what it reveals is incomprehensible to the human brain. But I keep all these worries to myself and this book. I don't even tell Cederic because he has enough worries of his own and there's nothing he can do about mine.

9 Shelet

It's working. It really is. People have begun seeing flashes of something when they try to work the pouvra, like...well, no one's really agreed on what they're seeing, but it's nothing we've ever seen in working pouvrin before, *and* the Castaviran mages are seeing it too! That was one of the things we weren't sure of, whether we could make the pouvra have an external effect rather than just affecting the mage working it. This is incredibly heartening.

10 Shelet

The pouvra keeps collapsing, probably because we're trying too hard. It's so exciting, feeling so close. It's also that the pouvra is the strangest shape any of us have ever seen. It's like it's trying to exert an influence on the world around it, but not in the sense of working magic, like the fire pouvra influencing the world by creating fire. From what I've seen when it's my turn to observe rather than work the pouvra, I'd say it's trying to create some kind of field that alters vision, like a lens or heat haze. That tells us it's working, since it would make sense it would need to change our perceptions. I wonder if the magic is out of sync with the world, or if it's just invisible. Out of sync might suggest a solution to bringing magic together, but it's too soon to make plans based on unsupported assumptions.

11 Shelet

We did it. We just don't know what it means yet.

We (the mages) had breakfast together this morning because Cederic left at dawn to ride with the generals. I don't know what they find to talk about all day, and I'm not sure I want to know, if their lengthy discussions mean they're having trouble coming up with strategies to defend Colosse. We mages have a strategy of our own: we break up into groups centered on the fourteen of us who can work the revelation pouvra, with everyone else observing. This is hard but necessary, because when you're bending your will to manifest it, you can't pay attention to anything else or it slips away as if you'd tried to force it.

So seven of us work the pouvra and the rest of the group watches and takes notes, and then when the mage gets tired, the other one takes her place. We have to break for rests frequently, and for some reason this pouvra makes you hungry, so I feel like I'm eating all the time, probably because I am. In general it feels like trying to climb a slippery wall; you have to move slowly and watch where you put your hands, or you slide backwards and have to start over. Fortunately, climbing walls is something I have experience with.

I was partnered with Jeddan—I love working with him—and it was his turn to work the pouvra while we watched. This gets boring fast, so I didn't realize the blurriness in my vision was anything more than eyestrain until somebody near me drew in a sharp breath, not very loud, but enough to be heard over the creaking of the wagon. I blinked a few times and realized the blurriness was extending outward from Jeddan in all directions, a faint haze that was like the finest gauze you could imagine, finer than anything human hand could produce. I realized I was holding my breath and let it out slowly, not wanting to disturb Jeddan's concentration.

Then Jeddan said, "I'm feeling a buzzing numbness in my feet and hands. I'm not concealed, am I?"

"No, it's working—don't get excited!" I said.

"I'm not," he said. His voice sounded remote, like he was thinking about something other than what he was saying. "Don't tell me what it looks like. I've got the shape of the pouvra surrounding me and I'm afraid if I try to picture something else, it will fall apart."

I waved everyone else to silence (unnecessarily) and watched as the haze spread. Then other shapes appeared within the haze. They were round, globular really, and the color of mud, as if someone had mixed together a dozen colors of paint and dunked them in it. It was...underwhelming. I'd hoped for something beautiful, but this didn't even look like magic. Then I wondered if it *was* magic at all. Maybe we'd revealed something else.

"Nobody tell Cederic I did this," I said, and I reached out to grasp one of the blobs. Nothing bad happened to me or Jeddan. The blob went through my fingers as if it were just an image of a blob. Then the haze shrank in on itself, and Jeddan opened his eyes. "I think I dispelled it," I said.

"I don't think so. I had to let it go because the tingling was turning into fiery burning," Jeddan said, tucking his fingers under his arms and flexing his feet in their sturdy boots. "What did it look like?"

"Ugly blobs," Tobiak said. "Are we sure it's really magic?"

"I had that thought, but what else could it be?" I said. "There are people who study the nature of the world—if it was made up of blobs, you'd think we'd have heard about it."

"And they're too big and too dispersed to be part of people, or animals, or even plants," Relania said.

Jeddan stretched. "So we know what it looks like," he said. "Next we need to make it do things without being absorbed by pouvra or th'an."

"I couldn't touch it," I said, "so it will have to be magic that does it."

"Sesskia, see if you can manage it. I want to see them," Jeddan said. "Try bending your will before picturing the pouvra. I felt as if it were sliding into place around me, like it was there the whole time and I just couldn't see it."

"I'll try that," I said. I settled down cross-legged with my hands resting on my thighs, closed my eyes, and let my mind sink into the state where my will is pliant and able to take on the shape imposed by the pouvra. I did as Jeddan suggested and bent my will without having a shape in mind, which is harder than it sounds. You have to reject all the impulses that come to mind, hunger and thirst and muscle pain, and accept that those things are part of who you are and willing them away is only temporary. You have to...I don't know. Become humble. Bow before the implacable power of reality.

And it worked. I saw the pouvra as if it were angular shapes rising out of the sea, taking the place of the volition I'd given up, shaping me to their desire. My feet and hands started tingling, but I stayed relaxed and examined the pouvra as if I were looking at my own body, something so familiar I wasn't surprised out of my reverie. It was smooth, and flowing, like water through a reed contorted in ways no real plant could have mimicked, not and still let water flow freely. I flexed that immaterial shape and saw it bend and try to whip away from me, so I made myself relax again and it steadied. Then I watched it, not trying to interact with it.

It didn't give any hint as to what it was for any more than any other pouvra does. It's not as if the fire pouvra has flames surrounding it or the concealment pouvra looks like it's made of glass. I wondered what it would be like to observe the other pouvrin this way, but realized it would be impossible because when you work a pouvra (normally, that is) it shapes the magic and then disappears. So the fact that this one persists tells me it really is maintaining what-ever field or lens it is that makes magic visible. It's very strange, and if we weren't becoming so desperate, I'd want to examine it more closely.

Eventually my hands and feet started to hurt, and I had to release the pouvra and open my eyes. "Well?" I said.

"If that's magic, it's just a bunch of blobs floating around," Jeddan said. "We can't touch them, and the only time we saw them respond to anything was when two of them drifted close together. They didn't join together, they sort of pushed each other apart."

"It was like the wrong ends of two magnets," Tobiak said. "They didn't even touch each other, but they moved apart really fast once they came close enough together."

"I think we can assume magic isn't supposed to look like that," Terrael said, "because we already know magic hasn't come back together. Maybe whatever made those blobs stay apart is what's keeping that from happening."

"Let's see if anyone else has made progress," I said, "teach them the key to the revelation pouvra, and start making plans. We need to work out why they repel each other, we need to learn if that's what's keeping magic apart, and we need to find a way to overcome that."

So we spent the rest of the day working on the revelation pouvra, with the result that all fourteen of us could work it and maintain it by dinnertime, at which point we were all so exhausted we never wanted to think about magic again. Right now I feel as if I'd walked all day instead of riding in the wagon, which isn't well-sprung but is better than nothing. Though I found out Thistle came back with us, and I suppose I could have ridden her if I hadn't needed to work with the mages.

I can't believe I even considered that.

CHAPTER NINETEEN

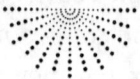

12 Shelet

We reached the Myrnala River early this afternoon and it took most of the time until dinner to get everyone across. I didn't realize there was some worry about whether we could cross it at all, given that the landscape has changed and the river might be wider or deeper, and maybe the bridge wouldn't even be there. But the Myrnala was actually narrower than it used to be in either Balaen or Castavir, I gathered, and the bridge was still there.

We made a huge procession going through Narness, which is the town at the eastern side of the bridge, and people came out and cheered, though I don't know what they thought they were cheering. I guess it's not obvious there's more to us than just the Balaenic Army. I wonder what they'll think when the Helvirite Army comes through. Unless they came through ahead of us. That would be wonderful. I probably should have asked Cederic whether they have or not. It's a big army and couldn't possibly have left no traces of their passing.

More experimenting. More discussion. Rode with Cederic for a bit and learned something of the tactical situation at Colosse. We have two plans, one for if the God-Empress is there when we arrive and one for if she isn't. I already knew Colosse isn't a very defensible city, but I didn't realize what a problem it would be trying to fight street to street. And our goal is to protect the people. So we're hoping to get there soon enough to set up between the city and the God-Empress's army.

I'm worried the Helvirite Army won't get there in time and we'll be crushed between the army and the city, but apparently there are things we can do to mitigate our being at a numerical disadvantage. One of those things, as Cederic pointed out, is for our mages to practice battle magic. So much as I hate giving up research time (because, frankly, I think it's going to be more important in the long run) I have to admit Cederic's right. We're going to compromise and divide our work day in half—mornings working battle magic, afternoons studying the revelation pouvra. This isn't the most practical use of our time, since we're going to be so tired from our morning work we'll have trouble with the revelation pouvra, but if we did it the other way around we'd definitely be too exhausted for battle pouvrin and kathanas.

If we aren't in time, and Colosse has already been overrun...then it gets difficult. Then we get to street-to-street fighting to force them out of the city, and a lot of non-combatants will die, not to mention soldiers and mages. And that's going to make the mages less effective, too, because they'll have to be so close to the fighting they can be killed before working magic. I've started mentally urging the army to move faster. Too bad there's not a pouvra for that. I'd flit ahead to see where the God-Empress's army is, but it would take too long.

We proved the blobs are what magic truly looks like—well, I say "proved," but Terrael calls it a hypothesis that's subject to further investigation. I had to soak his head again. The idea was to see if we could use th'an to make the blobs move the way we want them to. So someone (Jeddan) worked the revelation pouvra, and our Castaviran mages stood inside the haze and drew the mind-moving th'an—the plan was to move on to the mind-moving pouvra if the th'an didn't work.

What happened was as soon as the mages started scribing, blobs would drift in their direction, and eventually they would stretch and contort until they matched the shape of the th'an, and then they'd disappear and the th'an would activate and make a breeze as it moved the air away from the mages' boards.

It was fascinating. They looked like mud-colored taffy, and when they stretched thin, you could see brighter colors here and there like strands of yarn. We did some ~~playing around~~ experiments with different th'an, and then with pouvrin, and the blobs were attracted to both. So I don't care what Terrael says, we've succeeded in making foundational magic visible. We just don't know what it means.

We aren't sure, either, what it means that it takes so long for the blobs to activate th'an or pouvrin. It might be they're moving more slowly than usual, or it might mean there aren't as many of them as before. But no one's been able to come up with a way to prove which of those is true (unless it's something else entirely). Maybe the problem will solve itself if we can work out how to bring the magic back together.

13 Shelet

Good news—the Helvirite forces *did* cross ahead of us and we'll catch up to them just outside Colosse. I really hope the God-Empress's troops aren't there, or that General Garatssen will be smart enough not to engage with them if they are. That's a stupid thing to say. General Garatssen is excellent at what she does. She and Mattiak together are probably another one of our advantages over our enemy.

We're so out of practice with the offensive pouvrin we're almost back to where we were when we started learning them. Cederic was right to insist we work on them. We took our wagons well out of the line of march and practiced starting fires, testing our ranges (I'm still at 600 yards, but some of the others are going to surpass me soon), and they emptied out a wagon and gave it to the mind-movers to practice lifting with. I wish I knew how many battle mages the God-Empress has. If it's only the Viravonian Army's mages, we outnumber them, but we don't know how many other Castaviran forces she's accumulated. Not something I want to worry about, so I won't.

14 Shelet

Battle practice as expected. Terrael is working on a kathana that will magnify the effect of the revelation pouvra and maintain it longer than a mage working the pouvra can. More difficult is figuring out how to experiment on the blobs without them being sucked into the th'an or pouvra to fuel it. Terrael says he has some ideas but doesn't want to talk about them until he's certain, for fear of losing his focus. This probably means it's something abstract and complicated pertaining to Castaviran magic and I wouldn't understand it anyway.

I've been putting off having a conversation with Audryn about her not participating in the fight. The problem is while she's hugely pregnant, she's also one of our most versatile and creative battle mages, and it would be a huge loss if she had to sit out the war. But I feel uncomfortable asking her to risk her baby. On the other hand, if we lose, the God-Empress's troops aren't going to spare her just because she's pregnant. So maybe I'm not thinking about this the right way. I think I'll talk to her and see what *she* wants to do, though knowing her, sitting out the fight hasn't even occurred to her.

15 Shelet

We're only two days from Colosse and the scouts report it hasn't been attacked yet. I think everyone's pushing themselves harder now. Our battle mages seem confident in their abilities, but we're still practicing. We don't want to be complacent. Me, I'm not sure what I will do during

It's really late now, but I have to write this down. Terrael interrupted me just there. He was beyond excited. "I figured it out," he said. "We can do it tomorrow."

"Figured what out?" I said.

"The kathana," he said. "If we create the kathana first and let it absorb as many blobs of foundational magic it needs to activate, then —it has to be th'an—we put the th'an close together in positions where the magic they attract has to cross paths. We can force it to join. And that might—I'm pretty sure about this—teach, maybe that's the wrong word, but teach the rest of the blobs how to join. They look like they're independent, but they're all functionally part of one thing or they wouldn't be able to exert an influence on the world."

"I'll take your word for it," I said. (I actually had to make him repeat himself, and I asked him a lot of questions, before I understood even that much of what he was saying. So what I wrote above is my intelligible version, written so it reflects some of his excitement.)

"I'm right about this, don't worry," he said. "And if we can do this tomorrow—"

"We can restore magic in time for it to make a difference in the war," I said. "What do you need?"

"We can't do this in the wagon, because it will need the biggest kathana circle anyone's ever drawn," he said. "So we'll lag behind the army, but I'm sure we'll be able to catch up quickly. And it's going to take all of us, and we don't have time to practice. But I don't think it will require much practice, just teams of two Castaviran mages working in tandem. And the Balaenic mages who can work the revelation pouvra. I wish we had more of you."

"Then let's gather everyone and get started," I said.

We were tired enough that under normal circumstances, we wouldn't have had the energy to do anything Terrael suggested. But his excitement was infectious, and I certainly felt invigorated enough that the revelation pouvra wasn't difficult. Terrael paired up the Castaviran mages and showed them the th'an they had to do and the order they had to do them in, and explained how the pouvrin came in—it wasn't only the revelation pouvra, it was the walk-through-walls and the mind-moving pouvrin too, and Terrael was right, it was the most complicated kathana I'd ever seen, which I realize isn't saying much, but the Castaviran mages said the same thing.

Writing this has calmed me down. It must be before midnight still, because Cederic hasn't come to bed yet, but I think for once I'd prefer to fall asleep alone. I don't know why. Maybe it's that magic has always been a solitary act for me, and this is the biggest magic I've ever participated in. Which isn't to say I'd kick my husband out of bed if he did come right now, just that I feel the need for solitude and I'm glad to have it right now.

16 Shelet

I wish for once things would just go smoothly for us. I'm tired of writing "I'm so discouraged." So instead I'm going to write "We're making progress" and hope writing it makes it come true.

We (the mages, Terrael, Cederic, and I, Cederic having declared he wasn't about to let me do something potentially dangerous without him nearby) set out before dawn to the place we chose for the kathana circle. I don't think I mentioned we're traveling through thick forests and there aren't a lot of clearings large enough for what we wanted. But yesterday we passed through a little Castaviran settlement, not even big enough to be called a town, and they'd cleared a lot of the forest out for their crops. So we talked to one of the farmers and asked if we could use a fallow field, and he didn't like the idea until Cederic handed over far too much money. Then he didn't care what we did.

We used the mind-moving pouvra to clear a flat space, then the Castaviran mages drew out a double circle and filled the space between them with inert th'an. The Balaenic mages spread out around the outside of the circle, as evenly spaced as we could get— we were supposed to be close enough to spread our arms and barely touch our neighbor's fingertips, but some people have longer arms than others—and settled on the ground in whatever position we felt most comfortable. Then we waited for the Castaviran mages to finish and take up positions standing behind each of us. That was so uncomfortable, feeling hovered over.

The rest of the Castaviran mages, and the Balaenic mages who wouldn't be working the revelation pouvra, stood inside the double circle, which from my position looked like the rim of a giant magnifying glass, which was a good image considering we were trying to magnify foundational magic. Or something.

"Begin," Terrael said, and I started to bend my will to meet the revelation pouvra. This time, I kept my eyes open; I've gotten good enough at it that I'm not easily distracted. So I could watch in an idly curious way as mages began scribing the active th'an and the kathana began to resonate. It was something Terrael had incorporated into the inert th'an so we could immediately tell if it was working—the circle gave off a hum that made the tingling in my fingers and toes weaker. I could see the haze forming around the other mages (you can't see the one you produce yourself, don't know why) and spreading outward in all directions. We'd thought about trying to direct it into the kathana circle, but decided we didn't have time to learn a new technique and risk losing effectiveness. So we made a huge, misty dome that completely surrounded us, each mage's pouvra overlapping with the next. For some reason that didn't thicken the haze at all the way gauze gets more opaque the more layers there are of it. Strange, but fortunate for what we were doing.

We saw the muddy little blobs, ranging from pea-sized to the size of Jeddan's enormous fist, floating and darting around. Some were drawn to the edge of the circle, where mages were still scribing th'an, drawn to it and then stretched out to match the th'an. Others neared the circle where the active th'an were and were repelled by them. It was all fascinating in a dreamlike way, or so I felt from my abstracted state.

Then Terrael said, "Go," and the pairs of mages raised their boards and began scribing. And about twenty of the blobs floating within the circle started quivering as if they were being shaken apart. I knew from Terrael's explanation the mages were scribing pairs of identical th'an, a variation on the mind-moving th'an, on opposite sides of a blob. The idea was that the th'an would absorb magic and activate, then the central blob would be repelled by one and then the other and be unable to escape, and the th'an would guide it toward another blob and force them to unite.

It seemed to be working. I focused on the blob nearest me and watched it, dreamily, as it drifted through the air (this one was about five feet off the ground, because they don't only move in straight lines parallel to the ground, but in all directions at every angle). It seemed to move with purpose now, which made sense because it was basically being driven, and I couldn't help thinking of it as alive, which made me sad for it, but only for a few seconds and then I realized I was being foolish.

It started shaking harder—that's probably what made it seem alive, it seemed to be shivering as if it were cold, or afraid—and I could see flashes of color when it stretched and snapped back together. It was fascinating. The mages were moving it toward another blob that was somewhat lower and closer to me. The other one was shivering too, and then they were shaking so rapidly they looked like sea urchins, spiny and spiky but with the spikes expanding and retracting fast enough they looked like flashes of dull color.

Then they exploded, and those spikes flew in all directions. I shrieked and ducked, the pouvra disintegrated around me, and my face felt as if a hundred needles had pierced it. I reached up to touch my face and felt nothing, and soon the sensation passed. All around me I heard similar shrieks, then Cederic's arms were around me and he was saying, "Are you hurt, Sesskia? Show me your face."

I removed my hand, and he touched my face gently. "You look as if someone has given you freckles," he said. "Does it hurt?"

"Not anymore," I said, rubbing at my face as if I could feel the spots, but my skin felt as smooth as always. "It felt like being jabbed by needles."

"They are fading now," Cederic said. "I cannot see any other marks."

"Did you get it?" Terrael said. I looked up, but he wasn't talking to me, he was kneeling next to Audryn, who held a notebook in her lap.

"I think so," she said, "but I can't tell if it failed or if it just recorded an image that doesn't make sense."

I got up, with Cederic's help, and went to her side. "It's a th'an that collects an image and draws it on a page," Terrael said. "I thought it would be a good idea to record whatever was visible, if anything, and this is much faster than drawing by hand."

"There's some of the blobs, the ones we weren't manipulating," I said, "but what's all this?"

"It appears to be the kathana circle, but something is wrong with it," Cederic said.

"And I don't know why it drew it this way," Audryn said, running her finger over the page. "It's as if it shaded in the spaces and left the th'an and the kathana circle lines empty. It should look like a line drawing."

I walked around to face Audryn so I was looking at the image upside down. "This isn't our kathana circle," I said. "Look. You can see there's another circle just visible in the corners. It's showing a circle *within* our circle."

"But we didn't draw another circle," Audryn said.

"Audryn, may I see that?" Cederic said. Audryn tore it from the notebook and handed it to him. He rotated the page, stared at it for a while, then handed it to me and said, "Pencil, please, and may I use that notebook?"

Audryn gave him the notebook, and Terrael found a stub of a pencil in his trouser pocket. Cederic began sketching. "I am not certain of this, and I would like your confirmation, Terrael, but I believe I know what that kathana is," he said. We waited silently for him to finish drawing. When he finally handed the notebook to Terrael, I said, "What is it?"

"I don't know," Terrael said. Then he blinked, and said, "This can't be right." He snatched the image from my hand and held each at arm's length, rotating them slightly. "It *is* right," he said. "How did you see it?"

"I don't know," Cederic said. "Something about it roused a memory, perhaps. But you agree with me?"

"If you don't tell us what it is," I began.

"I beg you, do not finish that threat," Cederic said with a smile. "It is the divergence kathana. Or some of it."

I gaped at him. "How is that even possible?" I said. "Wasn't it destroyed when it separated the worlds?"

"I don't know," he repeated. "Either it was not, or this is some remnant of it still in existence after a thousand years or more. This image indicates that the fragments of shattered magic were repelled by its lines, which is why the kathana appears inverted."

"If it—but it can't—this explains so much," Terrael said. "If—no, I need to study it more, this isn't enough information—"

"But we don't have *time*," I said. "We're going to face the enemy any day now, and we're needed in battle. Even if this is more important in the long run, it won't do us any good if we're dead."

"You don't need me in the battle, Sesskia," Terrael said. "And Audryn shouldn't fight."

"I'm not an invalid, Terrael," Audryn retorted.

"I wasn't going to keep you out of the fight," I said, "but I think Terrael may need you more than we do. If he discovers anything, he won't be able to do anything about it unless he has a mage to help him."

"You know I'm one of the best battle mages, Sesskia," Audryn said, but it sounded weak.

"You are. And you also work better with Terrael than anyone else," I said. "I'm going to assign you a few more mages, Terrael. We can spare a few. And if you can figure out why the divergence kathana appeared just now, and what we can do with that, the rest of us will join you. I'm sorry, Cederic," I said to him, "but you know how important this is. If we can't stop the magic from diminishing, we won't be able to fight at all."

"I agree," Cederic said, "and I think we should rejoin the army. You will have another day or possibly three to solve this problem before we face Renatha Torenz's army. Let us pray it is enough."

Having passed the word about what we'd discovered, we rejoined the army, catching up to them just after noon. Nobody was in the mood for practicing battle magic; everyone was full of speculation about the divergence kathana and what it meant. We passed the image around so everyone could have a look, and Relania and Terrael got into a heated discussion—it was almost funny because their annoyance was directed at the problem and not at each other—which ended with them huddled over the notebook, Terrael drawing and Relania offering criticisms.

I still don't know what they came up with, because I rode the rest of the day with Cederic and the general staff, me explaining what we'd been doing when we weren't practicing battle magic and then all of us discussing strategies for if the mages had to leave the battle. None of the generals were happy about this, probably because they'd seen battle mages in action and wanted to have the ability to defend against them, but Cederic convinced them that even if they didn't really understand how important our other work was, we were doing the right thing. (I'm annoyed they didn't take their Empress-Consort's word for it, but they are Balaenic generals and this is war and I am, after all, only a woman and know nothing about fighting. I can't *wait* for them to meet Garatssen.)

We'll reach Colosse by tomorrow evening. The scouts still tell us the God-Empress isn't there. That worries me, because from the maps I've seen it's not that far from Duberin to Colosse, so what's she doing that keeps her from advancing? Again I have to tell myself, this is a good thing, this is progress. I wish I had more faith in what I tell myself.

CHAPTER TWENTY

17 Shelet

We reached Colosse late this afternoon to find the Helvirite Army already in position. Actually, they're several miles away from Colosse, and this sparked a huge argument between Mattiak and Raewyn Garatssen. I was riding with him and Cederic when we neared the camp, and heard him swear. "They're out of position," he said, and kicked his horse into a gallop. That left us behind, because I don't trust myself to stay on Thistle at a gallop, and Cederic wasn't going to leave me behind. So we missed the first part of the argument. When we got to the Helvirite camp, we could hear Mattiak's raised voice and it led us to Garatssen's command tent. We couldn't hear her voice at all, though there were pauses in Mattiak's speech that told us someone was responding to him.

"You are stretched too thin and unprepared to meet attack," Mattiak was saying when we entered the tent.

"We're in a perfect defensive position for a small force to engage with a much larger one," Garatssen said in a level voice. They were both speaking Castaviran, and I was impressed that Mattiak had gotten fluent enough to have a loud argument in a language not his own. "Since we had no idea when our reinforcements would arrive and our scouts say the former Empress is less than a day away."

"Reinforcements?" Mattiak bellowed. "You are third our size! If anything, *you* reinforce *us*!"

"It's our capital we're defending, General," Garatssen said. Now her voice was strained. "We're grateful for the assistance—"

"It is capital for both of us, if we win," Mattiak said. "Or do you suggest we are not as dedicated to defend it because we are Balaenic?"

"Generals, please take your seats," Cederic said calmly. "We need to strategize, and quickly, if we are to face the enemy so soon."

Mattiak scowled at Cederic, but found a seat. Garatssen sat down as far from him as she could get. The other generals and Cederic and I joined them. "I see I was unclear as to our combined armies' command structure," Cederic continued. "General Garatssen, I have made Mattiak Tarallan Commander General of the Army of Castavir and Balaen, as most of our forces are Balaenic and do not speak Castaviran. General Tarallan, General Garatssen commands the largest division of the Army and is an experienced leader. I expect the two of you to extend respect to one another and to contribute equally to the plan for our defense of Colosse."

Mattiak scowled again, but nodded. Garatssen's nod was much smoother and respectful. "General Garatssen, I appreciate your preparations," Cederic said. "I take it the strategy will change now the entire Army is present?"

"Of course," Garatssen said. "And we're glad you arrived when you did. We're lucky to have gotten here before Renatha Torenz. The word is that her Army's progress was slowed because she's been 'pacifying' the cities in her path, and she's had to pass through the new forest as well. Even so, we don't have much time. I contend this is the best ground to make our stand—or do you still disagree with that, General Tarallan?"

"No," Mattiak said, reluctantly, "it is as good as we hope for. Forest to south hems in potential for attack on that side, which lets us concentrate on western and northern defenses. We will split Balaenic forces into divisions and assign positions, giving them flexibility of acting independent. We have five divisions, General Garatssen," he said, addressing her, "and I think Helvirite Army serves best by covering west, given that it is larger than any two divisions combined."

"I agree with that, General Tarallan," Garatssen said. "We are equipped to handle a frontal assault, if that's what Renatha Torenz chooses."

"Then we plan our defense," Mattiak said. That was where I chose to make my escape, because there's nothing I can contribute to that kind of planning. I hope Mattiak and Garatssen can learn to get along. I know he can overcome his prejudices if he tries, but I don't know how much of a problem Garatssen's obvious competence will be—I don't *think* he's the sort of person who feels threatened by anyone as good as he is, but with her being a woman, I don't know.

I checked on Terrael's group briefly, making sure they had what they needed. They're set up pretty far back from the rest of our camp, so the fighting won't interrupt them. Terrael was confident but distracted, which told me he was deep in thought about the problem. That was a relief.

Then I went back to where the rest of our mages waited and divided them, with Jeddan's help, into five groups and told them which division they'd report to in the morning (not six, because the Helvirite Army has its own battle mages, and that reminds me I have to go talk to them and make sure they understand magic really is diminishing and it's not just them). Everyone was very alert and determined to make a difference, even the Balaenics who don't have a personal attachment to Colosse. I didn't assign Jeddan or myself to one of the groups, reasoning we might be needed elsewhere, and I won't know that for sure until I've talked to Mattiak in the morning. I figure that's enough time for them to decide on a strategy and give me our instructions.

I hate going to war. But I hate even more the thought of the God-Empress overrunning all of us and then Colosse. And I'm so worried we're (the mages) going to be completely ineffectual, if magic continues to diminish. Right now I'm praying Terrael's group comes up with a solution soon enough to benefit us.

18 Shelet

We've been fighting for maybe eight hours and it's dark enough that the enemy's withdrawn for now. They did exactly as Mattiak and Garatssen predicted—made assaults on the north and south like a giant pincer, trying to envelop us. So far we've been successful at driving them off. The southern forces (Gray and Brown) even managed to push them back against the forest—those ones withdrew quickly. Kalanik says the Blue Army, which is on the west in front of the Helvirite Army, barely saw any fighting at all. Garatssen says this will likely change in the coming days, as soon as they feel they've softened us up.

I stayed with the Helvirite Army and felt totally useless all day, since nobody passed the Blue Army to reach us. Mattiak says it's a deep defense, though I'm not sure what that means other than they aren't strung out along a single thin line. I spent a lot of time going back and forth between Terrael's group, flitting until I was sick of it. They're still not making progress. I eventually had to stop going there because I was so impatient I was afraid I might shout at them. I tried the binding pouvra while one of the mages was working the revelation pouvra—still nothing. I felt even more useless after that.

19 Shelet, early

Exhausted. The God-Empress started hammering on the Blue Army two hours ago even though it was still full dark—war wagons and mages summoning fire. I went to join the Blue Army mages and we managed to disable most of the war wagons, but the Blue Army is in shambles and we're not sure they'll be prepared to meet a full assault at dawn, which is almost certainly what's going to happen. Lots of shifting around, lots of me reassigning mages. It's not much comfort to know the enemy doesn't outnumber us by a lot, given how much of an advantage the war wagons give them.

I have to sleep for a while now. I know they need me, but I don't have any more to give right now. Working pouvrin feels like hauling a ship into dry dock with a rope and my own two hands and nothing else.

Hah. I must be lightheaded, because I just imagined those little blobs of magic actually being alive, and me coaxing them with bread-crumbs like they were ducks.

19 Shelet, forty minutes later

Damn. I *was* just lightheaded. The stupid blobs aren't alive, and we can't coax them to move any faster. Or, we sort of can, but it takes so much magic to do so it's a net loss. Now I really am going to sleep.

19 Shelet, afternoon

Taking advantage of a lull in the fighting to eat something and write for a bit. I haven't seen Cederic for a while, but I know he's still at the back of the Helvirite Army since I'm near the front. We can't risk both of us. (Cederic doesn't want to risk *either* of us, but he knows where I'm needed. I should probably find him and reassure him I'm all right.)

The assault shifted this morning to the western position. The God-Empress is still sending her troops out on both sides in that pincer formation, trying to engulf us and take the center from behind, but those divisions are all holding firm. The Blue Army, to my surprise, is also holding firm, though they've moved back some-what and the Helvirite Army has moved forward some. As exhausting as working magic is, our mages are still effective, can still act in concert unlike the God-Empress's battle mages, and morale is high. I haven't been to talk to Terrael today—no time. Maybe I'll do that after I eat and find Cederic.

19 Shelet, sundown

Cederic was happy enough to see me I know he'd been close to going out to look for me himself. "Please come to me every four or five hours," he said after hugging me so tightly it almost hurt. "I need to know you are not dead."

"I will, if I can," I said.

"That is not reassuring," he said.

"I mean I can't leave the battle if I'm personally engaged in a fight," I said. "I'll return as often as I can."

"I wish I could go with you," he said.

"You could visit Terrael," I said, "if you need something to distract you. And I'm sure you'd be more useful there than on the front lines."

"I dislike feeling helpless, Sesskia," he said, but he came with me to talk to Terrael. I wish he'd been able to give me better news, but they still hadn't made any progress; everything they try just soaks up magic and can't direct it anywhere. I'm so close to telling him to give it up and bringing our mages forward to help in the battle. But we need this. It's taking us far too long to work pouvrin, and the Castaviran mages are having to scribe th'an several times before they'll activate. It's small comfort the enemy battle mages are having the same difficulties.

19 Shelet, after dinner

After I wrote the last and the fighting stopped for the night, Cederic and I had dinner and then he said, "I have decided to aid Terrael in his efforts. I am little more than a figurehead here, and I think I have been stupid not to remember I am still Kilios and should not be wasting those talents."

That eased the knot in my stomach quite a bit. "I'll join you," I said. We found Terrael, who was in the middle of his own meal and very happy to see us.

"I haven't wanted to draw you away from your other duties, Cederic," he said, "but honestly, I could use your perspective." He set his plate aside and led us to where they'd laid out the kathana circle. It's not so big as the one we drew in that field, but it's still big, and I know it took them a long time to make it. They dug a shallow trench about two inches wide and filled it with scrap metal, forks and coins and some pewter cups someone managed to cut into strips. Then they used th'an to melt everything until it ran together. That means it's mottled silver and copper and gold and has this strange beauty to it. Terrael, of course, only cares that it's circular and uninterrupted.

"We draw the th'an as thickly as we can around the circle, leaving only the smallest gaps," Terrael said, kneeling down and drawing a few th'an on the ring as an example. "It's like penning the magic inside the circle. When they activate, they repel the magic. It's like filling a cup with water and then freezing it; if you try to add more water, it just runs off. Then we try as many th'an and pouvrin as we can to make the magic come together. But the best we can do is get them to deflect each other. At worst, the th'an and pouvrin absorb the magic and activate. Eventually we've used it all up and have to start over. But we've eliminated dozens of possibilities. I haven't given up hope."

"Is it possible to attract more magic before...penning it?" Cederic said. "If it masses thickly enough—"

"It's too thin on the ground," Terrael said. "We've found we can attract it with pouvrin by working one and letting it draw magic to it, then releasing it before the magic can activate it. But it takes so long, by the time we've collected some magic, more of it has drifted away."

"I have some ideas for that," Cederic said. "I apologize for not joining you sooner. I am afraid you will have to bear with me as I ask questions for which you have already found solutions."

"You'll see things none of the rest of us have seen, though," Terrael said, grinning, "and it really is only a matter of time."

I was going to stay with them, but I was so tired—I'm falling asleep as I write this—so I left the two geniuses at work and came back to our tent. I can hear the sound of the remaining war wagons going off and wish we had some of our own. Garatssen hadn't even heard of them. I guess they're a new weapon only the main army has. The main army and the Viravonian Army, that is.

I wish I knew what was going on down there. We haven't been able to decide what to do about Viravon when this is all over. Cederic wants us to give them independence, which I'd agree with if not for the Balaenic cities within Viravon's borders, especially Calassmir, who are going to have a hard enough time with a new ruler of their own country without being told they're now part of a completely different one.

I don't think we're going to win.

I don't think we're going to succeed at bringing magic together.

I can only admit this in the privacy of these pages, but I feel so discouraged. Maybe it's being so tired all the time, but it feels as if the

God-Empress has endless troops to pour into this attack and it's only a matter of time before we're overwhelmed. But I'm going to put on a brave face and be confident. These people need to know their rulers have faith in them and in our cause. And I do. I'm just not sure faith is enough.

20 Shelet, noon

Keonn collapsed this morning and won't wake up. Two other mages succumbed an hour later. I made everyone stop for a rest, sent runners to the other armies with the same instruction and told them to send any mages who collapsed to the rear of the Helvirite Army for care. I really just want them under my eye because if this means they're permanently unable to work magic, I want to know about it. Enemy mages still pounding away, damn them.

20 Shelet, evening

I sent everyone back to the front (fronts) with more instructions: no more than half an hour working magic of any kind, then half an hour rest and something to eat. I have no idea if it will help at all. Three more mages collapsed. None of them have woken yet, though the surgeons assure me their breathing and heartrates are normal.

I didn't do any magic this afternoon, just observed the mages in my group. I never realized before that some of them are struggling less than others. It's as if they're—I don't know what to call it. Stronger, I think, because it reminds me of how some people (Jeddan) can lift the corner of a laden wagon off the ground, and others (me) are lucky to be able to haul a fifty-pound backpack, well-balanced, for more than a mile or two without becoming exhausted. At any rate, I think there's a connection between that strength and who's collapsing, as if people are simply coming to the end of what they can handle and then trying to exert themselves past that. I wish I knew if there were some signal that could tell someone she's reaching that point, but no one seems to know. The best I can do is make them rest frequently and hope they're replenishing themselves, as if this really were a question of physical endurance, which I'm not convinced is true.

Went to see Terrael and found Cederic there too, but neither of them had much attention to spare. Cederic said they were making progress, and I know he wouldn't lie to me, but Terrael's been saying the same thing and he wouldn't lie to me either and damn it we're *not making progress.*

21 Shelet, afternoon

So very tired. The northern flank—the Black Army, I mean—collapsed under the assault and let the God-Empress's troops past. The Green Army was barely able to hold until the Helvirites came charging in to the rescue, at which point the main force of the God-Empress's army made a push through the center. We were able to repel them, but the northern front is barely holding and has been pushed back by that arm of the pincer. Five more mages collapsed during the assault, and I pushed myself and the others to our limits. Found out the closer we are to each other, the weaker we get, and I realized it's because we were using up each other's supplies of local magic. So that's it for concentrated attacks in unison. Small comfort that my fires are as large and devastating as ever and Saemon's trick of throwing battle mages into each other still works. He's more cautious than the rest of us about exerting himself, but then he's already collapsed once in battle and knows

Oh, I'm so stupid. I should have him explain how to know what it feels like when you're reaching your limit.

22 Shelet

Cederic and Terrael had me try the binding pouvra again. They seem convinced, since it's the only magic that incorporates both Castaviran and Balaenic (being a pouvra based on th'an) it's more likely to have the right effect. So tonight after dinner I stood in the middle of the kathana circle and watched the blobs of magic become visible around me. They really are ugly. I hope the restored magic is prettier.

"All right, Sesskia, work the, mmm, the walk-through-walls pouvra, then release it before it activates," Terrael said. I did as he asked and watched the blobs drift toward me. It's strange to keep the shape of a pouvra inside you without it doing anything, like when you tug on your hair but not hard enough for it to hurt, but it's everywhere. I released it before any of the blobs could reach me and saw them continue to drift through my body. It looks strange, but you can't feel anything.

"Now," Cederic said. All the mages began scribbling th'an on the metal circle as fast as they could. Blobs floated in that direction both from inside and outside the circle, and soon it began to glow, here and there, until the metal was lit softly along its whole circumference, like moonlight. I saw muddy blobs bouncing off it and off each other—or near each other; they still never touch.

"Sesskia," Cederic said, "you will need to work the binding pouvra and maintain it for as long as possible."

"It will just activate when the magic touches it. Or not activate, since it doesn't do anything," I said.

"Try to see it not as the fire pouvra, but the walk-through-walls pouvra," he said. "Make it into a container."

"I don't know if that's possible," I said, but I bent my will to the pouvra and felt it take shape around me. Blobs drifted in my direction and I could feel it when they reached me, felt the pouvra absorb them. I kept myself relaxed, though the temptation to exert my will was enormous. I'm so impatient for success I want to *make* it happen, and I know that's not how pouvrin work. The pouvra continued to absorb magic and the pressure of being tugged on from all directions increased. "I can't," I began, and the pouvra fell apart without doing anything. Just like it always does.

I shook my tingling fingers and toes out and said, "I'm sorry. I don't know how to do any better than that. If I try to force it, it will only fall apart faster."

Cederic rubbed out some of the th'an and the silvery light vanished. "We need to try once more," he said, "this time with the concealment pouvra."

So we repeated the whole thing, and this time I couldn't keep the pouvra from activating once the first magic touched it. I was discouraged, but Cederic and Terrael seemed pleased. "I promise we've learned something important," Terrael told me, "but if I try to explain it to you, you'll just soak my head again."

"If I had any energy left," I said, but it cheered me up. So I'm going to sleep now, and hope things look better in the morning.

23 Shelet, afternoon

Cederic,

I hope you never see this letter. With luck, I'll be back in a few hours, and I'll tear this page out and destroy it. But if, as you've often put it, my God-given reserves of luck have finally run out, I want you to know why I did this.

For a long time, I believed the former God-Empress's death wasn't my responsibility. That there were others who could make it happen, and that it wouldn't keep her generals from continuing to fight. But this morning I stood and looked out at her banner in the middle of her army, and I thought about why we're fighting this war. Someone's going to win, and that person will rule our two countries—our unified country.

I know from what Mattiak said that we're still evenly matched, so there's no way to know what will happen in the next few days. But if we lose—I'm trying not to be superstitious about writing that—an evil woman is going to take the throne, and our country is going to suffer. And I can't let that happen.

If the God-Empress is dead, it will throw her generals into enough confusion you'll be able to defeat them. All those excuses I made are no longer valid. Right now I'm the only one who can safely cross this battlefield and get close enough to her to kill her. And I'm probably the only one who can survive doing it.

I know you don't think I'm a killer—truthfully, I don't think I am either. But I am the Empress-Consort, and this is how I can serve our country. Serve all those people who don't deserve to be ruled by a madwoman. So it's what I'm going to do.

I know what you're thinking, and it occurred to me too: if magic is so hard to work, I might not have the ability to conceal myself *and* work the see-inside and mind-moving pouvrin. That's the chance I have to take. I'm still the strongest mage we have, and if anyone can manage it, I can. I don't think that's bragging. You know I always think things through, and I'm confident that I'm coming back from this. I believe in preparing for the worst, and I know this letter represents the worst.

I'm leaving all my books behind, just in case. I know someday you'll be able to read Balaenic, and I hope you'll read this record and it will give you comfort, as much as that's possible. Every moment of our life together is in these pages, right from the first time we met and you twisted my arm behind my back and looked so smug and superior I wanted to slap you.

All those first times—I'm sorry it also has our last times, and that I didn't know they were last times. I didn't know when I kissed you this morning before going to the front it would be the last kiss. I'm sorry the last thing I said to you was "You have butter on your chin." So this can be my last thing, instead: I love you. I wish I could elaborate on that, but I think you already know everything I mean, and if I write anything else it will sound stupid. So it's just—I love you.

Rule wisely. Be patient. Never forget me.

Sesskia

CHAPTER TWENTY-ONE

Karoli 27th

I should not be writing this in Sesskia's diary, in a language she cannot read, but I must do something or run mad. Though this is, in a sense, a violation of her privacy, I cannot help but think that this, too, is part of her record, ~~and someday~~

I did not realize Sesskia was gone until she was brought to the command tent. We had separated as usual that morning, I to join Terrayel and Audryn at the kathana circle, she to meet with her mages at the front of the western advance. I am never happy to see her go into danger, but we both knew if we did not win this war, having remained safely out of the fighting would not matter.

It is hard, now, to remember how optimistic we—Terrayel's mages —were that morning. We had narrowed our search for pouvrin that could affect the foundational magic to the binding pouvra invented by Sesskia, and were prepared to experiment with it. We believed maintaining it for extended periods of time, longer than we previously have, would enhance the collection of magic and allow its direct manipulation. I wish with all my heart I had insisted on Sesskia returning with me, as she is the most experienced with that pouvra, but I rejected what I knew was a selfish impulse to keep her near me. How differently things would have transpired!

The first we at the back knew of any unusual events was at nearly sunset, when we heard a tremendous explosion, followed shortly afterward by a wave of force so powerful we could not stand against it. We immediately left our camp and went to join Generals Tarallan and Garatsen where they stood observing the enemy. We saw no smoke, no sign of fire or explosion, only a great deal of activity, soldiers fleeing in all directions except toward Colosse. Those troops attacking on the west seemed confused, and our armies were taking advantage of that confusion to press them hard. As we watched, Renatha Torenz's army broke and fled, and General Tarallan shouted orders that our soldiers were to pursue cautiously, in case this was a ruse meant to draw the defenders out where they could be overcome.

I wish I had known to scribe the memory kathana. I have no idea how Sesskia was able to record conversations so accurately; my memory is not nearly as good as hers is. So I can only summarize: General Tarallan explained later that our armies moved forward and to both sides, encircling the north and south pincers and cutting those troops off from their fellows. Between that and the demoralizing retreat of the main body of their army, those troops immediately surrendered and were taken prisoner. The Blue Army pursued Renatha Torenz's forces, while the Helvirite Army remained to defend the city.

I, of course, was required to stay behind. My impatience at that came both from my eagerness to *do* something as well as my fears for Sesskia, whom I believed to be with the Blue Army, as I had heard General Tarallan give orders for all the mages to join in the pursuit.

We received word shortly afterward that the army had in fact been routed, and several officers had been captured, but nothing of Renatha Torenz (this was before Sesskia and the madwoman were discovered) or Garran Clendessar. I believe him to be still in Venetry, and I hope it does not mean we will have to lay siege to that city. The Gray Army has been sent to investigate the situation at Venetry, and we will not know for days yet what must happen.

Nor do we know what the remaining Castaviran—that is, Renatha Torenz's officers who remain free will do. They do not have the resources to come against us, but most of them realize their lives are forfeit for following her. I intend to pardon as many as I can; I do not wish my reign to begin in more blood than it already has. Gael Regates surrendered without a fight. I wish I could spare her life.

Then General Tarallan returned, bearing Sesskia in his arms, and at first I thought her dead and felt as if I had been stabbed through the heart. Learning the truth, that she was merely unconscious, was a profound relief. I could not have guessed how much despair her condition would leave me in.

I left her with the surgeons and healers so I could investigate the place where she was found. It looks like a crater, but one with no depression; there are simply lines some twenty or thirty feet long radiating from the center. Near this lay the body of Renatha Torenz, blackened and contorted as if something had tried to escape her body in all directions at once. Three other bodies similarly blackened lay just outside the crater.

I ordered Renatha Torenz's body returned to Colosse for examination, though thus far no one has been able to tell what actually killed her. It was nearly twenty-seven hours before I returned to Sesskia's side and found the surgeons and healers unable to tell me why she is unconscious or when she might wake from that state. There is nothing any of them can do for her, because her body is not damaged, and magic no longer works.

We have tried everything we can, thousands of th'an, dozens of pouvrin, and they simply will not activate. Either the magic has finally dissipated to a point we can no longer harness it, or it has stopped responding to our efforts, or the fragments of the divergence kathana have once again exerted their power over it, but magic certainly does not work. And without magic, we cannot even discover why. Terrayel's hypothesis is that whatever explosion occurred in the enemy camp is related to this loss, but he cannot prove it; all we know is, according to General Tarallan, Sesskia was at the heart of it.

It makes me laugh to think of it. Sesskia always did find a way to put herself at the center of whatever crisis might occur, regardless of the danger. Would that I could have protected her—but she would not be who she is if she did not risk herself in helping others. If she was in the enemy camp, it was almost certainly because she believed her actions would stop this war, and I suspect—I fear—she was attempting to defeat Renatha Torenz personally. Apparently she succeeded. I should be grateful it was not at the cost of her life, but I can only feel anger and sorrow that she is not beside me now, awake and strong. My foundation.

It has been three days since she was found at the center of the devastation. She has not woken, has not stirred no matter what we do to try to rouse her. Yet she does not exhibit any of the symptoms of someone who has fallen into an unnatural slumber; she breathes normally, her flesh is rosy and not sunken with dehydration, and when we lift her eyelids her pupils contract as they should. She simply will not wake up. I refuse to believe she will never wake again.

Karoli 28th

I wish I were yet only a man of no rank who might reasonably spend all his days sitting by his wife's bedside, holding her hand and speaking softly to her in the hope she might hear and return from whatever distant land her mind wanders in.

My visits to Sesskia are rare, because pulling this new nation together requires so much of my attention. Unrest has erupted in the southeast and the west, the army has moved to defend our western border from the Fensadderian refugees, and reconstructing a government that satisfies the citizenry and the former rulers of both countries is proving even more difficult than we imagined, which means it is nearly impossible. These are the things I tell Sesskia when I sit with her, and try not to think that my stories may be driving her further away, for who would willingly embrace such a world?

I have sent messengers to Endellavir, explaining the situation and requesting Lelaina's allegiance. I hope she will see sense now Renatha Torenz no longer holds power. If she does not, I will be forced to send the Brown and Gray Armies to take command of the Endellaviran forces, because all our troops are needed to put down the insurrection Arron Domenessar is at the heart of. He is raising the southeast in his own name, and although he has few forces, he is inciting rebellion among the people and I am afraid we will be forced to turn our weapons on them. I have sent more messengers to Lirilla and Garwin, demanding their allegiance in the name of Sesskia Daressar. They do not need to know her current condition.

We have yet to make contact with anyone in Viravon who can speak for the country. Their King, Wilsum Peletor, has been in hiding for years; I hope he will see my sincerity in wishing to meet with him. I think he will be unhappy with the proposal I will make, but Viravon's independence can only come at a price. I have no idea what he will choose.

Karoli 30th

Sesskia remains unconscious but healthy despite not having eaten for a week. My prayers are more frequent and more fervent these days. I have never been much for religion, feeling the discontinuity between the ecclesiastical rank bestowed on me by virtue of my magical talent and the sense that a true priest should perhaps have a vocation, but I have always believed in the existence of God.

I have also always wondered how such a being could allow someone like Renatha Torenz to continue to falsely claim divinity, and have concluded God gives us challenges to see what we will make of them. What I am supposed to make of the challenge that is the loss of my wife, however temporary, eludes me. Perhaps I am wrong, and there is no God, and I pray simply because I can do nothing else. But now the former Empress is gone, I feel as if my "priesthood" is more real than I had imagined.

I wish I could read this aloud to Sesskia, but I fear what might happen if my worries and doubts were overheard. The Emperor cannot indulge in weakness, even though this Emperor's strength lies silent and unmoving in this bed. I wish I could curl up next to her—I would certainly sleep better than I do now—but that would also show weakness, so I sit with her for the half-hour that is all I can spare, and write, and pray.

Edmonti 1st

Today I announced the redistricting of our combined countries. No more Castaviran Empire, no more Balaen. The new Empire is divided into four Kingdoms, which are further divided into districts centered on major cities, all of which are to be governed by the men and women who were formerly Lords Governor or consuls. This has proven to be the most difficult of all the tasks my government has faced, for there are not enough positions of responsibility for everyone who was formerly a ruler. Some of them, such as Brisson Rialen, were clearly unfit to govern and have been pensioned off, others have been offered positions on my new Council, but there are some for whom there is simply nothing, and I deeply regret not being able to reward all of those who deserve it.

We have taken the names for our new countries from an old language Terrayel says comes from as close to the time when our worlds were united as anyone can understand. Caelan Crossar governs in Venetry as king of Tenerrin, which encompasses the northwest. Granea Amelessar rules as queen in Calderrin, what used to be Endellavir in the northeast. Lelaina stepped down without a fight. She and I both know I cannot allow anyone who did not support my claim to the Imperial throne to continue to rule. I am considering naming her to my Council, because I would regret losing her advice completely.

Dugan continues to rule in the southeast, though as king of Medirrin rather than Helviran. I have named Morton Taisatus to rule in Davarrin, the southwestern part of the Empire, as I have decided there will be no consul in Colosse. Two Balaenic and two Castaviran rulers, though I have not given up hope of finding Wilsum Peletor and making a final disposition in the matter of Viravon. I long for the day when we will no longer make the distinction, but I am afraid it will not happen in my lifetime, nor that of my

Sesskia, wake soon.

Edmonti 4th

I will no doubt go down in history as the most autocratic ruler of the Essarian Empire. It is a name that means "unity," and at the moment it feels like wishful thinking. We have had to pacify Barrekel in order to gain access to its printing press, because our kathanas, of course, do not work, and it is essential we send word throughout the Empire of new laws, new rulers, new decisions...I should not be grateful Arron Domenessar was killed in the fighting near Garwin, but I shudder to imagine how difficult our task would have been had he lived to stir up resistance in his city.

Of course everything must be printed in two languages, which means devising new...they appear to be engravings, but raised rather than incised, with each piece representing a single letter so they can be arranged and rearranged endlessly. Naturally they had none of these in the Castaviran alphabet, which means yet another task to be performed before many others become possible.

Master Ustanz and her corps of translators have spread throughout the Empire, explaining, encouraging, teaching, even fighting on occasion. It will be years before the people accept the reality that is our new world, and those years will be ones in which I will have to demand obedience to these new laws that will allow us to live together in peace. I think I will not be a well-loved Emperor. I take heart in how most of the Empire's rulers, Caelan Crossar included, are united in trying to bring this country together. They do not always agree, and some of them are more self-centered than I would like, but they all understand the need for...unity.

Mattiak Tarallan and Raiwyn Garatsen are frequently at one another's throats. I wonder if there is not something else going on beneath that antagonism. General Tarallan cannot stop watching General Garatsen, who in turn ignores him so pointedly it is clear she is very aware of his presence. I hope the two of them will find their way to a better understanding, and not only because I would like General Tarallan to stop looking at my wife as if she is his unattainable hope of happiness. Though he has not been to see her, to my knowledge, since the day he brought her back to me. Sesskia often said to me she wished he might find someone who would love him as she did not. She is far more generous of spirit than I.

Sesskia's condition has not changed. Roda Daressar sits with her often, which eases my mind because I do not like leaving her alone, even if she does not realize it. I have asked Roda to serve on my Council and she declined the honor, thanked me for it, and said she would prefer to wait until Sesskia wakes to make any decisions about her future. I have instructed Caelan Crossar to restore her family's title and status and to discover if Roda has fortune or property in the Daressar name. He didn't argue.

Edmonti 5th

I have decided a new royal residence will be constructed rather than housing my family in the old palace. We still have concerns about assassination attempts, and the palace warren is indefensible against such attacks. However, I have ordered its reconstruction to move forward, though I do not yet know to what use we will put it. Perhaps something will suggest itself when we know how much can be reclaimed.

I have for the moment claimed a residence near Morton's former home, a large mansion with plenty of room not only for myself and Sesskia but for everything I need in my role as Emperor. Perce Aselfos approved of the choice and is, I think, relieved that we will not be living in the palace, even though I am certain he regrets losing his secret passages. Part of me would like to make this our permanent home, but it will be better if we live somewhere central, where we will not be accused of partiality toward the wealthy (though we are one of the wealthy, so I am not certain of the logic of that choice). And I think Sesskia should have some say in the decision. Any day now, she will wake.

Edmonti 6th

We brought Sesskia from the Firtha thanest to our new home, since the healers cannot do anything for her. If anyone tries to harm her, she will be safer here, with Aselfos's men and women watching for danger. And I can visit her more often, which was my true reason.

Edmonti 7th

The Gray Army returned with Garran Clendessar and a handful of Renatha Torenz's generals. The former King of Balaen was brought before me this morning. He was utterly terrified and begged for his life in a way that embarrassed all of those present. I ordered him confined, though not in a cell, and am trying to decide what his fate should be. It should be obvious: he raised arms against his rightful Emperor, even if he did so in defense of his own rank, and as a potential rallying point, he is dangerous. But I think it is unlikely anyone would choose to rally around him, unless someone like Caelan Crossar decided to use him as a figurehead. I fear I will have to have him executed.

I wish I had Sesskia's advice right now. She is capable of great generosity and yet can see to the heart of what is just and right. I can only see that quivering, sobbing figure, and try to find a way to spare him when my own heart is telling me it is impossible. At least this is a decision I can defer until a later time. We are not prepared to hold trials as yet.

The Council has become fractious lately, with a few of its members arguing over precedence, Balaenic and Castaviran, and others being drawn into the squabbles until I am forced to raise my voice to end the "debates." We waste time that should be spent making decisions about how to defend ourselves against the Fensadderian wars that threaten to spill over our western border. No one knows what changes may have occurred there, as in Castavir that territory was mostly unoccupied desert, but I am told Fensadderius has been at war with itself for a generation and I can't imagine the convergence lessened its strife.

General Tarallan and General Garatsen have gone from antagonism to a peculiar kind of mutual disinterest, but I have seen them look at one another and I conclude they have become lovers. I am not certain why they think they need to conceal this—it is certainly no Castaviran custom, and I don't believe it is Balaenic either. It may have something to do with their military ranks, since General Tarallan is nominally her superior. In any case, I don't think I should interfere, but I hope I can wish them joy of their union soon.

I slept in Sesskia's bed last night and was driven from it in the predawn hours by nightmares of waking to find myself lying with a corpse. Dear God, if you are listening, let her wake soon.

Edmonti 12th

I meet with Terrayel and Jeddan every evening to learn of their progress in discovering what has happened to our magic. I am so grateful for their friendship, grateful to Sesskia for teaching me how to gain it. Terrayel is optimistic, Jeddan more pragmatic, but neither of them can tell me any more than we knew from the start: no form of magic works anymore. The Balaenic mages, in attempting to work pouvrin, report seeing strange colors like endless ribbons when they bend their will, but trying to lay hold of the ribbons is futile, for they simply slip away from their grasp. No one knows more than this.

The mages are currently employed in teaching their Castaviran fellows to fall into the meditative state necessary to perceive the ribbons. Experimentation shows the restriction on using magic that limits it to those with green-gray eyes is still in force, as only those mages are capable of perceiving the ribbons. Terrayel remains undismayed by this and says it was to be expected, and encourages me to take heart in this evidence that magic does still exist. He and Jeddan are convinced that with time, they will solve this new mystery. They are both very determined men, and I have faith

I have no faith. Sesskia's unnatural slumber is the only sign that there is magic left in the world at all, for what else could cause an unconsciousness in which the victim does not eat or drink or urinate, nevertheless remains not only alive, but healthy? She will never wake, we will never find the answers, and the strife in Fensaddarius will cross the borders of our newborn Empire and tear apart the fragile consensus we have built. Unless the discord on my Council and the dissatisfaction of those who feel entitled to rank and privilege tear us apart first.

I cannot do this alone. I have to do this alone.

Edmonti 14th

The last Council meeting nearly ended in violence. I do not think it is prideful to say that anyone but I would not have been able to control the fractious members of the Council who are more interested in personal power than in serving this country. I am ashamed to write that I lost my temper—that I am under enormous pressure is no excuse—but it was, to my surprise, the most effective thing I could have done: I reminded them all that they serve at my sufferance, that I have the power to eject any or all of them from the Council, and that I will not tolerate disrespect of my office or my person.

Then I warned the three worst offenders that if they persisted in such behaviors, I would strip them not only of their Council positions but of their personal rank and fortune. I am, again, ashamed to admit I would like one or more of them to disobey, because it felt good to release some of the pain and sorrow I feel as anger. I am reasonably certain I will have to carry out that threat soon. I intended to make the transition of power easier by giving authority to as many of the former rulers as possible, but I see now too many of them are like Dainen Radryntor (who is *not* a Council member), obsessed with maintaining their old power and uninterested in building consensus. Today was the only warning I will give them.

Sesskia continues healthy and unconscious. I visit her more frequently now, and struggle not to make it even more frequently than I do. Sometimes I imagine grabbing her by the shoulders and shaking her, screaming her name to wake her, and at those times I pace up and down the stairs of this mansion, pushing my body to exhaustion. I miss her so much.

Edmonti 18th

I dismissed five Council members today. I discovered they had been meeting secretly to collude in gaining power over the Council and, ultimately, over me. I should perhaps be pleased that three of them were Castaviran and two Balaenic, and therefore they were capable of putting aside their bigotries to unite against me, but I am still too angry to take pleasure from any part of this idiocy.

I had them put under house arrest and will have to investigate the situation to see if it was actual treason they plotted or simple greed. In any case, they will lose their titles and political positions, and although I have reconsidered my earlier threat to take their fortunes as well—I think exercising that power against any who are not convicted traitors will cause outrage even among my supporters—I will certainly fine them. And then I will have to watch them carefully, guard against them raising a rebellion which I have no time to put down, and that will be just one more thing for me to fret myself to sleep over.

Still no change in Sesskia's condition. When I sit with her, I pretend she is awake and can respond to my whispered conversation. I can almost hear

CHAPTER TWENTY-TWO

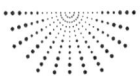

15 Dorinet

Cederic wants me to record this somewhere public, because it's an important part of how the world is now, but I'm going to write it down here first, because it happened to me and that makes it mine before it belongs to anyone else.

~~This morning~~ On the morning of 23 Shelet (it feels like it was just this morning—I can't believe I was unconscious for three weeks) I had breakfast with Cederic and then went to where I could look across the battlefield. Nobody had clashed yet, not where I was, and it was unnaturally still. All I could hear was the sound of our battle standards snapping in the wind, which was a little nippy, and the murmurs of people talking nearby. It didn't feel like war. It felt like it does when you're on the road and you wake up before everyone else and the light is somehow different. I saw the God-Empress's banner in the distance, right next to the Castaviran ones, and I strained but I couldn't make out individuals at that distance. Not that I expected to see the God-Empress. I figured she stayed well back from the fighting. I wondered if the King was with her. I wondered what she thought when she looked at us. Something insane, probably.

Then everything happened at once, soldiers shouting and racing out to meet the enemy. Things had gotten bad enough for the mages that we could only manage one attack before we had to stop and wait for—all right, I called it the magic coming back to us, like it was a herd of sheep and we drove them away every time we pulled a sheep out of the flock (I don't know which is right, herd or flock) and had to wait for them to come running back. I don't care if Terrael thinks that's stupid. I wish I'd had enough magic to soak his head.

Anyway. We could each do one blast of fire, or hurl one projectile, and then we had to wait ten or twenty minutes before we could do it again. I ended up not doing any magic, just going down the line of mages and reassuring them. Not something I ever imagined myself doing, but then none of that was something I'd pictured for myself. But all the time I kept looking out at that banner with the falcon head and the glyphs, and picturing the God-Empress directing her troops.

And I realized we were thinking about this the wrong way. I'd thought about killing the God-Empress before and decided against it not only because I'm not a killer, but because it wouldn't have made a difference. Her generals would still be in a position to choose a new God-Emperor and continue to attack. But the point wasn't just to win the war. The reason we were fighting was so *Renatha Torenz* couldn't rule both countries.

And she couldn't rule anything if she were dead.

I turned that thought over and over in my head for a couple of hours, waiting for my brain to decide it was a ridiculous idea and get rid of it. But it never went away. Yes, I wanted us to win because I think Cederic is the best choice for Emperor. But what I really wanted—what I was increasingly convinced we needed—was a guarantee the *worst* choice couldn't take the throne. Even if the God-Empress's death didn't throw her army into confusion (and I wasn't totally convinced it wouldn't do this) it would eliminate the one outcome that would be fatal for the new Empire. And once I realized I was right, I also knew I was the only person who could make it happen. Not even Nessan could make it across that battlefield unharmed. Just me.

The idea made me so sick I couldn't eat lunch. I went off by myself and stood where I could see the banner. I'd convinced myself I couldn't deliberately kill anyone else with the see-inside and mind-moving pouvrin; I'd even come to think of them as healing pouvrin rather than for assassination. But the more I thought about it, the more convinced I became that if I were able to do it at all, it would be to save my country. All those people, even the ones who didn't give us allegiance yet, didn't deserve to be ruled by a woman who thought of them as things, and when I was crowned I'd sworn, as Cederic did, to serve the people.

It felt so stupid, thinking in such grand terms, so I looked out over the fighting at the soldiers, to where there was a knot of stillness in the middle of the battle. It was too distant, and too muddled, for me to make out individuals, but there was a place where no one was moving, and it looked strange against the turbulence of the battle. I don't know why those men weren't fighting there, but I thought *I can just about manage to remember I'm doing it for them* and that gave me the resolve I needed.

So I went back and wrote Cederic that letter—I haven't decided yet whether to tear it out, since on the one hand, he never had to read it, but on the other, he did think I was almost dead...I don't know. But I wrote the letter in our tent, and then I left the books on our bed so he'd see them right away, and went back through the camp to the south, where the fighting hasn't been as heavy.

(Speaking of heavy, I didn't realize how much those books weighed until I wasn't carrying them anymore. They're not big, not more than the size of my hand, so maybe it's their emotional weight I was feeling.)

Then I concealed myself, which took forever and I was really afraid someone would notice what I was doing, and followed the forest around and to the west.

Maintaining concealment turned out to be easier than I'd expected, which suggested to me that this pouvra, at least, used magic when you first worked it, but then didn't require any extra magic to maintain. I didn't think too much about it because I was afraid the magic might change its mind and I'd be left completely visible in the middle of the God-Empress's camp. But it didn't, and I passed the fighting and kept on walking until I reached the place where they'd set up the big tents, including the God-Empress's traveling palace.

At that point I had to depend on my thief's skills, because I was afraid if I tried to work the walk-through-walls pouvra while concealed, I'd lose control of one or both of them. And it was *hard*. I don't know why there were so many people there in the camp instead of out fighting, and yes, I probably should have been grateful for that, but with my fingers and toes numb from the concealment pouvra I was mostly just frustrated every time I had to duck out of someone's way. I had to crouch behind a couple of barrels for about fifteen minutes because two soldiers were flirting just far enough apart I couldn't duck around them. Stupid soldiers. But finally I was outside the command tent and trying to find a way to see inside.

The door flaps were open, but too many people kept going in and out for me to stand in the doorway and look to see if the God-Empress was there. So eventually I stood to one side and listened. She was inside, talking to some of her officers, and I had begun to despair about how to kill her without being instantly captured myself when I remembered her traveling palace. It made far more sense for me to wait in there for her, since I doubted any of her officers were allowed inside. So I (taking the long way around, stupid soldiers) went to her tent, waited for a lull in the traffic (because her tent door was shut) and quickly ducked inside.

It looked exactly the way I remembered, down to the ridiculous marble statue, and I nearly dismissed the pouvra before I realized I'd want to stay concealed so she wouldn't raise an alarm when she entered. So I sat down on the chair and waited. For a long time. I don't know how long it was, but my hands and feet were really numb by the time the flap opened and the God-Empress entered.

She was as beautiful as ever, even though her roots were showing. She wore a pink satin gown embroidered with black roses that was completely out of place in a war camp, with glittering pink topazes set in silver bezels dangling to her navel and more of them woven through her hair and pinned to the silver coronet she wore. The first thing that went through my mind was *It's too bad she doesn't look crazy or all of this would have been over years ago*. I wonder now how much people put up with in her because they couldn't believe anyone that beautiful could be evil. Or maybe not. It doesn't matter anymore.

I tried to work the see-inside pouvra as she came toward her dressing table—I had to get out of the way quickly—and sat down, but I felt the concealment pouvra shake and gave up. She didn't seem to have anything in mind, just played with her hairbrush, shifted a few things around. Then she swiveled in her seat, looked at me, and said, "I wondered when you'd come, Sesskia."

I was so startled that she'd seen through the concealment—and apparently with no difficulty—I couldn't think of anything to say. Her words had the same archaic structure they always did when she spoke to me, which added to my confusion. When I didn't say anything immediately, she added, "I missed you. We always have such fun together."

"Fun for you, maybe, but not so much for the people you order killed," I said. I dismissed the pouvra and wrung feeling back into my hands.

"God dislikes waste," she said with an understanding nod, "but God cannot allow blasphemy and disrespect. You should understand that."

"I don't understand anything you do," I said. "I'm here to stop this war."

"No one can stop it," the God-Empress said. "It is a cleansing war. It will wipe away sin and disobedience. Even yours, Sesskia."

I went to stand next to her and worked the see-inside pouvra. "If you were the true God, it would be disobedience," I said. Her heart and lungs looked like anyone else's. I'd have thought they would be blackened, sooty lumps. "But it's not wrong to protect what you love from someone evil."

The God-Empress stood up. "No one understands me but you, Sesskia, and that's why you're my favorite sister," she said, reaching out to grasp my hand. Reflexively, I pulled away, and her eyes went from being vaguely unfocused to being acute and very, very aware of me. "I swore I would see you die," she said, "and die slowly, like all our other sisters."

This was where I realized how stupid I'd been. I knew I had to wait a while after working the see-inside pouvra for the magic to build, and I was prepared for that. But I'd thought I could work the see-inside pouvra while I was concealed, which would have given me plenty of time to wait. I also hadn't counted on not being able to keep the God-Empress from attacking me during that time. She opened her mouth to call for soldiers, and just as I had months ago in the palace, I grabbed her, stuffed my arm into her mouth, and bore her to the ground.

I couldn't conceal us both the way I had that time, but since she didn't have any minions around, it didn't matter. What mattered is she fought me like a crazed shark, thrashing and biting my arm and flailing at my face. The only thing that kept me from losing control of the see-inside pouvra were the hours I'd spent practicing it until I could almost do it in my sleep. I tried the mind-moving pouvra, felt my vision go blurry, but nothing happened. Too soon.

I tried to keep her pinned, but she got in a lucky blow to my head, and while I was dizzy she managed to roll out from under me. Her mad eyes were blazing, and she struck me again and again while I defended my face with my free arm and tried to keep her from getting on top of me. She seemed to have forgotten about getting help. I was sure she was going to batter me until I was dead.

I kept trying to use the mind-moving pouvra and coming up with nothing. It was like trying to scoop water with a sieve, because I could feel the magic there and it just kept slipping away. I knew I wasn't going to be able to manage the assassination pouvrin before she either got free or knocked me unconscious. So I began casting about for some other solution.

I remembered what I'd done the night before in Terrael's kathana circle, working the mind-moving pouvra to attract magic into the circle. Except I couldn't work that one, I already knew that. So I bent my will to the binding pouvra instead. It was one I knew well, it was simple and basic, and I figured even if it absorbed some of the magic it attracted, there would still be plenty left over for me to stop the God-Empress's heart.

Without the revelation pouvra, I could only tell the binding pouvra was working when the sensation of being pulled at increased, slowly, as it gathered the local magic together. I pictured its angular, impossibly curved shape as hollow glass pipes filling up with those muddy blobs that moved faster as more of them entered the shape and started repelling each other. I released the pouvra and immediately worked the mind-moving pouvra—and nothing happened. The magic I'd "collected" was gone and there wasn't anything else to hold onto. It was confusing and discouraging and I wanted to scream at how stupid it all was.

So I did it again. I was so tired I was conscious of the God-Empress's attack only as a series of blows to my face and shoulders and a tension in my hands and arms where I held her fast. This time, I made myself maintain the binding pouvra until I thought my whole body might come apart under those invisible hands tugging at me. My whole body was burning with the effort, as if I were running and running and had passed the limits of my ability and had to keep going. The God-Empress had one hand on my throat and was squeezing, and I knew if I didn't kill her soon, all of this would have been pointless.

Then my vision blurred, and the see-inside pouvra slipped away. I snatched at it, but all I could see was the neck of the God-Empress's pink gown instead of the heart and lungs pulsing beneath her skin. I cried out—I couldn't help myself—and tried to work it again, because I couldn't work the mind-moving pouvra on her heart if I couldn't see what I was doing, but I couldn't remember how, as if the shape had been completely driven out of my memory.

That was the closest I've ever come to true despair. Cederic hating me, Bridie dying alone, those were nothing compared to how I felt rolling on the ground trying to keep the God-Empress from killing me, knowing I'd wasted my—our—only chance to ensure the Empire wasn't ruled by an evil, insane woman who would corrupt it to suit her whim. I decided I had only one option left to me: I would have to turn the fire pouvra on her and hope I could maintain it long enough to kill her with it. It would mean my death as well, and that terrified me, but I didn't think I had another choice. Maybe if I'd had time, I could have come up with something else, but I was exhausted and in pain and barely able to focus on my enemy. So I released the binding pouvra and groped about for the other shape.

Except I couldn't. The binding pouvra felt as if it were locked into place inside me, pushing and pulling and putting me under such enormous tension I thought I might shatter. I tried again to release it and the tension increased. I could almost feel the magic being pulled into me, vibrating with the effort not to touch any of the other pieces.

I fought it, exerting my will on it so it would fall apart, and the tension increased *again* and I screamed, not even thinking about the attention that would draw. Distantly I was aware of the God-Empress tearing herself out of my hands and grabbing my hair and throat to drag me upright, but those pains were so small compared to everything else they were like pinpricks. I was blind No, that's wrong, I remember seeing the God-Empress's face contorted into a snarl, but it's like my mind made a picture of that moment, like Audryn's magic notebook th'an, and my memory of it is at a remove. It's more as if I was so consumed by the pouvra my senses couldn't behave normally.

The ground tilted—I don't know if this was real or not—and I grabbed the God-Empress's shoulders to keep my balance. Spots appeared in front of my eyes, crowding together so I could barely see the spaces between them, and even though I knew they should be invisible I also knew they were the magic, forced closer together by the constraints of the pouvra even as they tried to push each other away.

The God-Empress could see them too, I could tell by how her snarl of fury turned into confusion and then fear. She raised her hand and her fingers began to move in that strange th'an she'd used to flee Colosse before the convergence. I let go her shoulders and wrapped my arms around her chest, pulling her close to me and binding her arms to her sides. If the magic were going to kill me, and I was sure it would, I was taking her with me.

The God-Empress screamed and thrashed in my arms, and I tried to work the see-inside pouvra again, hoping there was enough magic to let me kill her, or at least subdue her. Pain shot through me, worse than before, as if I'd managed the fire pouvra and immolated both of us. I screamed again, and someone took hold of my shoulders and tried to pull me away from the God-Empress, and then two of the blobs of magic touched each other and I exploded.

Again, I'm not sure if that actually happened, or if it was the only way my mind could comprehend a pressure beyond anything the human body is meant to endure. I wasn't conscious of having a body at all, just wave after wave of magic coming into contact with more magic and bursting apart into infinitely long strands of color, like flowers blooming at high speed, like fireworks over the main harbor at Thalessa. It spread outward from me faster than I could perceive and at the same time slowly enough that I could wonder at the brightness of the color and the way each strand had its own thickness and texture.

They wrapped around whatever was left of me, and I felt—I can't explain this well, but it was as if I were glowing, and I could *feel* I was glowing rather than see it. I wondered how I looked to everyone around me. Then I wondered why I couldn't see anyone else when I knew I'd been clinging to the God-Empress and someone else had taken hold of me. And only then did I think to wonder if I was dead.

I mean, it's not as if anyone knows what the true God does with the part of us that is immortal. Maybe (I thought) what I was seeing was the afterlife. But then I remembered all these strands had appeared because of the pouvra, and if it really were death, it wouldn't have just come into being because of me. Even so, I didn't seem to have a body, and that frightened me.

So I began looking around for something that wasn't colorful magic strands, and I found...well, pieces. Not as if I'd been dismembered, ew, but—segments of memory I recognized as belonging to me. Memories of people, of my parents and sisters, of Cederic and all my friends. Memories of places—so many places I'd been in my travels. Memories of awful times and pain and loneliness, memories of joy and laughter. All the secrets I keep inside, ones I try to forget and ones I cherish and, astonishingly, a secret I didn't even know I had. Everything that made me who I am surrounded me, and I—the core of me, the part that knows and observes and understands how those memories fit together—began twitching at the strands to bring those pieces together.

They came together the way the magic had, only drawn to one another rather than repelled, and as they did I came to understand the way the strands worked, how they could be shaped to do anything you could imagine. I worked the strands again and felt my body settle into place around me.

(I'm looking at my hands now and they look perfectly normal. There's even the scar across the fleshy part of my palm where I carelessly sliced my hand with a scaling knife thirteen years ago. So I don't think my body is made of magic. But I could be wrong.)

Eventually I felt whole again, body and memory, and I stretched and felt the strands move with me. I almost began to worry I wouldn't be able to find my way back to the...not the real world, because this was realer than anything I could imagine, but the place where my human body belonged. But I knew the magic so well at that point I couldn't feel afraid of anything related to it.

Even so, it took me a few tries before I figured out how to make my awareness of it fade so I could see anything else. And when that happened, I opened my eyes and found myself in an enormous, too-soft bed, covered by a heavy down comforter (and feeling overwarm) and wearing only a thin nightgown with nothing underneath (as I discovered when I moved). I felt incredibly weak and hungry, as if I hadn't eaten for days, and achy, but I stretched and began to feel better.

I was able to get up and totter across the bedroom, which was as enormous as the bed, and found and used the chamber pot outside the equally large kiorka, though my bladder wasn't very full. When I came out, I startled a woman with a basin of water and some towels. She dropped everything, and without thinking about it I took hold of one of those strands and used it to stop the basin from spilling.

They're at the edge of my vision all the time now, though if I bend my will I can bring them into focus without completely losing my normal sight. I'm not sure I can manipulate them consciously yet, now that I'm awake, but I expect—I hope—that will come with practice.

Anyway, the woman gasped, dropped her burden, said, "Your Majesty!" and ran out of the room before I could say anything. I followed her to the door and looked out. It opened on a wide hallway lined with pedestals bearing vases of fresh flowers between other doors, all of which were painted a soft blue and outlined with gilt.

It was opulent and a little intimidating, and I shut my own door and contemplated my nearly-naked condition. Then I went into the dressing room and rooted around for something less revealing. Someone had put what few clothes I own away in the drawers, and the Imperial getup was hanging in the closet, so this was clearly my room, but I'd never seen the place before and it made me nervous.

I'd just put on underwear and was debating between two shirts when the door banged open and Cederic shouted my name. "I'm in here," I said. "Do you think—"

That was as far as I got before Cederic burst into the dressing room, snatched me into his arms, and held me so tightly I squeaked. "You're awake," he said, then kissed me as if he hadn't seen me for a year.

"Yes, and I have so much to tell you," I said after a few long, satisfying moments. Then I said, "You look terrible." He did. He looked as if he hadn't slept well for the same year he hadn't seen me, and while I don't think Cederic is ever less than impeccably turned out, he was as close to looking unkempt as I'd ever seen him.

"Sesskia, you were unconscious for more than three weeks," he said. "I thought...I was afraid you might never wake again."

"It didn't feel like three weeks," I said, stupidly. Then I remembered I was still in my underwear, and while I normally enjoy that when my husband is around, at the time I didn't feel up for anything more vigorous than hugging. "Let me get dressed, and I'll tell you—wait." I was filling up with questions. "Is the God-Empress dead?"

"Renatha Torenz is decidedly, thoroughly dead," Cederic said, grimacing, "and I hoped you would be able to tell us how she and three others were found contorted into near-unrecognizability when you lay unmarked nearby."

I shuddered at that and finished doing up my trousers. "I only know what happened to me," I said, "and I'm hungry."

So Cederic made me get back into bed while he called for food, and right about then was when people started crowding in at the door, Audryn and Terrael and Jeddan and Mattiak and about a thousand others, all wanting to see me, and they all seemed so happy and relieved it made me cry. Then Cederic shooed everyone away and said they all could have the day off, and we sat together talking while I ate, and then talked some more. I told him everything I'd experienced, and he asked a few questions, chief among which was, "Can you show me how the magic works?"

"I don't know," I said. "I felt as if I made it work by accident, not by conscious thought. It was just—like making my hands move. You don't have to direct them, you just do it."

"By instinct," he said. "That may well be the desired end state, but achieving it will have to take deliberate effort."

"I only know when I bend my will, it becomes visible," I said.

He pulled his knees up beneath his chin, disrupting my tray, and clasped his hands loosely on them. "Our mages have learned to perceive the magic, if that is indeed what those colored ribbons are," he said. "But they have yet to make it do anything. Of course, it has only been four days since they discovered its true nature."

"It apparently took me three weeks to learn to perceive it, and to use it on some level," I said. "Maybe I can turn that to our advantage. If I can figure out how to teach it. I don't know if three weeks is fast or slow, but it felt like only...actually, I didn't have any sense of time. But what matters is learning it, period, even if it takes some of us years."

He moved my tray to the floor and put his arms around me. "I am glad it took you no more than three weeks," he said. "I had no idea it was possible to feel as bereft as I did while you were unconscious. We could none of us work magic to even discover what was wrong with you, let alone bring you back out of that state—"

266

"That would have been a very bad idea," I said, "if it had interrupted what I was doing. It might have killed me."

"Just as well magic did not work, then," he said. "We hoped your unnatural slumber, in which you did not eat or drink yet stayed perfectly healthy, meant there was still magic and we simply could not access it."

"And now it's combined again, and the worlds are fully united," I said.

"Yes. Though it is only the beginning of bringing our *countries* together," he said. Then we talked about what he'd been doing during those three weeks. The details are all in the pages I can't read yet, the ones he wrote in Castaviran while I was unconscious. It breaks my heart to think of him struggling, unable to tell anyone about his doubts and fears without making himself look weak when he needs to be strong for everyone. I hope I can learn about our government quickly so I can be a true help to him. I foresee a lot of reading in my future. In Castaviran too, if I can collar Terrael long enough for lessons.

We spent most of the day in here—there was so much to talk about—and I ate a lot, and then Cederic had to go take care of some business (I don't think Emperors get days off) and I wrote all of this. I feel as if I've left out too much, because we had such a long conversation, but I think I remembered all the most important things.

Tomorrow I'll teach the mages what I know about working magic the new way, what I learned while I was in that state. I can't wait to work with them again, with this new direction we all have. I wonder if this really is how they used to do magic before the divergence. If it is, I'm stunned they could ever want to change it. Though...it makes more sense now, that they'd want to make it available to everyone, because it feels like touching life itself. So maybe those long-dead mages weren't so self-centered after all. Not that I think they were right. But I think of Terrael, and I can understand how it feels to want to share this with the people you care about.

Cederic's right that this is an important part of our history now, the convergence and how we all worked so hard to keep our worlds from destroying each other, but I hope he doesn't suggest my books go into a library somewhere—how embarrassing for all my pettiness and mistakes to be on public display! Even when I thought of myself as keeping a record for others, it was always only other mages I thought would read it, and I wasn't really serious about it then.

But even though we've started something new—building an Empire, bringing people together, changing the government, fighting wars small and large—it feels as if this is the end of something old. It's not as if this book is full—there are maybe twenty pages left—but this is what we set out to accomplish, all those months ago when I first came to Castavir. And nothing went the way any of us expected.

When Cederic comes back, I'll share my most wonderful, beautiful secret with him. I never did tell him I stopped using the contraceptives after the assassination attempt, when I was afraid we might need an heir, if the worst happened. I didn't actually think *anything* would happen. It's a measure of how desperate we all were I didn't even realize something had.

If it's a boy, I want to name him Alenik.

PRONUNCIATION GUIDE AND GLOSSARY

General note: in Sesskia's language (Balaenic), long A and long O are usually written "ae" and "oe," and she writes Castaviran words and names as they would be spelled in Balaenic (i.e. Coell (Coll) River)

aenemica (ay-NEM-i-cah) – in Balaen, a name one uses for one's enemy to avoid referring to that person in a way that might indicate a positive or friendly relationship

baezrel (BAYZ-rel) – two-wheeled transport like a bicycle, but for one to four passengers

Balaen (bah-LAIN) – Sesskia's home country

Barrekel (BEAR-uh-kel) – second largest city in Balaen; in conflict with Castaviran city Teliarne

Castavir (CAS-tah-veer) – Empire formerly ruled by the God-Empress Renatha Torenz; also the central country of that empire

collenna (coh-LEN-nah) – engine, either self-propelling or attached to a loenerel

Colosse (col-LOSS) – capital city of the Castaviran Empire

Darssan (DAR-san) – combination school and research organization for Castaviran mages

Edmonti (ed-MON-tye) – Castaviran month equivalent to Balaenic month Dorinet (May)

Endellavir (en-DELL-uh-veer) – country annexed a century ago by the Castaviran Empire

Helviran (HEL-veer-an) – country in the Castaviran Empire

Karoli (kah-ROH-lye) – Castaviran month equivalent to Balaenic month Shelet (April)

kathana (ka-THAWN-ah) – ritual or spell composed of th'an

Kilios (KEY-lee-ohs) – "highest master"; a mage who has mastered all known th'an and all kathanas that can be performed by a single person

Lethess (leth-ESS) – coastal Balaenic city, resort town, ruled by Granea Amelessar

loenerel (LOH-neh-rel) – a train-like vehicle that runs on any surface, not on rails

Pfulerre (FOO-lair) – coastal Castaviran city, ruled by Daenen Radryntor

pouvra, plural pouvrin (POW-vrah, pow-VRIN) – a form of magic requiring no words, gestures, or th'an, that is instead manifested through the mage's will

praenoma, (plural) praenomi (pray-NO-ma, pray-NO-mee)—Balaenic first name; reserved for the use of close friends and family

Sai (sigh) – "great master"; a mage with advanced knowledge of magic

Teliarne (TEE-lee-arn) – capital city of Helviran; in conflict with Balaenic city Barrekel

th'an (TH-AWN, with a glottal stop at the apostrophe) – magical pictogram or rune; may refer to a single rune or a simple combination of three or four

thanest (THAWN-est) – in Castavir, a place where magic is available to the public, usually for a price but sometimes for free

Venetry (VEN-uh-tree) – capital of Balaen

Viravon (VEER-uh-von) – country annexed by the Castaviran Empire over a century ago; in rebellion to gain their freedom

THE BALAENIC CALENDAR
Winter:

Hantar (30 days)

Jennitar (31 days)

Teretar (30 days)

Spring:

Shelet (30 days)

Dorinet (31 days)

Auret (30 days)

Summer:

Evray (30 days)

Senessay (31 days)

Lennitay (30/31 days)

Autumn:

Coloine (30 days)

Nevrine (31 days)

Seresstine (31 days)

THE BALAENICS

(NOTE: the surnames of the noble houses all end in –ssar; these are the people who are allowed to serve as Chamber Lords and as Lords Governor of the major cities of Balaen)

Sesskia (SESS-key-ah) – Balaenic mage of ten years' standing, Cederic Aleynten's wife and Empress-Consort of the Castaviran-Balaenic Empire

Jeddan (JED-un) – Leader of the Balaenic warrior mages, Sesskia's friend

Mattiak Tarallan (MAT-tee-ack tar-ALL-un) – Commander General of the Balaenic Army

Alenik (ah-LEN-ick) – Sesskia's father (deceased)

Cessily (SESS-ih-lee) – Sesskia's mother (deceased)

Roda (ROE-duh) – Sesskia's older sister

Bridie (BRY-dee) – Sesskia's younger sister (deceased)

Garran Clendessar (GAR-un CLEN-des-ar) – King of Balaen

Caelan Crossar (CAY-lun CROSS-ar) – Chamber Lord of Defense

Merdel Lenssar (MUR-del LEN-sar) – Chamber Lord of Commerce

Jarlak Batekessar (JAR-lack BAH-teh-keh-sar) – Chamber Lord of Agriculture

Debarra Jakssar (deh-BAR-uh JACK-sar) – Chamber Lord of Transportation

Relania Phellek (ruh-LAIN-ee-ah FELL-eck) – mage of several years' standing, pacifist and spy

Tobiak (toe-BYE-ack) – mage created by the convergence, spy

Jerussa (juh-RUE-sah) – mage created by the convergence, master of the flitting pouvra

Arron Domenessar (AR-un do-MEN-uh-sar) – Lord Governor of Barrekel

Roebart Gradden (ROH-bart GRAD-un) – General in command of the Black Army at Barrekel

Soessen Ellert (SOH-sun EL-ert) – General in command of the Brown Army at Barrekel

Granea Amelessar (GRAY-nee-ah AM-el-es-ar) – Lord Governor of Lethess

Orenna (or-ENN-ah) – mage in the service of Granea Amelessar

THE CASTAVIRANS

Cederic Aleynten (SED-er-ic ah-LEN-ten) – Kilios, Sesskia's husband and Emperor-elect of the Castaviran-Balaenic Empire

Terrael Peressten (ter-RAIL per-ESS-ten) – mage who can no longer work magic, Sesskia's friend, married to Audryn; Cederic's aide and inventor of kathanas

Audryn Engilles (AW-drin en-GIL-is) – mage and friend of Sesskia, married to Terrael; Terrael's partner in invention

Sovrin Ustanz (SAW-vrin uss-TANCE) – mage who can no longer work magic; head of the translator corps and Sesskia's friend

Jaemis Quallen (JAY-mis QUAH-lun) – mage, expert in transmutation kathanas

Dugan Lerongis (DOO-gan leh-RON-gis) – King of Helviran in the Castaviran Empire

Joena Lerongis (JOH-nuh leh-RON-gis) – Queen-Consort of Helviran, Dugan's wife

Lelaena Osther (leh-LAY-nuh OSS-ther) – Queen of Endellavir in the Castaviran Empire

Moerton Taissatus (MOR-ton TIE-sah-tus) – Consul of Colosse; chief of the consuls of the Castaviran Empire

Veneta Amaleten (ven-EE-tah ah-MAH-leh-tun) – chief Sai of the Firtha thanest in Colosse; Cederic's former teacher and most high priestess

Renatha Torenz (reh-NAH-tha tor-ENCE) – deposed God-Empress of Castavir

Gael Regates (GAIL reh-GAH-tes) – Commander of the Castaviran Army; former conspirator against the God-Empress

Perce Aselfos (PERSS ah-SEL-fus) – Renatha Torenz's former spymaster, responsible for removing her from the throne

Brisson Rialen (BRIS-un rye-AH-len) – consul of Teliarne, Dugan Lerongis's cousin and heir

Raewyn Garatssen (RAY-win ga-RAHT-sen) – Commander General of the Helvirite Army, Dugan Lerongis's half-sister

Daenen Radryntor (DAY-nen RAD-rin-tor) – consul of Pfulerre

READ ON for some bonus scenes from Cederic's point of view!

The Coronation (15 Hantar)

Cederic examined the Imperial crown where it rested on a purple velvet cushion. It was burnished gold lined with white satin, studded with pearls the size of his thumbnail. A single central diamond that would look like the wearer's third eye winked in the low light of the reception chamber. The satin lining was yellowed toward the bottom, where it had rested against Imperial heads over the centuries. Emperors, Empresses, down to Renatha Torenz, who had betrayed its trust in her evil madness.

And now it was his.

He put his hands behind his back to keep himself from picking it up, feeling he ought not before he'd actually been crowned. He had worn it briefly, very briefly, when Veneta Amaleten had put it on his head to test the fit—he didn't want it slipping down over his ears during the ceremony and distracting everyone from the gravity of the moment. It had been a perfect fit. Veneta hadn't made any comment, but he knew her well enough to read her expression. *Like it was made for you*, she'd been thinking. Cederic tried not to feel superstitious about that.

He felt he was, if not the last person anyone would have chosen to rule an empire, certainly far down on the list. His family was of modest means, he was scholastically gifted, he'd spent his life in magical pursuits. Had the convergence and Renatha Torenz not intervened, he would have founded his own thanest and pursued his studies until old age forced retirement on him. It was not false modesty when he felt himself inadequate to the role he now intended to fill. He played the part well, but in the dark of night, when his doubts tormented him, he wondered why no one else saw how much he still needed to learn.

Someone stepped up beside him. "The Consort's crown is far too big for me," Sesskia said. "They had to pad the lining so it didn't fall off. Some of those Emperor-Consorts must have had enormous heads and ears that stick out by a mile."

Cederic smiled at the image. "The Consort's crown is not so gaudy as the Emperor's. It suits you."

Sesskia shuddered exaggeratedly. "I never wore jewelry in my life until about four months ago, but I like to think I have better taste than that."

"The crowns are only for state occasions. It is unlikely you will wear it more than a handful of times during our reign. Be grateful we were married before the coronation, because Imperial weddings are one of those occasions."

"You're so foresighted." Sesskia hooked her arm around his elbow. Cederic took a moment to appreciate his wife's figure, resplendent in her green and gold wedding gown. She wore her beautiful dark blonde hair loose around her shoulders, framing her round face. On impulse, he stroked her hair once, and she glanced his way and smiled. "I hope they call us soon. I'm getting hungry."

"I fear my appetite has disappeared. Unfortunate, as I understand the feast prepared for us after the coronation is quite lavish."

"I'll eat for both of us." Sesskia sighed and rested her head on his shoulder briefly. "I suppose it's too late to run."

"You don't want to run."

"Not really, just...it's hit me recently that this means I'll live the rest of my life in the open, no more hiding. It's an uncomfortable feeling. I wouldn't be able to do it without you."

"You would not have to do it if not for me."

"That sounded close to bitter, Cederic. You don't think I blame you, do you?" She squeezed his arm lightly. "This was the best choice, for us, for everyone. I may not love the idea of being a public figure, but being Empress-Consort doesn't frighten me. If that makes sense."

The door opened. "Your Majesties?" An older man with a square face and wispy brown hair entered the room. "They're ready for you." He stepped past Cederic and picked up the purple cushion bearing the crown. A younger woman, following behind him, reverently lifted the cushion with the Consort's crown. The two crossed the room to a second door, almost invisible in its unobtrusiveness, and carried their burdens out.

Cederic caught Sesskia's eye. She was smiling again, with that look that never failed to make his heart beat faster with love. "Walk with me?"

"Always," she said.

A spiral staircase rose from the corridor beyond the reception chamber, just broad enough for the two of them to walk side by side. Th'an scrawled on the walls glowed with amber light, casting strange shadows as they passed. Music came faintly to his ear, as well as a distant murmur like an oncoming storm that filtered in from above, making Cederic picture Marloen Hall filled to capacity. Today they would make history, he and Sesskia, first Emperor and Empress-Consort of an Empire that hadn't existed for centuries, possibly millennia. Sesskia's hand rested loosely on his arm. She didn't seem worried at all, and it comforted him. Of all his fears, the one that she might find all this too much, and reject him, was both the least rational and the most terrifying.

They emerged from the staircase and through a narrow door into the grand foyer of Marloen Hall. Crimson drapes fringed with silver tassels shrouded the windowless walls, turning the parquet floor dull and dark and giving the entire room a funereal look. Cederic had attended a number of musical performances there and had never become accustomed to its somberness. It was empty, the main doors closed but guarded by men in Balaenic Army uniforms. They had not been able to find the right garb for Imperial attendants, all of the existing costumes being intended for service directly to Renatha Torenz, so General Tarallan had pressed some of his men into service. Cederic thought it a good symbol, a reminder that even though their fragile new empire as yet had no name, he was Emperor to both Balaenic and Castaviran.

The two soldiers bowed their heads as he and Sesskia approached, respectful but not servile. It was a comforting gesture. He paused before the doors, let out a long breath, and said, "Now, if you please." The soldiers took hold of the ornate brass handles and pulled the doors open. The music, something grand by one of his less-favorite composers, swelled to full, then cut off, leaving the chord unresolved. It was not a mistake—that was where the phrase ended —but it made Cederic uncomfortable nonetheless, as if the music demanded a response he was powerless to give. The swishing sound of a thousand people turning to look at him and Sesskia filled the space where the music had been. Cederic counted silently to three, then walked forward.

It was the longest walk of his life, longer even than the day he had left the kathana chamber, humiliated by his "old friend" Denril Vorantor. He kept his eyes focused on Veneta, who stood at the center of the dais below, dressed in the honey-gold silks and satins of the most high priestess. It had not been a difficult decision, granting her that rank, though there were likely others as qualified and deserving. Facing years of conflict and antagonism from men and women challenging his decrees, he had wanted to have at least one ally who would support him completely. Not that she would not argue with him if she felt he was growing arrogant, but that was itself a kind of support.

The uncanny stillness made it hard for him to keep a measured pace. Even his boots were quiet on the red velvet carpet. Sesskia's gown rustled, barely audibly. Her hand gripping his forearm was the only sign she was not as inwardly placid as she appeared to be. She hated being the center of attention—well, she'd said it, that was no longer an option. What might have happened if they had not fallen in love? Would he still be here, pacing this interminable aisle alone? The idea of facing this challenge without her support filled him with horror.

The aisle ended at the dais steps, seven of them, shallow and broad and glossy with varnish. Cederic released Sesskia, who squeezed his hand in brief reassurance. It would be her turn to ascend soon enough. Keeping the same slow pace, he strode up the steps and stopped at the dais's edge, some fifteen feet from Veneta. She was expressionless, her eyes fixed on his.

"Who comes before God at this time, in this place?" she exclaimed. The exquisite acoustics of Marloen Hall, honed by carefully placed th'an, carried her voice to its farthest reaches.

"Cederic Aleynten," he replied, his deeper voice reverberating off the walls.

"Speak your will, Cederic Aleynten," Veneta said.

"I come before God to claim the right of rule to the Empire of Castavir and Balaen." It was an awkward phrase, but they hadn't had time to come up with a name for the new empire, and Cederic felt it would be off-putting to the people to impose a new name to go along with a new country, with all the other impositions.

"Step forward, Cederic Aleynten, and be judged of God."

Cederic walked forward and went to one knee before Veneta. He had knelt like this before Renatha Torenz and burned with fury at having to do so. He did not consider himself a particularly religious man, but he believed in God, and resented the madwoman's usurpation of divinity. Now, kneeling in front of the most high priestess, he felt unexpected peace tug at his heart. Whatever his reservations, he was confident God knew the sincerity of his desires.

"Cederic Aleynten," Veneta said, "you who would be Emperor, do you judge yourself worthy of this honor?"

"I have served the Empire all the days of my life," Cederic said, "as mage, priest, Sai, and Kilios. I have never sought recognition for its own sake, but have sacrificed my own needs for those of the Empire. So far as I may humbly divine, I am worthy of the Imperial crown."

"God recognizes your claims and acknowledges the truth thereof." Veneta raised her head. "If anyone would dispute the right of Cederic Aleynten to lay claim to the Empire of Castavir and Balaen, speak now."

Silence. With his back to the audience, Cederic couldn't help but feel their eyes like daggers boring into him. If someone chose to speak up, he didn't know what he'd do. They hadn't planned for that contingency, choosing instead to pack Marloen Hall with men and women who were Cederic's loyal supporters. He closed his eyes, praying for no interruptions. Nothing happened.

He felt Veneta's hand rest atop his head, and opened his eyes. "Cederic Aleynten," she said, "will you take oath before this company as Emperor?"

He swallowed to moisten his dry mouth. "I will."

"Do you swear to fill the office of Emperor to the utmost of your ability?"

"I so swear."

"Do you swear to uphold the laws of the Empire without fear or favor, granting justice to all who come before you?"

"I so swear."

"Do you swear to serve the Empire for all the days of your life?"

"I so swear."

"Do you swear to put the needs of the Empire above your own?"

"I so swear."

Veneta removed her hand. "God hears your oath, and is satisfied." She turned away, and when she turned back, she had the Imperial crown in her hands. "Cederic Aleynten, as God's voice and with the witnesses of those present, I crown you Emperor of Castavir and Balaen. May your reign be long and just."

The crown was heavier than it looked, weighing down his head so he bowed before Veneta. He continued to kneel as spontaneous cheering and shouting broke out throughout the hall, afraid he might stagger if he tried to stand immediately. A long and just reign. He'd settle for one that outlasted the defeat of Renatha Torenz.

Veneta made a little "get up" motion with her hand, shielded behind his body so no one else could see it. He smiled, rose, and turned to face the crowd. That only made the cheering redouble. His eye fell on Sesskia, waiting at the foot of the dais, smiling broadly. The ceremony wasn't over yet.

He let the cheering go on for a few seconds longer, then gestured to request their silence. When stillness once again lay over the assembly, he said, "An Emperor's strength is in the hands of his Consort. Sesskia of Balaen, join me."

Sesskia strode up the steps, raising her skirts to avoid tripping over them, and knelt gracefully at his feet. "Sesskia," Cederic said, and to his astonishment found himself tearing up. He cleared his throat. "Sesskia, do you judge yourself worthy of the honor of Empress-Consort?"

"I have risked my life in the service of Balaen and Castavir," Sesskia said in a clear, ringing voice. "I want our countries to live together in peace. I want this Empire to flourish. In all humility, I believe I am worthy of the honor of Empress-Consort."

"As God's representative, the Emperor accepts your claim. Will you swear oath before this company as Empress-Consort?"

"I will."

Cederic laid his hand atop her head. "Do you swear to fill the office of Empress-Consort to the utmost of your ability?"

"I so swear."

"Do you swear to support the Emperor in all his doings, all the days of your life?"

"I so swear." She smiled at Cederic, and he almost forgot what came next.

"Do you swear to uphold the laws of the Empire without fear or favor, granting justice to all who come before you?"

"I so swear."

"Do you swear to serve the Empire for all the days of your life?"

"I so swear."

"Do you swear to put the needs of the Empire above your own?"

"I so swear."

"As God's representative, the Emperor accepts your oath." He removed his hand and half-turned to take the Consort's crown from Veneta. "Sesskia of Balaen, as Emperor and with the witnesses of those present, I crown you Empress-Consort of Castavir and Balaen. May your reign be long and just."

The crown seemed not to weigh on Sesskia as it had on him; she continued to smile at him as the cheering recommenced. Cederic thought it might be louder for his wife than it had been for him. The years ahead would be difficult, and he was fully aware he would not be popular, so it was just as well one of them would be. He offered her his hand and helped her rise and face the audience. "And so it begins," he murmured.

"It still doesn't feel quite real," she murmured back. "You'd think the cheering would be enough. Or the weight of the crown."

So she did feel it. "It is a first step, the first of thousands. Someday I imagine we will wake to the realization of what we have sworn this day."

"The sooner, the better." Sesskia gripped his hand more tightly. "We don't have to wear these things throughout the meal, do we?"

"I am certain Sai Amaleten will want them whisked away for safe-keeping." Cederic guided Sesskia down the stairs and, hand in hand, they proceeded up the aisle. This time they waved and smiled at the crowd, though Sesskia did it more easily than he did. It would likely be years before he felt comfortable enough to really smile in public.

The crowd bulged and swayed as people moved to follow them, though no one ventured onto the ribbon of carpet that unrolled straight as a furrow from the dais to the doors. The Balaenic soldiers who stood sentry at the doors headed toward them, gesturing at the people to stay back. Cederic put his left arm around Sesskia and limbered up his fingers in preparation for fending overeager subjects off. It would look bad for him to turn magic on his people, but worse for them to be mobbed.

Someone stepped onto the carpet as if pushed by those behind him. Cederic registered the knife as it began its descent. Without thinking, he put himself between it and Sesskia, raising his hand to work the mind-moving pouvra on the man even though he knew no gestures were needed. That extra second was all it took for the knife to plunge into his chest.

Cold agony shot through him. He opened his mouth to shout a warning and heard a pained, wordless cry emerge instead. The man raised the knife for another blow, and Cederic tried once again to work the mind-moving pouvra, but it slipped away as if oiled. Dazed, he saw the knife glitter oddly before falling to the ground. Two men, the soldiers, tackled the assailant. They went down in a pile, but slowly, as if time no longer had meaning.

Cederic realized he was on the floor. The carpet was not as soft as it looked. Sesskia had hold of the front of his embroidered tunic, her mouth opening and closing as slowly as the soldiers had fallen. She looked like a fish, a beautiful blonde fish. He tried to tell her this— she would find it funny—but his mouth wouldn't respond.

His head was so heavy, probably because of the crown...but no, it lay on the floor some distance away. It must have fallen off when the knife struck him. If it was damaged, Veneta would never let him forget it. Cederic blinked slowly as the crown grew fuzzy in his vision. He smelled blood. A lot of blood. Sesskia was covered in it—oh, no, had the assailant hurt her too? He tried to sit upright, grabbed Sesskia's wrist, but his fingers were as numb as his mouth. His chest burned, his heart beat erratically. *I'm dying*, he thought. He tried to keep his eyes open, feeling madly as if in closing them, he might never open them again, but they were as heavy as the crown, and he slipped into unconsciousness.

He came to himself in a dry, cool room filled with the oily smell of a lot of magic all in one place. Opening his eyes turned out to be difficult, so he let his ears and nose build up a picture for him. He was in bed, not one that was familiar to him, and the pillow felt rough, so he wasn't anywhere luxurious. The smell of magic meant this was probably a thanest, possibly the Firtha thanest, though why was he in a thanest instead of at Marloen Hall?

He forced his eyes open and raised his head from the pillow. Sesskia sat next to his bed, her eyes and nose reddened and her hands clasped in her lap. Blood soaked the front of the green and gold gown, its coppery scent faded behind the smell of magic. Terror struck him, made his heart lurch. She jerked, startled, as he moved. "Sesskia," he croaked, "are you all right?"

Her eyes widened, then filled with tears. "Am *I* all right?" she sobbed. "Cederic, you nearly died! That man—I should have stopped him, I can't forgive myself—"

"Sesskia, don't cry," Cederic said, aghast. He lifted his hand—it seemed to weigh a hundred pounds—and clasped her interlocked ones. "Don't cry."

She drew a shuddering breath and blinked tears away. "I'm sorry. It's just...they told me you would recover, but there was so much blood. I did my best with the healing pouvrin, the healers said they saved your life, the pouvrin did, but I—" She breathed in again. "You're still weak. I shouldn't upset you."

Cederic let his head fall back onto the pillow. It, too, felt as if it were made of lead. "I do not remember an attack. My last memory is of raising you to your feet and accepting the accolades of the crowd."

"Some raving bastard tried to kill you, halfway up the aisle," Sesskia said. "I don't know if he was after you or me, because you put yourself between me and the knife, but he...I made him drop the knife, and the guards killed him."

Cederic closed his eyes again and let her words sweep over him. He felt so tired. That made sense, if he'd been stabbed and then healed. For once it was he who took injury, and not Sesskia. Gratitude carried him off into sleep again.

The Big Blow-up (18 Teretar)

Lady Radryntor's cook was indifferent at best, producing bland meals heavy with fish and other seafood. Cederic had been born far inland, and fish had not been part of his boyhood diet. Even in

Colosse, where the chefs *had* been excellent, they had rarely cooked fish, and those only river trout. Shrimp had been a delightful discovery three and a half weeks ago. Now he was tired of it. Steak, that would be wonderful, or even a simple baked potato with butter.

He dutifully forked up another bite of shrimp in cream sauce, grateful for the self-control that kept even the slightest hint of distaste off his face. To his left, Lady Radryntor dug in happily, making the little humming sound she did when she was eating something she enjoyed. Cederic was certain she had no idea she did it. He appreciated it because it made her seem human, an ordinary woman and not the hardened bigot she actually was. He needed to deal with her fairly, and the humming made it easier. Easier, but not effortless.

Lady Radryntor's hostility to his cause grew daily. It took every ounce of conciliatory civility he possessed to keep her placated, keep her energies turned toward preventing her people from clashing with the Balaenics. He was increasingly convinced it was an exercise in futility. When they first arrived in Pfulerre, his presence had done much to soothe tensions between Lethess and Pfulerre, but Lady Radryntor's bigotry had infected the populace. Cederic feared the day when he would have to call on the Balaenic Army to put down a riot. *That* would only make matters worse.

At night, he would lie awake pondering the problem. Would it be better to force the issue, command Lady Radryntor to obey him, or wait for her to challenge him so she would clearly be in the wrong? He would listen to Sesskia's quiet breathing and contemplate waking her to discuss it, craving her company as well as her opinion. But she looked so tired, all the time, that he could never bear to disturb her sleep. He couldn't remember the last time they'd made love. Well, soon they would perform that all-important kathana, and time would be theirs again.

"I won't join you for the judgment session this afternoon," Lady Radryntor said abruptly. "My stewards have business for me to attend to. Questions of tariffs, which the Balaenics still aren't paying."

Cederic was glad his mouth was full, as it gave him time to control his first reaction, which was to hurl accusations of bigotry and disobedience at the woman. "The citizens of Lethess are under no obligation to pay tariffs on goods merely traveling through your city boundaries," he said. "As I believe we have discussed."

"These are tariffs on their trade, your Majesty, not on their traffic," Lady Radryntor said, a trifle smugly. "They resist paying what I believe is a fair tax on foreign goods."

"I think—" Cederic caught himself before he could criticize. He was willing to bet Lady Radryntor's "fair tax" was unfairly weighted. "I will discuss the matter with Lady Amelessar. I am certain you and she can come to an accommodation." Though if they did, it would likely be because Granea Amelessar gave in. Lady Amelessar was a better administrator and a nicer person than Lady Radryntor, but she also had governance of a city a third the size of Pfulerre, and was aware of the position that put her in. Even so, Cederic knew Granea's patience with Lady Radryntor was wearing thin.

"Let's hope so. I have been nothing but reasonable with regard to those people." Lady Radryntor took another bite and the humming began again. Cederic realized he was gripping his fork tightly enough that the tendons stood out on his hand and made himself relax. After this meal, he would go in search of Sesskia. Was today the day they were performing the kathana? He couldn't remember. He would...no, he had to sit in judgment in Pfulerre that afternoon, much as he wished he could delegate that responsibility. *After* that, he would find Sesskia, and the two of them would sit together, talk, possibly do more than that.

The gauzy blue-green curtain hanging in the arched entrance parted, and a Balaenic soldier entered. "Your Majesty," he said, then seemed to lose sight of the rest of his sentence.

Cederic laid his fork down. "Yes?"

"Your Majesty," the man continued, "there is something...your presence...your Majesty, something terrible has happened. The magic they were working, the kathana, it...failed." He said "kathana" like it was a word in a foreign language, which for him, it was.

"Failed?" Cederic said, dread rising within him. Failure was bad enough, but this man looked as if he had had a glimpse of hell. "How, failed?"

"What is that man saying?" Lady Radryntor said irritably. "How dare he interrupt this meal?"

"People died," the soldier said, ignoring the words spoken in a language he did not understand. He swallowed hard. "They...I've never seen—"

The dread hardened into a knot of horror. "Sesskia?" Cederic choked out.

The man shook his head. "No, your Majesty, but others—"

Cederic pushed back his chair and stood. "Where is she?"

"I don't know, your Majesty. Jeddan sent me to tell you...he said you should know. They...I've never seen more horrible deaths."

"Excuse me," Cederic said to Lady Radryntor, and left without waiting for her response.

He ran through the halls of the consul's palace and across Pfulerre, drawing on th'an to replenish his aching muscles and relieve his heavy breathing. Rain fell in a light drizzle, dampening his hair and shoulders, but he had no attention to spare to do anything about it.

The space outside the military camp where the mages had prepared the kathana circle was empty of people, though the circle remained. It was mostly whole except where one of the clay runes had been scrabbled out of the ground and crushed into black fragments that lay scattered across its surface. It showed no sign that anything had gone wrong with the kathana, no blood or anything that might indicate people had died there.

He debated briefly with himself, then ran back to the consul's palace. Someone in the camp might know what had happened, but he was far more likely to learn the truth from the mages themselves. He hoped they had returned to their quarters—many deaths? What could possibly have gone so wrong?

The wing of the palace set aside for the mages' use was unnaturally silent. Normally a low hum filled the air, the sound of dozens of people talking quietly. Cederic pushed aside the drape covering the doorway and entered the common area. The curtains were drawn back from the tall windows, letting in watery sunlight that illuminated the giant slate boards where the mages drew plans for kathanas. Low seats like flattened mushrooms dotted the floor. A few men and women, strangers to Cederic, occupied them, one or two curled up into tight balls with their eyes open and staring at some invisible horror. Seeing them, Cederic's horror tightened inside his chest.

"Where is Sesskia?" he demanded, then regretted how harsh he'd sounded. Whatever these people had experienced, they did not deserve to be harassed.

Silence reigned for a long moment. Then one of the women sitting nearby said, "She was caring for the bodies. I think she went to her room after that. I haven't seen her since—" Tears spilled from her eyes, and her shoulders shook with suppressed sobs. Cederic mumbled something in thanks and left the room. Once in the hall, he sprinted for his bedchamber.

The door hung ajar, and no sound came from within. Cederic pushed it open, moving silently. He felt as if he were creeping up on some woodland creature who might flee if startled, though he had no idea why that was the image that occurred to him in connection with whatever tragedy his wife had endured. Shutting the door quietly behind him, he walked to the bed. Sesskia lay there, curled on her side in sleep. Both her fists were clenched as if she were fighting demons. She looked so beautiful, her thick hair spilling across her back and over her shoulders, her dark lashes resting on her cheeks like a silken fringe, her brows drawn down in that so-familiar fierce expression, that the knot in his chest relaxed. Surely it could not have been so terrible, if she could sleep.

He sat beside her and thought about leaving her to her rest. *No,* he thought, *we have been alone for far too long,* and gently shook her shoulder to wake her. Her eyelids fluttered open, and she looked up at him without comprehension. The momentary sensation that she didn't know who he was filled him with guilt at having left her alone for so long. "Sesskia," he said, "wake up. Tell me what happened."

She sat, and his hand fell away from her shoulder. "I don't want to talk about it." Memory returned to her, and a look of bleak horror crossed her face. Cederic clasped her hands, wishing he could erase that look as easily. He remembered how she had looked back in the palace at Colosse, months ago, bearing the burden of the God-Empress's evil alone, and it broke his heart.

"Sesskia, you look as if you are being eaten from within," he said. "You need to talk about it. Please, love, let me share your burden."

She blinked. "Share my burden?" she whispered. Then she shouted, "Share my burden? *Now* you want to share my burden? Where the hell have you been, all these weeks when I *needed* you and you just...just *ignored* me? Should I be grateful that you've finally decided I'm more important than all your damned responsibilities, or did you just find yourself with five minutes in your schedule and thought 'well, I have this wife, maybe I should see how she is'? Damn it, Cederic, *nine people* are dead—is that really what it takes to get through to you? I don't know why you bothered, since it's not like they're coming back!"

Her words struck him like shards of ice, sharp-edged and painful. All his worst nightmares, that she would suddenly decide being married to the Emperor was too much, came true in a single long moment. The hard, derisive tone of her voice, the look on her face— he was never going to forget it. He withdrew his hands from hers and stood, feeling his face had frozen into a dispassionate mask. He found himself at the door without knowing how he'd gotten there. Sesskia had fallen silent, for which he was grateful. He shut the door behind him and stood there, struggling for composure.

She was right. He'd ignored her, and this was the price—this terrible, agonizing guilt and the crushing heartache of being spoken to so cruelly by the woman he loved. He tried to muster anger, because he was sure he did not deserve it, not all of it, anyway. But all he could feel was pain so intense his eyes ached with the tears he never dared shed.

Distantly, he heard the sound of Sesskia weeping—no, that was far too gentle a word for the sounds tearing out of her, the howl of someone pushed past enduring into a grief that could not be expressed any other way. He took a few steps away from the door. He would let her cry it out, return later when she had regained control, and maybe they could forget what had passed between them.

No. No more separation. She needs me more than ever, no matter what she said.

He went back into the room and again closed the door quietly, though it was unlikely she could hear him over the sound of her sobs. She had her face buried in the pillows and her whole body shook with her tears. Once more, he sat on the bed and gathered her into his arms, holding her close with her wet cheek pressed against his. "I'm sorry," he murmured. "I'm so sorry." He wasn't sure whether he was apologizing, or expressing his pain at her sorrow, but he could feel in his heart there was nothing else he could say.

Sesskia shuddered, then flung her arms around him and clutched him like a drowning woman offered a rope. She cried, and he held her for what felt like forever, until her tears turned into shaking, dry sobs. They held each other, not moving, not speaking, and Cederic stroked her hair and wished he knew what to say to comfort her further.

"I'm sorry," Sesskia finally whispered. "I shouldn't have said any of that. I didn't mean it."

"I may have deserved some of it," Cederic said. "I have been a fool for not realizing how little we were seeing of each other. Lady Radryntor has occupied so much of my time I told myself my own needs could wait. But I never thought of your needs, nor that my needs are to some extent those of the Empire and should not be neglected.

"Even so, I should never have spoken to you that way," Sesskia said. "Please forgive me."

"As you forgave me, once."

She lifted her head so she could look at him. Tears still sparkled on her thick lashes. "I should have pushed harder," she said. "I knew we were drifting apart, but I was selfish. I figured since I was exhausting myself, you should be the one to make the effort. So I never did anything beyond trying to stay awake until you came to bed."

Cederic smiled and wiped away a few of her tears. "You don't know how many times I thought of waking you," he said. "But I knew you needed your rest, and I told myself eventually there would be time."

"I wish you'd woken me."

"I wish I had, too. But we have nothing but time now." He kissed her, and felt her respond with such desire it drove the rest of his doubts and sorrow away. The judgment would wait. Nothing was more important than her.

"Even if Lady Radryntor decides to evict us from Pfulerre?" Sesskia said, twining her fingers in his hair.

Cederic gestured, and a heavy chair flew across the room and wedged itself under the doorknob. "She will need several men with large axes to do that," he said between kisses, "and if she is able to get past that door, there are more chairs in this room I will use as projectiles."

Sesskia started unbuttoning his shirt. "Are you sure your concentration can be divided like that?"

He slipped his hands under her shirt and unfastened her breast band. "No, but I thought you might like the reassurance of knowing I am so committed to making you cry out in pleasure I would attack the servants of one of our vassals to ensure it."

"That is the most romantic thing you have ever said to me," Sesskia said, and pulled her own shirt off over her head.

It felt like the first time all over again, as if they had been so long separated they had forgotten the feel of each other's bodies. Cederic was experienced enough to recognize his partner's desperate need for reassurance, for something that would replace whatever awful events had transpired in the kathana circle, and took his time, giving her pleasure without asking anything in return. It was the most marvelous experience. He loved her so much.

After, when they lay twined together, Cederic said, "Do you think you can tell me about it now?"

291

Sesskia curled closer. "It was a disaster," she whispered. "I still don't know what happened, and I don't want to think about finding out, not today, anyway. The eight keypoint mages were killed by their magic, crushed or burned to death, and Jaemis—" She drew another shuddering breath. "We couldn't even tell Jaemis had been human."

Cederic's throat and eyes ached with sorrow. He had known Jaemis Quallen for seven years, since before he was Kilios. They had been as close to friends as Cederic ever was with any of the mages. He had been a brilliant student of transmutation, which was why he'd been at the center of the kathana. The thought of him dead made Cederic's heart hurt.

"I made sure they were all taken...where they could be readied for burial," Sesskia went on. "I just keep thinking—what did we do wrong? Were we impatient, or were they the wrong mages at the keypoints, or..." She shuddered again and buried her face in his shoulder. "I can't stop thinking about it."

"I wish I knew what to tell you," Cederic said. "I should have involved myself more in the kathana, so I could be more help to you."

"I'm glad you weren't, because we might have asked you to take the central role, and maybe I'd be mourning you now instead of Jaemis. I couldn't bear that. Cederic, I feel as if I've done nothing but make mistakes for the last three weeks. Stupid mistakes, stupid wrong decisions."

He kissed her again, ran his hand down her side and over her hip, hoping to distract her and make the bleak look vanish. "There is nothing we can do about the past except move forward, and hope to do differently in the future. Together, this time. No more struggling alone."

"No, you're right, but I haven't even told you—Cederic, my sister is in Lethess."

His eyebrows went up. "Roda?"

Sesskia nodded. "She came to see me...just over two weeks ago. It was after they welcomed us to Lethess, you know, how we paraded through the city? She was there on business and she saw me, and she came to the camp. She looks just the same as always, small and dark-haired with Dad's eyes. She said...she said she'd looked for me, years ago, but I'd already left Thalessa and she couldn't find anyone who remembered me. She asked me to forgive her so we could be a family again. I sent her away."

Cederic twisted a lock of Sesskia's hair around his finger and waited. Finally, Sesskia said, "Well?"

"I was not sure whether you wanted advice, or just a listening ear."

"I don't know. I guess I want reassurance."

"That you did the right thing?" Cederic propped himself on his elbow so he could look more directly at her. "If you are looking to me to tell you whether or not to forgive your sister, you will have to ready yourself for disappointment, as I think it is not my place to tell you what to do with your pain. But I think you are wrong in believing that forgiveness means behaving as if the sin never happened."

"Then what does it mean?" Sesskia said.

"What did it mean when you forgave me the cruel things I said to you in the palace?"

Sesskia averted her eyes. "That was different," she said. "That wasn't years of pain and abandonment." She looked up at him through her lashes and smiled. "Besides, I was in love with you and I wanted a reason to forgive you."

He laughed. "The two may be different in, let us say, intensity," he said, "but the principle is the same. You chose to let go of the resentment you might justifiably have harbored against me. That is not the same as pretending it never happened. Much as I personally would like not to have that memory."

"And it meant being able to love you, so it's not as if nothing good came of it."

"That is true." He sighed. "It's up to you to decide whether something good came of Roda's actions. But I think, if you choose to let the past bury the past, you may feel happier. And your happiness is paramount to me."

Sesskia put her arms around his neck. "Show me," she said. With a smile, Cederic drew her close and kissed her, long and sweet.

ABOUT THE AUTHOR

In addition to Convergence, Melissa McShane is the author of The Extraordinaries series, beginning with BURNING BRIGHT, the Crown of Tremontane series, beginning with SERVANT OF THE CROWN, as well as COMPANY OF STRANGERS and many others.

After a childhood spent roaming the United States, she settled in Utah with her husband, four children and a niece, four very needy cats, and a library that continues to grow out of control. She wrote reviews and critical essays for many years before turning to fiction, which is much more fun than anyone ought to be allowed to have.

You can visit her at her website **www.melissamcshanewrites.com** for more information on other books.

For news, new release announcements, and other fun stuff, sign up for Melissa's newsletter **here**.

If you enjoyed this book, please consider leaving a review at your favorite online retailer or on Goodreads.

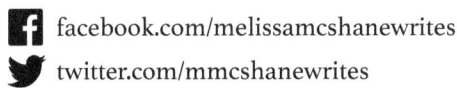

facebook.com/melissamcshanewrites
twitter.com/mmcshanewrites

www.ingramcontent.com/pod-product-compliance
Lightning Source LLC
Chambersburg PA
CBHW070307260626
47160CB00003B/748